"Look, we g[...]
wearing, but the [...]
to take a week, [...]
we can lift some ~~prints and verify. If~~ we can get prints.
There's no guarantee."

"What are you getting at, Doc?"

"According to the tags, the guy was Sergent Roberto
Ruiz."

"Yeah, I already knew he was military. Where was he
stationed?"

"That's just it. He wasn't stationed anywhere. According to the Army's records, the stiff can't be Roberto Ruiz
because Sergen Ruiz was lost in Vietnam about twenty-five
years ago. Listed as MIA, presumed dead, body never
recovered."

Johnny shook his head slightly, thinking of Pham's murder and the threat he'd just received and what Doc was
telling him about a second MIA. "You know, Doc, something really strange is going on here. How can an MIA just
suddenly drop into the middle of the Mojave Desert?"

Praise for *Blue Rain*

"Offbeat. . . . Freadhoff puts a different spin on the Vietnam POW story, and in Johnny Rose he has created a
character who is comforting in his normality, a man
whose plodding pace is more impressive than a superman."

Orlando Sentinel

"The terrors of Vietnam come ever closer. . . . Freadhoff
conjures up enough paranoia to chill readers, all the
while offering an insider's take on how a good reporter
goes about digging out the facts, no matter what the
obstacles."

Publishers Weekly

BLUE RAIN

CHUCK FREADHOFF

HarperTorch
An Imprint of HarperCollins *Publishers*

HARPERTORCH
An Imprint of HarperCollins*Publishers*
10 East 53rd Street
New York, New York 10022-5299

Copyright © 1999 by Chuck Freadhoff
ISBN: 0-06-109727-6

First HarperTorch paperback printing: September 2000
First HarperCollins hardcover printing: April 1999

HarperCollins®, HarperTorch™, and ❦™ are trademarks of HarperCollins Publishers Inc.

Printed in the United States of America

Visit HarperTorch on the World Wide Web at www.harpercollins.com

10 9 8 7 6 5 4 3 2 1

For Dave Miller

ACKNOWLEDGMENTS

I had a lot of help with this book. I want to thank Scott Carrier of the Los Angeles County Coroner's office for his help and advice. A special thank you goes to my friend and fellow author Paul Bishop for his encouragement and advice, my friend Paul Escoll, who provided keen insight and invaluable help in refining the plot and Doris Miller for her tireless copyediting. A special thank you to Jane Preuss, who helped me understand Jimmy's character. I especially want to thank my agent, Matt Bialer, who never lost faith in the project and encouraged me to strive constantly to produce a better book.

1

In the distance Johnny could see the flashing lights atop a sheriff's car at the edge of the two-lane dirt road. Filtered through the heat waves rising off the desert floor, the alternating red and white flashes seemed to waver and had none of the urgency they command in the city's penned-in concrete streets. Out here miles from the nearest paved road, the lights seemed languid, almost lazy. He could make out a few people, too, although they were little more than blurry outlines standing in a cluster at the side of a van out of the direct sun.

Inside Johnny's aging 240Z the temperature was rising as the air conditioner struggled against the desert heat. Last spring his mechanic had said something about the Freon needing to be recharged, but Johnny hadn't done it, and now he cursed himself for ignoring the advice. Sweat trickled from his armpits down the sides of his body, and even with the AC on high his back stuck to the seat. He drove slowly, but the car still jolted over the ruts and the tires slipped on the rocks and sand. Johnny eased off the accelerator for a moment, then drove on, keeping the Z in first gear.

It was a strange place to find a body. Over the years, Johnny had seen bodies in many places: sprawled in garbage-strewn alleys behind working-class bars; locked in the twisted wreckage of cars as firemen worked methodically to cut away the steel tomb; in body bags being loaded on gurneys and wheeled out of the charred remains of houses; and once he'd even been there when the cops popped the trunk of a car and found a mob enforcer who had been missing for ten days. But he'd never been to the desert to cover a story like this.

The road crested a small rise, and he could see the yellow police tape flapping in the breeze perhaps fifty yards or so off the dirt road. He could see the van better. It was a white television vehicle with a small disk antenna mounted on the top. He also saw a black-and-white patrol car and a copper-colored Chevy Caprice, all parked at the edge of the road. He eased his car down an incline and a few minutes later pulled to a stop behind the last car in the line. The heat and wind hit him as he stepped from the car. He blinked and turned his head for a moment, turned back and walked slowly up to the group of three men and a woman standing beside the TV news van.

The woman was dressed in a V-necked white blouse and black slacks. Johnny recognized her as a reporter for one of L.A.'s independent television stations. Her blonde hair was pulled back in a ponytail. Her cameraman, dressed in jeans, a T-shirt and floppy hat, stood at her side. The other two men wore deputy sheriff's uniforms. The van blocked the wind, and Johnny understood why they were clustered together at its side.

He looked at the taller of the two deputy sheriffs. "Hi, I'm Johnny Rose. I'm with the *Chronicle*."

"Hi." The deputy nodded back. He was taller even than Johnny, and thin with a long face and a small black mustache. Half-moons of sweat had soaked through his uniform at the armpits and his face glistened. Johnny guessed he was about thirty, no older.

"I'm surprised you guys are still here. I figured by the time I drove out from L.A. you'd be long gone."

"Coroner's wagon broke down. It'll be here soon. At least they keep telling us that."

"You catch the call?" Johnny asked.

"Yeah."

"Who found the body?"

"Couple of guys in a dune buggy. Just out banging around the desert. Almost ran over the guy."

"So who's running the show?"

"Sergeant Martinez." The deputy cocked his head toward the waving yellow plastic tape. Johnny looked and saw two men in street clothes, one standing behind the yellow tape watching a second man who was kneeling in the dirt inside the roped-off area.

"Thanks."

Johnny stepped out from the van's protected side and was hit with a sudden gust of wind. A moment later the wind died to a steady breeze and the heat seemed to jump immediately. In mid-September, while the rest of the nation was raking autumn leaves, enjoying Indian summer and thinking of putting on snow tires, nothing much changed in the desert north and east of Los Angeles. The heat could top 100 degrees and rain was as rare as meteors.

The yellow police tape was strung in a loose triangle between two yucca trees and a pile of rocks. Johnny recognized the man standing at one point of the triangle even before he turned around. It was Steve Hounds, an AP reporter. In his mid-fifties, he had a barrel chest and thinning reddish-gray hair. They'd covered the same stories and shared beers after deadlines off and on for more than twenty years. He glanced over his shoulder as Johnny walked up.

"Who'd you piss off?" Hounds asked.

"What?"

"No one drives out to the Mojave in the middle of the day this time of year unless they have to."

Johnny shook his head. "No. It was my idea." He looked past Hounds to where the other man was kneeling in the sand, then looked back at the AP reporter. "Thought this might turn out to be Billy Osborne. Could make a good column."

"Osborne? That missing stockbroker?"

"Yeah."

"Well, I hate to break this to you, Johnny, but Osborne took off with his clients' money and his wife's best friend and I can pretty much guaran-damn-tee you he didn't come out here. As I remember it, you did a couple of columns on it yourself."

Johnny shrugged. "Yeah, but you know how it is. I always need copy. Besides, I had nothing better to do."

"Yeah," Hounds said and looked back at the body. Johnny's eyes followed. It was facedown, legs spread slightly and wearing Nike sneakers, pointed outward. The body was clad in lightweight pants and a polo shirt. The edge of the shirt, pulled free from the waist, flapped in the light breeze. One pant leg was pushed above the ankle, exposing a once-white sock, now gray with dirt and sand. The exposed arms were brown and leathery, the skin pulled tightly against the bone.

As he looked at the scene Johnny sensed something odd, out of place, but wasn't sure what. He watched the man kneeling next to the body for a few minutes, then looked around the roped-off area, letting his glance drift from the base of the yucca tree over the rocks and sand and back to the body. He felt a small nagging at the back of his skull. He looked at the body again and the nagging grew, becoming more insistent.

"You see anybody move anything?" he asked Hounds.

"What?"

"This is just the way they found the body, right?"

"Yeah, I guess. Why?"

"Oh, I don't know. Just wondering."

Hounds turned and looked at Johnny. "Come on, don't bullshit me, Rose. What are you thinking?"

"Maybe the coyotes dragged the body around, that's all," Johnny said. If Hounds didn't see it, that was his problem. Johnny wasn't going to help him. Away from the job, the AP reporter was a friend, but out here he was also a rival. If the AP moved the piece on the wire, Johnny could lose his edge, lose a column.

Before Hounds could say anything the detective stood and walked to the other side of the corpse. The newsmen stopped talking and watched as he knelt again, going down on his hands and knees, bending close to the ground while looking like a Muslim in prayer. He seemed to be looking at something strung around the body's neck. A moment later he stood and, still looking down at the corpse, pulled latex gloves from his hands.

Johnny watched him as he walked toward them. The sleeves of his white shirt were rolled above his wrists and his tie was loose. He was short and stout and his stomach slipped over his black leather belt. He wore jeans and cowboy boots. His skin was a deep brown and his thick black hair was combed straight back from his forehead. He wore dark aviator glasses that hid his eyes, making it tough to guess his age.

As he approached, Johnny looked past him. In the distance khaki-colored hills rose gently off the desert floor to the stark blue, cloudless sky. There are those, he knew, who talk of the beauty of the desert and how it teems with life, but at that moment, looking from the desiccated corpse to the detective approaching them and the land behind him, Johnny saw only the harsh, unforgiving sun and dirt that seemed to stretch to infinity.

"I'm Johnny Rose, with the *Chronicle*," Johnny said as the man reached the tape. "This is Steve Hounds with the AP."

"I'm Sergeant Martinez."

Hounds and Johnny pulled their notebooks from their hip pockets. The wind whipped the pages, forcing them to cling tightly as they wrote.

"What can you tell us?" Johnny asked.

"Not much. Body's an adult male. No way to tell the exact age yet. Could be Hispanic, judging by the black hair, but again it's pretty hard to tell."

"How about an ID?"

"I've got a tentative ID but we still have to confirm it, so I can't release any information yet."

"Any idea how long he's been here?"

"It's been a while. I mean, he didn't die yesterday or anything like that. I'd guess a few weeks, minimum.

6

The coroner will have to make the final determination."

"You have any idea how he died?" Hounds asked.

Martinez shook his head. "No. Not yet. But with any case like this, we treat it as a homicide. I'll say this, though, right now there doesn't seem to be any indication of foul play."

"Is it possible he was killed somewhere else and dumped here?" Hounds asked.

"Well, anything's possible, but like I said, there doesn't appear to be any indication of foul play."

"You recover a weapon?" Johnny asked.

"No."

"So if he wasn't murdered, what killed him?"

"My guess is he died of exposure."

"Any idea what he was doing out here?" Hounds asked.

Martinez shook his head. "Nope. I'm hoping we'll know more after we contact the family."

Hounds exhaled deeply and shook his head slowly. "Jesus, it's hot." He paused, then went on. "When will you be releasing the name?"

"Soon, I hope. Just want to confirm the ID, that's all."

"Okay, look, I gotta get to a telephone and file this. Let me get the correct spelling of your name, okay?"

Johnny moved away as Martinez and Hounds talked. He walked along the yellow plastic tape, making his way around the perimeter of the marked-off area. He studied the scene carefully, then found the place where the tape was nearest the body and stood looking at the figure. He could see the head, the burned skin pulled tightly against the bone. The man's shirt and slacks were bleached almost white by the sun. It made Johnny conscious of the heat again, and he licked his lips and swallowed. He squatted down for a better view and looked at the man's legs. Part of the pants were gone and a chunk of leg was missing where a desert animal had torn away a hunk of flesh. The breeze puffed the rear pockets in the corpse's pants. Johnny saw that they were empty and wondered how Martinez had made a preliminary identification. He stood and as he did, the sun suddenly glinted off something in the dirt at the man's throat. Johnny knelt down in the dirt as he'd seen Martinez do earlier. His cheek brushed the ground and he shaded his eyes and looked across the sand at the corpse. He saw a small piece of metal hanging on a chain around the man's neck.

When Johnny looked back Martinez and Hounds were already walking toward the parked cars and TV van. Johnny stood near the tape waiting until he saw Hounds leave and the TV van drive slowly down the narrow road. He didn't want to ask his questions with other reporters around.

He crossed the desert to the patrol cars and found Martinez behind the wheel of the Caprice. The engine was running, and when the detective rolled down his window, Johnny could feel the air conditioning.

"Let me ask you something," Johnny said. "This is off the record since you're not releasing the ID yet anyway, okay?"

"Okay."

"This guy have a wallet on him?"

Martinez smiled and shook his head. "No, not that I saw."

"Then how were you able to make a preliminary identification?"

"Well," Martinez paused. "This is off the record, right?"

"Yeah, I won't use it until you officially release the name."

Martinez leaned close to the window. "He was wearing dog tags."

Johnny stood up and looked across the top of the car to the yellow tape swaying in the breeze, then bent and looked in the car window at Martinez again.

"Well, he sure wasn't wearing fatigues and those weren't jump boots he had on. Those are Nikes. They look good on the street, but I sure wouldn't try and cross the desert in them."

"Yeah, I know what you mean."

"Guy didn't have a jacket, either."

Martinez grunted. "Hey, man, it must be a hundred and ten out here. Who needs a jacket?"

"It gets cold at night."

"Yeah, I see your point. He was dressed pretty lightly for this climate."

"You know, there's something else that bothers me."

"What's that?"

"You find a backpack or anything like that?"

Martinez smiled again and Johnny knew the sergeant had already asked himself the same questions. "Nope."

"How about a canteen?"

"No, nothing. Just the body."

"So what was he doing out here? Where was he going?" Johnny asked the questions but didn't expect an answer. Martinez shrugged. "Is there anything near here? Any towns, mines, settlements, anything?" Johnny asked.

Martinez shook his head slowly. "There's nothing for fifteen, maybe twenty miles."

"So how'd he get here?"

"My guess is he walked."

"Walked? You think his car or dune buggy broke down and he was trying to walk out and get help?"

"I don't know, but I doubt it. We've searched the area and haven't found any vehicles."

Johnny waited a moment, then looked at the sergeant, staring hard at him, trying to see through the lenses of Martinez's sunglasses. "So what you're telling me is, this guy just dropped out of the sky, is that it?"

Martinez nodded. "Sure looks that way, doesn't it?"

2

It was pushing five o'clock, getting close to the early
deadlines, when Johnny pulled off the freeway and
called the *Chronicle* from a pay phone on the edge of
a McDonald's.

"Metro desk, this is Krammer." The voice was low,
raw and stained with decades of nonfiltered cigarettes.

"It's Rose," Johnny said.

"Rose? You calling 'cause you got something? Was it
Osborne?"

"No. They won't release the name yet, but it wasn't
Osborne. The stiff had black hair. Osborne's blond. But
I'm not sure it'll make a column, so I figured I'd dictate
a couple of graphs. Went all the way out there, might as
well get something out of it."

"Okay, hold on. I'll have Riley take it," Krammer
said and the phone went dead. As he waited, Johnny
surveyed the parking lot, filling up in the late afternoon.

It was freshly paved, the parking lines still white, the blacktop not yet smeared with catsup, spilled soft drinks and cartons thrown from car windows. The air was heavy with the smell of hot grease and fried food, and overhead plastic pennants dangled listlessly from ropes strung between the roof and the light poles at the parking lot's edge. The small triangles flapped idly in a weak breeze like a flock of lazy multicolored birds.

"Hey, Johnny, it's Riley. What do you want to call this?"

Johnny turned his attention back to the phone. "Slug it 'DEADGUY.' You ready?"

"Shoot."

He kept the story short, knowing it was only filler destined for an inside page. An unidentified dead body way beyond the *Chronicle*'s circulation area deserved no more. He could hear the keyboard clicking on the other end as Riley typed. Johnny dictated at a slow, even pace, stopping twice to glance at his notes and give Riley a moment to catch up. Seconds after Johnny dictated the last sentence, Riley stopped typing.

"That it?"

"Yeah."

"No name yet?"

"No, not yet. Shouldn't be too long. Cops say they have an ID. Just want to notify next of kin before releasing it"

"Okay, I'll send this through."

"Hey, before you go, look and see if the AP moved anything. Steve Hounds was out there. Check the state wire." He heard the keyboard again, then Riley said, "Here it is. You want me to read this? It's pretty short, only a couple of graphs."

"Sure."

Los Angeles County Sheriff's deputies are investigating the death of a man whose partially decomposed body was found in the Mojave Desert this morning. The man appears to have been dead for several weeks, according to Sergeant Henry Martinez of the Los Angeles County Sheriff's Office.

Martinez said there was no evidence of foul play and it appeared the man died of exposure. Police have made a tentative identification of the body but have not released the name, pending notification of the next of kin.

The body was found by two men driving a dune buggy through the area for fun. Martinez said the police are working on the theory that the man became lost while on a short walk in the desert and died while trying to hike out. "The body was lightly dressed. Obviously the man wasn't equipped for an extended hike. So we think he must have gotten lost somehow and wandered out here," Martinez said.

"That's all there is, Johnny. Pretty much what you have."

"Okay. Tell Krammer I'm heading home. If the desk has any questions they can call me at my place. I'll be there in less than an hour."

Johnny bought his dinner, a roast beef sandwich and a carton of coleslaw, at a delicatessen a block from his apartment. At home he parked the Z in the carport and walked up the narrow walkway to his door.

He held the white paper bag with the sandwich and slaw in his left hand and juggled his keys in his right. He struggled to unlock the door, then shoved it open and stepped back a moment and waited. A second later, his cat, little more than a black blur, shot past his foot into the apartment.

Johnny watched the cat run to the kitchen at the back of the apartment and leap gracefully to the counter. It sat like an imperial porcelain statue and watched its supplicant close the door and carry the bag across the dark living room to the kitchen table.

"Hey, Weird Harold, how are things on the streets today?" Johnny asked the cat and reached out to scratch its ear. Immediately the cat hissed and swung, claws out. Johnny jerked his hand back uninjured.

"You know, someday you're going to really piss me off," Johnny said, although he knew it wasn't true. In fact, Johnny liked the cat's stubborn refusal to play house pet or ever acknowledge its reliance on Johnny's charity. Besides, Johnny and the cat had coexisted in the apartment for almost five years. From the first day that Weird Harold had strolled into the apartment and leaped onto the counter like he owned it, the cat had never been friendly and Johnny admired that stubborn, independent consistency. The cat stood and paced to the edge of the counter, yowled once and sat again.

"Sorry, Harold, you'll have to wait. I'm going for a run," Johnny said. He flicked on the dining room light and put his dinner in the refrigerator. When he walked past the kitchen table on his way upstairs, Weird Harold had curled into a ball near the center of it, feigning a total lack of concern about the delay of dinner.

Johnny dressed in running shorts and a sweatshirt with cutoff sleeves that had worn thin over the years.

He stretched quickly, and started running slowly north toward San Vicente Boulevard. For the first two blocks he was stiff and his breathing labored. In the last few months, the pounding on the pavement had started to aggravate his knees, and he felt a dull ache under his right kneecap. He looked down at his shoes and again promised himself he'd get new ones in a day or two. He'd been running in these for almost a year.

The slope of the street steepened slightly as he approached San Vicente and Johnny picked up his pace. The pain in his hips and knees had eased a few blocks before. The late afternoon air was warm and sweat glistened on his face. As he ran, he pulled the bottom of his sweatshirt up and wiped the moisture off his cheeks. A moment later it was back.

He turned west and ran in the gutter, waiting for a break in the traffic, then sprinted to the wide grassy median. He followed the path beaten in the grass near the curb. The boulevard descended as it neared the ocean and Johnny fell into an easy rhythm. As he ran, he thought briefly of the body in the desert, but his mind quickly wandered. He could never concentrate on one subject when he ran, his mind pinballed from topic to topic.

At Ocean Avenue he turned and began the long uphill trip back. He ran more slowly but kept a steady rhythm. By the time he reached his apartment, he'd run almost six miles. He stretched, showered and dressed in cutoff jeans and a T-shirt.

Downstairs, Weird Harold had moved to the couch, but when Johnny entered he stood, stretched, wandered to the counter and leaped up. He sat and waited. Johnny got the deli bag and a long-necked bottle of beer from the refrigerator and sat at the table.

Weird Harold moved to the table and sat at the edge, watching Johnny intently as he pulled out the sandwich and slaw, flattened the bag and ate quickly leaning over the white paper.

Slivers of roast beef and pieces of cabbage covered in mayo dripped onto the paper as he ate. Finished, he shoved the paper across the table to Weird Harold, who momentarily abandoned his haughtiness to lick the paper and eat the beef.

Johnny poured dry cat food into Harold's bowl on the floor near the refrigerator, then got another beer, moved to the couch and switched on the television to ESPN. The Dodgers were in Colorado, two hours ahead of L.A. The game was already in the sixth inning when he turned it on and the Rockies had a 9–4 lead. The Dodgers rallied and eventually won 14–12, but as the game wore on and the hits and runs piled up, Johnny lost interest. Sitting in the semidarkness, the living room lit only by the television and light spilling from the dining room, his mind left the baseball game to return again and again to the mystery of the man in the desert, a man who had seemingly fallen to earth with nothing more than dog tags glistening in the sun to tell the world he had ever existed. It would make a hell of a column, he knew.

After the last out, Johnny turned off the TV and sat looking at the dark screen. After several minutes he got up, hit the light switch, leaving the dining room dark, and climbed the stairs to the bedroom. Harold was already curled in a ball in the middle of the bed. When Johnny slipped under the covers, the cat hissed and batted his legs through the blankets, then turned in a circle, lay down again next to him and went back to sleep.

Johnny looked at the clock, then closed his eyes and went to sleep thinking of the column and planning his phone calls for the morning.

The newsroom already had a sense of tightly wound, caffeine-fired energy when Johnny got in the next day. The police scanners at the edge of an assistant editor's desk squawked constantly, but no one seemed to be listening. It was, Johnny knew, a learned skill—hearing only the important calls, the murders and fatal accidents and big fires, while letting the others flow past unnoticed, unheard. When Johnny approached, the assistant editor glanced up from his screen and nodded.

"Hey, Johnny, what's up?" The man was in his mid-thirties, thin and handsome, with thick black hair cut short.

"Not much," Johnny said. "When's Krammer due in?"

"Any minute now. You got a column for tomorrow?"

Johnny nodded. "Yeah, I filed it yesterday. When Krammer gets in, tell him to see me. I wanted to talk to him about that body in the desert. It could be a pretty good one for the weekend." He turned and started toward his desk, but stopped when the editor called.

"Hey, Johnny, Barsh wants you to cover a campaign speech by Geld tonight. It's at the Sheraton downtown. He's supposed to speak about nine."

"Me?"

"Yeah. He said to send you."

"Why am I getting this?"

"Jacobson's out sick, abscessed tooth, and McCoy's on vacation. That doesn't leave anyone, well—no one but you."

"Yeah, okay," Johnny said and took two steps, stopped and turned back. "Hey, tell me something. Would I be covering this if Geld didn't own the paper? I mean, is this a real news event?"

The assistant editor shrugged. "If you don't like it, take it up with Barsh."

"Yeah, right," Johnny said and headed for his desk. It sat in the far corner of the newsroom, a sprawling space with worn industrial carpet, a dropped acoustic tile ceiling and hanging fluorescent lights. The reporters' desks were formed into pods of four, leaving narrow aisles between them. The shoulder-high partitions that divided the desks offered the reporters a sense of privacy but did little to reduce the noise.

Johnny dropped into his chair, leaned back and listened to the reporter next to him interviewing someone. He could hear the questions and the click of the computer keys as she took her notes. After a moment, he tuned her out, becoming lost in his own thoughts, letting the noise of the newsroom insulate him like a thousand layers of gauze.

He considered the assignment he'd just received and the man who'd made it, Robert Barsh, the *Chronicle's* new metro editor. He'd been brought in only a few months before by the paper's new owner, Gordon Geld, with a mandate to cut costs, improve quality and boost circulation. Johnny wondered if Barsh was taking the first step to pulling him in, ending his days as a columnist?

Technically Johnny was still a general assignment reporter and could be assigned to political speeches and school board meetings at the editor's whim. In reality, his only assignment was a column three times a week. He could write about whatever he wanted. He developed his own ideas, following whatever interested him, and the editors left him alone, parceling out the man-bites-dog features, the car crashes and city council meetings to the young, hungry reporters.

It was, Johnny knew, the best deal on the paper and the source of some friction on the staff. The young reporters busting their humps on small, inside-the-paper stories simultaneously resented and admired him. Why, they wondered, was Johnny Rose keeping his own hours, free of the yoke of grunt work? Why was he writing just three pieces a week when some of them were writing two a day? He knew they thought his freedom came from his writing talent and his ability to report, to dig harder and get more information than others thought possible. But Johnny knew it wasn't just talent that bought freedom. In fact, it played only a small part. Johnny got his column by seeing stories others didn't see, by looking for angles others never thought of. He got his column because he had a sense of what people wanted to read.

One story had won Johnny the column. A young, distraught mother had killed her four children, all under the age of six, and then turned the gun on herself. Several reporters beat Johnny to the scene, but he was the first one, the only one, to interview the ambulance driver who was the first man in the house, arriving even before the cops. The man had four kids himself. In Johnny's story, the readers saw the children and their mother through a eyes of a man who had witnessed a seemingly endless succession of tragedies and could still weep. The story, in the words of the newsies, "sang."

—

Johnny had used the piece and a job offer from the *L.A. Times* to get the column. He struck a deal with Dale Cavanaugh, the former metro editor. He'd stay, write the column and be free of day-to-day reporting duties. He knew his deal wouldn't make sense to the young reporters the *Chronicle* hired. He'd never make as much as the *Times* was offering, and the *Chronicle* would never have the respect the *Times* did. But Johnny didn't care. He had almost total freedom to write what he wanted, something the *Times* would never offer but something he cherished.

Now Johnny wondered if Barsh was about to break the unwritten contract and for a fleeting moment considered not following up on the story of the body in the desert. He knew Barsh would have little interest in it. There was no local angle, nothing to "speak to the lives of our readers," in Barsh's words. But Johnny knew it was a story people would read. It was, in his view, the perfect elevator story; a piece casual acquaintances would chat about in an elevator. *"Did you read the story about that body that showed up in the middle of the desert with nothing for miles around?"*

He glanced around his cubicle. His eyes passed over the stacks of papers, press releases and unfiled clippings on the surface of his desk and came to rest on a bumper sticker he'd tacked to the partition wall more than five years before: HUMPTY DUMPTY WAS PUSHED. Johnny liked the bumper sticker because of the message it sent, a message the best reporters seem to understand intuitively: conventional wisdom is crap.

He reached for the phone and called an old friend.

"Coroner's office."

"Hi. I'm trying to reach Roy Whetmore."

"Sorry, buddy, you just missed him. He's gone. He may not be back for the rest of the day. You want me to take a message?"

"Sure. Tell him Johnny called, would you?"

"Okay. Anything else?"

"No. That's all."

He called the sheriff's substation next. But Martinez wasn't in and he had to leave a message. Next he dug a California state map from his desk drawer, pinpointed the spot where the body had been found and looked for nearby military installations. The nearest one was Edwards Air Force Base. It wasn't really close; it would be a long, grueling hike from the base to where the body was found. As Johnny looked at the map, he asked himself again, Where was this guy going?

He tried the public affairs office at Edwards but was told no airmen were missing. He called March Air Force Base in Riverside and tried the Marines at Camp Pendleton near San Diego. By early afternoon, he'd tried almost every military installation in Southern California. But at each base the answer was the same. No military people were missing. No one was AWOL. The body in the desert didn't belong anywhere. So why was he there?

In frustration, Johnny threw his pen on the desk where it bounced against a copy of the *Chronicle*'s early edition then rolled to the edge of the desk and fell to the floor. He sighed, bent and picked it up. He tried Martinez again and had to leave his name and phone number a second time. He had just hung up when his phone rang.

Within minutes of answering it, Johnny had forgotten completely about the body in the desert.

"Johnny Rose here."

"Johnny?"

He recognized the voice instantly. It was Pham Lich, a Vietnamese man Johnny had met while doing a story on immigrants. Over the years they had become friends.

"Hey, Pham, how are you?"

"Johnny, I have problem. Maybe you help."

"What kind of problem?"

Pham was silent for nearly a minute and, but for the background noise of the kitchen where Pham worked, Johnny would have thought the line dead. When he spoke again there was an urgency tinged with fear in his words.

"I see him, Johnny. It him."

"Who, Pham? Who did you see?"

"Captain Loveless. Air Force."

"Wait a minute, Pham, I don't get it. Who's Captain Loveless?" Johnny leaned forward into his desk and flipped open his notebook wearily. He picked up a pen, ready to write.

"Kyle. He pilot in Vietnam. Plane go down. Missing. POW."

"Yeah, so?"

Johnny could hear the exasperation in Pham's voice as he struggled to make Johnny understand. Pham paused, then his words came in a rush, the accent growing thicker as he spoke.

And suddenly Johnny understood. He leaned forward with a jolt and scribbled notes quickly, flipping the pages as Pham spoke. Finally, Pham just stopped. It took a moment before Johnny realized he had finished speaking.

"Look, Pham, why don't I come by the restaurant tonight and we'll talk about this. I have to cover a story,

Geld is giving a speech, but I can probably be there around closing time."

"No, no, you no come here. Maybe dangerous."

"Dangerous? What do you mean? How can it be dangerous?"

"No come here, Johnny."

"Okay, where do you want to meet?"

"The park near house."

"Yeah, I know it."

"We meet there."

"Okay, fine. I'll do a little checking in the meantime."

They agreed to meet about eleven and Johnny hung up and flipped the pages of his notebook, rereading his notes slowly. But as he read, doubts quickly surfaced. What Pham said seemed absurd. An American pilot, a POW who had never returned from the war, was now walking around L.A.? This wasn't the type of story a Vietnamese immigrant runs across. This was the stuff of spies, the CIA and Senate subcommittees. Briefly he considered dismissing it, just letting it slide. But Pham had seemed so certain, and the fear in his voice was very real.

Johnny stood and stretched his arms high over his head and arched his back. He was tired, hungry and sick of phone calls that led nowhere. But he could probably make one or two more, get the answer, wrap it up and go back to his other story. There had to be a clear, easy explanation.

He called information for Washington, D.C., then dialed the number. He was transferred three times but finally got the right office: Air Force Public Relations in the Pentagon. The man who answered the phone said his name was Captain Greene. "That's Greene with an *e* on the end."

"Right, I got it."

"So what can I do for y'all?" He spoke with the drawl of a born southerner.

"I need to get some information about a POW from the Vietnam War, a pilot shot down over Laos near the end of the war. His name was Kyle Loveless."

The captain paused for a moment, then said, "Well, I can check for you, of course. But to tell you the truth, your best bet is to try the National League of Families. They're here in D.C. They keep excellent records. I've got the number right here."

Johnny jotted it down. "Okay, thanks."

The woman from the National League of Families was polite but perfunctory. Yes, they had records. Yes, she'd be happy to check. It would just be a minute. Could he hold? But before he could answer, the phone was filled with silence. Less than a minute later she was back.

"Okay, I found the file," the woman said and Johnny leaned forward again in his chair and took notes as she talked. "Captain Kyle Loveless was shot down over Laos in late December 1971. Nearby planes saw him take a hit in the left wing and go into a slow descent. Two parachutes were seen but no beepers were heard."

Johnny listened intently, remembering what Pham had said.

"So what's his status now? He still missing, or was he rescued at some point?"

"Rescued?" She seemed surprised. "No, his status was changed. He's listed as presumed dead. There are no Americans still listed as POWs or even missing. All those who didn't return are now listed as presumed dead."

"Presumed dead? I, ah . . ." Johnny stumbled, not quite sure what to say. "You know, a friend of mine swears he saw Captain Loveless just a few days ago. But what you're telling me is that's not possible."

"No, there's no way that's possible. Look, I'll tell you something but it's got to be off the record, okay?"

"Sure."

"There are more than two thousand Americans listed as missing in action in Vietnam. About six hundred of those are missing in nearby countries. That's just to give you an idea of the size of the problem. These days all we're looking for is a full accounting. Now that we have reestablished relations with Vietnam, we should be able to get an accounting for some. That's really all we want. But we'll never get it for all of them. I'm sure you understand what I'm saying."

"Yes, of course." Sure, Johnny understood. The league was saying they'd given up hope of anyone else ever coming home. There were no POWs alive over there. "So my buddy was wrong?"

"Absolutely."

Johnny leaned back and tossed his pen on the desk again. This time it rolled under the edge of that day's paper and stopped.

"Can you tell me where Captain Loveless is from?" It was a throwaway question. Something to keep the conversation going while he tried to think of something smart to ask. But the answer shocked him.

"Los Angeles. Didn't you know? I assumed that's why you were calling about him."

Johnny scrambled to cover his surprise. "Ah, yeah, sure, but L.A.'s a big place. Was he from the city proper or surrounding area, do you know?"

"All it says here is Los Angeles."

"Okay, well, thanks. You've been a big help."

"You're welcome."

"Oh, one more thing. Can you tell me if he was married?"

He heard the pages flip and then she spoke. "Yes, yes, he was."

"Great, can you tell me how to get in touch with his wife? Is she in L.A., too?"

"I'm sorry, Mr. Rose, but we don't give out the names and addresses of family members. If you want, I'll take your address and phone number and pass it along. That way, if she wants to contact you, she can. That's the way we work it here."

"Okay, sounds fair to me." Johnny spelled his name and gave her his home and work numbers and address.

He hung up and looked again at the words *presumed dead* and thought about what the woman had told him without really saying it. There were no POWs, no Americans left alive in Southeast Asia. Even the families understood that now.

So Pham had been mistaken when he thought he saw Kyle Loveless. But if he was wrong, why did he think it was so dangerous? Johnny glanced again at the bumper sticker tacked to the wall of his cubicle. The message hadn't changed, but it suddenly seemed more ominous.

3

All three sets of double doors to the banquet room were closed by the time Johnny arrived. He opened one and slipped through. He was standing at the back of a ballroom filled with round tables spaced across the carpet like perfectly shaped white lily pads in a huge red pond. A long rectangular table stretched across the front of the room on a dais raised about eighteen inches from the floor. Geld sat in the middle on the right. Johnny scanned the crowd and saw politicians and bankers, actors and musicians, entrepreneurs and businessmen, the old money and the new. All of them, he knew, had paid five hundred a plate. For a fleeting moment he felt out of place dressed in jeans, corduroy jacket and maroon tie that he'd pulled from the glove compartment and tied in a sloppy Windsor knot moments before entering the hotel.

He moved along the back of the hall until he found a

chair in the shadows and sat down to wait. A few moments after he'd taken out his notebook, a man he didn't recognize moved to the podium. He wasted little time. He welcomed the guests and launched straight into Geld's introduction. He told them that Gordon Geld was an entrepreneur turned publisher, a businessman and visionary, a man with new ideas who could lead California back to the forefront of economic prosperity. The crowd clapped and Geld walked to the podium.

He wasn't tall, perhaps five foot nine, and was thin. His white hair was elaborately combed to cover a balding head and his face bore the long ago scars of acne. Not at all a candidate from central casting. Yet when he spoke, he drew the audience in and the people listened intently.

Johnny stopped writing once to watch the crowd and saw that the people were caught in the rhythm of Geld's speech, taken up in the allure of the easy answers and quick solutions Geld promised. In a tone tinged with the arrogance of self-made wealth, Geld warned them about the costs of welfare, the state's poor education system and the threat of illegal immigration. As Geld talked about the porous border that allowed a tidal wave of illegal immigrants to pour into the state, Johnny watched the red-jacketed waiters, almost every one Latino, slipping around the edges of the tables, silently clearing away dirty dinner plates and uneaten desserts. Moments later they were back, pouring coffee and decaf, as unobtrusive as a soft summer breeze. The waiters seemed as oblivious to Geld's words as he was to their very existence.

The audience clapped enthusiastically when Geld finished and returned to his seat, smiling and waving to the tables as he went. Despite the enthusiasm he saw, Johnny wondered if Geld really had a chance of winning his third-party bid for the governor's seat. It was one thing to pack a hotel ballroom in L.A., quite another to win a statewide race. Was Geld an egotistical fool playing with his money or a brilliant visionary who understood something no one else saw? The election was still almost two months away. The polls showed Geld trailing both main-party candidates, but not by much. The race was still open.

The man who had introduced Geld took the podium again and thanked everyone for coming. A few moments later, the rear doors swung open and the people milled and flowed and slowly emptied the room. Johnny sat, hunched over his notebook, rereading his notes and fashioning a lead. When he looked up, the room was almost empty. He stood and turned to leave but stopped and looked back at the head table. Geld was reaching across the table to shake hands with two supporters. They chatted briefly, then Geld turned and moved to the far end of the dais and stopped next to a tall, thin man with dark hair. The man looked out at the ballroom; his eyes lingered on Johnny for a moment and then he bent down, his mouth inches from Geld's head, and began speaking.

It took a moment before Johnny could place the man. But then he had it. He was Charles Raby, head of security for Geld Enterprises Inc. As Johnny watched the earnest conversation another man, a security guard in a white shirt, dark blue blazer and gray slacks, moved along the floor until he was standing just below Geld and Raby. He stood watching the empty ballroom, his hands folded neatly in front of him, and bounced slightly on his toes. Johnny watched Geld and

Raby lost in a world of hushed conversation and guarded exchanges for a moment; then he put his notebook in his jacket pocket and left the ballroom.

He found a bank of pay phones in a hall and called the *Chronicle*. He looked at his watch and knew he'd be lucky to get to the park by eleven. The night metro editor assigned a young, inexperienced reporter to take Johnny's dictation. Three sentences into the story, the reporter was saying, "Hey, slow down, man, I can't type that fast."

Johnny clenched his jaw and looked at his shoes as he waited for the reporter to catch up. Again and again he had to stop and listen to the *tap, tap, tap* as the reporter struggled to get the typing done. Waiting to dictate the last paragraph, Johnny checked the time again and knew he'd never make it. Finally, twenty-five minutes after he began, Johnny hung up and hurried from the hotel.

Traffic was light on the 101 freeway and he reached the Valley in twenty minutes. Still, it was well past eleven when he pulled to the curb and got out of the Z. He stood near the car and turned slowly, searching the park for Pham, but did not see him. Two tennis courts were lit by powerful lights high overhead, but the rest of the park was shadows and darkness.

He cut across the grass to a sandy path along the park's northern edge and followed it to the top of a small knoll near a cement-bottomed pond. He scanned the darkness for Pham.

That was when he saw the murder.

Johnny was about eighty yards away when he first saw the men. He stood for a moment, frozen. He leaned forward, trying to peer through the darkness across the baseball diamond and wide grassy field at the two dark, struggling stick figures, unsure of what he was seeing. The two appeared to be little more than shadows locked in some odd, jerky dance moving to music only they could hear.

The bigger one, the taller of the two, was behind the second man now, pulling on something around the smaller man's neck. They were moving in the hazy edge of light spilling from the huge lamps high above the tennis courts not far away. They shifted, not more than three feet, the taller man dragging the shorter one back into the shadows. The shorter man was struggling violently, his feet kicking, his legs flailing like overdone spaghetti.

In the second before he moved, Johnny could hear the slap of the tennis ball and the giggle of the young woman he'd seen only moments before on the tennis court. He could hear a car idling at the intersection not far away and feel the clinging warmth of the late summer evening. But he couldn't hear a sound from the two men, their actions all pantomime.

He glanced at the couple on the tennis court, but they saw nothing beyond the boundaries of their own well-lighted world. He ran, breaking into a sprint, his long legs stretching, his heart pounding. Almost immediately his lungs screamed and his cold leg muscles, suddenly forced into action, ached. He wanted to shout, but the hard sprint had cut his wind. He was gasping and had no breath for it. Halfway there, maybe forty yards away, he found a rhythm and picked up speed.

The smaller man slumped to the ground and the bigger man turned and saw Johnny running at him. The man moved quickly away, dodging the picnic tables and running easily toward the street beyond.

Johnny altered course, taking an angle toward the street. The man was through the thicket of cement tables, breaking into the clear and heading toward the curb.

Johnny was closer, gaining on the fleeing man. The man was at the curb as Johnny rounded the last of the picnic tables. He heard the car door slam. He was crossing the grass, not thirty feet from the curb, still running hard, his own breathing the only sound he made.

The engine caught and the vehicle sped away. Johnny pulled up and suddenly bent double as exhaustion swept through him. He gasped for oxygen, his lungs raw, painful as he breathed. He slumped to the ground, resting on his hands and knees, his head bowed. A wave of nausea swept over him. His stomach muscles tightened and for a second he believed he would vomit. The feeling passed and he sat up straight.

He looked again down the street but saw only asphalt, curbs and parked cars. The attacker was gone. He'd seen enough to know he was driving a sport utility vehicle, maybe a Blazer or a Bronco, but the license plate, everything else in fact, had been a blur.

Then one detail suddenly leaped out. Johnny didn't even know how it entered his brain. Perhaps when he ran close to the body he'd seen it, not realizing what it was. The pants. The victim's black-and-white-checked pants.

Johnny stood quickly, suddenly in a hurry to see if the man in the checked pants was still alive. He retreated quickly through the picnic tables, his legs rubbery, unsteady, his eyes fixed on the mound in the grass. He reached the man, who was lying facedown in the grass. Johnny touched his neck and felt the thin wire that had been wrapped around his throat. There was no pulse. He grabbed the man's shoulder to turn him over but withdrew his hand and looked back across the park, past the baseball diamond and tennis courts to the street.

There was still a chance Pham was just late, later even than Johnny had been. He might show up soon, maybe he was pulling to the curb at that moment. But Johnny could see there were no cars stopping. He looked again at the body. He didn't want to go on. He didn't want to know.

Damn Pham. Where was he? Why was he so late? He'd been so upset on the phone.

Suddenly the tennis court lights went out and the park was swallowed by darkness. Without light, sound seemed to travel faster and farther. The young tennis couple was talking as they stowed their gear and unlocked their bikes. Their voices carried to Johnny's ears like ill-disguised whispers.

He turned and looked at the lump in the grass in front of him. A thought played at the edge of his mind, a thought so awful Johnny refused to let it in. But it became insistent, demanding. He held it at bay until it demanded he admit whom he was looking at.

Johnny was breathing fast, his heart pounding. There was no question who it was. The checked pants and the white shirt, the black hair. He hesitated a moment, then took a deep breath and rolled Pham's body over. Johnny sucked air deep into his lungs as Pham's head fell sideways, almost free from his body. A thin wire stretched between pieces of dowel had cut a deep gash through the flesh of his neck, leaving a neat slice and a trail of blood. Even in the darkness Johnny could see the scratches near the wire where Pham

—

must have dug deep into his own neck as he fought for his life. His mouth was open, contorted in a grimace, and his eyes bugged out like balloons inflated to the limit. An ounce more pressure and they would burst.

He stared at the face and fought the panic that swelled in his chest. He breathed deeply, then grabbed the dowel and unwound the wire and laid it aside. He pulled back, sitting on his haunches, and shivered violently for a moment, fighting desperately not to puke. He looked away, forcing himself to be detached, rational, to try to understand. Still, he was shaking, his hands trembling, his legs twitching.

A woman screamed, a guttural cry of horror. The sound ripped into Johnny's ears. He looked up. The tennis players stood straddling their bikes, staring at him only a few yards away. The woman screamed again. The two stood there frozen, just staring at him, their faces full of fear as though he would kill them next. Suddenly the man moved, jerking his tennis racquet from the back of the bike and holding it in front of him, swaying it back and forth like a club.

"Stay away. Stay away," he said, his voice loud, his eyes canyon-wide with fear.

The woman screamed again. Johnny just crouched there, Pham's body in the grass in front of him, looking at the two of them.

And then the man grabbed something small and square off the back of his bike. A phone. Still swinging the racquet in his right hand, he punched three numbers.

"I need the police. A man's been murdered," he said.

Johnny shook his head. "No, you don't . . . I just got here," he pleaded to the couple, suddenly desperate to make them understand, to believe. The man stepped in front of the woman, swinging the tennis racquet, letting his bike fall with a crash as he talked, telling the police where they were.

Johnny raised his hands, palms up. "Hold on there. I didn't do this." He kept his eyes glued to the man, swinging the racquet frantically while trying to tell the police where he was. The woman had stepped behind him and stared over his shoulder at Johnny as if he were a gorilla escaped from the zoo. Johnny watched the couple for a few moments more, then turned his back to them and moved to Pham.

He pulled his sports coat off, then squatted down and laid it over the body of his friend. He sat, his legs pulled up and his arms around his knees for a moment, and tried to distance himself from what he'd just seen.

Pham Lich, a Vietnamese immigrant who fought his way from a living hell to the land of the free, was murdered last night in a San Fernando Valley park less than a mile from his home.

Johnny began shaping the column he would write. The words formed in his mind like a well-rehearsed prayer, offering him reassurance, making him think he was in control. The words put him back on the other side of the line. No longer a player, just an observer.

Two uniformed officers, a white man with a crew cut and biceps the size of cantaloupes and a young black woman, arrived about ten minutes later. They spoke briefly with Johnny and the tennis couple and told all three to wait for the detective. He didn't arrive for nearly thirty minutes. By then Johnny was sitting on a bench at a concrete picnic table, trying not to look at Pham's body or at the uniformed cops who had arrived and strung yellow plastic tape around the scene.

Johnny saw the detective climb out of an unmarked police car and walk slowly toward a uniform. Despite the warmth of the evening, the detective took a moment to shrug his sports coat into place and tug on his shirt until the cuffs peeked out. He moved easily, all the time in the world; a man in control. He stopped and turned to look at Johnny for the first time, then looked away again.

It was another ten minutes before he approached the picnic bench. "I'm Detective Earl. I'd like to ask you a few questions."

Johnny nodded.

Earl hesitated a moment, looking back across the diamond and playground to Johnny's 240Z parked at the curb, then back to Johnny. "Let's start with your name."

"Johnny Rose."

"Mr. Rose, you have any identification?"

Johnny pulled out his wallet and handed Earl the license.

"According to this you live in Santa Monica. Why are you out here in the San Fernando Valley in the middle of the night?"

"I was supposed to meet a guy. The man over there. His name is Pham Lich." Johnny nodded toward the body.

Earl reached into his breast pocket then and removed a small notebook and pen. Earl looked directly at him and nodded slowly, as though he'd already known what Johnny would say.

"Yeah, so, go on."

"I was walking along the path over there." Johnny turned and waved across the park. "Near the cement-bottomed pond. Then I saw these two guys struggling. It looked like the bigger guy was trying to beat the shit out of the shorter one. I ran over but the big guy got away." Johnny wanted to tell it straight, give the short, dapper cop enough to satisfy him.

"How'd he get away?"

"He jumped into his car and took off."

"You get a look at the car?"

"It was a Jeep or something like that, maybe a Bronco or Blazer. Dark color, blue or black. I didn't see the license plate."

"Then what?"

"I went to look at the body. That's when the lady started screaming and her boyfriend called you."

"Hmmmm. Okay, so why were you meeting Mr. Lich?"

"He said he had a story he wanted to talk to me about."

"A story?"

"I'm a writer for the *Chronicle*."

"This is a little outside your circulation area, isn't it?"

"Yeah, but I've known Pham for a few years. I trust him. He wanted to talk, so I came."

Earl said nothing for a moment, just nodded as he stared at Johnny, letting the silence hang in the air and lengthen.

"But you never saw him here, didn't talk to him?" he finally asked.

"No, I never talked to him. I just parked and was walking over there when I saw the two guys fighting. I ran over but I got there too late. He was already dead."

Earl had stopped taking notes, and when Johnny finished he looked at him. A car cruised by on the boulevard, music blasting, its huge bass speakers vibrating like a thousand-watt earthquake. Earl didn't even look. He just waited until the noise faded.

"But you never saw him alive tonight, didn't meet him here?"

"No." Johnny exhaled. Jesus, didn't this guy get it? He hadn't seen Pham until it was too late. How many times did he have to go over it before the guy understood?

Earl nodded like he was taking it all in. "But you know for a fact that the victim is Mr. Lich?"

Johnny looked at the cop. The guy was neat, almost anal. His black hair was short enough to measure in millimeters, a precise part cut down the left side like a border between hostile nations. No hair strayed over the line. The creases in his blue slacks were sharp and his black tasseled loafers gleamed.

Johnny looked at the cop and knew he couldn't afford to underestimate the guy.

"Of course I'm sure. I turned the body over. His head almost came off in my hands, for Christ's sake." Johnny gestured, mimicking his actions as he rolled Pham onto his back. He saw the blood then. First on his hands, then the dark stain on his shirt. No question Earl had already seen it.

Something crossed Earl's face. For a second Johnny thought it was a smile, but then it was gone.

"How long have you known Mr. Lich?"

"Four years, maybe five."

"A pretty good friend, was he?"

"Yeah, he was a good friend."

"Where did you meet him?"

"I was doing a story on Vietnamese immigrants a few years ago. I went to the Vietnamese restaurant where he worked. He was a cook."

"And you came out to the park just to talk. He had a story for you? That it?"

Johnny shifted on the bench, keeping his eyes on Earl. "Yeah, that's it."

"Must be a hell of a story if he had to tell you in the middle of the night in a park."

"Like I said, I had to cover something else first. Eleven was about as early as I could get there."

"But why here?"

"I think he was scared. He told me not to come to the restaurant. He said it was dangerous."

"What was he afraid of?"

"I don't know. He just said it was dangerous. He said he'd tell me tonight."

Earl nodded. "It have anything to do with this story he wanted to tell you about?"

"Maybe. Probably." Johnny wondered then how much to share with Earl. The odds were pretty high he'd never believe the story. Johnny wasn't even convinced himself.

"Okay, so what was this hot story anyway?"

Johnny exhaled and looked across the baseball diamond and field to the street on the other side of the park. He spoke to the darkness. "He said it was about a guy named Kyle Loveless."

"Go on."

"Kyle Loveless was a pilot Pham knew in Vietnam. He was shot down over Laos and when the war ended he was listed as MIA. Body never recovered."

"Okay, I'm listening," Earl said.

"Pham told me he saw him. Swore that he saw Loveless here in L.A. just a couple of days ago."

He looked at Earl. In the darkness he couldn't see his face well. But he didn't have to. His posture said it all. He stood there with his arms crossed against his chest, his head bent slightly forward, his eyes on the ground, like a priest hearing the worthless promise of an unrepentant sinner. Earl had listened to his words, Johnny knew, but he hadn't believed a single one of them.

4

It was after 3:00 A.M. when the coroner arrived, loaded Pham's body onto a gurney and wheeled it into the van and left for the morgue. Johnny had answered Earl's last question long before but had waited until the doors on the van slammed shut and it began slowly rolling across the grass toward the street before he left.

As he crested the Sepulveda Pass and joined the flow of early morning traffic down the San Diego Freeway to L.A.'s west side, he could feel the exhaustion radiating throughout his body. The sprint across the baseball diamond, the emotional shock of seeing Pham and the tough police questions had drained his strength and numbed his emotions.

He planned to drive straight home and climb into bed and fall into a black tunnel of sleep. Instead, without considering what he was doing, he took the Wilshire

Boulevard exit and almost immediately turned off the street into the sprawling Veterans Administration grounds. He didn't even fully realize what he'd done until he was driving along the grounds' quiet, deserted streets. He stopped in front of a light-colored three-story rectangular cement building.

All the windows were dark. Johnny sat in the car and looked at the building and thought of his brother, who just might be sleeping in one of the dark rooms. It was where he should be, but it was tough to ever know where Jimmy was. Sometimes he stayed in the dorms for months; then he would disappear into the freeway underpasses or the bushes of nearby parks or the overgrown arroyo that bordered the VA grounds. He could be gone for weeks.

Johnny wondered what his brother would think of Pham's claim that he'd seen a POW in L.A. There would be more than a little irony to it, considering how Jimmy spent his last tour in Vietnam. But Johnny also knew that his brother probably would say nothing at all. He seldom responded anymore. Words and ideas seemed to sink into him like stones into quicksand. Sometimes Johnny could watch Jimmy's eyes and see recognition. But an instant later the words and thoughts disappeared inside him. Jimmy could speak when he wanted to, but he seldom seemed to care to anymore. If Jimmy said anything he'd probably say Pham made a mistake. But, Johnny asked himself again, if it was a simple error, just mistaken identity, why had someone killed him?

Johnny sat for almost half an hour watching the building, thinking of his brother and searching for an answer to Pham's murder. In the end, though, he could find no explanation for the slaying. Nor did he go into the building to seek his brother. He simply started his car and drove home.

Weird Harold dashed from the darkness into the apartment the moment Johnny opened the door. He ran to the kitchen and leaped to the counter, where he paced and yowled until Johnny took the box of cat food from the cupboard and poured some into the bowl. While Weird Harold ate, Johnny slipped a Bill Monroe CD into the stereo and sat in the dark at his kitchen table sipping a glass of orange juice and listening to the high lonesome sound of one of America's greatest musicians. Later, when the cat jumped onto the table and sat looking at him, Johnny made no attempt to scratch his ear.

In the morning, the face Johnny saw in the mirror looked older, more tired than he'd remembered. The gray in his mustache seemed to be choking out the remaining black hairs like weeds in an untended garden. Had more lines appeared at the corners of his eyes overnight, or was he just noticing them for the first time? He shaved slowly, meticulously, still feeling the exhaustion from the night before and too little sleep. After he showered, he dressed in khakis with a plaid shirt, put a fresh necktie in the pocket of his coat. He carried the bloodstained pants and shirt he'd worn the night before to the Dumpster behind his apartment building and then drove to work.

Johnny had no set hours and arrived at the *Chronicle* late in the morning. He spent an hour reading the competing papers and scanned the wires for stories about Pham's killing but found nothing. He created a file and had just begun writing a column on his friend's death when he heard Barsh call him from across the newsroom.

Johnny looked up and saw him standing in the doorway motioning him over. Barsh's office was tucked in a corner of the newsroom, an L-shaped afterthought made of portable walls, the upper portion glass. Miniblinds hung on the inside of the windows. They were open. It meant Barsh was in. He kept them open when he was in the office and closed them every night, his last act before leaving. Like he was closing the curtains on a great drama.

"John, I'd like to see you," Barsh called again. His voice was a little louder this time, carrying across the newsroom above the low hum of conversations and keyboards and the muted sound of a television turned to CNN. Johnny stood and slowly worked his way past the reporters' pods, catching snatches of hurried conversations as he went.

"Please have a seat," Barsh said and motioned to one of two chairs sitting side by side facing a desk that filled the office almost wall to wall. Barsh was in his early thirties but almost bald. He combed the few strands of black hair neatly over his bare skull. From the day Barsh arrived, he and Johnny had kept their distance, a mutual distrust built more on incompatible chemistry than any real differences. Johnny respected Barsh's ability to edit copy. He could make a phone book interesting, Johnny once said. But he seemed to have the news judgment of a yak. Barsh had made it clear more than once that he disliked Johnny's refusal to join in "the *Chronicle* team" atmosphere he was trying to generate in the newsroom.

Johnny stood by the door and waited until Barsh had moved behind his desk before speaking.

"I gotta tell you about something I'm working. I got a call yesterday from a guy I know. A Vietnamese refugee named Pham Lich. He wanted to tell me something, but he said it was dangerous. So we agreed to meet at this park near his house last night. But when I went to meet him . . ."

"Hold on a second, John," Barsh said. He looked at him across the desk and Johnny started to speak again, but Barsh held up his hand. "Wait. Let me start by telling you I think we have a problem. I understand you were questioned about this by the police last night."

"Yeah, that's what I'm trying to tell you. The man I was going to meet was murdered. I think he had some information that someone didn't want out but he was killed before I could talk to him."

"That's why I called you in. I don't think this is a story for us and it's not something for you to follow. It's outside our circulation area." Barsh was looking at the wall behind Johnny, avoiding eye contact.

"Wait a minute, you don't even know what the story is." Johnny waved his hand briefly, as though he could easily dismiss Barsh's words. "When I talked to Pham yesterday, he said he'd seen a POW, an Air Force captain missing in Laos, here in L.A. I've already called the Pentagon and the National League of Families. This captain's widow is supposed to call me. I gave the league my phone numbers and address. I'm already working on it."

"That doesn't matter, John, this isn't something we want to follow."

Johnny looked at Barsh, not really believing what his editor had just said. No newsman would turn away from a story like this. "Listen to me for a moment," Johnny said, speaking more slowly, as though Barsh were a child. "The man was murdered to keep him quiet. To keep him from telling me something. Doesn't that mean anything to you?"

"It tells me someone wanted to kill him. It doesn't tell me anything else. You don't know that he was killed because of something he knew. Maybe it was a random mugging that went bad. We don't know, John. You never did get to talk to him out there at the park, did you?" He paused for a second, then looked directly at Johnny, a challenge in his eyes. "Did you?"

Johnny choked back his anger and struggled to understand the reason Barsh refused to go after this story. Even a brain-dead editor could see the story could be huge. Johnny looked at Barsh with no idea of what to say. Finally, he said the only thing he could think of. "Random mugging? Are you crazy? What kind of mugger carries a garrote around with him? It was a cold-blooded murder."

"You don't know that."

"I do know it. I saw it, remember? I can't believe I'm arguing with you about this. A source was murdered just before he meets one of our reporters. We should have everyone in the office working on this, digging into it, finding something." He could feel the heat in his face and knew he must be red.

"This is all speculation. You didn't talk to him out there, did you?"

"I told you, I talked to him on the phone."

"Yes, but for how long?"

"It was just a couple of minutes, but—"

"So the fact remains, we don't know a thing for sure, except that he was murdered and that the police questioned you. Right?"

"Yeah, right." Johnny looked out the door to the newsroom. His eyes fell on the television mounted on a shelf high above the metro desk. CNN was playing film of a battlefield and Johnny realized it could be any one of a dozen countries in the world.

"So, you understand? We don't have the manpower to chase ghosts, John. We just can't spend time on a murder outside our circulation area."

"Yeah, right, picking it up here, boss."

"What?"

"Nothing," Johnny said. "Is that it?"

"No. There's something more you should know, John. Someone also called Mr. Geld."

"What? What's Geld got to do with this? Besides, who the hell called him?"

"I don't know. He has a lot of contacts and someone thought he should know that one of his reporters had been questioned. He called me this morning. He's quite concerned."

"Why? Because it might look bad for his campaign? That's it, isn't it?" And suddenly Johnny thought he understood. "Geld's afraid to rock any boats until after the election."

"No. That's not true."

"Look, if we're not going after this because Geld's worried, tell him not to worry. I went out there to meet Pham Lich and somebody had murdered him. It's a hell of a story."

"Yes, John, as you said, you found the body. That's the whole point. You could be considered a suspect. I called Detective Earl this morning and—"

"You what?"

Barsh went on, ignoring Johnny. "I asked him if you were considered a suspect and he said right now no one can be ruled out. Stop and think about it. You found the body. You had blood on your clothes. Earl even told me someone saw you taking the garrote off Mr. Lich's neck."

"That couple didn't see shit. If they'd been looking, maybe Pham would be alive."

"John, that's beside the point. I can't have you covering a murder story in which you're a suspect. I'll have Sheridan do a couple of graphs for the inside. I don't want anyone thinking we're avoiding the story because of your involvement. Then, because you're convinced this is such a great story, I'll have him do some checking. That's fair, isn't it?"

Johnny didn't answer immediately, and Barsh asked again, "Isn't it?"

Johnny could see Barsh's logic. He *had* been involved. Besides, Sheridan was a good reporter. Young, hungry, aggressive. He'd been on the police beat for fewer than three years and already had better sources than most reporters get in a lifetime. Johnny finally nodded. "Yeah, okay," he mumbled.

"Good. But you're not following it. And I want you to know I talked to Mr. Geld about this and he agrees with me."

Johnny looked toward the door again, trying to calm himself, saying nothing, and Barsh went on.

"In fact, Mr. Geld thinks it would be wise for you to talk with the paper's attorney. I've made an appointment for five o'clock tomorrow. His name is William Bradley." Barsh reached across the desk and handed Johnny a piece of paper.

Johnny took it and moved to the door, but as he stepped out of the office Barsh said, "Wait." Johnny turned and looked back at him. "There's one more thing. Geld wants to see you personally."

"Oh, Christ. He going to give me a hard time about this, too?"

"No, I don't think that's it. I talked to his assistant, who said it doesn't have anything to do with your work. But he said Geld wants to talk to you personally. Said it was important. Said you should go to his house this afternoon about five or so. He's having a fund-raiser there. He'll see you before it starts." Barsh stood up and held out a paper toward Johnny. "Here's the address and directions."

Johnny stepped back to Barsh's desk, took the paper and turned to leave. He stopped just inside the door and focused on the door frame. He reached up and ran his fingers along the smooth metal. Without looking at Barsh, he said, "You know, when I walked in here, I thought this was a door. Now I think it's a looking glass."

5

Johnny walked out of Barsh's office and crossed the newsroom without looking back. He moved past the same cubicles he'd passed only a few minutes before. But this time he didn't hear the half-sentences of reporters asking questions or the snapping of computer keys. One reporter, his telephone headset hanging on his neck, glanced up and nodded as Johnny went past. "Hey, Johnny, how's it going?" he asked. But Johnny, lost in his own thoughts, didn't hear or see the reporter. He turned sideways to skirt a pile of newspapers on the floor at the end of the desk and kept walking. At his cubicle, he tossed the paper with the address and directions to Geld's house onto the desk and sat down. He reached onto the desk and picked up a paper clip. He leaned back in his chair and slowly unfolded it, then bent it back again and unfolded it a second time, thinking of what Barsh had said. It had to be Geld's influence; the man was so afraid that Johnny's brush with the law would somehow hurt his campaign that he was pulling in his horns.

Johnny tossed the paper clip into the wastebasket and, without consciously considering it, made a decision. He leaned across his desk and flipped through his Rolodex. He stopped at the *N*s, found the number and dialed.

"Ben Ng, please."

"Sorry, Mr. Ng busy." The voice had a heavy Vietnamese accent.

"Ah, this is Johnny Rose. Can you please tell him I'd like to stop by and see him in a little while and ask him if he'll be there?"

"Ah yes, Mr. Rose. You wait." Johnny could hear the clattering of dishes, the rhythmic sound of chopping and a general haze of commotion as he waited. Then the man was back.

"Yes, he say he be here."

"Great, thanks."

Johnny considered his decision for a moment, looking for a way to justify what he was about to do. Being out front on something like this would probably be the best thing that could happen to Geld's campaign, he told himself. It would make Geld seem like a real publisher, not just a rich industrialist who bought the *Chronicle* as a hobby. He'd thank Johnny when it was over.

It was several hours until he had to be at Geld's, but Johnny knew he couldn't waste the time. He had too much legwork to do. He picked up his reporter's notebook and saw a pink "While You Were Out" slip taped to his monitor. He'd been so lost in his own thoughts he hadn't seen it until then. "Doc Whetmore, from the L.A. Coroner's Office" had returned his call. Johnny thought briefly of calling him, but by now he'd lost all interest in the unidentified body in the desert. He had a much bigger story to follow. He balled up the note and threw it in the trash.

He took the rear elevator and rode to the ground floor. When the doors opened he walked down the hall and out onto a covered patio that extended to the parking lot beyond. To his right a half-dozen redwood picnic tables were spaced around the patio. Five of the tables were empty, but at the sixth, four pressmen in dark blue work pants and shirts ate hamburgers and tacos from a lunch truck parked at the edge of the lot.

One of the men looked up from the newspaper he was reading and waved casually. "Hey, Johnny, how's it hanging?"

Johnny looked at the man, who was in his mid-fifties with a blond beard and mustache and wore a baseball cap pulled low on his forehead, the bill bent into an almost perfect U shape.

"I'm okay, Phil. How are things with you?"

Phil shrugged. "I'll live."

"All right, take care," Johnny said and walked on into the parking lot. The black asphalt radiated the heavy afternoon heat, and the tar was sticky and soft where cracks had been repaired. He was only a few steps from his car when he remembered the directions to Geld's house. He'd left them on his desk.

"Shit," he swore under his breath and walked back to the door. He reached for his magnetic card to swipe over the electronic pad by the door and swore again. "Damn." His card was on his desk, too.

Johnny turned and looked at the pressmen finishing their late lunch. One man was gathering the paper plates and sheets of aluminum foil from the table top. Phil was bent over the newspaper.

"Hey, Phil," Johnny shouted, "I forgot my card, can you let me in?"

"No, he can't." The voice came from behind him. Johnny turned and looked at the security guard standing just a few feet away. "You know the rules. No one uses anyone else's card."

"Hey, Ducky, give me a break, would you? I just forgot my card. It's upstairs on my desk. It's no big deal."

The guard's name was Bryan Duckworth. His black hair, shot through with gray, was cut razor-short. He was about fifty and his stomach was starting to push against his belt, but he had a powerful upper body that testified to a life of labor. He and the other "white shirts," as Johnny called them, had arrived about a year before, when Charles Raby had become chief of security for Geld Enterprises. Unlike the last security company, which seemed to specialize in the lazy and incompetent, Raby's company appeared to be dominated by middle-aged men with no humor and dead eyes.

"You've got to fill out a report. Those are the rules, Mr. Rose. You know that. There's nothing I can do about it."

Johnny held up his hands in defeat. "Fine, no problem. I'll do it in the morning. I've got an interview."

"I'll leave a message at the front desk that you'll stop by," Duckworth said.

"Yeah, yeah, whatever," Johnny said, knowing that getting into the *Chronicle* without a badge wasn't particularly hard. As he turned to leave, Charles Raby walked out of the building onto the patio. He wore gray slacks, a navy blue blazer, a white shirt, a blue tie and black tasseled loafers shined to a glare. He looked at Duckworth, then glanced at Johnny.

"Ah, Mr. Rose. Will we see you tonight?" he asked.

"Yeah, sure."

"Good. I know Mr. Geld is looking forward to talking with you," Raby said and started to walk away.

"Well, there is one problem," Johnny said and looked from Raby to Duckworth and smiled. "The thing is, I was heading out to work on a story this afternoon and I forgot the directions upstairs. I don't have my pass, so maybe you could give me the address and tell me how to get there."

Raby stopped, looked at Johnny and turned to Duckworth.

"Let him in so he can get the directions."

"But—" Duckworth began to protest.

"Let him in." Raby's voice was flat, emotionless, but held an air of authority that Duckworth wouldn't challenge.

"Yes, sir." Duckworth stepped to the door and wiped his own card across the small black square next to the door. The lock clicked back and Duckworth pulled the door open and held it as he looked at Johnny and waited.

"Hey, thanks," Johnny said, but Raby just nodded and walked past him into the parking lot without speaking.

When Johnny went back out the door five minutes later, the pressman, Phil, called him again. This time, though, Phil sat alone and waved him over. "Hey, man, I want to talk to you."

Johnny crossed the patio, pulled a bench away from the table and sat, his legs straddling it. Phil smiled, showing his crooked teeth, and his bright blue eyes twinkled.

"Hey, what's up?"

"Couldn't hear what he was saying, but I figured I better warn you not to mess with that one. He's trouble, man. You don't want to screw around with him."

"Thanks, but Duckworth's not a really big concern, you know. I think he's a mean son of a bitch, but I got no reason to worry about him."

"It ain't Duckworth I'm talking about. It's Raby. Old Charging Charlie himself."

"Raby? I don't know, he seems harmless. Looks sort of like an ad salesman to me."

"He's no ad salesman and he ain't harmless. Like I said, I'd steer clear of him and Duckworth, too, I was you."

Johnny looked back over his shoulder at the empty parking lot and turned to face Phil again.

"You know him?"

"Know both of 'em. Met once a long time ago."

"Really, where?"

"Nam. They'd never remember me 'cause I only ran into 'em the once. Mean suckers. I never saw either one of them again until about a year ago when Raby showed up here. Then a few weeks later, Duckworth showed up. Recognized Raby the instant I saw him though. Duckworth took a little longer."

Johnny turned once again and looked into the parking lot, but saw only the afternoon sun glittering off the windshields and the cars baking in the heat. Charles Raby was long gone.

Johnny left the picnic table and headed toward his car. In the distance, perhaps half a block away, Johnny could see a billboard for Gordon Geld. His picture took up half the sign and the other half held only six words: GORDON GELD, HE GETS THINGS DONE. He looked at the billboard for a moment, Geld peering back at him from high above, turned and walked the rest of the way across the hot blacktop to his car.

6

By the time Johnny reached Chinatown, the sun had clamped a lid on the city, pinning the air to the ground as it filled with exhaust and shortened tempers. The smog-saturated air clung to the city's skyscrapers like a mist. Officials warned that little children and the elderly should stay inside. Across the city, people pulled their windows shut and turned their air conditioners to high.

Ben Ng kept the old window unit in his office cranked up. But despite its struggles, the air inside was as polluted as that hanging over the city. Ben himself made sure of that. He took a long drag on a Winston and exhaled. He stabbed out the butt and immediately lit another.

As Johnny watched him light up, he felt the old familiar tug. He'd given up smoking years ago, but when he was tired or tense he really missed it. He missed everything about it: rolling the cigarette between his fingers, inhaling and the feel as the smoke hit his lungs and the nicotine his brain.

Ng exhaled again, tilting his head back this time and sending the plume straight up. It didn't take much smoke to fill Ng's office. Just off the restaurant's kitchen, it was little bigger than a meat locker. It was a miracle Ng could squeeze himself in. Johnny wasn't sure how he did it. Ng was short and round with no neck; a chain-smoking, Indochinese Michelin Man.

"This is terrible. Very bad. Very, very bad," he said and waved his hand, the smoke streaming off the end of the cigarette. Ng was shoehorned in behind an old metal desk with round corners. Johnny's knees pressed against the metal as he leaned toward Ng.

It had been a year, maybe more, since Johnny had been to Ng's restaurant. The last time, he'd stopped by to say hello to Pham and have a quick drink on his way home from the Dodgers game. He ended up staying for hours drinking with Pham and Ben.

Johnny had liked Pham the first time he met him. He was straightforward, smiled easily and loved remarking on the absurdities of American life that only foreigners seem to notice.

"Why you have fifty-five speed limit when no go fifty-five?" he once asked.

"It's to keep people from going seventy-five," Johnny said.

"Ah, good idea," Pham answered, with a hint of a smile showing how silly he thought it all was.

Eventually they'd become good friends. Not best buddies, but close enough that when Pham finally got a driver's license, Johnny tried to give him a '75 Buick Century. It had been his mom's car before her death.

For two years it sat in the family garage, its hoses and belts rotting in the closed-up heat, the oil collecting in the pan and turning to sludge. By the time probate was finished, the Buick wouldn't even start.

But Pham had refused the gift, seeing it as charity. When Johnny realized he'd wounded Pham's pride, he said, "Look, take the car, fix it up and drive it. When you sell it or trade it in, we'll split what you get for it. I mean, it's worthless to me like this. At least this way you get some wheels and down the line, I'll get some money out of the deal, too."

Johnny had seen the Buick on the street near the restaurant that night and smiled to think it was still running.

After the last customer left that night, Ng had turned the window neon off, locked the door and joined Johnny and Pham in a booth, his legs barely touching the floor, his belly pressed against the table. The low light inside dimly reflected off the glass covering the tablecloth. Pham was hanging over the table, his white cook's shirt soiled and unbuttoned. Ng chain-smoked Winstons and slowly filled the ashtray with butts. Johnny, on the outside, slouched, his legs stretched straight.

Somehow the subject turned to Vietnam and the war. Pham's words came a little slowly and brokenly, but Johnny had no trouble following him, just sitting and listening as he talked of that time with a mixture of bitterness, pride and melancholy. Pham had been Special Forces, working with the Americans, going behind enemy lines to rescue GIs. Pilots mostly. He had been an officer, tough and on the fast track. Ng had owned a restaurant catering to the Americans.

Ng got out early. But Pham had fought to the end

while the forces around him and the corrupt regime they were propping up collapsed in on itself. After Saigon fell, Ho's boys had sent him to the camps. Years later he made it out with his family to the refugee centers in Hong Kong and eventually to California, where Ng gave him a job cooking in his Vietnamese restaurant on the cusp of Chinatown.

Pham and Ben Ng laughed that night remembering the parties they'd thrown in Ben's Saigon restaurant after pulling a pilot out of the jungle. At one point that night, though, Pham shook his head. There should have been more parties, there were more men, he said.

"What do you mean?" Johnny had asked.

Pham shrugged, keeping his eyes on the nearly empty water glass, the gin almost a memory.

"What are you saying? That we left people over there? Guys were alive that we never went after?" Johnny pressed.

"Need more parties," he said to the glass, his voice just above a whisper. "More men there. Need more parties."

That had been more than a year ago, but until yesterday Johnny had dismissed it as a bad mixture of gin and nostalgia. Not now.

Now Johnny looked at Ben Ng. "I was supposed to meet Pham last night. He called me, said he had to talk to me. But when I got to the park, he'd been murdered."

Ng took another drag, sucking hard on the cigarette. "Very bad," he said. He put the cigarette in the ashtray and immediately picked it up again.

"He told me he'd seen someone, a POW named Kyle Loveless. Pham knew him in Vietnam."

Ng's eyes narrowed slightly. "Yes?" His answer was both a question and an admission.

"I need to know about the man he saw. The captain. Was Pham absolutely sure it was Captain Loveless he saw?"

Ng looked at the desk, avoiding eye contact, and when he spoke his voice was low, forcing Johnny to lean forward. "Maybe. It could be."

"Who did he see? Was it Loveless?" Johnny pressed, demanded. He wouldn't let Ng dodge the question. "Did he see Captain Loveless?"

"This is all very bad. Yes. Very bad."

"Ben, I need to know."

"I don't want trouble." He waved his hands, the cigarette still between his fingers.

Johnny dropped his gaze to the desk. Ben's reaction didn't surprise him. The man was in a foreign country, probably scared to death, just had his friend murdered, didn't trust the police for a second. How to play this one?

Johnny played it easy, speaking gently, his voice soft.

"Ben, I told the police about Kyle Loveless, but they don't believe me. I've got to know what Pham saw. I want to find the man who killed him."

Ben Ng's hands came to rest on the desk. His eyes said he understood. "Yes."

"Have the police been here?"

Ben nodded, and Johnny continued. "Did you tell them about the pilot?"

"I want no trouble. They no believe me anyway."

Johnny felt himself sag. Ben hadn't told them, hadn't backed him up. He looked to the floor and waited a moment. When he glanced up, he saw a mixture of fear and pain in Ben's eyes. "That's okay. But you've got to tell me, Ben. Did he really see that pilot?"

"He see someone he think Loveless."

"Where?"

"Here."

"In the restaurant?"

Ben nodded.

"How? What did he do, just walk in?"

"Yes." Ng looked at Johnny, finally ready to tell it. He inhaled, pulling the smoke deep into his lungs, then blew it out and began. "Three men. One man skinny. He look old. They order much food. For take-away. They standing near bar, waiting. That where Pham see them. Most time Pham never see customers. He in kitchen. But that day, he come up front to speak to me. Tell me something. I don't remember. He see the captain at the bar with others. But he not believe it. He know the man dead, missing in Laos. So he not say anything. But he know the captain and Pham sure the man know him, too.

"Then later, Pham out back, smoking a cigarette, and see the men. They walking to car. He knew. Certain. He called to the captain. The men, they stopped and looked at him. Three men wait outside the car but the captain go inside. The two stopped Pham and told him he wrong." Ben mimicked a man pushing, his palm up, pumping against the air. Ng was warming up to the story now.

"They tell him go away. The man in the car never look at Pham. But Pham knew. Then he tell me. Ask me what to do. I tell him say nothing. Warn him. We work hard. We want no trouble."

"Was he absolutely sure it was this pilot, this Kyle Loveless?"

"He pretty sure."

"Did he tell anyone?"

"No. We don't want trouble."

"But then why did he call me? Why was he scared?"

"Two day ago, man came to restaurant. He said he from Immigration. But I didn't believe him. Pham a citizen now. Why Immigration care about him? The man ask me questions. Where Pham live? When he be at work? I tell him to leave. But it scare me and when I tell Pham, he call you. He want you help."

Johnny pressed his knees against the desk, the toes of his worn brown loafers squeezed under its edge. He rested his forearms on the desk's edge and looked at the bare off-yellowish wall behind Ben. Pham had called him for help. But he hadn't helped, he'd shown up late. He wanted to smash something, anything, strike out against the feelings of frustration and guilt. Instead, he looked at Ng, an idea forming.

"How did they pay?"

"What?"

"How did they pay? The three men. The day they were here. Cash, credit card? The men, the day they were here."

Slowly Ben Ng smiled, then his head began nodding rapidly like a doll in a car's rear window. "Wait," he said. He stood, turned sideways and slipped past the desk with surprising ease.

He was back in minutes, clutching the receipt. He handed it to Johnny, who pulled his notebook from his pocket and wrote down the name, "E & M . . ." The final word didn't show on the receipt.

"I can't read what comes after 'E & M' here. Can you make it out?" He slid the receipt across the desk and Ben studied it for a moment, then shook his head.

Johnny looked at the name again. "It looks like it

could be an *E* or maybe *B*." Ben shrugged. "There's no address, either. Any idea how I can find who this belongs to?"

Ben made an "I don't know" gesture. Johnny sighed deeply and stood, bumping his knees against the side of Ben's desk. He thanked Ben and left.

Outside, he glanced at his watch and knew that with rush-hour traffic on the Harbor and Pasadena freeways, he probably had just enough time to get home, change and drive back to Pasadena to Gordon Geld's house.

7

Johnny took the Orange Grove Avenue exit off the
Pasadena Freeway and turned south toward some of
the oldest and most expensive houses in Southern
California. He checked the address again and two
blocks later turned right onto a quiet, tree-lined avenue.
At the first three houses he saw signs in the front yard:
GORDON GELD: HE GETS THINGS DONE. Even without
the signs, though, Johnny knew he was on the right
street. Cars lined both sides for nearly a quarter mile. A
young dark-skinned man in black slacks, short black
jacket and white shirt with a red bow tie was running
along the long line of cars—BMWs, Mercedes, Jaguars
and Cadillacs and even a Toyota Land Cruiser—back
toward Geld's house. Up ahead Johnny could see a sign
in the street: VALET PARKING.

He pulled to a stop next to the sign and another

man, also in dark slacks and a short black jacket, stepped to the door and opened it.

"I don't plan on staying long," Johnny said. The man nodded, put a stub under the windshield wiper and waited while Johnny got out. He handed Johnny a ticket, then slipped behind the wheel and pulled away from the curb.

Geld's house was invisible from the street, set back and hidden behind a barrier of high, thick bushes. A driveway, protected by a rolling wrought-iron gate that had been retracted, gave access to the property. The driveway curved up near the house, then back to the street again. A wide stone porch with a waist-high wooden railing ran across the front of the house. A swing and two rocking chairs were beyond the railing. Johnny tried without success to imagine Geld lounging in a rocker, his feet propped on the railing, looking onto the wide lawn that ran down to the bushes. But the picture wouldn't fit.

As Johnny walked up the driveway, he wondered again why Geld wanted him there. Barsh had told him Geld didn't want him digging into Pham's murder. The publisher probably wanted to drive home the point personally. Make sure he didn't upset the campaign when it headed into the critical homestretch. Maybe he was just going to fire him. No chance he'd embarrass Geld then. Johnny tried to think of other, more likely reasons for the summons, but came up empty. Climbing the wide steps, he was aware of a gnawing curiosity and a slight dread in his stomach. Whatever Geld wanted, Johnny decided, it couldn't be good.

He paused on the porch and looked back toward the street. The air remained warm despite the setting sun, and Johnny shifted uncomfortably in his sports coat, wanting to take it off and loosen his collar. He could hear faint music from the back of the house, a muted version of "Proud Mary."

He turned and walked through the open door into the house. He was in a large room. He paused for a moment and looked around. Ahead on his left a staircase with a swooping banister led to the second level. The ceiling had been torn away to reveal darkly stained beams. The hardwood floor, its narrow boards as strong and beautiful as ancient tribal art, creaked slightly as he crossed the room to where a door led to a porch.

He stepped into a crowd of designer dresses and thousand-dollar suits and, just like the night before, was suddenly conscious of his own dress. More people were arriving on his heels, and he moved to the side of the wide stone porch and watched some of Southern California's wealthiest people file through. As they glided down the steps, Johnny understood that Geld wasn't just a fringe candidate. In the beginning, almost everyone had dismissed him as marginal, a multimillionaire on an ego trip. The polls showed he was still in third place, but the race was tightening and Geld was attracting some of the richest and most powerful people in Los Angeles. *Rich* and *famous* were the words that leaped to his mind. He watched an industrialist, a developer, L.A.'s mayor and a city councilman walk down the stone steps, their beautiful second wives at their sides. He saw two men walk by chatting casually, and Johnny realized that their latest haircuts had probably cost more than his first car.

"May I get you a drink, sir?" A waiter was at his elbow.

"Gin and tonic," Johnny replied. The waiter turned and disappeared.

Geld's house sat on the edge of an arroyo, and below it a backyard had been carved out of the hillside in three terraced levels. Brick steps switchbacked down the side to grassy areas. The dresses and suits flowed off the porch and down the steps toward the round white tables and umbrellas that dotted the first two levels. A swimming pool and deck consumed most of the third. The band played on a small stage near the end of the pool.

The waiter returned a moment later and held out the tray, and Johnny took the glass, moved to the edge of the porch and leaned against the railing, scanning the crowd for Geld. He didn't see him. He waited a little longer, then walked back into the large empty room he'd passed through a few minutes before.

A short hall led from the room to the kitchen. Johnny saw the caterer's workers arranging small sandwiches on silver trays and turned away. But as he did, he saw Raby cross the kitchen and disappear. Thinking Raby might know where Geld was, Johnny went down the hall and through the kitchen.

He was gone. Johnny stood near the end of a long table and looked around as the men and women in black slacks and white shirts filled trays and carried them out the back door. Johnny looked out back but saw no sign of Raby. Another door led into a dining room. A long, heavy Spanish-style dining table with eight chairs, four on a side, nearly filled the small, intimate room. Raby stood near the end of the table speaking to a short, thin Asian man in a dark suit that hung loosely on him. The man was at least six inches shorter than Raby and looked up at him defiantly.

"Next week," the man said, his voice thick with an accent Johnny didn't recognize.

"It takes time," Raby replied.

"Next week. No wait," the man insisted.

Johnny felt a heavy hand on his shoulder and turned. Duckworth stood behind him. He wore a short-sleeved white shirt and dark blue tie.

"What are you doing here, Rose?"

"I'm looking for Geld."

"Wait out on the porch."

Raby looked through the door then, saw Johnny and without speaking stepped to the door of the dining room and swung it shut.

"I'm supposed to see Mr. Geld," Johnny said.

"Wait on the back porch," Duckworth said again.

"Yeah, sure," Johnny said and walked back through the kitchen and hall and out to the porch. He sipped his gin and tonic and watched as three Iranian businessmen walked slowly down the steps to the pool. Raby came ten minutes later.

"Ah, Mr. Rose, sorry to keep you waiting. Sometimes looking after contributors takes the personal touch. I'm sure you understand. Anyway, I'm glad to see you made it. So you found the directions all right, then?"

"Yes, the directions were fine."

"So, if you'll follow me, Mr. Geld would like to talk to you in private. In his study. It's this way." He turned and walked back into the house. Johnny trailed him across the hardwood floor and up the stairs to the second floor. At the top of the stairs, he turned left down a corridor and stopped in front of the last door. He pushed the door open and looked at Johnny. "He'll be here in a minute," Raby said and walked away.

Johnny watched Raby disappear down the hall. He never looked back. The study was small, perhaps an architectural afterthought or the by-product of an earlier remodeling. But the builder had filled the west wall with windows and through the curtains Johnny could see the fiery orange sun slipping behind the hills on the other side of the canyon. The study's walls were bare save one huge poster, a *Forbes* magazine cover, blown up. It was a photo of Gordon Geld and a headline touting his Midas touch.

He heard footsteps and turned to see Geld walk in. Johnny guessed his age at sixty, maybe even close to sixty-five. He wore a long-sleeved light blue shirt, no jacket and no tie. His informality surprised Johnny.

"Hi, Johnny, I'm really glad you could come," Geld said. He crossed the room and held out his right hand. In his left he carried a tall glass almost full with ice cubes and a clear liquid. As they shook hands, Raby entered and closed the door. He stood next to it, his arms folded across his chest.

Geld turned and looked out the window. "Spectacular view, isn't it?"

"Yes, it is." Johnny waited, letting Geld take the lead. He'd asked Johnny to come. It was his show. Geld sipped his drink. Johnny noticed the sliced lime in the glass then. So Geld liked gin and tonics, too.

He stood next to Johnny looking out the window at the terraced hillside below them and the crowd milling under the umbrellas. All those rich people were waiting for Geld to show up. And where was he? Up here, in his private study watching them, devoting his time to Johnny. Johnny knew he should feel flattered, but felt only an odd suspicion. What did Geld want?

Geld sighed and turned away from the window, stepped back and looked at Johnny. He had to look up slightly, but if it bothered him, it didn't show. He smiled, his eyes holding Johnny's gaze. "You know, I really like your stuff. You're a fine writer."

"Thank you." The remark surprised him. Geld didn't strike him as someone who read bylines.

"There aren't a lot of people around like you anymore. Veteran news people who understand the way things work. People who aren't afraid to ask tough questions."

"It's part of the job. It's what I was trying to do with that story about Pham Lich. It would get a lot of readers," Johnny said. He watched Geld closely, judging his reaction.

"Pham Lich?" Geld seemed genuinely mystified.

"The Vietnamese immigrant who was murdered last night."

"Oh right, right. I spoke with Mr. Barsh about that. Told him to have you check with our lawyer, make sure the police don't give you a hard time." He appeared uninterested, as though Johnny were talking about a high school basketball game.

"Barsh told me not to work on it. Told me those were your orders." Johnny tried to keep the challenge out of his voice. Antagonizing Geld wasn't his goal.

Geld was silent for a moment, his eyes focused somewhere behind Johnny's right shoulder.

"No, that's not what I said. I told him you shouldn't work on it until the police have eliminated you as a suspect. If they clear you tonight or arrest someone tomorrow, fine. Then you can do whatever you want. But"—his eyes shifted directly to Johnny and narrowed slightly—"I will not have one of my reporters writing about a murder where he's considered a suspect. I don't think any newspaper publisher would stand for that. Don't you agree?"

Johnny held Geld's eyes and nodded. "Yes, I see your point."

"Good." Geld smiled and his mood seemed to shift instantly. "As I was saying, you're a good reporter. Most of the articles I read, it's obvious the reporters don't have any idea what they've writing about. Some of the stuff you see in the *L.A. Times* and the *New York Times*, stories on global warming and things. If you know anything about science, you know the writers don't know what they're talking about."

Johnny took a sip of his drink and said nothing. Geld's tone was sure, stubborn and arrogant, barely papered over with civility. But Johnny knew he wasn't there to argue with him. Not about global warming, anyway. Johnny had seen men like Geld many times, geniuses who make the mistake of letting their success do their thinking. No one ever won an argument with them.

"Well, Johnny, I know you're a busy man, so I won't keep you."

"Okay."

"As I'm sure you know, we're heading into the homestretch of this campaign. Our private polling shows it's pretty close. Personally, I think things are just starting to break our way." He stopped for a minute, and his voice lost the campaign quality and he spoke in softer tones. "I really believe we can make a difference. We can change things for the better."

Geld turned and walked halfway to the door, stopped and turned back to face him. Johnny looked past him for a moment and saw Raby. He was watching Geld and didn't see Johnny's glance, and in that unguarded moment, Johnny saw something he couldn't read or understand. Raby showed none of the boredom of a political aide who's heard it all, or even the adoration Johnny had seen in the eyes of so many true believers and hangers-on. Instead his eyes emitted an ill-disguised hostility like infrared rays that leaped across the room and bored into Geld.

"I asked you to come out here tonight because I need a press secretary." Geld's words brought Johnny back to the moment, and he looked again at the publisher. "In the last few weeks of the campaign, I need someone who understands the press. I think you'd do a good job for me. Do you think you might be interested?"

Johnny started to speak, then stopped. The question shocked him. Press secretary? Of all the things he'd ever considered doing in his life, press secretary for a politician had never been one of them. "Ah, I really don't know. This catches me kind of by surprise. Do I have to decide right now?"

"Of course not. But let me tell you, when I win the election I plan on taking my staff with me to Sacramento. No promises, mind you, but you could find yourself press secretary to the governor."

"Ah, well . . ."

"Money's another consideration. How much did you make last year?"

"I don't know exactly."

"It was $43,728. I know because I checked. While the campaign's under way I'll pay you at the rate of $88,000 a year. That's double what you're making now."

Geld crossed the few feet to the windows again, stood next to Johnny and gazed across the arroyo. The far hillside was deep in shadow. Geld reached up and put his hand on Johnny's shoulder. His voice barely

—

above a whisper, he spoke as though he were sharing an intimate secret.

"It's not very often that you get a chance to make a real difference in the world and be well paid for it, too."

"I know. It's a very generous offer."

Geld looked at Johnny. His gray eyes showed a surprising intensity. "I want the best and I get what I want, Johnny. Take a day or two to think about it. But don't take too long. I need an answer. If you want the job, you can start immediately. You won't have to give notice at the *Chronicle*. I'll take care of all that. And remember, offers like this don't come along very often. Don't make a mistake."

"I'll think about it carefully."

Geld smiled. "Good. Now, if you decide to join us, you'll report directly to Mr. Raby and me, no one else. There's not a long chain of command in my campaign," he said and nodded to Raby.

"Right," Johnny said, because he could think of nothing else to say.

"Well, I'm sorry to leave you, but I have to go. Have another drink. Stay as long as you want."

"Thank you."

Geld turned abruptly and walked from the room, but Raby stayed a moment longer. He smiled, but the smile barely moved the corners of his mouth.

"I think you should take the offer. Like Mr. Geld said, don't make a big mistake here." He pivoted, a perfect ball-of-the-foot swivel, and was gone down the corridor. He left the door open.

Johnny stayed in the small study and thought about Geld and Raby as he drank the rest of his gin and tonic. When the slice of lime stuck to the glass, he stuck a finger in and slid the fruit into his mouth. He felt the small jolt as the sourness of the lime hit his taste buds.

Geld had never spoken to him before, but now, in the heat of his campaign, he offered him a job. Double what he was making. Why? Geld could hire an experienced pro, someone who knew politics, someone who knew elections. So why was Geld asking him? And why offer him so much money?

He glanced at the open door and thought again about Raby's strange expression. It wasn't just hostility Johnny had seen. There was something else, a strange condescension, the look of a parent watching a neighbor's spoiled child, knowing his children were so much better.

The whole meeting had a down-the-rabbit-hole feel to it, and Johnny shook his head trying to get his equilibrium back. He turned to the window again. He saw Geld making his way down the steps, shaking hands and smiling as he went. He wore a coat and tie now and there was no drink in sight. Raby was at his elbow, bending close to the shorter man, talking as they walked, the king and his chamberlain. They paused on the steps for a split second and Johnny thought he saw Geld glance back up toward the window. But the publisher was moving through the shadows and it was difficult to see.

Maybe, Johnny thought, he'd imagined the whole damn thing.

This time Weird Harold wasn't waiting for him. Johnny stood on the small cement porch and held the door open for a few moments. But when the cat didn't come, he stepped into his apartment and pulled the door closed behind him. The living room was filled with fading daylight. He crossed the living room to the kitchen area and pulled open the refrigerator. Inside, the shelves were almost bare. A large plastic jug of orange juice and a quart carton of milk and one bottle of beer were on the top shelf. On the next shelf were two packages of ravioli—boil for five minutes and serve—a stick of butter on a saucer, an unopened package of American cheese slices, a loaf of wheat bread and a dark, almost black avocado.

He took out the jug of juice, bumped the door closed with his hip and leaned against the counter as he tipped the jug up and drank. He considered putting on his running shorts and shoes and putting in four or five miles. But when he leaned forward to put the orange juice back in the refrigerator, he noticed the red light blinking steadily on the answering machine at the edge of the counter.

He flipped on the light, punched the button and listened to the machine's mechanical voice: "You have three messages." The tape whirred, stopped and played. But there was no message, nothing but a long stretch of silence followed by a click. The second message was the same silence. Johnny listened. He could hear no breathing, but he knew someone was there, listening, waiting for him to answer. Then the click came and the caller was gone.

The third message was straightforward. "It's Cavanaugh. I got Dodgers tickets for tomorrow. Call me."

The tape rewound and stopped with a jerk. Johnny looked at the machine for a moment and called his former metro editor.

"Hello."

"Hey, it's Johnny."

"Hey. What about tomorrow night, can you make it?"

Johnny exhaled deeply and looked through the sliding glass door to the small fenced-in patio in the back, then at the dining room table. He shook his head as he said no. "I don't know. I better not. I got a couple of things I gotta look after."

"Okay, no problem. Next time."

"Right, next time. Hey, before you go, let me ask you something. You didn't call earlier and hang up without leaving a message, did you?"

"No, of course not, why?"

"Oh, it's not important. Listen, I gotta go."

As Johnny set the phone in its cradle he heard a scratching and loud yowl from the patio. He slid the door back and Weird Harold strolled in, brushing his side against Johnny's leg as he came. The cat paused a moment, and leaped to the counter and paced along its edge. Johnny reached over and scratched the animal's head gently. Weird Harold pressed his head into Johnny's hand, then with a swift and sure swing, batted Johnny's finger, its claws breaking the skin.

"Damn," Johnny said as he jerked his hand back and looked at the short red line forming on his finger. He stared at Weird Harold for a moment and exhaled sharply through his nose, a half-grunt. "I guess you won that time," he said. The cat simply stared at him.

Johnny turned to the cupboard, pulled out the box of food, poured it into his dish and refilled the small water bowl. Weird Harold dropped to the floor and walked casually to the food, took two bites, then walked away.

Johnny put the orange juice back in the refrigerator, considered running again and decided against it. Instead he walked to the living room, picked the remote off the coffee table, flicked on the twenty-seven-inch Sony and flopped onto the couch. Geld's picture filled the screen and Johnny hit the Mute button.

Johnny had seen the commercial enough times already. It was an ad man's sketch of the life of the *Chronicle*'s publisher, beautifully photographed and well scored. A chemist by training, Geld had started working for a big chemical company, then eventually started his own firm, Bio-Analysis Inc., which developed fertilizers and pesticides. But that was just the beginning. Later he moved aggressively into gene splicing, became Fortune 500 rich and began building Geld Enterprises, a collection of businesses around the state. He'd added the *Chronicle* to his empire two years before.

"I know him," Cavanaugh had said when the purchase was announced. "He's no publisher, he's just a savant of the periodic table."

A savant who could become California's next governor, Johnny thought. Would he go with him to Sacramento?

Johnny changed the channel to ESPN and watched a baseball game. He watched the pitches and swings, the groundouts and the runs, without concentration. Instead he thought about Geld and his sudden offer. By the late innings, Johnny was no closer to understanding the man or knowing what he would say to the offer.

He knew he needed help to understand Geld. Maybe then he'd know what to say when he had to give the publisher an answer. Johnny went to the kitchen and took the cordless phone from the counter. He sat at the table and dug through his wallet until he found the business card he wanted. A telephone number written in pencil, faded and blurry, was on the back.

Bill Lewis had been the *Chronicle*'s chief financial officer when Geld bought the paper. A button-down Mormon with a keen sense of business and a quick judge of people, he'd lasted less than a year.

When Lewis answered the phone, Johnny recognized his strong tenor voice immediately. They talked briefly, a casual conversation filled with questions about the family and Lewis's new job. Finally, Johnny told him about Geld's offer.

"Well, congratulations, I guess," Lewis said.

—

"I wondered what you thought."

"Why are you asking me? I haven't worked there in over a year."

"Yes, but you're the only one I know who ever worked that closely with Geld, you know, day to day. Close enough to know the man."

"Well, it's true I worked with him, but I don't know if I'd say I know him."

"Either way, tell me, what do you think? I mean, why would Geld offer me a job as his press secretary?"

"How should I know? I gave up trying to figure out how that man thinks about three minutes after I met him. It's funny, I can still remember it. He came into my office and in about five minutes told me everything that he was going to do to make the paper more profitable. Never asked any questions. Didn't need to. He already had all the answers. After he walked out the door I thought to myself, 'Well, he's quite mad.'" Lewis laughed as he said it. "I think I started sending out résumés the next day."

"So what you're saying is he doesn't seek a lot of advice? Wouldn't really be asking me my opinion, right?"

"Let me put it this way. In the time I worked for him, I don't think he ever asked me once what I thought about something."

"I'm going to have to give this some thought, I guess. I don't think I'm cut out for PR, but on the other hand, the money would be really nice."

"You know something, Johnny, ever since we started talking you've been waving red flags at me. I think maybe you already know your answer."

"Yeah, you're probably right. But tell me, does he really have a chance of winning?"

"If he keeps spending money the way he has been, I'd say he has a shot, sure."

Johnny paused for a moment and glanced across the apartment at the television, where one of the players struck out and threw the bat down in silent anger. He turned his attention back to Lewis.

"You know, there's something else I wanted to ask you about."

"What's that?"

"What do you know about this Charles Raby? He and Geld are thick as thieves, but I got a weird feeling that Raby doesn't like Geld very much. Seems strange, that's all."

"Who knows with those two. They're both weird. I'll tell you this, though, Raby sure doesn't fit the mold. Geld surrounds himself with yes-men. I don't really know Raby that well, but he sure didn't strike me as a yes-man. I didn't think he'd last more than a month. Shows you what I know."

"You have any idea how the two of them hooked up?"

"A couple of years ago, Geld became obsessed with the idea that someone was stealing secrets from Bio-Analysis and selling them to the competition. But then Geld always thought the place was full of spies. Anyway, Raby owns a private security company. Strictly top-notch people, or so he says. Hires only ex-cops and ex-military. Well, Geld heard about him somewhere and hired him to find the leak. They never did find anybody, but somewhere along the way he hired Raby and his entire organization. They've got some kind of exclusive contract. That's when we got all the new guards. And now Raby's chief of security for all of Geld Enterprises."

"Yeah, the new guards. I call them the white shirts."

Lewis laughed. "Brownshirts is more like it. Let me tell you a story I heard. I don't know if it's true or not, but a guy in my church told me this and he swears it's true. A few years ago, some other big company hired Raby to find an industrial spy, just like Geld did. Raby found the guy all right and went to the cops. They were all ready to arrest the guy, but get this, Raby wouldn't sign a complaint. He waited until the day the guy's daughter was getting married. Then Raby had him arrested and dragged out of the reception with his hands handcuffed behind his back. The guy was eventually acquitted, but he never got over the humiliation. He had a heart attack and ended up living on disability. That should give you an idea what kind of man Charles Raby is. Plays for keeps and plays by his own rules."

"So what's he doing for Geld?"

"Keeping the place free of spies, I guess."

Johnny thanked him, hung up and sat in the silent apartment. The cat walked past his legs, rubbing his side on Johnny's ankles, but Johnny ignored him. He pushed his chair back, stood and stretched. But as he stood, he thought he heard something. He stopped and listened and heard it again.

There was a quiet knock at the front door.

Johnny crossed the living room to the door and glanced through the peephole. A woman standing alone on the narrow walkway was looking back at him, waiting.

The small hole distorted everything, like looking at a carnival mirror. Even with distortion, though, Johnny thought he was looking at someone he'd never seen before. He stood peering through the peephole, feeling his warm breath rebound at him off the door.

Now who was this lady? Only one person. That eliminated Jehovah's Witnesses. Sure wasn't the Avon Lady. It was way too late for any kind of door-to-door sales.

He turned to walk away from the door. He wasn't in the mood for company. Neither was his place. Newspapers and magazines were piled on the coffee table, an empty glass there, too. The whole apartment was messy. Not filthy, but not visitor-ready, either. But then he never had people over, didn't invite anyone into his privacy. He decided to pretend he wasn't home.

He took a couple of steps from the door, then heard the soft, tentative rap again and stopped and looked at the door, letting his curiosity pull him back. He moved to the door. Later he would wonder what would have happened if he hadn't. How it all might have been different if he'd just ignored the woman on the sidewalk.

But he didn't. Instead he jerked open the door and said, "Can I help you?"

She was looking away as he opened the door, and the sudden movement seemed to frighten her.

"Oh, ahh, hi, ahh, I'm sorry, you startled me."

Johnny nodded but said nothing, taking a long look at the woman. She was pretty, with blonde hair down to her shoulders, a white blouse with a princess collar, a brooch at the neck, a dark jacket and a skirt that reached to mid-calf. A little too conservative for his taste, but still nice.

"I'm looking for John Rose. I think this is his apartment but half these doors don't have numbers."

"It's rent control."

"Pardon me?"

"It's the rent control. The landlord refuses to fix anything because he can't raise the rent."

"Oh."

"Anyway, I'm Johnny Rose. How can I help you?"

She seemed uncertain what to say next. "I was given your name. Told you wanted to talk to me."

Johnny squinted at the woman, trying to see her face better in the blend of last rays of daylight and soft yellow from the porch light. No. He'd never seen her before.

"I'm sorry, you are?"

"Oh!" She gasped. It came out as almost a squeak. "I'm sorry. Forgive me. I'm Susan Loveless. You wanted to talk to me about my husband, Kyle."

Johnny blinked, fighting not to show his surprise. "Oh, right, yes. Please come in." He stepped aside, holding the door open.

"If I'm catching you at a bad time, I can come back." She bit her lower lip.

"No, not at all." He tried to sound lighthearted, casual. The last thing he wanted was to see her walk away. If she left, she'd never be back. He'd bet on it. Years of experience had taught him that. If someone's willing to talk, you have to listen. There are no dress rehearsals in life.

She stepped past him into the apartment, and he gently pushed the door closed behind her and walked across the living room to the kitchen. Susan Loveless, though, stopped just inside the door and looked around.

"Maybe this isn't a good idea," she said and chewed her lip again.

Johnny turned and saw the look on her face. "Oh, yeah, sorry about the mess. The cleaning lady only comes every other generation. She seems to have skipped mine." A forced smile turned up the corners of her mouth.

"Look," Johnny said, "come on in and I'll make us some coffee and we can talk. You don't have to tell me anything you don't want to. Okay? Give it ten minutes and if you're still uncomfortable, you can go. And listen, why don't you open the front door, this place could use a little ventilation."

"Okay," she said. Turning, she pulled open the door slightly, just enough to let in the fresh air, then crossed the living room to the round table in the dining area and sat down. As he poured water into the coffeemaker, Johnny stole glances at Kyle Loveless's widow. She used makeup well, and thoroughly. Expensive clothes, too. But she seemed an odd combination, as if she couldn't decide who she was. She had the dress-for-success look of a hard-as-nails boss but the demeanor of a nervous nail-biter in the typing pool. Strange.

"Cream or sugar?" he asked.

"Black's fine."

As he set the mug in front of her, Johnny looked at her hands clenched together on the table. She wore a diamond wedding ring, he noticed. He wondered if she'd remarried. He sat down and sipped his coffee, being casual, trying to calm this frightened woman.

"I appreciate your coming by. I'll admit I'm a little surprised. I didn't really expect to hear from you, especially this soon. The lady at the league didn't give me much hope."

His comment seemed to surprise her. She started to speak, stopped and then nodded. "Yes, well, I wanted to come." She wrapped her hands around the mug and looked at them.

"Mrs. Loveless." Johnny paused for half a beat. "It is still Mrs. Loveless?"

"Yes. I never remarried and please call me Susan."

"Okay, Susan. I'll come right to the point here. I know this may sound really strange, but have you had any contact with your husband or do you have any reason to believe he's alive?"

She looked at her coffee cup as she spoke. "No. Kyle is dead."

"Mrs. Loveless, ah, Susan, I know this is hard, but a friend of mine, a man who knew Kyle in Vietnam, swears he saw him in L.A. just a couple of days ago."

"Oh, Mr. Rose, I was afraid of this. I almost didn't come because of it, but I knew I had to talk to you. I couldn't take the chance." She seemed on the edge of tears.

"I don't think I understand. Couldn't take what chance?"

"You don't know what it's like to have your hopes raised, to allow yourself to hope, to hope for just a second that your husband really is alive. If you write an article in your paper saying Kyle is alive, it will become a circus again. The phone calls, the TV people in front of my house standing on the lawn, just waiting for me to come out. One woman I know, they went through her trash. Dug through her garbage!"

Her hands squeezed the mug tightly, her knuckles white. Slowly she raised her eyes and looked at him. "I've seen Kyle myself, you know. Dozens of times, maybe even hundreds. I've seen him in shopping centers and on the street and even caught a glimpse of him in the crowd at the Hollywood Bowl." Her voice quivered, then came back strong, defiant. "I once stopped in the middle of a busy intersection to get a closer look at a man sitting on a bus bench. All the time the cars around me were honking their horns and people were yelling. I just sat there, knowing it was stupid, but I had to look . . . he looked so much like Kyle. So, you see, I know what it's like. I also know your friend was mistaken, Mr. Rose. Kyle is dead."

Johnny hunched over his own untouched coffee. He wasn't ready to let it go. He couldn't. He'd seen Pham's body, turned it over. If Kyle Loveless was dead, then Pham was murdered for nothing. Somehow that seemed to make it even worse. "My friend was very sure."

Suddenly her shoulders dropped and she seemed to slump. She sipped her coffee for the first time and set the mug gently back on the table.

"Mr. Rose, I lived with false hope for almost twenty years. I kept telling myself that he was alive and that he would come home again." She shook her head slightly and exhaled deeply. "You know, it's almost funny. All those years it became like a religion, an article of faith." She paused, then asked, "Did you know Kyle grew up in Southern California?"

"No. I didn't."

"Well, he did. Played baseball all the way through high school. But he was never much of a Dodgers or Angels fan. For some reason Kyle loved the Chicago Cubs. I don't know why. But for all those years, I kept track of the Cubs. I always knew where they were in the standings and if they had any hot rookies so I could tell him how they were doing when he came home. Then one night a few years ago, I was driving home from work and I was listening to the news and the sports came on. Chicago had lost again, they were always losing, and I said to myself, don't worry, Kyle, we'll get 'em next year and suddenly I knew. I just knew. It didn't matter what happened to the Chicago Cubs. Kyle was never coming home. He was dead.

"All those years I spent with that faith at my core, checking everything against that central belief that Kyle was alive somewhere. Then that stupid baseball score slipped right past all my defenses and I knew. I just knew. I guess I'd known for years but hadn't admitted it. Not until that moment. It was an epiphany for me. And you know how I felt? I wasn't sad or depressed or anything like that. I wasn't even angry because of all the years I'd wasted. I just felt empty. It was like I'd been in a hospital for twenty years and was suddenly released. I went home that night and swore I was starting my life over again. That part of it was over. Kyle is dead and I have to get on with my life."

She stopped talking for a moment and wiped a tear from the corner of her eye, making a dabbing motion with her index finger.

They sat quietly for a moment. Johnny said nothing. He was thinking about Jimmy. He thought about his second tour, of his letters and his one phone call home. He'd gotten a new assignment. He was still on the choppers, still working the door, but this was a special unit, he said. All it did was go after downed pilots and guys lost in the jungle. He knew what it was like being down there, looking to the sky for rescue, Jimmy said. A very special unit. They were doing good things. Guys just like Jimmy probably went looking for Kyle Loveless, Johnny thought.

She looked at him, her eyes almost begging. "Please, Mr. Rose, don't put anything in your paper about Kyle being alive. I've started my life over. I can't take that again."

Johnny looked at Susan Loveless, unsure of what to say. He wanted to comfort her, reassure her that he would let it go, drop the story. But he couldn't.

"Susan, I can assure you that I'd never write anything that I can't verify. I would never write something that I didn't know for sure was true."

She stood suddenly. "I have to go. I've said too much already. Maybe I shouldn't have come." She pulled her purse off the back of the chair where it hung and started to the door.

"I'll walk you to your car," Johnny said, standing abruptly and pushing his chair back.

She was halfway across the living room and Johnny hurried to catch up. He stepped in front of her to open the door wider.

"Thank you," she said and stepped out to the sidewalk. She paused and waited while Johnny pulled the door closed. He fell in beside her as she walked toward the street.

"Thanks a lot for coming. I know it wasn't easy for you," Johnny said.

She seemed more relaxed; maybe just glad to be leaving.

"The thing is, I know Kyle, or knew him. You have to understand we were very much in love. If he were here, if he were alive, he'd contact me. He would. So if anyone in the world would know that Kyle was alive, especially if he were here in L.A., it'd be me, not some Vietnamese refugee."

"Yeah, I understand. I hadn't thought of that," Johnny said.

They reached the curb and she walked to a black VW Jetta. She dug in her purse for her keys, but as she pulled them out they fell to the sidewalk, and Johnny bent quickly to pick them up. They dangled from a round yellow disc with a happy face painted on it. The words "WE'LL KEEP YOU SMILING, S&J SHELL" and an address around the edge. Funny, Susan Loveless didn't strike him as the happy face type.

"Thank you," she said as she took the keys. She smiled slightly and looked at him, holding his eyes for a second. "Please," she said, turned and got in the Jetta. It pulled away from the curb and Johnny walked back to his apartment.

He dropped into the chair at the table and looked at the mug she'd clutched. What she said made sense. Maybe if she'd remarried, had kids or something. But Susan Loveless hadn't remarried. Had centered her life on a belief that her husband was alive. She'd carried the torch for the guy for more than twenty years and what did he do? Nothing. Not even a postcard. No. It didn't make any sense.

He sat at the table, looking at the two cups of now-cold coffee. Her visit made it tougher. Harder to keep it all balanced, be fair to Susan Loveless and Pham both. No, maybe that wasn't true. Maybe she made it easier. Being fair and balanced always gave you an edge. It kept you apart, on the sidelines. The words were like a chalk line on the field. You cross the line and words won't help. Cross the line and you have to play the game.

He stood, picked up the cups and carried them to the sink. He rinsed them idly, then turned them upside down on the counter to dry, thinking of Susan Loveless. Everyone insisted her husband was dead, his bones decomposing in a jungle in Southeast Asia. Everyone except Pham, and now he himself was dead.

There was no debate over that. Johnny had the blood-stains to prove it.

Maybe there was a logical explanation. Maybe Pham hadn't really seen Kyle Loveless. Maybe Susan Loveless was right; Pham was mistaken, just the latest mistake in a tableau of mistakes that had cost 50,000 American lives. Johnny was beginning to believe he'd never know.

As he thought again of Susan Loveless, something she'd said bothered him. He tried to remember, but he couldn't focus on it.

Suddenly he felt very tired, exhausted. He needed to sleep. He climbed the stairs to his bedroom. He was about to flip off the light and get in bed when he glimpsed the framed photo atop the dresser. He crossed the room and picked it up. Perhaps it was stupid to have a picture of his ex-wife on the bureau in his bedroom. But he kept it, he told himself, because it was the last good picture he had of Jimmy. And he knew it was the last good picture he had of himself. The last time he'd still had hope of holding on to the only two people he loved.

It had been shot at the beach, late on a September afternoon. The three of them stood near the water's edge facing west, squinting into the sun and smiling foolishly. Johnny and Jimmy were on the outside, Crystal sandwiched between them. He and Jimmy had their arms draped across Crystal's shoulders and she hugged each around the waist.

Johnny looked at Jimmy and remembered that the trip to the beach had been Crystal's idea. Less than a month before, Jimmy had committed himself to the hospital. It might help, she'd said, and Johnny, still believing his brother might recover, hadn't argued. His gaze moved from Jimmy to Crystal and he thought again of their marriage, which had collapsed after four years.

When she'd finally left there was no blowup, no huge fight, no top-of-the-lung curses. Their marriage hadn't died a fiery death full of recriminations. It had simply dried up and withered from lack of time, attention and care. He was chasing stories, she was chasing a career. When the end came, they parted with a civility as fragile as bone china. He had even helped her pack and carry her boxes from the apartment to her car. After the last box was in the backseat and Crystal had driven away, he'd come back into the apartment, sat on the couch and felt the heavy weight of loneliness, as if he were the only person on an intergalactic space ship light-years from human touch.

He put the photo back on the dresser, sat on the edge of the bed for a moment, then lay down and rolled over, turning his back to the picture.

9

Johnny walked into the *Chronicle*'s morgue at just after nine the next morning. A young black woman with large shoulders, a round face and hair cut close to her scalp sat at a desk near the door. She was bent over the *L.A. Times,* spread open between a pile of books and a computer terminal. She did not look up when Johnny came in.

"Hey, Jaunique, how are you?" he said as he approached. He stood next to the desk, his thigh brushing its edge.

She glanced up, then down to the paper again. "Hi, Johnny. I'm okay, but I'll be better after I finish my coffee." She tapped the lip of a mug a few inches from her hand with her index finger.

"So, Jaunique, you think maybe you could do me a favor?"

"Maybe. Depends on what it is." She kept her eyes on the paper as she picked up the coffee and sipped it.

"I need you to run a search. Our files, maybe the *L.A. Times*, the *Register*, the *News* and the other locals. I'm looking for a company with the initials E and M. Maybe E and M Incorporated or something like that."

She looked up finally. When she did, she smiled and her white teeth gleamed against her dark brown lips. "What city's it in?"

"I don't know. Around L.A. somewhere, I think."

"What do they do? What kind of business is it?"

"I don't know. All I've got are the initials. Nothing else."

"E and M. That's it? That's all you've got?"

"I'm afraid so."

Jaunique folded back the paper, picked up a note pad and wrote the initials. She looked at Johnny. "Mr. Jonathan Rose, do you ever do anything the easy way? When was the last time you came in here and had something that didn't take my whole morning?"

"That's why I come to you. Because you're so good at it."

She shook her head. "Boy, just because you say nice words to me doesn't mean I'm going to be doing all your work for you. You know that now, don't you?" Johnny smiled but said nothing. "Okay, that with an ampersand or is the *and* written out?"

"Ampersand."

She made another note, then looked up. "Well, that's not much to go on, but I'll try. No promises."

"I'll take whatever you find." He turned and looked at the shelves. "Mind if I look around a little myself?"

"Help yourself," she said and lowered her eyes to

the paper. She showed no sign of starting the search as Johnny walked down the narrow aisle to the back of the room. Halfway along the shelves he found the stacks of yellow telephone books. The books for L.A.'s west side, central division, the San Fernando Valley and the San Gabriel Valley were mixed together with those of other counties. Johnny worked left to right, pulling each directory off the shelf, holding it in his right hand and balancing it on his arm as he scanned the pages.

An hour later he closed the last book and looked at the list of more than two dozen names and phone numbers. There was an E & M Automotive, an E & M Advertising, an E & M Machine Tools, E & M Sandblasting. There was an E & M Exterminators and an E & M Business Consultants, an E & M massage parlor and more than a dozen others. But none of them was in downtown L.A., near Chinatown or had offices near the city's center. Johnny closed his notebook and walked to the front of the morgue.

"Hey, Jaunique, you having any luck?"

"I don't know. I found some stuff, but none of it looks too good. I checked our database and the *Times* and the *Register*, just like you asked. Went back three years. I found, let's see." She flipped through a computer printout on her desk. "Oh, I don't know, probably six dozen references to an E ampersand M. There was a double murder in a bar called the E & M out on the east side two years ago. There was an E & M Foundation giving money to buy computer equipment for the schools out in the Valley. But most of the articles were about some fertilizer company that had a tanker car derail up north near Lancaster. They had to evacuate the whole surrounding area. Happened about a year and half ago. You remember it? Made the TV news."

"No, not really."

"Well, that's about all I've got. There are some others. You know, the usual stuff, businesses opening or a robbery or burglary. Usual stuff. It's all on the printout, name of the company, and first two lines of each story. If you want, I'll check some more."

"No. That's fine. Can I take this?" He motioned to the thin pile of paper with the perforated edge.

"Please do."

Johnny took the printout, folded it, stuck it in his outside coat pocket.

"Thanks, Jaunique. I owe you."

"It's what they pay me for, but you can owe me anyway," she said.

He took the elevator to the newsroom on the fourth floor and wandered back to his desk. The reporter in the cubicle next to him was hunched over her keyboard, interviewing someone on the phone, typing her questions and answers as she went. She didn't look up as Johnny walked by.

He moved into the relative privacy of his own cubicle and unfolded the printout on top of the other papers on his desk. He blocked out the noise of the newsroom, the high-pitched voice of the reporter next to him and the constant buzzing of the telephones around him and read each line twice. As he went over the list of businesses and locations, he wondered if one was where an American pilot had chosen to reappear after rising from the dead halfway around the world.

As he started down the list a third time, his phone rang. Without looking away from the list, he fumbled for the receiver and picked it up.

"Johnny Rose," he said, still concentrating on the names, only half-listening to the phone call.

"You be careful and it stops with the slope." The voice was male, older and raspy.

"What? Who is this?"

"Leave it alone, Rose."

"Who the hell is this?"

"Leave it alone, you saw what happened to Lich. The same thing could happen to you in a heartbeat. Let it go." And the phone was dead.

Johnny stared at the phone, hearing the dial tone coming from the receiver like an insistent, low-voltage fire alarm. His heart was racing. Why would someone threaten him? He remembered the story about Pham's murder and a sense of dread seeped through him. The story had been short, straightforward and run deep in the paper. It had carried no byline and had never mentioned him. But the caller knew to call him. How?

He grabbed his notebook and wrote down the conversation, re-creating it word for word as accurately as possible. The moment he finished, Johnny picked up the phone again and called the newsroom receptionist.

"Sarah, did some guy just call and ask for me or say he wanted to talk to the reporter who wrote about a Vietnamese man being murdered?"

"What? No. When?"

"Just two minutes ago?"

"No, no one's called and asked for you today and no one asked about any murder story. Why?"

"Oh, nothing. Thanks."

Johnny hung up and called the paper's main reception desk. It took a few minutes for the woman to ask the four people answering the phones, but she called back with the same answer Sarah had given him moments before. No one had asked for him or called about the story. The man had called him direct.

Somehow the killer knew whom to call. He must have gotten Johnny's name from the cops. There was no other possible explanation. Unless. Johnny stood and looked over the tops of the partitions, scanning the newsroom from cubicle to cubicle, settling on one reporter, then another. Was someone at the *Chronicle*, a reporter, a copyeditor, the receptionist, connected to Pham's murder?

He sat down and instantly the phone rang. He looked at it for a moment and snatched it up after the second ring.

"Johnny Rose." He listened intently.

"Johnny, it's Doc."

He exhaled. He had been holding his breath. He could feel his heart beating, reverberating in his chest. "Oh, hi. How are things at the coroner's office?"

"Hey, Johnny, you okay? You sound kind of strange."

"Yeah, I'm fine, I just got a weird phone call, that's all. No big deal."

"Okay, if you say so."

"Yeah, really, I'm fine.

"Okay, and now that you ask, things are busy as hell here. You know, there's never a shortage of corpses that need toting, tagging and cutting. That's why I was a little late in getting back to you. I called yesterday and left a message."

"Yeah, sorry I didn't get back to you. But the thing is, when I first called, I was working on a column and figured maybe you could help me out. But now I'm not doing anything on it anymore. I'm working on something else."

"I'll bet you called about John Doe Number One-sixty-five. The body in the desert, right?"

Johnny sat a little straighter in his chair. "How'd you know that?" There was a long pause before Doc responded.

"I just took a guess. You know, with Jimmy and all, I just figured this would be one you'd be following up pretty hard."

"Jimmy?" What was Doc talking about? "What does Jimmy have to do with this?"

"It's what he did the second time around. That's why I thought you called in the first place."

"No." Johnny shook his head. "Doc, I don't know what you're talking about." He leaned forward, resting his elbows on his desk, and thought of the decomposed body in the desert and the dog tags glittering in the sun. And he thought of his brother, who had spent his second tour in Vietnam with a special unit whose sole job was to hunt for Americans lost behind enemy lines.

"Doc, what are you talking about?" he said again.

"The dead guy in the desert, Johnny."

"Yeah, I know that. But I don't know what you're getting at here. Let's start at the beginning. Was he murdered or what?"

"No, looks like he died of natural causes. Exposure. He'd been out there maybe three weeks or a month."

"So what's the big mystery? And what's all this talk about Jimmy?"

"Look, we got a tentative ID off some dog tags he was wearing, but the body was so badly decomposed it's going to take a week, maybe ten days to rehydrate the fingers so we can lift some prints and verify. *If* we can get prints. There's no guarantee."

"What are you getting at, Doc?"

"According to the tags, the guy was Sergeant Roberto Ruiz."

"Yeah, I already knew he was military. Where was he stationed?"

"That's just it. He wasn't stationed anywhere. According to the Army's records, the stiff can't be Roberto Ruiz because Sergeant Ruiz was lost in Vietnam about twenty-five years ago. Listed as MIA, presumed dead, body never recovered."

"But—" Johnny stopped, remembering Pham's certainty that he'd seen Kyle Loveless. "That's not possible, is it? I mean, what's the guy's family say?"

"We haven't contacted them yet. We have to wait for a positive ID, especially with something like this. And this is strictly off the record, Johnny. You can't run anything until we get a positive ID."

"I understand that. Where's he from?"

"I don't know. It's not my case, I'm just giving you what I picked up around here."

Johnny shook his head slightly, thinking of Pham's murder and the threat he'd just received and what Doc was telling him about a second MIA. "You know, Doc, something really strange is going on here. How can an MIA just suddenly drop into the middle of the Mojave Desert? What's he doing out there in the first place?"

"I don't know, it could be anything. Maybe the Army's records are screwed up. Maybe the guy deserted and somehow got home and then ended up out there. I don't have any idea. It could be a lot of things, but I thought you'd find it interesting."

"Could someone have faked it for some reason? Made it look like Ruiz?"

"If they did, they knew what they were doing. The Army records show Ruiz enlisted in 1967. And I know for a fact that right after that, in 1968 I think it was, the Army started issuing dog tags with Social Security numbers instead of serial numbers. Ruiz's tags had the original serial number, not a social. So it looks authentic."

"This doesn't make any sense at all."

"Yeah, I know. That's why I thought you'd find it interesting."

Johnny started to speak again, but didn't. He dropped his gaze to the gray metal desktop, focusing on an old coffee stain where his mug had left a ring, then shifting to the printout he'd received from Jaunique.

"Tell me something, Doc. You did a tour in Nam. You think we left anyone over there?"

"I don't know. But if we did, they'd all be dead by now. But maybe you're asking the wrong guy."

"You were there."

"Yeah, like you said, I did one tour. Jimmy did two." Johnny was silent. "Maybe you should ask him."

"Yeah, maybe."

"You been by lately?"

"No. You know how it is. It's hard."

"Well, it ain't easy for him either."

"No. I know. Maybe you're right. Maybe I should go talk to him."

"Couldn't hurt. If anybody would have a good idea about it, he would."

"Thanks, Doc. And let me know if you get a positive ID or a hometown, okay?"

"Of course."

Johnny hung up, picked up a pen and pulled the cap off and replaced it several times absentmindedly as he stared at the computer screen, thinking of his conversation with Doc. Was the body in the desert another

MIA? Or was there a simple, logical explanation for that, too? But if there were, why had someone threatened him? He put the pen in his pocket, picked up his notebook and went to Barsh's office.

The metro editor was behind his desk, his side to the door as he typed at a terminal.

"Hey, you got a minute, I need to talk to you," Johnny said.

Barsh half-turned and looked across his body at Johnny. "Of course, come on in. I was going to call you anyway."

Johnny stepped into the office but didn't sit. He flipped open his notebook and scanned the notes he'd taken a moment before.

"Listen to this. Someone just called me and threatened me. Told me to stay away from Pham Lich's murder. Quote, the same thing could happen to you in a heartbeat. End quote."

"You have any idea who it was? I mean, did you recognize the voice?"

"No, none at all. It was a man, I know that. He had sort of a raspy voice." Johnny turned and looked through the glass that made the wall to Barsh's office. His back was to the metro editor's desk. "There's something more to it."

"What?"

"I didn't write the story, I'm not even mentioned in it. But the guy called me. Called me direct. He knew my name." He turned back to face Barsh.

"Maybe it came through the switchboard and Sarah assumed you'd written it."

"No, I asked her. Called the main switchboard, too. No one called asking about Pham. No one called asking for me, either."

Barsh swiveled and faced Johnny completely. He laid his arms on his desk and looked at Johnny. His expression changed slightly. The concern of a moment earlier was gone, replaced by a look Johnny couldn't interpret.

"You know, John, I don't like what I think you're saying here. Do you think someone here's involved, is that what you're saying?"

"No. I don't know what I'm saying." Johnny turned and looked through the glass at the newsroom. "Really, it could have been anyone. A cop, a paramedic, the guy who drove the coroner's wagon. Any of those people could have gotten my name. But I didn't give my direct number to anyone but that detective."

"You're right, it could have been anyone. But let me ask you something else. Did anyone else hear the conversation?"

Johnny turned back from the window and looked at Barsh. He shook his head slowly side to side, thinking of the reporter next to him, lost in her own interview. "No, why? What difference does it make?"

"I got a call from Detective Earl this morning."

"Yeah, so?" Johnny knew something was wrong now, he could sense it in Barsh's tone. He looked at the editor woodenly.

"He asked me a lot of questions about your going out to the park." Barsh's eyes were focused in the middle of Johnny's chest. "He asked if I gave you the assignment, if I knew about it before you went. Stuff like that." Barsh shifted his eyes suddenly and looked up, returning Johnny's stare. He spoke with urgency. "John, he asked if I knew about the POW story."

Johnny dropped his arms to his side, the notebook still open in his left hand. "What did you tell him?"

"The truth. I told him I didn't know about it in advance but you had carte blanche to follow anything you wanted without checking with me first. Then I asked him if all these questions meant you were a suspect."

"And what'd he say?"

"Not much. He said it was all routine, but I don't believe him." Johnny looked at him, the question obvious on his face. "Sheridan's been checking with some of his sources. Johnny, they found your fingerprints on the dowel that was part of the garrote."

"Of course they did. I took it off Pham's neck. I told him that. Look, I'll call him and tell him about the phone call. Why would someone threaten me, if I was involved in the murder?"

"John, even if we can prove you got that phone call, we can't prove you were threatened."

Johnny smoothed his hair with his right hand, rolled his shoulders and looked at Barsh again. "Why the hell would I make up a story about getting a threatening phone call?"

"I don't know. But Detective Earl might think you—"

"Think what? Think that I made it up to cover myself?" Johnny could feel anger swelling inside, his stomach twisting in knots. "Tell me this, then. What possible motive would I have to kill him?"

"Look, I'm sure there's a logical explanation. Just stay away from it."

"Logical explanation. You know, everyone keeps talking about logical explanations. I'm beginning to wonder." Johnny put his notebook into his pocket and turned to leave. "I've got a column I'm working on."

"Stay away from this, John. You understand that?"

Barsh's voice was strong and carried across the news-room as Johnny walked out.

He stopped at the receptionist's desk on his way to the elevator. Sarah, a young blonde with a thin face and stringy hair, looked up and smiled. "Hi, Johnny, heading out?"

"Yes, if anyone's looking for me, tell 'em I had to go talk to someone about a story. I don't know when I'll be back."

He started to turn away when she looked at her board of blinking lights and said, "That's your line. You want me to get it?"

"Sure."

"*Chronicle*." She paused. "He's away from his desk at the moment, just a minute, I'll try to find him. Who should I say is calling?" She listened, then hit a button on the phone and looked at him.

"Susan Herbert. Says you were trying to reach her."

He considered the name for a moment. "Doesn't ring a bell. Take a message, would you?" He turned and walked to the elevator.

As he waited for the elevator, he considered the name again. Susan Herbert. He was positive he hadn't called her. How important could it be?

10

The Veterans Cemetery in West Los Angeles is separated from the sprawling grounds of the VA hospital by the San Diego Freeway, a giant swath of continuous motion and noise dividing the dead from the ill.

Jimmy thought it was funny. "Hey, no point in getting me a hearse when I die, just throw my body in a wheelbarrow, push me over there and dump me under a bush." He'd said it the first time Johnny visited him at the hospital.

Johnny hadn't laughed. He had been unwilling to accept what Jimmy had understood so clearly from the first day there. This was the last stop. This was Jimmy's home now. Forever. Johnny had still been hoping it would be different, that somehow someone could glue the pieces back together.

It took Johnny only about twenty minutes to make it from the paper to Wilshire Boulevard. He drove slowly through the VA grounds, remarkable for their unhurried pace. Mayberry with palm trees and a military twist.

He turned north, following the road for a few minutes, then parked not far from Jimmy's residence hall. Built of concrete, the hall had the look of a Depression-era building constructed by the Works Progress Administration back when the nation was struggling to put itself back together. Today the people living there were doing the same, but with less hope and less time. And now Johnny had come here himself seeking help, looking for a way to make the pieces of a strange and deadly puzzle fit together. He'd come looking for guidance from his brother, who understood Vietnam and MIAs better than anyone Johnny knew.

A group of seven men sat at a picnic table in front of the hall. Two were playing a game and the others, including two black men on folding metal chairs at the end, were watching. A small boom box sat on the edge of the table. It was tuned to an oldies station. Sam the Sham and the Pharaohs were singing.

As Johnny got closer, he saw they were playing dominoes. He stood back for a moment watching the play, then approached, stopping next to the far end of the picnic table. None of the men seemed to notice him.

"Hi, I'm looking for Jimmy Rose, you know if he's in?" Johnny asked.

"No." One of the dominoes players answered. He sat in a chair at the end of the table. He looked about sixty, with a long beard and thick hair that stuck out from under a baseball cap and curled on his collar. "He's not in," the player said and looked up at Johnny, studying him for a moment. "You're his brother."

"Yes."

"Yeah, figured so," the man said. "You look like him. Haven't seen you around before, though."

"You know where he is?"

"I ain't seen him."

Johnny looked at the men, letting his gaze slip from man to man. They were all staring back at him now. He stepped closer and realized that the man who had spoken was in a motorized wheelchair, not a folding metal one like the others. After a moment the man turned back to the dominoes and the others shifted their gaze back to the little black bricks.

"How long since you last saw Jimmy?" he asked.

"Three days, maybe more, I don't know."

Three days. Who knew when he'd be back. "Okay. Thanks," Johnny said.

He turned and walked back to his car. As he neared the Z he could hear the radio again. This time it was Johnny Rivers.

He pulled away from the curb and went to find his brother. He cruised slowly through the streets, looking at the men sitting on the benches and walking the streets and rolling along the sidewalks in their wheelchairs. He was certain he wouldn't see Jimmy and he didn't. He continued westward until he reached a parking lot at the western edge of the VA property and stopped. The nose of the Z nudged the chain-link fence that marked the property's border. He got out and looked at the canyon on the other side of the fence. It wasn't particularly deep or even that wide. Johnny could see the tall eucalyptus trees and the backs of the private homes across an expanse of weeds, tall grass and stubby trees. Still, in an area of twelve million people, it had the feel of the country. The canyon's rocky ground dropped steeply, then rose to a narrow plateau before dropping and rising again to the back of the private land.

If Jimmy had gone back in-country, this was probably where he'd gone. He'd done it often over the years. In the beginning he'd sometimes found himself a place out near the freeway where the trees and ivy grew thick on the sloping shoulders of the elevated roadway. But there were others out there. Some like Jimmy, decades later, unable to move fully back to "the world," as they'd called home when they were fighting and dying halfway around the globe. And there were those who had never served but haunted the intersections claiming to be vets, holding up cardboard signs, begging. More now, it seemed, than ever. Finally Jimmy had found his own place, this place, away from the walls and the other vets, where he could be alone with his own private demons. He'd taken Johnny there once, shyly but proudly showing how he'd cut the fence, peeled it back, followed a path to some trees and made a camp.

"Jimmy. Jimmy, it's me, Johnny," he shouted and turned slowly, scanning the horizon for his brother.

Johnny leaned against the side of the car, watching the fence. Occasionally he turned from looking at the clump of trees to watch the sidewalk and buildings for his little brother. As Johnny waited, he thought back to when they were kids growing up, Jimmy always trying to keep up, running a little harder to stay with his older brother.

Some of Johnny's earliest memories were of looking after Jimmy, helping him with his fights, helping with his studies, telling him about girls, giving him advice. Always the big brother.

Vietnam changed that. Changed everything, in fact. Johnny was only fourteen months older, but two years ahead in school. He wasn't around to protect his little brother those last two years, keep him straight, keep him in school and out of the military. Johnny was in college studying, working part-time and protesting against the war. Busy, full of important things. Saving the whole world and losing sight of his own.

It was different for Jimmy. He dropped out after only a few weeks at a community college and joined the Army. A year after accepting his high school diploma, he was in Vietnam, a helicopter door gunner.

His letters always told Johnny not to worry. He was having a good time, seeing the world. There really wasn't much danger. They never really saw much action. Then, nine months into his tour, his crew was on a mission to pick up a patrol. It was years later before Johnny finally learned what happened.

The chopper set down in a clearing. The patrol scampered out of the grass and started boarding.

"I gotta take a piss, just be a second," Jimmy yelled and jumped from the ship, running across the grass, normally higher than his head, now beaten to the ground by the wind of the blades. Finally he got just beyond the helicopter wind and unzipped. The first mortar round hit then. It was near the chopper. The second one hit a second later, even closer. Jimmy turned and watched as the helicopter lifted up, shooting skyward as quickly as it could, fighting for altitude. He could see a GI from the patrol, half in the chopper, on his belly, his legs dangling, kicking against the sky. Two others were on the ground wounded, screaming. And he saw them. VC. Suddenly the place seemed alive with them. They rushed into the clearing where the chopper had been moments before, shooting at the fleeing aircraft.

Jimmy dived to the ground. He burrowed into the tall, thick grass and hid, hearing the mix of the wounded men screaming and the VC yelling. The noise of the chopper faded and he heard two shots and the screaming stopped. There was nothing except the chatter of the VC.

Lying in the grass, Jimmy told himself the chopper would be back. They knew where he was, where they'd left him. But he wasn't sure. Maybe they thought he was dead, too. Maybe they'd just let it slide, not bother taking the chance to come for him. No, they wouldn't abandon him. Would they?

And then the weather closed in. Fog and rain. There was no visibility. Nothing flew and the VC hunkered down. He could hear them out there, beyond the thin wall of grass through the veil of fog, chattering away in their singsong babble. Sometimes they seemed so close he was certain that if he just reached through the fog he could touch them. A hundred times he started to reach for the sidearm he carried, ready to start shooting and get it over with. But each time he forced himself to hold back and in the end, cloaked by the thin, impenetrable veil of grass, he was safe. They never saw him. For four days Jimmy lay hidden, drinking rainwater, eating bugs and grass. After two days they left. Jimmy was alone and still the choppers didn't come and he waited with a growing certainty that they would not come, that he would die there.

When they arrived, the gunships hovering overhead while a chopper put down in almost the exact spot the other had fled days before, Jimmy didn't run from the grass and leap aboard. He emerged from the brush slowly and calmly. He climbed aboard, nodded to the soldiers and moved once again behind the door gun. "I'll take it," he said to the gunner, who saw the look in Jimmy's eyes and moved aside. Three months later his tour ended and he immediately signed on for another year. He joined a special force whose sole mission was to pick up downed pilots. Twice they'd led raids on suspected VC prisons where American POWs were believed held. Both times they'd been too late.

Later, when Jimmy was back in the States trying again to get sober, to be clean, he and Johnny had sat on lawn chairs in their parents' backyard one night and sipped iced tea, and Jimmy had told him what it was like being a door gunner.

"They loved to hide in that tall grass, but if you know what you're doing you can smoke 'em out. You get the pilot to fly over real low and rock, sending that grass flat in waves. First one direction, then another." He held his hand out, palm down, and slowly rotated it, mimicking the chopper's action. "And you just sit up there and wait for the little fuckers to run. You see something in black and you open up. Wham, wham, wham. Shit, man, you do it right and you can get a dozen with one good pass. Man, you feel like an eagle just waiting for the mouse to move. It scurries and then bingo, you're on it. You should feel it, Johnny, the way that big gun feels in your hands, kicking and bucking and you know you're in control. You're the man then. You're God almighty."

Johnny looked at Jimmy and almost cried. His brother's words were those of a braggart and his face was hard as Rushmore, devoid of expression, yet tears from wells buried deep in his soul streamed down his cheeks. Johnny watched as Jimmy's eyes widened and focused into the distance. He was gone, a million miles away.

Johnny began to understand that night that Jimmy

would never be whole and that he might never know his little brother again.

He stayed at the VA hospital until just before five o'clock. Jimmy never showed and Johnny finally left. But as he drove off the grounds of the hospital, Johnny wasn't thinking about Jimmy anymore. He was thinking about a long-held and very valuable marker. It was time to cash it in.

11

It was less than half a mile from the fence at the edge of the VA grounds to the Federal Building in West L.A., but it took Johnny almost ten minutes to fight through the traffic on Wilshire Boulevard and turn south on Veteran Avenue and into the parking lot.

As it turned out, there was no hurry. Johnny stood next to the Z, leaning back against its side, for almost an hour, waiting and watching. Johnny knew he would wait until midnight if he had to. Eventually Ken Hightower had to walk out of the Federal Building, down the steps and into the parking lot. And from where he stood, Johnny would see him.

Johnny had known Hightower, an FBI agent in the L.A. office, for almost a dozen years and over that time they had gained a grudging respect for each other. But they had never been friends and never would be. They lived in different worlds within the same city. Johnny was single, ambivalent about most things and carried a deep skepticism about organized religion. Hightower was a church deacon, a man with a rock-solid dedication to family, God and country. But none of those differences mattered now, because Hightower owed him and Johnny was determined to collect.

Two years before, the daughter of a Bel Air lawyer who specialized in defending drug runners and dealers had been kidnapped. A cop Johnny had known for years called in the middle of the night to tell him. The girl was the fourth kidnapping in two years that fit the same pattern. The target was the son or daughter of someone rich, someone who had a source of money the IRS couldn't trace. Someone who probably would deal rather than go to the police.

The FBI had heard about the kidnappings, but there was never a complaint. The first three paid. The lawyer didn't. He called the FBI. Only a few cops knew about the abduction. Johnny called Hightower at six the next morning and asked about the case.

"Well, Johnny, you know we don't comment on things like this," Hightower said.

"Since when? You're always commenting."

"We never comment on a case."

"Does that mean the Bureau's working this?"

"I have no comment on that."

"Look, I know the girl was kidnapped. I've got that cold. All I want to know is if you've been called in, that's all."

"Look, Johnny, I'd help you if I could. But there's nothing I can do," Hightower said.

"Come on, Ken, if I have to I'll track down the father's ex-wife or neighbors or business partners. Give me an hour and I'll have enough to write a story. I'll end up saying something like the FBI isn't talking about the case. Then everyone will think you're involved anyway. Unless you want to flat-out deny it."

"I'm sorry, but it's like I said. I can't help you."

"Okay, then tell me about the other three. I understand the Bureau figures it's the same guys. That true?"

There was a long silence, then Hightower said, "Can you come over to my office?"

"I'll be there in twenty minutes."

They'd sat in an interview room high in the Federal Building. The room was small but clean and bright, with posters for the '84 L.A. Olympics on the walls. Hightower laid it out. Yes, the girl had been kidnapped. The Bureau believed her life would be in jeopardy if the kidnapping became public. With any luck, the kidnappers didn't know yet that the FBI was involved. If Johnny wrote a story, the kidnappers would kill the girl.

"So I'm asking you, please don't run it. I mean, we're talking about a kid's life here."

Johnny nodded his silent consent. But there would be a price, he said. After it was over, when the girl was safe, Johnny would break the story about all four kidnappings. That was the deal. He'd sit on this story and break the bigger one. Hightower hesitated, then agreed.

But Johnny didn't break the story. Six hours later, the agency rescued the girl and arrested the kidnappers. The Special Agent in Charge of the L.A. office, a man named Hanley, held a press conference just in time for the five o'clock news to announce that the FBI, working closely with local law enforcement, had smashed an organized kidnapping ring and arrested two men and a woman. The woman, an IRS employee, had tipped the kidnappers to those the IRS suspected of illegal sources of income.

Johnny stood at the back of the crowd of reporters, watching his exclusive evaporate as it was flashed around the world. He was seething and scanned the crowd for Hightower. He found the agent after the press conference.

"We had a deal, you son of a bitch." Johnny barely held his anger in.

"There was nothing I could do. I told Hanley about our deal, but he didn't care. I swear, Johnny, there was nothing I could do."

Johnny stood glaring at Hightower in his charcoal gray suit, white shirt and dark blue tie. He knew if he didn't walk away, he'd probably hit the agent. "You owe me," Johnny said, and jabbed Hightower's chest with his finger.

"Yeah," Hightower said and nodded. "Yeah, I do."

"I'll collect," Johnny said, turned and walked away.

Now Johnny stood on the hot asphalt watching closely as the people flowed from the tall, white, rectangular building. Some straggled out alone, coming down the steps with the slow-footed slog of weary trench fighters. Others came in small groups, chatting easily and even laughing as they walked. Johnny saw them all and just waited.

The daylight was beginning to fade and the lot was nearly empty when Hightower finally descended the steps alone and approached the parking lot. Johnny recognized the gait, a slow side-to-side sway that marked Hightower even at five hundred paces.

The agent saw Johnny coming when he was still about thirty yards away. He set his briefcase on the cement and waited at the edge of the parking lot.

"Johnny," he said with a nod. He didn't offer his hand, Johnny noticed.

"Agent Hightower."

"What brings you by?"

"I need something, information."

"Oh?"

"Look, is there someplace we can talk?"

Hightower glanced back and up at the Federal Building, then looked to the parking lot again. "How about my car? It's just over there."

"Yeah, fine."

They crossed the blacktop in silence and stopped at a white Chevy Caprice. The car was hot from the all-day sun, and Hightower started the engine and let it idle as he turned the air conditioning on high. The initial blast of air was warm and smelled of Freon, but a moment later it began to cool and Hightower turned down the blower. Even with the cool air, Johnny could feel his back and legs beginning to sweat and stick against the hot Naugahyde seats.

"There, that's a little better," the agent said, then turned sideways and looked at Johnny. Hightower was probably in his late forties, with short, dark hair. A small pink mole grew next to his razor-cut sideburn near his left ear. He turned slightly, reaching back across his body to press a button and lower his window a crack. He looked back at Johnny. "Okay, let's hear it," he said.

"I need you to look into something for me."

Hightower was silent for a moment. The only noise in the car was the low hum of the air conditioner. Johnny felt the cool air blowing against his face from the dashboard vent. In the distance he could see a young woman walking her dog, a big white husky suffering from the summer's heat, its tongue hanging out.

"What are we talking about?" Hightower asked.

"You told me once you'd done a stint in domestic counterintelligence."

"Yeah. So?" A note of suspicion had crept into his voice.

"You still have some friends there? A contact or two?"

"Maybe. What's this all about, Rose?"

"It's about a body found in the Mojave Desert, tentatively identified as Roberto Ruiz, who's still listed as MIA in Nam. And it's about a pilot named Kyle Loveless, MIA in Laos. But a friend of mine swore he saw Loveless in L.A. a couple of days ago. Only nobody can talk to my friend anymore because he's been murdered. I want to know what's going on. I want to know if either one of these guys, Ruiz or Loveless, ever got home. If they did, how come there's no record of it?"

"POWs? This is about POWs?"

"You got it."

"I think you've gone around the bend, Rose."

"I want to know what's going on."

"So what? I'm supposed to drop everything and check out a couple of guys that have been dead for twenty-five years? It's probably just a case of mistaken identity."

"Listen, you owe me. I'm not asking that much. I just want you to check. Kyle Loveless and Roberto Ruiz. If they're home, how come no one knows? Is the government running some kind of secret game here? The CIA bringing people back?"

"I think this is stupid."

"If they're home, how come no one knows? That's all I want to know. I'll find the rest myself."

The car was silent for a moment, then Hightower reached over and flicked off the air conditioner. Instantly the cool breeze hitting Johnny's face fell away. Johnny could hear the rumble of the San Diego Freeway in the distance. One row in front of the Caprice, a brown Toyota pickup backed out and drove away. Finally, Hightower nodded slowly and said, "Okay, I'll check it. Give me a couple of days."

Johnny knew Hightower thought it was a dead end, an easy way to pay his debt. But he also knew the agent would be thorough. Johnny was counting on it. He started to push the door open when Hightower said, "Wait." Johnny turned and looked at the agent but didn't pull the door closed.

"This wipes the slate clean. We're even. You know that."

"Yeah, I know." He pushed the door open and then turned back. "I'll call you in a couple of days," Johnny said, still looking at the agent, awaiting a final commitment. Finally, Hightower nodded and said, "Okay."

12

Johnny pulled the Z into the carport at the rear of his apartment building, leaving plenty of room between his car and the green Chevy Kingswood station wagon in the next stall. Huge and heavy, a dinosaur of a car built when gas was cheap, it boasted a 464-cubic-inch engine, one of the biggest ever put in an American passenger car.

Ethel, his neighbor, owned it. She was probably responsible for half the dings in the Z's right side. Elderly and frail, she either couldn't control the Kingswood's heavy doors or didn't care.

As he got out of the Z, Johnny glanced at the rear of the wagon. It was almost full; a mixture of newspapers and black plastic bags of aluminum cans filled the car above the windows. Ethel used the Chevy as a recycling bin. Then, once a month or so, she'd climb behind the wheel like a kid mounting a Clydesdale and back the monster up until the rear bumper kissed the cinderblock wall across the alley, turn and head toward the street and the recycling center.

Johnny checked the distance between the two cars and, satisfied, headed up the narrow walkway leading from the carport to the apartments' front doors. At his place, he put the key in, turned it, and jerked back, pulling hard on the knob. The deadbolt slipped across and the door popped open. Johnny had complained about the door a dozen times, but the landlord never got around to fixing it.

As he pushed the door open, someone called his name. He looked up the walkway toward the street. Detective Earl and another man were moving casually down the walkway toward him. Johnny turned his back to the open door and watched the two men approach. They stopped a few feet away.

"Mr. Rose, this is Detective Krieg."

Johnny nodded at the man. He was young, perhaps thirty, over six feet, and blond, with wide shoulders and a slender waist. He wore a blue sports coat unbuttoned, white shirt with no tie, black pants and cowboy boots. He radiated a not-too-subtle confidence, a certainty about what he was doing. The man loved being a cop. Johnny could see it in a glance.

"What can I do for you?" Johnny asked. He looked from Krieg back to Earl. He remembered what Barsh had said. They'd found his fingerprints on the dowel.

"Well, we just had a couple more questions," Earl said. He flashed a tight, quick smile. "You mind if we come in?"

"We can do this here," Johnny said.

"Okay. You said you and Mr. Lich were pretty good friends, that right?" Earl asked.

"That's right."

"You ever lend him any money?"

"No."

Krieg nodded, a barely visible head movement, like a tired clerk at the refund counter who's heard it all before. "Well, Mr. Rose," he said, "we found a book in the glove compartment of Mr. Lich's car. It was like a diary or a ledger, I guess you'd call it. It was written in Vietnamese and it took a little while to get it translated." He stopped and looked at Johnny, waiting for a comment. Johnny said nothing. "Well, according to Mr. Lich's records, he owed you a couple of thousand dollars. Apparently he bought a car from you but never paid you. Is that true?"

Johnny returned Krieg's stare, holding his eyes, knowing if he looked away, he'd be giving the detective the edge. He felt a tingle of fear in his legs and his heartbeat accelerated. "I wanted to give him the car. But he wouldn't take it, so we made a deal. He'd fix it up, drive it and when he sold it, we'd split the proceeds."

"That's pretty generous of you. Why'd you want to give him the car?"

"It had been my mom's car. When she died, it was part of her estate. Took a couple of years to finish probate and the car just sat there. By the time I was ready to sell it, it wouldn't even start. It would have cost me more to fix it up than I could get for it. Pham needed a car. He was pretty good with his hands. I figured he could get it running again. It seemed like a good deal for both of us." Johnny's mouth was dry as he spoke and swallowed hard to keep his voice from cracking.

"Why wouldn't he take it when you wanted to give it to you?"

"I don't know. Pride, I guess."

"So Mr. Lich was going to sell it later and split the money with you?" Earl asked.

"That's right."

"How long ago did you two strike this deal?"

"Couple of years ago."

"And he never paid you?"

"No, he still has, ah, had the car. Look, you're getting this thing all wrong. I didn't give a shit about the money. Like I said, I wanted to give him the car in the first place."

"So you never asked him for it?"

"No."

"You didn't see him that night and talk to him about the money he owed you?" Earl asked. "Maybe argue about it?"

"No. I already told you I didn't speak to him that night."

"That's right. You went there to talk to him about POWs in Vietnam. That's when you saw him get killed."

Johnny nodded but said nothing. He folded his arms across his chest and waited. "Is that all?"

"For now," Earl said.

Johnny half-turned to the open door and was about to enter his apartment but remembered the threat that morning and turned back.

"You know, there's something I should tell you. It might help. Someone called me today and threatened me. Called me at the *Chronicle* and told me to stop working on the story. Said the same thing could happen to me that happened to Pham."

The detectives looked at Johnny for a moment, then Earl flipped open his notebook. "You recognize the voice?"

"No."

"Any idea who it might have been?"

"No."

"About what time was this?"

"About ten."

"You didn't by any chance record this?"

"No, I don't record my calls."

Earl nodded. He'd made only a few notes. "Think it might have been a crackpot? You know, someone who saw your name in the paper and called you?"

"No." Johnny hesitated a moment, knowing how stupid what he was about to say would sound. "I didn't write the story about Pham's murder. Another reporter did. My name wasn't even in the piece."

"But this mysterious caller called you, not the guy that wrote the story?"

"Yes, that's right."

"How'd he get your name? I mean, if your name wasn't in the paper, how'd he know to call you?"

"I don't know."

"So you don't know who it was or what this guy's connection to Mr. Lich was? He didn't tell you any of that?"

"No."

Earl folded his notebook and put it in his pocket. "Well, that's very interesting."

"Now, if that's all, I've got some things I've got to do," Johnny said.

"Sure. Thanks for your time."

Johnny stepped into the apartment and closed the door. He stood in the warm, stale semidarkness of the living room. Light filtered through the blinds on the west-facing window, leaving the room only half-lit.

"Jesus," Johnny whispered to himself, "they think I did it. The bastards think *I* killed him."

He climbed the stairs to his bedroom replaying the conversation in his head, hearing Earl's voice and seeing Krieg's nod, thinking of hundreds of things he should have said. By the time he reached his bedroom, his fists were closed in anger and frustration, his fingernails biting into his palms.

He changed into his running shorts, T-shirt and shoes. He stretched for less than three minutes and left the house. Powered by his anger, he ran too hard, his legs pounding, his arms swinging at his sides like a sprinter's. Within two blocks his breathing was labored and a pain throbbed in his side. The street climbed slightly and Johnny picked up his pace, trying to run off the side ache, to pound his frustration and fear into the pavement. But the pain only intensified and his legs jellied. He slowed, trying to find a rhythm, determined to slip into a flow that would carry him for miles. But he was barely a mile from home when he had to turn back. He'd spent his reserves early and foolishly.

Three blocks from his house, he walked. He was physically spent. His knees and ankles ached and his legs wobbled, but the frustration was barely tempered. Weird Harold was waiting for him on the step and dashed into the dark apartment when he opened the door. He stood for a moment and watched the cat leap onto the counter and pace along the edge, waiting for Johnny to fetch his dinner. Johnny smiled. At least some things were consistent.

"Give me a minute to shower, then you'll eat," he said to the cat.

He started up the stairs and the phone rang. He crossed the living room back to the kitchen and grabbed it on the third ring.

"Hello."

"Hi, Mr. Rose, it's Charles Raby."

"Oh, right, hi."

"Mr. Geld asked me to call. He's particularly anxious to know if you've reached a decision on his offer."

Johnny turned and leaned against the counter, the edge hitting him just below the waist. He looked back across the dark living room and hesitated a moment. He saw the big TV and thought of the Geld commercials he'd seen. "Gordon Geld, he gets things done." The guy could very easily be the next governor, Johnny thought.

He said, "Thanks for calling. I was planning on getting in touch with you tomorrow. I want to thank Mr. Geld. It was a very generous offer, but I don't think it's the right thing for me right now."

"Oh? What could be more important than helping elect the next governor?"

"I'm not saying it's not important," Johnny said. "It's just not for me. I appreciate Mr. Geld thinking of me, though."

"You know, Johnny—may I call you Johnny?"

"Sure, everyone does."

"This could be a once-in-a-lifetime offer. You really should consider it carefully. I don't want to see you make a mistake here."

Raby's tone had changed, a subtle shift that caught Johnny's attention. Was the guy trying to tell him something? He waited, but Raby said nothing more.

"Well, like I said, I appreciate the consideration, but it's not for me."

"If it's a matter of money, I'm sure we can work that out."

"No, it's not the money. Mr. Geld's offer was very generous."

"Is there anything we can do to persuade you?"

"No, I'm afraid not."

"Okay, thank you, Johnny," Raby said and hung up. Johnny looked at the phone in his hand for a second, replaying the conversation, then turned and set it down. It rang again instantly.

"Johnny Rose."

"Hello, Mr. Rose?"

"Yes?" He listened carefully, trying to place the woman's voice.

"I'm sorry to bother you at home, but I tried your office a few times today and couldn't reach you."

He was sure now, he didn't know her. "No problem. What can I do for you?"

"This is Susan Herbert, I was told you wanted to interview me and I thought maybe we could set up a time."

Johnny squinted a half-scowl. It was the same woman who had called the *Chronicle* earlier. He struggled to recognize the name but still came up empty. "Ah, you'll have to forgive me, the last couple of days have been rather hectic. I really don't remember the request. Who are you with?"

"With? I'm not with anyone. The National League of Families called and said you wanted to talk about my husband, Kyle Loveless."

He froze and unconsciously tightened his grip on the phone.

"Wait a minute. What was your name again?"

"Susan Herbert. That was my maiden name before Kyle and I got married. I started using it again several years ago. After Kyle was declared dead."

Johnny stood perfectly still. Through an open window he could hear a car alarm beep in the distance.

His eyes were fixed on the table where the woman had sat; the woman who had convinced him she was Susan Loveless. He hadn't doubted her for a moment. He'd believed every word and even felt slightly guilty about following the story.

"Ah, I know this is going to sound pretty strange. But we've never met, is that right?"

"No. Not that I know of, why?"

His glance shifted to the table again. He could see her sitting there, gripping the coffee mug, her knuckles turning white as she begged him not to write a story.

"Mr. Rose? Are you there?"

"Yeah, pardon me. I was just thinking that, well . . ." And suddenly he knew what she'd said that bothered him, playing at the edge of his consciousness but never quite in view until that moment. If Kyle were alive, she'd be the first to know, not some Vietnamese refugee. But he'd never mentioned Pham, referring to him only as a friend. He hadn't told her that his friend was a refugee. He hadn't even mentioned Pham to the League of Families. But she'd known about him, known he was a Vietnamese refugee. It was a setup.

"Yes, I, ah, I'd really like to talk to you. I think it's pretty important. Could I come see you tonight?"

"Ahh, well, I hadn't planned on something quite this soon."

"It's very important."

"All right. Why not?"

Johnny took the small pad of paper and pen next to the phone. "Great, why don't you give me your address."

He hung up and put the pen down, turned and

leaned back against the counter. He looked again at the table and thought of the woman who had visited his home and easily convinced him she was the widow of a downed American pilot and knew he could take nothing at face value again.

13

Susan Herbert lived on a quiet street of mature trees and older tract houses that had been modernized with dens added and pools dug in the back. They'd built houses like these as fast as they could in the 1950s, tearing out Southern California's orange groves, laying sewer lines and pouring concrete at a breakneck pace. The developers' signs had bragged that the houses were built with "genuine lath and plaster" and there were "garbage disposals in every house" and "E-Z payments."

They were meant for the immigrants from across the United States newly arrived in the land of opportunity and perpetual sunshine. Blue-collar homes, white-collar homes, it didn't really matter. An easy mix of frame and stucco houses anyone with a steady job could afford. Today, the neighborhoods were filled with two types: people who had bought thirty years before and yuppies who had bought a couple of years ago and parked their Saabs in the driveways.

Susan Herbert answered a few moments after he rang the bell, as though she'd been sitting, waiting for him to arrive.

She was probably five-ten and slender. She wore sandals, blue jeans and a long-sleeved white shirt, the sleeves rolled to the elbows and the tails hanging out. Her reddish-blonde hair, which she wore tied back, was thick and generously streaked with gray. Her skin had the pink tinge and the light scattering of freckles typical of natural redheads. She wore no makeup to hide the lines that spread from the corners of her eyes to her hairline and cracked the surface of her cheekbones.

"Hi, I'm Johnny Rose."

"Please come in." She held the screen door open and Johnny stepped into the house. "We can talk in here," she said and led him to the living room.

Johnny looked at the sparsely furnished room for signs that this woman, this house, were fakes, a Potemkin home conjured up to provide authenticity. The room had polished hardwood floors and a brick fireplace on the front wall. A sofa covered with a sturdy light brown fabric was pushed against the far wall and a maple coffee table and matching end table were next to it. A Kennedy rocker across the room from the couch completed the furniture. At the side of the fireplace an antique popcorn popper, a small black enclosed wire basket at the end of a long handle, leaned against the bricks. Next to it was a faded red round wooden tub, filled with magazines.

As Susan Herbert walked to the sofa, Johnny stepped to the fireplace and studied the two framed photos on the mantel.

Both were of a young man. In one he appeared serious, almost brooding. He looked about eighteen. But in the second, clad in the gown and mortarboard of college graduation, he smiled and his eyes seemed to cheer. There was no picture of a pilot, nothing, in fact, to hint that the woman now sitting on the couch had ever been married to a U.S. Air Force officer.

"Please have a seat," she said and motioned to the Kennedy rocker near the fireplace. As he moved to the rocker, Johnny noticed dust balls collected in the corners and a few strands of an abandoned spider web strung from the edge of the popcorn popper to the baseboard. A layer of dust covered the floor of the fireplace. Johnny began to believe that Susan Herbert was exactly who she claimed.

"So what can I do for you, Mr. Rose?" she asked. Her question was businesslike, crisp. Johnny nodded to her, suddenly aware of the distance that separated them. He leaned forward, arms on his thighs, in an attempt to reduce the gulf of polished hardwood planking that flowed between them like a swift current.

"Well, to tell you the truth, I'm not really sure where to start," he said.

"The woman at the League of Families told me you wanted to talk about my husband. Isn't that why you're here?"

"Yes, that's true. That's why I came. But I need to back up a little bit."

Susan Herbert was quiet for a moment, and Johnny could feel the late-evening breeze seeping through the two screened windows, barely disturbing the warm heavy air in the room. Outside he could hear the hiss of a sprinkler spraying the neighbor's lawn.

She nodded and said, "Okay."

"Two nights ago a man named Pham Lich was murdered. He was strangled to death in a park in the San Fernando Valley."

"Yes, I saw it on the news. But what does that have to do with my husband?"

"Pham was a friend of mine. I'd known him for several years." Johnny paused and looked straight at Susan Herbert, focusing dead on her eyes, weighing her reaction as he spoke. Did she already know this? Did she know that Pham believed that he'd seen her late husband? If so, she gave no sign. Her eyes were blank, masking her thoughts. He glanced at the floor and looked back at her again. "I'd talked to him earlier in the day and he told me he'd seen your husband in L.A. a couple of days ago. Said he wanted to talk to me about seeing him."

"Seen Kyle?"

"Yes."

She shook her head, a slow turning from side to side. But her face and eyes were still blank. She said nothing for a moment, but when Johnny failed to break the silence, she said, "Well, I don't know what he was talking about, Mr. Rose. I know he couldn't have seen my husband. Kyle's dead. And frankly, if that's all you needed to know, I could have told you that on the phone."

Johnny sensed a subtle shift in her tone, a harder edge that had crept in as though being civil were a struggle. He sensed he was close to losing the interview, close to alienating her. And for a reason he didn't quite understand, he didn't want to do that. Without knowing why, he'd already begun to believe her.

"Yes, I know. But, well . . ." Johnny paused again,

unsure of how to proceed, not knowing where this would lead. "The thing is, I saw Pham murdered. I went out to the park to talk to him about seeing your husband. But I got there just in time to see him being killed."

"That's awful."

"Yes."

"Did the police catch the killer?" Her question struck him as perfunctory, as though she were asking about the family of a casual acquaintance. For a second he thought of telling her that he was the prime suspect, but didn't. He was having enough trouble with the interview.

Johnny felt like a mountain climber searching for a fingerhold, a two-inch crevice he could jam his fingertips into to keep from plunging off the sheer face. He rolled his shoulders and looked at her.

"No, not yet. But that's not all of it. Look, I know this is going to sound strange, so stay with me for a moment, please." He waited, but she said nothing, gave no sign of acceptance or rejection. He went on. "Last night, a woman claiming to be Susan Loveless, claiming to be you, came to my apartment and asked me to stop working on the story about Pham. She almost begged me not to write it."

Susan Herbert's eyes narrowed and she looked at Johnny with suspicion. Her lips pressed together into a line as narrow as a knife blade. She was quiet, and Johnny could feel the weight of the silence in the room. Outside, the hissing of the sprinklers stopped and a moment later he could hear another one gurgle and erupt to life. But he waited for her, forcing Susan Herbert to respond to what he'd just said.

"I don't know anything about your friend or any

woman who claimed to be me, and frankly, I think this is all rather strange."

"I didn't mean to upset you, but I—"

"You didn't upset me," she said, and Johnny could see it was true. Susan Herbert wasn't upset, but he knew her anger was building. "Mr. Rose, I got on with my life years ago. I loved Kyle very much, but I made peace with the truth. I don't know why your friend thought he saw Kyle or why he was murdered or why that woman doesn't want you to write about it, but I can assure you it has nothing to do with me or my dead husband. There has to be some other explanation."

Johnny nodded slowly. "Yes, I'm sure you're right. It's just, well, Pham was so positive."

"We all make mistakes, Mr. Rose."

Johnny waited half a beat and nodded, then smiled at her. "Please, call me Johnny. It's what everyone calls me. You know, these days kids call everyone by their first names. But me, I'm old enough that when I was growing up you called every adult Mr. or Mrs. So when someone says Mr. Rose, I think they must be talking about my father."

She smiled slightly. "All right," she said, and Johnny sensed he'd gained a small edge, discovered a crevice in her tough exterior. Still, he noticed she didn't ask him to call her by her first name. He believed her now simply because she didn't seem to care if he did. The other woman had worked so hard to convince him. Susan Herbert, it seemed, couldn't care less if he believed what she said.

"Let me ask you this, Ms. Herbert. Have you ever heard of a man named Roberto Ruiz?"

She shook her head. "No, not that I can think of. Why? What does this have—" Johnny held up his hand

and she stopped and waited for him to continue.

"A couple of days ago, a man's body was found in the desert. He'd been there for three or four weeks. He was wearing dog tags that identified him as Roberto Ruiz, an Army sergeant. But the Army's records list Ruiz as MIA in Nam."

Susan Herbert's eyes appraised Johnny openly. Perhaps she was wondering if she'd just invited a maniac into her living room. Her eyes held a strange blend of anger and curiosity. Johnny was quiet, letting her take the lead.

"Mr. Rose, ah, Johnny, do you know how absolutely absurd all this seems? A stranger comes to my house and tells me a man was murdered just after seeing my husband, who's been dead for more than twenty years? And a second man, who's been missing since the war, is found dead in the desert. Is this someone's idea of a cruel practical joke?"

Johnny didn't answer at first because he didn't know if she were making a statement or truly asking a question. But she seemed to be expecting a reply.

"I assure you this isn't a joke. I know it sounds strange, but it's true and I'm just trying to make some kind of sense out of it, that's all."

Susan shook her head, a quick wiggle back and forth as if she were dismissing everything Johnny had just said. She brushed a strand of hair from in front of her eyes.

"Well, I don't know what to tell you. My husband is dead and I don't know anything about that Vietnamese refugee who was killed or that dead man in the desert. Frankly, I don't see how I can help you."

"Yes, I understand. I guess I . . . well . . ." He hesitated, not knowing what to say, how to proceed.

Susan Herbert, it now appeared, was a dead end. "I guess I've taken up your time needlessly. I apologize. Thanks anyway for letting me come over." He stood up and looked at her, still seated on the edge of the couch.

"I know this all sounds strange, but I've got to chase down every lead. It's the only way I'll find out what's going on. I hope you understand."

Her shoulders seemed to drop slowly and the muscles in her face relaxed. She stood up.

"Look, would you like something to drink? Maybe a cup of coffee or a Coke or something?"

"Sure, a Coke would be great."

She walked toward the kitchen, stopped halfway across the floor and looked back at him. "You want it over ice?"

"Sure."

She waved him to the kitchen. "Let's sit in here. It's not as formal."

It was a large room with tile counters, a double sink and a breakfast area in a windowed corner. The refrigerator stood just inside the door. Susan took two cans out, turned and put them on the counter. She took glasses from the cupboard, got ice from the freezer and filled the glasses.

She handed him the Coke, leaned back against the counter and faced Johnny, who stood in the doorway. Susan sipped the Coke and said, "You know, I checked you out."

"Pardon me?"

"Before I called you, I checked. I'm a researcher at the Center for Modern Studies. It's a think tank in Santa Monica. You'd be amazed at the stuff we can dig up." She smiled, letting the statement hang in the air, giving Johnny notice of something. He wasn't sure what.

"Oh?"

"I almost never talk about the war anymore and I never liked being interviewed. But when the league called, I was intrigued. Why now? Why after all these years did a reporter want to talk about Kyle? So before calling you, I did some background work. I read some of your stories. I liked them, especially the series about the homeless living in Palisades Park. You seem to care about what you're writing about."

"It seemed like an important story."

"It was, I liked the series. After I read it, I asked some friends who know the *Chronicle* and they told me about you. That's why I agreed to talk to you."

"Well, thank you. I'm glad you did."

She half-turned and set her glass on the counter behind her. She leaned back again, folded her arms across her chest and looked back at him. The smile was gone and her eyes held the blend of curiosity and anger he'd seen earlier.

"Look, it's been more than twenty years since Kyle's plane went down. The first few years were horrible. My son, Will, was born just a few months after I got the news and then there were all the false hopes. There was going to be peace, then there wasn't. Then all the men came home and Kyle wasn't among them and eventually it became obvious Kyle wasn't coming home. I just got on with my life. I started using my maiden name again because, frankly, I was tired of being the war widow. There's more to life than grief and memories."

"Yes, I know. We have to live our own lives." He thought of Jimmy.

"You know, I'm still curious. Even with all this stuff

about murders and bodies in the desert, I still don't know exactly why you're here. I don't know what you expected to learn from me."

She looked straight at him, her stare intense as she waited for an answer.

"I was hoping you could help me," he said. "I don't know who Pham saw, it could have been anybody. I thought maybe it was your husband and the records were wrong. I just didn't know. But I did know after Pham called me, he was murdered. Like I said before, I have to track down every lead."

Just then the back door opened and the young man whose pictures were on the mantle walked in. He was at least six-five, with broad shoulders and thick red hair. Johnny knew instantly from the red hair and bright green eyes that he was Susan's son.

"Will, this is Mr. Rose, the reporter I told you about."

Will stepped closer and extended his hand. "Hi, nice to meet you," he said. The grip was strong.

"Nice to meet you, too, Will."

"I've got to get going, I've got an early start tomorrow," Will said. He turned to Johnny. "Mr. Rose, it was nice to meet you."

"Please, call me Johnny."

"Okay. Well, nice to meet you. I'll give you a call," he said to his mother, then walked into the living room. A moment later Johnny heard the screen door shut. He looked back at Susan.

"Will's rebuilding a car out in the garage. His father was pretty mechanically inclined, too." Johnny nodded and she continued. "You want to sit?" She motioned to the table in the kitchen's corner.

"Sure," Johnny said.

"Tell me something," she said as she pulled a chair away from the table and sat. "What did she look like?"

"The woman who claimed she was you?"

"Yes."

"Well." He paused for a moment, remembering the woman at his door and seeing her at his table. Susan watched him for a second, then lowered her eyes to the glass in front of her.

"I'd guess about five foot seven, slender, maybe a hundred-thirty. Blonde hair to her shoulders. Bangs. Thin face. Conservatively dressed with a dark skirt below her knees, white blouse with a princess collar and a brooch. Wedding rings. A pretty woman. Wore a lot of makeup, but handled it well. Eyeliner, lipstick, powder."

"You don't miss much."

"It's a habit."

"Well, it doesn't sound like anyone I know."

"I was afraid of that. I've got to admit, she had me totally convinced, except she said something that I didn't catch until you called. She said if Kyle were alive she'd be the first to know, not some Vietnamese immigrant. But I had never mentioned Pham to her. Didn't even mention his name to the league."

"But she knew about him?"

"Exactly. She already knew when she got to my apartment."

"But why? I mean, why would anyone want to impersonate me? I still don't understand that."

"She didn't want me digging into the story. She wanted me to stop. I guess maybe she thought if she could convince me Pham was wrong about seeing Kyle, I'd let it go."

"Yes, of course. But why go to all that trouble? I mean, Kyle *is* dead. So why bother?"

"I don't know. That's part of why I'm here. I'm hoping you can help me."

Susan was quiet for a moment, her eyes fixed on her glass as she slowly ran her fingertip around its lip, a thoughtful caressing motion, not nervous, agitated. Suddenly she stared at Johnny. "I'm having a very hard time with this."

When Johnny asked the next question, his words were low and coaxing, not demanding or challenging. "Ms. Herbert, do you think there's any possibility that Kyle's still alive, that he's here in L.A.?"

When she didn't respond immediately, didn't quickly dismiss the idea out of hand, Johnny sensed a subtle change and hoped she was about to offer him a hint, a clue to unraveling the logical explanation that everyone assured him lay behind it all. He waited quietly, patiently, like a farmer waits for a late-afternoon rain. He knew from years of watching and listening to people that something was coming. He knew the way a farmer can feel and smell the rain and knows he only has to wait. The faucet dripped and Johnny could hear the small splash of water on enamel suddenly loud in the kitchen. The ice cubes in Susan's glass shifted, clinking as they settled. Finally she shook her head gently, side to side, and said, "You should really call me Susan."

"Okay." He waited for her to continue.

"Well, the answer to your question is no." She paused a moment. "You know, Kyle never saw Will. I was pregnant when he left for Vietnam. If he was in L.A., nothing could keep him from seeing his son. Absolutely nothing. I'm convinced of that."

Was that really everything she had planned to say? Johnny wondered. "Tell me about him, about your husband," he said.

"Why?"

"No specific reason except, well, I don't know why Pham thought he saw him and I don't know why that woman came to my apartment. But I know that the more I can learn, the better chance I'll have of getting at the truth. That includes learning more about your husband."

Susan nodded and looked at him, and he knew she was deciding how much to tell and then she began. "Kyle went through college on some kind of Air Force scholarship and really believed he had a responsibility to be as good a pilot as he could be. That's the type of person he was. He believed you should always do the right thing. The funny thing was, he didn't even want to be a pilot when he got out. But he was a very good pilot. You know, I think there's an old saying about it being a curse to be good at something you don't enjoy. I think about that now and then. I mean, look where it got him."

She stopped for a second and slowly shook her head. "Oh, I don't know. It was all so long ago," she said and looked at Johnny. For the first time, he realized that she was a pretty woman.

"Yes, it was."

"You know, I wanted to ask you something after reading that series on the homeless. Were you there, did you serve?"

"No," he said. She waited, but he said nothing more.

"Your stories had a passion, it seemed that you must have been there."

Johnny shook his head no. "I had a brother who was there. Army."

"He was killed there?"

"No, he came home."

"Oh, you said you *had* a brother, so I just thought . . ."

"He's still alive but, ah . . . we don't see a lot of each other."

An awkward silence filled the space between them for a moment and then Susan said, "Sometimes I think we've forgotten all about Vietnam and then other times, like tonight, there it is again, right in your face. I don't think those of us who lived it will ever forget. God, I hope not."

"You're right. It takes generations to pay off a war. It's like alimony after a bad marriage. It goes on forever."

She raised her eyebrows and looked at him quizzically.

Johnny laughed and held up his hands, palms out. "No, I'm not speaking from experience. I'm divorced but I didn't have to pay alimony. She makes more money than I do."

"I was twenty-two when I got married," Susan said without prompting. "Fresh out of college and so sure of so many things. Someone asked me once why I got married at that age. Without thinking, I just said, 'young and stupid.' It's not that I wasn't crazy in love with Kyle, it's just that, well, now I realize at that age you really don't know enough to make those kinds of important decisions."

The kitchen was quiet, and Johnny didn't know what to say or how to proceed. He'd asked his questions and found no answers. He enjoyed talking to someone who knew the personal price the Vietnam War was still exacting. But the conversation had drifted, and now as they sat in silence, he knew it was time to go.

"Listen, I really appreciate your taking the time and helping me like this. But I'd better get going."

"Sure, I understand," she said.

They walked to the front door without speaking, and Johnny stepped out to the porch. He looked back at her through the screen. "Thanks again."

"You're welcome. You know, it's funny. When you first called, I didn't want you to come. I was pretty sure I was through with all that, that I didn't want to relive it again. Now I'm glad you did. It was good for me to think about it again, even if I wasn't much help."

"Actually, you were a lot of help. I haven't really talked to anyone like that in a long time."

"Well, if I can help any more, please let me know."

"Sure thing."

He turned to go, but before he could step off the porch, Susan called, "You know, there's something I don't understand."

"What?"

"How did she know you'd called the league?"

"What?"

"The woman. How'd she know to show up at your house and pretend to be me?"

Johnny looked back at the screen door, unable to see her face through the thick dark mesh. He had absolutely no idea how to answer her question.

"I don't know," he finally said. "I really don't know."

14

The most interesting story in the *Los Angeles Times* the next morning was L.A. Mayor Paul Apodaca's endorsement of Gordon Geld. Johnny read the article, which ran below the fold on the front page, as he carried the paper from the front door to the table. He finished the story while he drank his first cup of coffee.

Apodaca's endorsement would be a big help. Although the L.A. mayor's office was officially nonpartisan, the mayor's party affiliation was always known. Apodaca was a moderate Republican, pragmatic and very popular. He had powerful friends and connections throughout the state. Geld's candidacy had just received a shot of adrenaline.

Johnny read the story and a sidebar on the latest polls, completed before the Apodaca announcement. They showed Geld still in third place, with the race tightening. Johnny finished the story, glanced at the poll results and pulled out the sports section. He'd just started the story on the Dodgers when the phone rang. He shoved his chair back and stretched to reach the phone without standing.

"Hi, this is Susan Herbert, I hope I'm not disturbing you," she said.

"Oh no, not at all. In fact, I was planning on calling you. I want to thank you again for helping me last night."

"I'm afraid I really wasn't much help."

"No, no. You were. Really."

"Well, anyway, that's why I called. After you left, I started thinking about that man you asked me about, Roberto Ruiz. I know his wife. Well, I mean, I met her once. But she called her husband Bobby. I guess that's why I didn't make the connection at first. But I know where she lives or at least where she used to live. Do you have a pencil and paper?"

"Sure, but wait, before you go on, let me ask you something. Have you had breakfast yet?"

"Breakfast? No, why?"

"Let me buy you breakfast. You can tell me about Sergeant Ruiz there."

"You mean now? This morning?"

"Sure, why not?"

"Well, I don't know if that's a good idea."

"You know John O'Groats on Pico?"

"I think so. It's near the Rancho Park Golf Course, on the south side of the street, right?"

"That's it. They have great homemade biscuits. How about meeting me there at nine? That's, what, an hour and a half? Can you do that, or do you have to be at work at a certain time?"

"No, I can pretty much set my own hours." She

paused and Johnny waited, hoping she would agree. "Okay, nine would be fine."

Johnny was smiling as he put the telephone back in its cradle. He headed for the stairs to take a shower.

He dressed in khakis and a blue long-sleeved shirt but didn't bother with a tie. He arrived before her, and he put his name on the list and joined a small crowd waiting on the sidewalk.

Susan came a few minutes later. She wore a long, lightweight, dark skirt and a white blouse. Her hair fell free to her shoulders and this time, Johnny noticed, she wore lipstick and a hint of eye shadow.

"Hi," he said as she walked up. The lines of their relationship were still unsettled and Johnny didn't know if he should shake her hand or hug her, and after an awkward moment did neither. The conversation was strained at first, sticking to the safe, neutral ground of traffic and weather. But then, like an engine warming slowly on a winter's morning, they slipped into an easier flow and talked of work and books and music.

Johnny was in the middle of a sentence when he stopped abruptly. Susan followed his eyes. He was looking at a man walking toward them. The man was about forty, perhaps a little older, and wore a dirty white baseball cap. His yellow-white hair curled out from under the cap and stuck out like a fright wig. He was short and his too-long jeans dragged on the ground. He wore a burgundy USC T-shirt that hung loosely on him. His face and arms were burned the red of new bricks and he had a long, thin, ill-trimmed goatee. When he reached the small crowd on the sidewalk, he began.

"Hey, I'm trying to get something to eat, can you spare a little change? Can you help me out here? God

bless you. I just need a little something for breakfast."
He held his hand out as he looked from person to person, trying for eye contact. He began to raise his hand
as he looked at Susan. "Excuse me, ma'am, can
you . . ." But his words died in his throat as his eyes
met Johnny's. He looked away and moved on without
speaking to the others on the sidewalk.

Johnny was still silently watching the man when
the young woman who had put his name on the waiting
list called them inside. They walked into a two-room
restaurant of small, square, wooden tables and a garage
sale mix of chairs that made it look like a college student's dining room. The room smelled of strong coffee
and bacon, sausage and freshly baked biscuits. A hum
of conversation filled the room, blending with the clatter of silverware and dishes. Johnny heard the muted
buzz of a phone ringing and saw a customer in a suit
pull his briefcase from the floor, open it and take out a
phone.

The woman led them to a table on the west wall, near
an old sideboard. They had to squeeze past another table
to reach it. They ordered and the waitress brought them
biscuits and coffee while they waited for the rest of their
breakfast.

Susan tore the lid from the thimble-sized container of
half-and-half and poured it into her coffee. She sipped
the coffee and reached down to her purse on the floor
next to her chair. She took out a square envelope and slid
it across the table. It had a Christmas stamp on it.

"It's Sandra Ruiz's address," she said. "I met her
once at a conference for the families of POWs. Later
she sent me a Christmas card. For some reason I kept
it."

Johnny turned the envelope, smudged and yellow

with age, in his fingers and looked at the return address written in a small, neat hand.

"Where's Arvin, California?"

"Up near Bakersfield."

"Any idea if she still lives there?"

"No. I only met her the one time. You can call the league and ask them to contact her if they have a current address."

Johnny shook his head. "No, I think it would be better if I just drove up there this afternoon."

"Why don't you call first? Save yourself the drive."

He grinned. "No, people can blow you off on the phone. But it's a lot harder in person."

"Is that why you were so anxious to come over and see me personally last night? You were afraid I'd blow you off on the phone?"

"Well, that was part of it," he said, smiling. "And I wanted to judge your reaction. Watch your face when I asked about your husband."

Her laugh surprised him. "That's why I let you come over," she said. "I wanted to meet you in person, find out who was asking these questions about Kyle."

Johnny glanced away, his gaze resting on the envelope for a moment. When he looked at her again, she was watching, a look of caution in her eyes.

"What is it?" she asked.

"I wasn't totally honest with you last night."

"Oh?" In one syllable she'd opened the distance between them again.

"You asked if the police caught Pham's killer. They haven't. But because I found the body, I'm probably a suspect. The thing is, I don't think they believe me about why I went out to see Pham. That's another reason I need to find out who or what Pham saw. It may be the only way I can prove I had nothing to do with it. I'm sorry I didn't tell you last night. I know I should have, but I was afraid you wouldn't talk to me if you thought I was mixed up in Pham's murder."

"So why are you telling me now?"

"It's important that you understand."

She looked directly at him, the challenge obvious in her eyes. "Is there anything else you didn't tell me?"

"No, I swear."

"Well, frankly, I can understand why the police don't believe you. It all seems pretty far-fetched."

"Look, I don't know who Pham saw. But if the cops dismiss what he told me out of hand, they'll never find the killer."

"Okay, let's assume for a moment Pham saw someone he thought was Kyle. How are you going to find the man he saw?" she asked.

But Johnny didn't seem to hear her. He was staring past her, a look of anger filling his eyes. Susan turned and followed his gaze. Through the large window she could see the crowd on the sidewalk. A moment later she also saw the man with the baseball cap and scraggly goatee begging again. She watched as a man gave the beggar a dollar, then she turned back to Johnny.

"Do you know him?"

"No. I've seen him, but I don't know him."

"But . . ." She glanced through the window again and turned back to Johnny. "I just assumed, I mean, the way you looked at him."

Johnny spoke in a soft voice that carried a surprising amount of pain. "He reminds me of Jimmy, my brother. They all do. The guys with the cardboard signs, the ones that look like they haven't eaten in a week. I look at them and I see my brother. I'll admit I'm not real rational about it."

"Is he living on the streets?"

Johnny exhaled deeply, and his mood seemed to shift and he seemed to focus on her again. "Jimmy, a street person? No, not strictly speaking he's not. He's, well . . . well, it's a long story."

"I have time."

Johnny picked a small sugar packet from the bowl on the edge of the table and spun it around with his index finger on the table's glass top, nudging it forward and back as he debated what to tell this woman he'd only met the night before.

"Jimmy did two tours in Vietnam, did 'em back to back, and when he came home, it was obvious from the beginning that he had some really bad problems. I don't think there was a drug he didn't try over there or when he got home. Alcohol, cocaine, heroin, LSD. Man, you name it, he was taking anything he could get his hands on. Finally he tried to commit suicide. We spent a small fortune on psychiatrists and counseling and finally, after he tried again, he committed himself voluntarily to the VA hospital. That was years ago and he's still there."

Johnny stopped for a minute and watched a woman in a flowered print dress with a white apron wiping down the horseshoe-shaped counter as two women in tights slid onto stools. He heard the waitress set the silverware in front of them and ask if they wanted coffee.

"Johnny," she said, "at some point you have to let go. One of the hardest things I had to learn out of all this was that sometimes there's just no one to blame. You have to accept it and move on."

Johnny knew the truth of what she'd told him. "Sometimes it's not that simple. I didn't put him in that hospital, but, well . . ." Johnny shrugged and said nothing more.

"But what?"

"Nothing."

"No, I won't accept that. If you expect me to talk about Kyle and about my life, you can't hide things. It has to be a two-way street. It's that or nothing at all."

Johnny nodded slowly. "Okay," he said. "The thing is, I haven't been there for him. I kind of gave up on him. My mom never accepted Jimmy's condition as permanent. She insisted he'd get better and we'd all be a family again. But to tell you the truth, after a few years, I got sick of it. I got sick of him. I got sick of trying and not getting anywhere. But I'd never let my folks down, so I did what I could. As long as Mom wanted me to do it, I was gonna do it. I helped with the medical bills, went to visit him. I did whatever I could. Then a couple of years after Jimmy was committed, my dad was killed by a drunk driver. My mom died a couple of years later. I was going through my divorce about the same time and I . . . I just wasn't thinking much about my little brother.

"There wasn't much of an estate. Mom and Dad had spent pretty much everything they had on doctors and hospitals for Jimmy. But the thing is, my dad had been a weekend musician. He was actually pretty good, played the violin and the harmonica. Jimmy had played the violin in high school and he was pretty good, too. When my dad was killed, mom had held on to his instruments. She said she was keeping them for when Jimmy came home. But a few weeks after her funeral I went out to visit Jimmy and took him the violin. It wasn't a great instrument, but it wasn't bad, either. Probably worth a few hundred, not much more than that. Lot of sentimental value, though. I told myself I was hoping it would help Jimmy. You know, maybe somehow playing the violin would help. But he sold it, pawned it and used the money to buy some speed." Johnny shook his head slowly from side to side, his gaze on the tabletop.

"You can't blame yourself for that. You were trying to help."

"No, I wasn't. I think I knew all along that's what he'd do. But I gave it to him anyway and then when he sold it, I used it as an excuse to give up on him. I knew my mom would never forgive me for letting go. But after he did that, after he sold Dad's violin for drugs, it was easy. I had the perfect excuse and I pretty much just stopped going."

Johnny glanced away, watching the woman in the flowered dress behind the counter. He straightened his shoulders and looked at Susan again. "It's not something I'm really very proud of."

"Johnny, there's only so much you can do. We all find ways to cope."

The waitress, a young dark-haired woman in tight black jeans and a white T-shirt, slid past the next table, which was less than two feet away, and put their plates in front of them. A moment later she filled their coffee cups. As she left, Susan held Johnny's eyes.

"You know, none of us has a monopoly on doing things we regret. Always taking inventory of your faults and shortcomings doesn't do anyone any good."

"I guess you're right. You know, being an adult is a real pain in the ass sometimes."

Susan smiled. "You're right. But there's not really much choice, is there?"

"No, not really. Now, you'd better eat your omelet before it gets too cold. Besides, if I'm going to Arvin, I want to get there before the heat of the day."

"I think out there the heat of the day starts around eight o'clock in the morning," Susan said.

Later, standing on the sidewalk, Johnny again felt the awkwardness of the unknown boundaries of a budding relationship. Only this one was complicated because Susan was part of a story. But before he could say anything, Susan spoke. "Will you call me tonight? Let me know what you find?"

"Sure," he said.

"Great. Talk to you then, and thanks for breakfast. It was really good." She turned and walked away without looking back. Johnny watched her and thought she was as pretty as a sunrise.

15

It took Johnny almost two hours to climb out of the
L.A. basin, cross the Tejon pass and drop down to
where the Mojave Desert blends into the hot, dry and
fertile Central Valley, the great green swath in the middle of every map of California. But it took only about
three minutes to drive Arvin's main street from one
edge of town, past the new McDonald's, the old theater,
the one stoplight and the empty storefronts, to the
liquor store on the other end of town. He turned in the
store's parking lot and headed back into the town. He
stopped at the light and looked up and down the cross
street.

As he drove through Arvin, a sense of familiarity and
knowledge settled over him. He'd visited small towns
and tiny hamlets like this all his life. Every summer his
family drove to Oklahoma to visit relatives. They'd stop
at the small motels on two-lane highways and eat in

truck stop diners with jukeboxes featuring Elvis Presley and Perry Como. Johnny had seen rural America in the 1950s and 1960s, before Motel 6 and fast food and unleaded gas. And as he drove the main street of Arvin, nearly deserted in the heat of the day, he felt a kinship and familiarity with those days of childhood expectation and certainty.

According to the sign on the edge of town, Arvin had almost 10,000 residents. But it didn't seem that big. It reminded Johnny of all the towns he'd seen in the Texas Panhandle, Oklahoma and New Mexico. They all appeared the same, these farming and ranching towns built on the plains with nothing to stop the wind and no clouds to block the glaring sun. The elements seemed to leach the energy out of Arvin just as slowly and surely as they faded the paint of the town's wooden buildings. For a moment he thought *desperation* would be a good word for the town, but then thought better of it. No, Arvin wasn't desperate. It was resigned.

He turned north and a couple of blocks later seemed to pass through some invisible border where no one checks for papers but everyone knows if you belong. He had entered suburbia: cul-de-sacs with ranch-style houses and neat green lawns that ran together, bicycles in the driveways and small kids in blow-up wading pools. Houses like this fetched at least two hundred grand in L.A. Instinct told him this wasn't where he'd find Sandra Ruiz, and he turned back downtown.

On the main street, Johnny stopped at a Quick Gas and filled the Z. He paid in advance and went inside to get his change. He looked at the envelope Susan had given him and asked the cashier how to find Howard

Street. It was a few blocks south of Highway 223, Arvin's main drag, and Johnny drove slowly, watching the house numbers.

From the new houses and cul-de-sacs to Howard Street was less than two miles, but it seemed light-years away. The new homes had AC units on the roof and one or two had satellite dishes. On Howard Street he was looking at aging swamp coolers and rusted TV antennas. But it wasn't just the appliances. It was the houses and the yards. The homes were smaller and older, with waist-high chain-link fences separating one yard from the next.

He found the house and parked. There was a gate across the driveway, but it was open and he walked in. He crossed the small lawn of dried crabgrass and stepped onto the porch. A wooden screen door sagged on its hinges, the inside door open. He could hear a TV tuned to a Spanish-language station somewhere in the darkened interior. He knocked gently on the screen door. It shivered under his rap. When no one came, he leaned close and called through the screen, "Hello." He knocked again.

A moment later a woman, short and squat with graying black hair and wearing a flowered rayon dress, stepped close to the door. In the half-light of the interior, it looked as if she was wearing slippers.

"Yes?"

"My name is Johnny Rose. I'm looking for Sandra Ruiz. I was given this address. Is she your daughter?"

Her hands flew to her mouth and her eyes seemed to fill with tears. She said nothing.

"Ah, I, ah, well . . ." Johnny stumbled for a moment, then stared, trying to see through the screen, to grab the woman's eyes, to gain some fraction of understanding there. "I'm a newspaper reporter from Los Angeles. I was given Sandra's name by a woman whose husband was also listed as missing in Vietnam. I wanted to talk to Sandra. Is she here?"

Johnny spoke slowly, almost haltingly, his mind racing ahead of his words, trying to understand the reaction of this old woman.

"No English. *No hablo inglés*," she said, the words coming quickly, spilling from her mouth. She turned then and shouted back into the house. "*Ven! Pedro, ven aquí.*" She stepped farther back into the shadow of the living room.

A moment later there was another shadow, a man, next to her. The woman spoke rapidly in Spanish and the man stepped forward to the edge of the light.

"Who are you?"

"My name is Johnny Rose. I'm a reporter for the *Chronicle* in Los Angeles. I wanted to speak to Sandra Ruiz. I was given her name by Susan Herbert, another woman who lost her husband in Vietnam. I'm working on a story."

"Our daughter is gone." The man stepped closer, his left hand resting on the edge of the door. Johnny could see him clearly now. He wore a red-and-white-checked, long-sleeved cotton shirt, jeans and cowboy boots. His face was dark brown and deeply lined. His barrel chest ended in a large protruding stomach above a large silver buckle.

"Gone? Where? Maybe I can call her."

"We have lost our daughter." And with that the man slammed the door. Johnny stood for a moment staring through the screen at the peeling white paint of the door. He thought about knocking again, trying to explain he meant no harm. But he knew it would be useless. Even through the screen he'd seen the strength and pride in the man's face.

He left the yard and walked next door. There was no grass, just dirt and shrubs. The front door was closed and there was no answer when he knocked. He moved on, trying the next house. There he found an elderly woman who spoke no English and couldn't understand his stumbling, rusty high school Spanish. Finally, in frustration, he just turned and walked away.

He stopped at the sidewalk near his car and looked back toward the Ruiz home. Across the street three small brown children in their underwear darted in and out of a listless stream of water spouting from a slowly rotating sprinkler. Johnny crossed the street and stopped at the fence. The laughing children paid him no heed.

"Hello," he called toward the house. "Hello." The children stopped and stared at him. They began their wobbly sprints through the sprinkler again a few moments later when a young woman in a loose T-shirt and jeans, stretched by her wide hips, stepped through the door to the porch. Her dark hair fell loosely to her shoulders. Johnny looked at the children and guessed they were all hers.

"Sorry to bother you, but I'm a reporter from L.A. I'm trying to find Sandra Ruiz."

"We just moved in. I don't know her."

Johnny noticed the boxes stacked near the door. He looked back down the street and then at the woman again. "Ah, the address I have is for across the street, but they said she's gone."

"You could ask the man a couple of doors down. His name's Al, I think. I only met him once. But he

told me he's lived in the neighborhood most of his life."
She waved down the street.

Al knew Sandra. Knew the whole family, he said.
They were relatives of some kind. Johnny didn't catch
the exact explanation. Al stood in front of a blue Toyota
pickup, a bucket of soapy water near its front wheel.
He sprayed the vehicle and bent to wash the fender.

"Sure, I knew Sandy all my life. Knew her old man,
Roberto, too. We all grew up together. But Roberto,
man, he got killed in Nam. She moved back in with her
parents after that."

Al was short and slight and wore a dark blue
athletic shirt and knee-length baggy shorts. His black
hair was combed straight back and a tattoo of an
eagle on his right forearm had faded almost to a blur.
He was barefoot. At first Johnny had figured him at
about thirty-five. But as he looked more closely, he saw
the lines at the corners of his eyes and guessed Al
was at least forty, maybe more. He squirted the soap
off the fender and hosed down the hood and started
washing it.

"Well, you have any idea where I can find Sandra? I'm
working on a story about wives of POWs. I got her name
from a widow in L.A."

Al stopped and looked at Johnny as if he'd just
crawled from under a rock. He held the hose at his
side, the water pouring onto the driveway.

"Shit, man, she's dead. I thought that's why you
were here."

Johnny thought about Sandra's mother, her hands
at her mouth, and the man standing behind the screen,
slamming his door in Johnny's face.

"Dead? No, I didn't know. I was given her name by
a woman in L.A. When did she die?"

"About three weeks, maybe a month ago." Al dropped the hose and pulled a rag from the bucket near his feet. He started washing the truck. Johnny stared at him, thinking of the body in the desert and what Doc Whetmore had said. It had been there three weeks or a month.

"How'd she die?"

"She drove her car into an irrigation ditch and drowned."

"Irrigation ditch? I don't get it. How could she drive into an irrigation ditch?"

"A mile or two west of town there's one that crosses right under the road. She must have gone off the shoulder. They found her car in there the next morning. Cops figured she fell asleep and the right front wheel got off the pavement and the car slid into the ditch. She was still strapped in. Funny. If she hadn't been wearing the seat belt she might of got out."

"So the cops checked it out? Figured it was an accident?"

"Of course, what else would it be?" He looked at Johnny now, perhaps wondering for the first time why he was asking all the questions.

"Hey, I don't know. Like you said, it just sounded crazy, that's all," Johnny said.

Al had finished washing the Toyota's hood and now walked back to the side, jerking the hose behind him. He sprayed the truck again, then picked up a thick rag and began drying it.

"Well, thanks a lot. I appreciate your help." Johnny said and started for the sidewalk.

"Hey, wait a minute." Johnny stopped and looked back at Al. "You're that interested, I got something inside. Hold on a minute."

He dropped the hose, the water still running, and walked up the driveway and disappeared into the house. A moment later he was back, carrying a newspaper.

"Here, I got a couple of 'em."

Johnny looked at the paper. The story with a photo was on the front page, below the fold. It was a straightforward rewrite of the police report, with a few personal details thrown in near the bottom. It mentioned her job at a nearby bank, that she'd graduated from the local high school and that her husband, Roberto, had been killed in Vietnam.

"Thanks. Can I keep this?"

"Yeah, sure." Johnny folded the paper under his arm and turned to leave when Al spoke again. "Let me ask you something."

He looked back over his shoulder. "Sure."

"You're working on a story about the POWs' widows, right?"

"Yeah, that's right."

"Well, you know if they ever caught those guys?"

Johnny turned completely around and looked at the man. "What guys?"

"Those guys trying to raise money to look for POWs. That's what that colonel said, anyway. Some kind of scam. Wanted to warn Sandra about it."

Johnny stepped closer. He could hear the water from the hose hitting the cement driveway and smell the lemon scent of the soap in the water Al had just poured out. "What colonel?"

"I don't know. Sandra said some Army colonel was out and asked her some questions about Roberto. Said some people were trying to rip off the families with some new scam. You know, promising to bring back their husbands. Pretty stupid scammers, if you ask me."

"Why's that?"

"Shit, man, look around you. There's no money here. Sandra was a bank teller. Lived with her folks. Where the hell they gonna get any money from?"

"Yeah, right." Johnny nodded in agreement. "She tell you the colonel's name?" Al shook his head no. "He from the Army?"

"Yeah, I guess."

"When was he here?"

"I don't know. Three, maybe four weeks ago." He stopped for a moment, then waved his finger at Johnny. "You know what, he was here the day before she was killed. I remember now. I saw her that morning and she told me about it then. Said this colonel had come by the house the night before. That same night she drove her car into the canal."

Johnny thanked him again and walked to the sidewalk and turned back. "Hey, I crossed an irrigation ditch coming into town from the west. That the one?"

"Probably. Head west on Bear Mountain Road, that's Highway 223, it's the first one you cross. You get to Edison Drive, you've gone too far."

In the car Johnny tore the article from the paper, put it in his wallet, drove to Bear Mountain Road and turned west. He could see the canal's low berm a quarter-mile away and pulled the Z off the road close to it. He walked the last few feet and stood next to the canal. Its sun-baked dirt banks rose only a few feet above the ground level. It looked about four or five feet deep and maybe five feet across. If there was a current, Johnny couldn't see it. The water seemed to sit between the winding banks like dirty tub water. Near the culvert, which carried the water under the road, bright green moss spread across the surface.

Johnny stood looking at the water and moss and slowly shook his head. It was, he thought, a terrible place to die. He stayed at the canal's edge only a few minutes, then got in the Z and began the hundred-mile trip out of California's farming belt across the mountains and into the city. As he drove he thought of Sandra Ruiz drowned and Roberto Ruiz dying of exposure in the desert and Pham strangled in the park, and wondered if there was such a thing as a good place to die.

16

It was late afternoon when Johnny turned onto the VA grounds and drove to Jimmy's dorm. The man in the wheelchair was alone outside the building. He sat next to the steps, smoking a cigarette and watching Johnny approach.

"Hi. You know if Jimmy's around, if he's come back in yet?" Johnny asked.

"He came by for a few minutes and went again. Seemed to be in a hurry. I don't think he's planning on coming in for a while. He had that look."

Johnny didn't ask what look. He'd seen it enough times to know. The light seemed to fade in Jimmy's eyes and they appeared to focus somewhere in the distance. Conversation with Jimmy was often difficult. When he was like that, he was in a different universe light-years away, and communication seemed to crawl across the space between them like an oxcart traversing the plains.

"When was he by?" Johnny asked.

"This morning sometime."

"So he's okay. I mean, he was then?"

"Yeah. I told him you wuz looking for him. He said okay."

Johnny thanked the man and followed the same route he'd taken the day before. He cruised the streets of the VA slowly, stopped to check the canteen and patients' library and stopped next to the fence. But there was no sign of him. Johnny knew that if Jimmy wanted to hide, finding him would be almost impossible. The VA grounds covered almost seven hundred acres; disappearing would be easy. Johnny searched for another hour but finally gave up and drove to the *Chronicle*.

At the paper, he searched the database for a story on Sandra Ruiz. He knew there was no chance the paper had covered the story, but AP might have moved something and the *Chronicle* used it for filler. In less than two minutes the message appeared on the screen. There was no story in the *Chronicle*'s files about Sandra Ruiz's death. He switched off his computer and leaned back in his chair, staring at the now-blank screen. The phone rang and he grabbed it.

"Johnny Rose." There was no reply. The line was open. He could hear someone breathing. "Hello, who is this?" The phone was quiet.

Johnny stood abruptly and scanned the newsroom, trying to see into every cubicle. Was it someone there, someone at the *Chronicle*, someone in the newsroom?

"Who the fuck is this?" he demanded. The line went dead. His arm dropped and he held the receiver at his side, scanned the newsroom again, rising to his toes, but it was impossible to see past the partitions and around the corners into most of the cubicles, and he slowly sat down.

"John, oh, John," Barsh's voice came across the newsroom loudly. "Can you step into my office for a moment?"

Barsh was in the doorway of his glass office staring at him and the moment Johnny met his eyes, the editor turned and walked into his office. Johnny waited a second and followed.

He crossed the newsroom slowly, looking back to see if anyone was watching him go, but everyone seemed caught up in their own jobs, bent over keyboards and talking on the phones. In Barsh's office, Johnny dropped into a chair and waited for Barsh to begin. The metro editor was sitting on the corner of his desk, one leg dangling, his toes just shy of the floor.

"You didn't come in today."

"I left a message with Rogers. Told him I was following up a lead on something."

"All he said was that you were out. He didn't mention what you were doing."

Johnny felt himself shrug, an almost imperceptible "what the hell do I know" gesture, and said nothing. He didn't want to tell Barsh or anyone in the newsroom about Susan Loveless or his trip to Arvin. A silence filled the distance between them until Barsh finally said, "Okay. Well, then, did you go see William Bradley?"

"Bradley? Who's Bradley?"

"The paper's attorney. I told you to go see him. I even made the appointment for you, remember?"

The attorney. He'd completely forgotten. "Oh, right. I got busy and couldn't make it. I'm sorry. I'll set up another appointment and go in the next day or two."

Barsh didn't respond. Through the glass Johnny could hear the muted voices of two reporters talking about the lead to a story. Barsh sat perfectly still and Johnny stared straight ahead, refusing to look at the editor. Barsh stood and stepped to the door. He closed it gently and moved behind his desk. He pulled out the chair, sat and looked across the empty surface at Johnny.

"John, there's something I have to tell you. Remember, I told you I would ask Sheridan to look into that murder in the park. Check with his sources in the department."

"Okay. He find anything?" He feigned nonchalance but could feel his pulse quicken.

"The police have found a witness. A homeless man who was sleeping in the park. He saw the murderer."

Johnny sat up straight and smiled. "That's great," he said.

"Not necessarily. He described the killer as a white male, tall and thin." Barsh stopped speaking and looked across the big desk at Johnny.

"Right, sounds like just what I told the cops."

"John, he didn't say anything about seeing you."

"Didn't see me, that's bullshit. I was there. I chased Pham's killer."

Barsh raised his hands, palms out, and gestured for Johnny to calm himself. "I believe you, John, but look at it from Detective Earl's point of view. He's got witnesses who put you with Pham's body, he's got your fingerprints on the dowel—"

"I told you—"

"And he's found a motive," Barsh continued, refusing to let Johnny interrupt him.

Johnny stood suddenly. When he spoke, his voice

was strained and sounded strange in his ears, as though it belonged to someone else. "They think I killed Pham for some two-thousand-dollar piece-of-shit car? I didn't even *want* the damned thing. I tried to give it to him, for God's sake."

"Sit down, Johnny. I'm not the one who thinks you killed him. I'm just telling you what the cops are saying."

"Yeah, well, it's all bullshit."

"That may be, but until this is over, I don't have any choice but to take you off the metro staff for a while. I want you to start working the night copy desk."

"What?"

"Just until this is over. You can start doing your column again as soon as this is all settled."

"But if the cops don't believe me about Kyle Loveless, they'll never find the killer. They'll end up chasing their tails." He stood abruptly again. "Am I the only one who understands what's happening?" He hesitated a moment and spun around to look out at the newsroom. Two reporters who'd been listening looked away. Had they been eavesdropping, watching him?

"I'm not working the copy desk. I'm not doing that."

Barsh's gaze dropped to the desktop. When he spoke his voice was quiet, barely above a whisper.

"John, don't fight me on this. I don't have any choice."

"I can't sit around here doing nothing until Earl decides he's got enough to put me in jail. Don't you see, I can't do that?"

"John, be here at six tomorrow night to work the desk or don't come in again." He'd drawn the line, it was up to Johnny to cross it or back down.

As he looked at Barsh, Johnny's eyes focused on details of the man's face; a patch high on his right cheek that he'd missed shaving that morning, a small discoloration near his nose where he'd probably had a mole removed. Suddenly Johnny thought of Geld. Maybe he should call him, ask him to intervene. Hadn't Geld told him personally how much he liked his work?

"Maybe I'll call Geld," Johnny said, playing his ace in the hole.

"Don't bother. I've already spoken with him. He agrees with me one hundred percent."

"You talked to Geld about this?" Johnny was stunned.

"When Sheridan told me what he found, I called Mr. Geld and told him what I planned to do. Like I said, he agrees with me. You'll report to the copy desk."

"You planned to move me to the copy desk even before we talked, didn't you?"

"John, I don't have any choice."

Johnny stood and slowly shook his head. "No," he said.

"What do you mean, no?"

"Send me my check."

"What?"

"I quit."

"You'd better stop and think about what you're doing."

Johnny looked through the glass into the news-room and again scanned the reporters' pods and thought of the phone call minutes before. He thought, too, of Detective Earl picking up all the wrong pieces and slowly building a fundamentally flawed case that would have just enough to it to send him to prison for life.

Johnny looked at Barsh and shook his head. "No," he said and walked out of the office.

It took about twenty minutes to clear his desk and empty his drawers into a box on the floor. He tossed the last few personal items into the carton, picked it up and stood.

"This looks permanent." The voice came from behind him and Johnny glanced over his shoulder. Ray, a photographer who'd worked at the *Chronicle* for nearly thirty years, was standing there, grinning. He was almost as tall as Johnny, with a barrel chest, powerful arms and thick white hair combed straight back from his forehead.

"I just quit."

"I was afraid of that. Not many of us left anymore." Ray held out his hand and Johnny suddenly realized the photographer smelled of developing chemicals. They'd been on a lot of assignments together, and Johnny never smelled chemicals without thinking of Ray.

Johnny shook his hand and Ray retreated toward the darkroom. Johnny surveyed the newsroom one last time. He realized then that he'd just said good-bye to one of the two or three people in the whole newsroom he'd miss. He picked up his box and walked out.

17

Johnny shoved the box in the rear of the Z and looked down at its meager contents: a notebook, a batch of outdated press passes, a Rolodex, a few clips, a coffee mug and the computer printout Jaunique had given him. Not much to show for more than ten years in one place. He closed the hatch, turned and scanned the parking lot, then looked at the rear of the building near the pressroom. The rounded noses of the trucks, lined up waiting for the papers that would start flowing off the press at about three the next morning, were barely visible in the loading bays. He studied the building next, slowly scanning the brick facade up the rows of windows past the editorial offices to the top and back down.

He'd always thought it would be hard to leave, not to be a reporter anymore, not to be part of the process of putting out a paper. But standing there staring at the building, he felt strangely empty. He knew he wouldn't miss it.

He left the parking lot without a glance back and drove without thinking, without planning, up one street and down the other. He drove past small ethnic eateries just warming up for the evening. He passed gas stations, their islands empty, and convenience stores with their parking lots full. He glanced into well-lighted donut shops and saw steel racks shining and coffeepots glistening behind them. He saw people waiting silently at the bus stops, staring at the passing traffic as though idle conversation with others nearby would be dangerous. At one stoplight, he thought of going home and even signaled for a turn. But when the light changed he turned in the other direction, shoved a Warren Zevon tape in the deck and sang along.

He drove for an hour, heading east, then south, and finally he turned back north and then west to Sawtelle Avenue and north again. He caught the light at Santa Monica Boulevard and a minute later was on the VA grounds. He knew even as he drove past the white pillars at the entrance that he was probably on a fool's errand.

But Johnny also knew he had to try because there was so much he didn't understand, so much about his brother and Vietnam and POWs that he'd simply never asked. And now, Johnny knew, it was probably too late. Years too late. Even if Jimmy had the secrets locked inside, he might never be able to get them out.

Jimmy's shrink had tried to explain it once. She said a part of Jimmy's brain had become disorganized. "For us," she said, "everything is organized. For people who have suffered like Jimmy, everything is scrambled. I recently read about a man who as a child survived the

Nazi death camps. He was adopted after the war and seemed to have adjusted. But the first time the family went skiing and the boy saw the chair lifts going to a small house on the top of a hill, he became hysterical. What he saw was all these children going up the hill, and the chairs coming back empty. He started screaming and clinging to his mother, absolutely paralyzed, because to him the most logical explanation was that this was a killing machine for children, and his parents were trying to put him on a chair. For your brother it's the same way. His brain has created its own order that to him is perfectly normal. To us it is bizarre."

Johnny had looked at the woman sitting across from him, Dr. Monica Goldman. She was almost sixty, maybe a year or two beyond, with gray hair cut short. She wore a dark suit with a white blouse. Her office was impressive, dark wood and a polished desk and comfortable sofa in the corner. But Johnny wondered how good she really was. Despite all the sessions, all she could say was that Jimmy's brain was "disorganized."

"So, is there any hope?" Johnny finally asked one day.

"I can't say. Sometimes people are able to learn to live with it. Other times, it gets worse. With your brother, I don't know. I just don't know."

"Okay, so tell me what can I do."

"Stop being so angry with him."

Johnny just looked at her. Angry? How could she think he was angry? He'd paid for the clinic to dry Jimmy out, paid the landlord when he was getting ready to evict Jimmy, was even footing a good part of her bill. Would he be doing that if he were pissed off at his brother?

"I'm not angry with him. I want to help him."

"Those aren't mutually exclusive remarks," the doctor had said. It had taken Johnny almost two years to understand the truth of what she said.

Now he was cruising the grounds looking for his kid brother again, knowing he had to talk to him. There had to be someone to listen as he tried to sort it all out. He drove slowly past the residence hall, past the canteen, and cruised on. At the baseball diamond he parked and searched the small crowd watching a slow-pitch softball game. He checked Jimmy's empty camp and returned to the car and started cruising again.

He found him sitting alone on a bench in a bus shelter.

Johnny walked up and sat on the bench, but Jimmy didn't react. He said nothing. It was what Johnny expected.

In the last few years their conversations had become trivial and almost always seemed to end badly. Sometimes Jimmy would say something sharp, even insightful, and a moment later slip back over the edge, leaving Johnny frustrated and angry with his brother.

He looked good, Johnny thought. His face still showed the wear of alcohol and he'd lost weight, but he was clean, his hair combed and his beard neatly trimmed. Even now, with so much difference between them, they still looked remarkably alike, Johnny thought. Brothers forever.

Then, without ever acknowledging his brother's presence, Jimmy started speaking, looking straight ahead as though he were talking to himself. "The captain came today." He seemed afraid as he said it.

"Pardon me?" Johnny said.

"The captain, I saw him. Talked to him." Johnny listened, hearing the edge of pain and fear in Jimmy's voice. Johnny could feel his stomach muscles tighten and his heart accelerate.

"Jimmy, who's the captain? Who is he?"

Jimmy was quiet for a moment, then his head turned and he looked right at Johnny. He smiled and nodded as though just seeing his brother for the first time. "You were here today. Sorry I missed you."

Johnny went with the flow, knowing he couldn't push his brother, couldn't force him into a conversation. "Yeah, I talked to a guy outside your place. They said they hadn't seen you in a few days."

"I'll just be out a few days. I'll be back in the hall soon." He seemed to shiver, then turned away and looked straight ahead again. "I don't want to see him again, Johnny. I can't do it."

"See the captain?"

Jimmy nodded. "I can't see him again."

"Jimmy, who's the captain? You've got to tell me. It's really important. I can help. I can make sure he never comes here again. But you've got to tell me." He was staring at his brother, willing him to look back. But his eyes were straight ahead.

Across the street, beyond a small grassy area at the rear of a building, a man in white pants and a white T-shirt maneuvered a cloth-sided laundry basket on wheels out the back door of the three-story building and across a wide cement loading dock. Jimmy turned and looked at him. "So, what brings you to the loony bin?"

"Jimmy, I need to talk to you. You've got to listen to me. Maybe the captain's involved. Can you listen to me?" Johnny said.

"Hey, today's your lucky day. I've got a few spare minutes with nothing to do."

Johnny looked up at his younger brother, knowing he was there then, lucid. He wondered how long it would last.

"Jimmy, first tell me who the captain is. Why are you so upset by him? What did he want."

But even as he spoke, Jimmy seemed to draw away, to be sinking back into himself, and Johnny scrambled to hold his attention. "Hey, we can talk about that later. I came here to tell you that I just quit my job."

"Oh? Why'd you do that?" His tone was flat, emotionless. Maybe he'd already slipped away completely.

He looked at Jimmy, dressed in blue jeans, worn-out running shoes and a loose-fitting T-shirt. "A friend of mine was murdered," he said.

"Oh. What happened?" There was no feeling, no emotion. Johnny's words seemed to have sunk into oblivion.

"He was strangled. Jimmy, listen to me now. It's very important. My friend told me he saw a POW. Saw a guy we left behind. Saw him right here in L.A."

"Yeah? Who killed him?"

Johnny shook his head. Didn't the guy feel anything anymore? Nothing at all? Didn't he listen?

"I don't know who did it."

"You doing a story?"

"I quit, remember?"

"Oh, yeah, I forgot."

"Jimmy, I gotta tell you about what's been going on with me. It's very important. I need to know what you think. Try to stay with me on this, okay?" Jimmy was silent. "Okay?" Johnny prodded.

His brother nodded, and Johnny started talking,

not waiting for anything more. He started with Roberto Ruiz's body, moved to Pham's phone call, wound his way through the visit to Susan Herbert, his trip to the desert and ended with the confrontation with Barsh.

The two brothers sat in silence for a few minutes when he finished. The evening was just beginning to cool and the night air was still, and against the background buzz of the huge metropolitan area, Johnny could hear a single radio playing a country ballad. For a few seconds he thought of the nights he and Jimmy had camped out in the backyard, waking in the quiet morning to find their tent thick with dew. He looked at his brother. "What do you think, Jimmy?"

"Me? I think the world's a fucked-up place. You go around talking trash like that and *I'm* the one in the nuthouse?"

Johnny felt himself sag, a collapse both mental and physical. What had he expected? Some grand insight from his younger brother who had to struggle to live someplace with a roof over his head for more than a few weeks at a time?

But it wasn't just Jimmy. It was everything. A refugee murdered, a phony widow, a woman who drowned in an irrigation ditch, everything. Maybe Jimmy was right; the world was just too strange.

Johnny reached over and grabbed Jimmy's arm. He had to try again. He couldn't leave it like this. "Jimmy, didn't you hear a word I said?"

"Life's a bitch and then you die. What can I tell you, bro? Danger's everywhere."

"I guess you're right," Johnny said and waited a moment before asking Jimmy again about the captain. But as he asked, Jimmy seemed to shiver and turn away. It was useless. Johnny stood. "Sorry I haven't been by in a while."

"Don't worry."

He stood and started to walk away, but then he heard Jimmy's voice and stopped. "He came right here and we talked. Just like before, like in Nam before we flew." Jimmy was looking at the loading dock across the street, talking to the night.

Johnny took a step back toward the bus stop, moving slowly, as if a sudden movement would send his brother's thoughts off their rails. "You mean the captain, Jimmy?" He could see the look of concentration in his brother's face and knew he was struggling to talk, to tell Johnny what he wanted to know.

"He asked about you. Asked all about you."

Johnny froze. "What did he ask you, Jimmy?"

"Where you were. Wanted to know like if you had a girlfriend or something."

"What did you tell him, Jimmy?"

"I told him to try the paper."

"Good. You did the right thing."

"Oh, I almost forgot. He's not a captain anymore. Did I tell you? He's been promoted since I saw him last time. He made colonel. Full bird."

Johnny walked to the bench and looked at his brother. His heart seemed so loud in his ears that he was sure even Jimmy could hear it.

"What's the captain's name, Jimmy? Who is he?"

Jimmy looked at Johnny and smiled. He seemed to be fading quickly away, as though the struggle to hold onto the world's version of reality had been too much. "He said he was bringing them home this time, Johnny. Really bringing them home." Jimmy turned away and sat straight-backed, staring ahead, his face immobile.

Johnny knew he could try to search the records, file a request with a bureaucracy someplace and wait, hope it came up with the name of Jimmy's commander. But how long would that take? Weeks? Months? His best chance was sitting right in front of him. Johnny reached over and touched his brother gently on the arm. "Jimmy, you've got to help me here. It's very important. Who's the captain? What else did he say about the POWs?"

But his brother didn't seem to hear a word Johnny said.

18

The road through the VA grounds dips where it passes below Wilshire Boulevard. As Johnny headed down the incline, the Z's headlights caught the side of the underpass, which had been painted with symbols of military outfits. He'd driven there dozens of times and never seen it before. But that night, Johnny pulled to the curb and looked at the huge mural caught in his headlights on the concrete: the black outline of a soldier, head slightly bowed, with a guard tower in the background and a line of barbed wire. The words "POWs/MIAs NEVER FORGOTTEN" were stenciled on the wall next to it. He thought of Jimmy's words. The captain told him, "He was bringing them home this time, really bringing them home."

Johnny sat and looked at the outline of the soldier, the Z's engine idling silently, then eased the car into the street again and drove out the south exit of the VA grounds onto Sawtelle Boulevard. As he left the grounds, he saw headlights in his mirror. Half a block later he looked again and saw the headlights jump as the car behind him accelerated to make the light at Ohio Avenue. It slowed again and then followed him at a safe distance south across Santa Monica Boulevard. Johnny's eyes flicked from the road ahead to the mirror and back. Suddenly he sped up and turned the corner, heading west on LaGrange Avenue. A moment later the car rounded the corner. Johnny turned south at the next block and watched as the car passed through the intersection heading west. He felt his shoulders slump and he relaxed his grip on the steering wheel. For a second he contemplated his mounting paranoia with a sense of embarrassment. But he knew it didn't matter if the goblins were real. He had to act as if they were. He turned west on Olympic Boulevard and stopped at a gas station on the corner of Olympic and Bundy Drive. He found a phone on the north side of the mini-mart and called Susan.

"Oh, hi. I'm glad you called," she said. "Was Sandra able to help?"

Johnny hesitated, thinking of the irrigation canal, the green scum floating on the water's surface. "Ah, Sandra Ruiz was killed a few weeks ago in an automobile accident. She apparently lost control of her car and drove into an irrigation ditch and drowned."

"Oh my God, that's awful."

"Yes, it is. But I'm not sure it was an accident."

"What?"

"She was killed just about the time Roberto Ruiz died, if that's who it was out there in the desert. My friend at the coroner's office said the guy had been dead about three or four weeks. She died exactly twenty-seven days ago."

"It could be a coincidence."

Johnny watched a Mustang convertible, its top down, stop at the island. A young man wearing dark glasses against the nonexistent sun got out and walked toward the mini-mart. Johnny turned his back to the lot and leaned into the phone.

"Yeah, it could be a coincidence, but there's something else. I talked to her cousin, a guy named Al who lives across the street. He told me an Army colonel had come to visit her the night before she died. This colonel told her there were some scam artists preying on the families and wanted to know if anyone had contacted her about her husband."

"That doesn't sound right. They wouldn't come to your house in person at night. They might send you a letter or they might call, but I'm not even sure about that. Still, I guess it's possible."

"Has anyone contacted you?"

"No, I haven't heard from anyone in the military in years."

"So maybe there is no scam. Maybe it's something else."

"Maybe, but Johnny, I . . ." She hesitated.

"But what? What is it?"

"Well, I've been thinking about all this, about what your friend Pham said and about the man in the desert."

"And?"

"Well, I keep asking myself if somehow, against all the odds, an American soldier, a POW, managed to come home, where's the parade?"

"Parade? What do you mean?"

"We both know that the first POW out of Vietnam would be worth millions. Just the book contract alone would be worth that. Then there'd be the TV appearances, the meeting with the President, the movie rights, all of that stuff. It would be huge news. So if there really were POWs back home, why is it a big secret?"

"But then how do you explain Pham's murder and the body of Roberto Ruiz?"

"I don't know, Johnny. I'm just telling you it doesn't make any sense to me."

"No. You're right, it doesn't make any sense. Why bring them home and keep it a secret?" He was quiet for a moment, and when he began speaking, his voice was softer. "I went by the VA tonight. I talked to my brother. Well, talked to him as best I could. It's never easy." Susan said nothing.

"The thing is, he told me some colonel came to see him. Talked about bringing the boys home. Now, I know my brother has all kinds of problems. God, do I know that. But he's never said anything like this before. Ever. And the way he talked, he knew this colonel. In fact, this guy, assuming for a minute that he's real, scared Jimmy. I mean really seemed to frighten him. I couldn't get Jimmy to tell me his name. I think he was too scared. And the whole time Jimmy was talking, I was thinking it was an Army colonel who visited Sandra Ruiz." Johnny waited a moment while he watched the young man in the Mustang leave the store and walk to his car.

"Oh, hell, this is all crazy. I shouldn't have bothered you."

"No, I'm glad you called, I really am. Besides, who

knows, maybe this is the story that's going to win you your Pulitzer."

Johnny could hear the smile in her voice as she spoke, the attempt to put the conversation back on an even keel. He closed his eyes and exhaled deeply.

"There's something I gotta tell you. I quit the *Chronicle* tonight."

"Quit? Why?"

"Oh, man, where to start?" He rubbed the bridge of his nose between his finger and thumb and looked back across the brightly lit islands, aglow in the pink-white lights of halogen lamps high above the lot. "A reporter at the paper, a guy named Sheridan, he works the police beat and has a lot of good sources, told Barsh that the cops have a witness to Pham's murder. The way this guy describes the killer it sounds like the guy I described, but the thing is, the witness, he's some homeless guy sleeping in the park, said he never saw me. Never saw me running over to try to save Pham."

"Okay. But what does this have to do with the paper?"

"Barsh wanted to put me on the night copy desk. Take me off the story."

"Well, is that so bad? I mean, that doesn't sound terribly unreasonable to me."

"Susan, I'm the only one who believes there's a connection between the man Pham saw at the restaurant and the murder. Detective Earl doesn't believe it. He thinks maybe I did it. I don't know what Barsh thinks. He probably believes I did it, too. Right now, I'm the only one who's asking the right questions and if I don't find the answers, I could end up in prison."

"You're not the only one who believes, Johnny. I

don't have any idea what this is all about, but I believe you."

"Thank you."

"You be careful."

Johnny said he would and drove home. As he drove, he felt the stirrings of a happiness he hadn't felt in years. He realized he was anticipating the next time he could see Susan, even the next time he would talk to her.

He was smiling when he turned the Z into the carport and the headlights lit up the body of Weird Harold dangling from a rope. One end was tied around his neck and the other was nailed to the roof of the carport. The body hung motionless over the middle of his parking space.

Johnny's breath caught in his throat and his foot jammed on the brake. The car was rocking on its springs as he shoved the door open. He knew the moment he saw the body that the cat was dead, but he still ran to it. He lifted the cat, taking the tension out of the rope, knowing it was futile even as he did it. He stood for a moment holding Weird Harold, feeling his soft fur. Johnny knew he'd lost more than a pet. He and the cat had been companions, independent and dependent on each other at the same time. He would miss the damned cat and his haughty demands and his stubborn refusal to show affection except on his terms.

He could feel an anger beginning deep inside. An anger for the killing of Weird Harold, and Sandra Ruiz and Pham. The anger fed off his frustration at seeing so much and understanding almost nothing. He realized suddenly that he and the cat and the rope were casting a long, grotesque shadow on the wall at the end of the carport. He lowered the cat slowly and let him hang again on the rope while he went to the Z and dug in the glove compartment to find an old pocketknife. He cut the simple cotton clothesline rope and put the body in a small box he found near the Dumpster.

He opened the door to his apartment and unconsciously waited and caught himself, realizing that Weird Harold wouldn't dash past him again. The apartment was dark and from the front door Johnny could see the flashing red light on his answering machine. He crossed the room slowly and stood next to the kitchen counter, looking at the light blinking rhythmically. He punched the button and listened to the three words.

"Get the message?"

Johnny stabbed the Stop button and stood a moment longer looking at it, listening to the whir as the tape rewound. He wanted to smash the machine, send shards of plastic flying through the air. He raised his fist but stopped. He should save the tape, he knew. He should save it and make Earl listen to it. He dropped his fist to his side and relaxed his fingers. There was no point. The tape proved nothing. "Get the message?" It could mean anything.

Johnny called Animal Control, left a message asking the agency to pick up Weird Harold's body, then opened the sliding glass door and stepped onto the small patio. He inhaled deeply and blew the air out, trying to ease the anger he felt. The air smelled of lighter fluid and sizzling steaks, and he could see wisps of smoke drifting from the patio across the small walkway in back. Beyond the redwood fence he could hear a young couple arguing in Japanese, the words nothing but strange sounds to Johnny's ears, but the emotion was as familiar as well-worn jeans.

The argument stopped for a moment and then, just as the man began speaking again, the phone rang. Johnny stepped through the open door, picked the receiver from its stand on the kitchen counter and waited.

"Hello, Mr. Rose? Hello?" It was a woman's voice.

"This is Johnny Rose. Who is this?"

"My name is Paula Marks. I'm the night supervisor with Medical Administrative Services at the Veterans Administration hospital. You're listed as the contact for James Rose."

"Yes, is there a problem? Has something happened to Jimmy?"

"Sir, can you come to the hospital? Your brother's been hospitalized."

"What? What happened?"

"Well, sir, he tried to kill himself."

The two single beds sat parallel in the room. The second bed, the one nearest the large window, was unoccupied. Johnny sat on it and watched his brother sleep. Two clear plastic tubes snaked out of Jimmy's nostrils and disappeared under the blue sheet tucked near his chin. Another tube ran from an intravenous bag hung above the metal headboard into the back of his hand, which rested atop the sheet. His head, hand and arm were all of Jimmy Rose visible to the world. The sheet covered the bulky casts on Jimmy's legs. The brothers were alone in the darkened room. The door was partially open and an occasional shadow would flicker past as a nurse or orderly moved to the nurses' station down the hall.

Even in the darkness Johnny could see that the

skin of Jimmy's arm showed the signs of constant exposure to the sun. It was brown, almost leathery.

Both his legs were broken and it had taken the surgeons more than three hours to stop the internal bleeding and set his legs. Jimmy was very lucky to be alive, the doctor had told Johnny.

Johnny watched his brother sleep for nearly an hour and then walked into the hallway. The linoleum gleamed and the ceramic tile, which stretched like wainscoting halfway up the wall, was bright and well scrubbed. Dr. Savarjian was at the nurses' station, leaning against the counter, reading a chart. The doctor was short, plump, dark complexion, with thinning dark hair, a small mustache and brown eyes behind thick glasses.

"Dr. Savarjian, I'm Johnny Rose. I think you treated my brother, Jimmy."

"Ah, Mr. Rose. Yes, I did. Your brother is a very lucky man."

"What happened? No one has told me a thing. I know he fell, but nothing more than that."

Savarjian looked at him for a moment, then crossed his arms, hugging the chart close to his chest. "Your brother didn't fall. He jumped. Off a building. Normally he would have landed on a concrete loading dock, but just as he jumped one of the men pushed a big laundry cart out the door. He landed in it and it broke his fall."

Johnny could see the loading dock and the tall building and remembered Jimmy staring at it as he talked. He cringed at the thought of his brother's leap to the concrete. "Is he going to be all right?"

"Well, the prognosis is good. He's resting comfortably now. I think he can look forward to a full recovery."

"How the hell did he get to the roof?"

"There's a window from the hallway on the top floor. If you're determined, you can get up there. One of the men saw your brother climb out a window. He called Security, but I'm afraid they didn't arrive in time. I'm very sorry."

"Can I stay for a while?"

"He's sleeping, but you can look in on him."

Johnny returned to the room and his perch on the edge of the bed. He sat in the darkened room and looked at Jimmy and remembered Dr. Savarjian's prognosis. Full recovery. What the hell did that mean, Johnny wondered? A life playing dominoes and sleeping in the weeds outside the fence of the VA hospital? But as he looked at his brother, Johnny knew it didn't really matter. He didn't care where Jimmy slept or how he spent his days. He just wanted him alive.

Jimmy opened his eyes the next morning.

"I'm thirsty," he said in a coarse whisper. Johnny moved to the other side of Jimmy's bed and picked up a cup from the small table next to him. He held the cup to Jimmy's lips so he could sip the water.

Johnny looked into his eyes and realized that Jimmy was alert, aware. He didn't know how long it would last.

"What happened, Jimmy?"

"It was all there again. Like I never left it."

"What, Jimmy? What was there? Nam?"

Jimmy nodded. "All of it. The choppers, all of it. He brought it with him."

"Who brought it, Jimmy? Was it the captain you told me about?"

"It hurts. God, it hurts."

"I'll get the nurse to give you something, okay?"

Jimmy nodded, but before Johnny could move away, he spoke again.

"I just can't live with it. I can't see it anymore, Johnny. I just can't. I just can't do it."

Johnny grabbed his brother's hand. "You don't have to live with anything, Jimmy. The war's over. So don't talk like that. You're not leaving me. You're not. You're in the hospital now. You're going to be okay."

Jimmy's eyes closed and he seemed to drift off. Johnny sat for several minutes listening to his brother's breathing, then stood and watched Jimmy for a moment longer. Finally he walked to the door and grabbed the knob, but paused and turned back.

Jimmy's eyes were open. "Did the captain find you?"

Johnny shook his head. "No, no one found me, Jimmy."

"He asked me where you'd be if you weren't home. Asked if you had a girlfriend. But I didn't know." Jimmy seemed confused, disoriented, as though lost amid a complex algebra problem.

Johnny let the door swing closed and returned to the side of the bed. He leaned close to his brother. "Jimmy, why did he want to find me?"

"I don't know. I didn't ask."

"Who is he? Tell me." But his brother seemed to drift away, his eyes closing slowly. "I'm going to go get the nurse."

Jimmy opened his eyes again, turned his head and looked out the window. "I need something to drink," he said.

Johnny picked up the cup and held it to his brother's lips again. "It's going to be okay, Jimmy."

Jimmy's eyes seemed to lose focus for a moment.

Then he nodded. "Yeah," he said, barely above a whisper. He blinked rapidly, as though answering the question took strength.

"You gotta watch out for him, okay? Be careful, Johnny."

"Don't worry, I will. But you gotta help me here. You gotta tell me who he is. Who's the captain, Jimmy?"

Jimmy hesitated, and Johnny could see his brother struggling, fighting to answer. His voice was barely a whisper. "He's a killer, Johnny. I know. I've watched him. He doesn't care." Jimmy's eyes changed then and dissolved quickly into a vacant stare.

19

Johnny stopped at a pay phone near the elevators and called the FBI. He half-expected Hightower to dodge him or be out of the office. But he'd been on hold for less than a minute when the agent picked up.

"Agent Hightower, how can I help you?"

"It's Johnny Rose."

The line was dead for a moment, then the agent said, "Hold on a second, will you?" Johnny could hear a muffled conversation; then the agent was back.

"Sorry for the delay. I had to finish something and I wanted to close the door."

Any other time, Johnny would have chatted briefly, making the small talk that is such an important part of the care and feeding of sources. But after a night in Jimmy's hospital room, he no longer cared about the formalities of his former job. He was blunt.

"You have anything for me?"

"You sound tired, Rose."

"I've been up all night."

"Well, let me start by giving you a little advice."

"I didn't call you for advice."

"Yeah, well, I'm giving you some anyway. I don't know what the hell you're doing, but I know you're in way over your head. Let this thing go, Rose. Whatever it is, just let it go."

Let it go. Was he crazy? Johnny gripped the phone, his palm moist against the plastic, and his voice came out strained and intense. "You have anything or not?"

He could hear Hightower exhale deeply.

"Okay, I heard one thing. Immigration spotted a man traveling on a false Thai passport coming through LAX a couple of days ago. They alerted Customs, who called us. Guy's name is Tran Vhin, he's the right-hand man for Khun Sa. We followed him, but lost him."

"What's Khun Sa?"

"It's not a what, it's a who. Khun Sa is the strongest warlord in the Golden Triangle, along the Thai, Laos and Burma borders. He controls all the opium produced in that area. None of the governments can touch him. Between you and me, I don't think they want to do anything about him. He's making them all rich. Lately, though, some rebel insurgents have been giving him a pretty hard time. We figure his man's in town to launder some money or make a weapons buy. Get something to put the upstarts in their place. That's why we were following him."

"So? What the hell does this have to do with Loveless or Ruiz?"

"Nothing, really. But it's the only thing with a Southeast Asian connection I found. It's what I got."

"If that's all you found, then you didn't look hard

enough, Hightower." The disdain was obvious in his voice.

"Don't give me that shit. I looked, all right." Hightower's voice filled with anger. "And as soon as I started asking about that pilot, that Kyle Loveless, I got calls from some heavy hitters back east. They wanted to know all about why I was asking."

"Heavy hitters. What the hell does that mean? Why does the FBI care about a couple of long-dead POWs? What's going on, Hightower?"

"I don't know. I really don't know what the hell this is all about and believe me, I didn't ask. I just answered their questions."

"What'd you tell 'em?"

"The truth. At least, pretty much the truth. I told 'em you'd filed a report of a live sighting. I was just following it up. That's it, Rose, that's the end of story."

"That's it? What do you mean, that's it?"

"That's all I've got."

"That's bullshit. I know you, Hightower. You're better than that. A lot better. You'd never let it go that easily. So don't try to blow me off. If you've got something, give it to me. You owe me that much."

"Hey, I checked and all I got for it was a full load of grief. So that's it."

"No, you got that wrong. That's not it. Listen to me. I want to know what you found. If I don't get it, I'll call your supervisor and tell him the whole story. I'll lay it all out, including the half-truths you told the heavy hitters back east. I'll tell 'em you're a source helping out a reporter without going through official channels."

"You do that and no agent will ever talk to you again."

"I don't give a shit."

"They'll never listen to you anyway."

"Yeah, maybe not. But you'll have a lot of explaining to do and probably a mountain of paperwork, too." Johnny paused for a moment and his voice came softer, less demanding. He turned and faced the wall, his back to the corridor.

"Look, Hightower, all I want is what we agreed to. Now, if you found something, let me have it and you'll never hear from me again, ever."

The phone was dead for a moment and Johnny waited. He looked past his shoulder and watched an elderly man in a motorized wheelchair with a flag on a whip antenna on the back roll down the hall and turn into the elevator. A moment later the doors closed and he was gone.

"Okay. I heard one thing before the lid slammed shut. So listen real carefully, I'm only going to say this once. Then we're even, right? This wipes the slate clean, right?"

"Yeah, we're even. What is it?"

"Twice they asked if you'd mentioned the Royal Hotel on San Julian downtown."

"The Royal? What does a hotel have to do with this?"

But Johnny's question hung in empty air. The phone had gone dead.

No intersection marks the heart of Los Angeles's skid row. There is no symbolic center, like Florence and Normandie, ground zero for the last riots. In the City of the Angels, the downtown simply fades from nice stores and steel-and-glass hotels with lines of cabs in front to aging brick hotels and older shops with samples chained down on the sidewalk outside the door. Finally, before the produce markets and warehouse district, come the transient hotels, the $400-a-month single rooms with bars covering the windows. The streets are filled with day laborers who work the nearby toy warehouses when they can find a spot and the homeless pushing shopping carts heaped with rags or bedding or filled with crushed aluminum cans.

San Julian was in the heart of the area. Johnny turned north on the street and saw a line of people, black, white and brown, sitting and standing on the sidewalk to his left. On the curb to his right an elderly black man, bent and frail, waved his arms as he spoke to a young overweight woman in shorts that stretched tightly across her fat buttocks. It was the only conversation Johnny saw. The others moved silently and anonymously along the sidewalk or sat alone on the curb tending their bottles in their invisible isolation booths. Only one person, a large brown man in baggy shorts and a loose athletic shirt, seemed to notice Johnny's car. He was walking on the sidewalk but stopped and stood perfectly still and watched Johnny intently as the car rolled past.

Half a block away Johnny passed a bar. Its open door led to a darkened interior like the entrance to a mine. The bar abutted an empty parking lot ringed by bars topped with razor wire. And next Johnny saw the Royal Hotel.

It was a two-story brick rectangle with a flat roof and small covered porch underneath a second-story balcony. The place was at least fifty years old. Probably more. Three narrow cement steps led from the sidewalk to a porch screened with heavy wire mesh. An iron door blocked the entrance. Sitting on the steps, leaning back against the door, was a man in dirty blue jeans ripped at the knee. Despite the heat, he wore a windbreaker zipped to the neck. His hair was long and stringy and stuck out from under a blue Dodgers baseball cap with a flat bill. A bottle, wrapped in a brown bag bunched at the neck, sat on the porch next to him. Johnny wondered if he were a resident or a drunk who'd perched on the porch steps while gathering strength to push on.

A plywood FOR SALE sign, bolted to the building just below the roofline, was weathered, its letters faded. Nailed across it was a new sign that proclaimed in bright letters: SOLD.

Johnny found a parking lot a few blocks away, paid the attendant five bucks and walked back toward the hotel. He moved slowly and cautiously along the cracked and dirty sidewalks, aware of the people around him. He passed the skeleton of a broken couch on the curb, its cushions gone and its exposed springs brown with rust. A block from the hotel he could see the drunk still sitting on the steps. Up ahead, past the hotel, he saw a police cruiser turn the corner and pull to the curb. A moment later, another one passed him from behind. Then a second. They jerked to a stop just across from the Royal. In an instant there were other cruisers and uniformed cops everywhere. The street people scattered like ants from a kicked hill. The big brown man ran down the middle of the street toward Johnny. Two cops chased him. The faster one, a woman, caught up and leaped on his back. The man staggered, then knocked her off and turned and swung at the other cop only a step behind. Instantly they were on the ground, rolling and throwing punches. The big man struggled to his feet and two more cops rushed up and pulled him down again. A crowd circled the officers and the brown man as they rolled on the asphalt. The crowd cheered as though they were watching a combination big-time wrestling match and *Jeopardy!*

The drunk on the steps to the Royal stood and moved to the top. He rose to his tiptoes to see over the crowd that circled the officers. Finally the man walked down the steps and sauntered to the edge of the circle. Johnny watched him go, then moved quickly to the hotel, pulled the iron door open, crossed the small porch and stepped inside the building. He was alone in a long narrow hallway with several doors on both sides. A worn red carpet stretched down the hallway like a path to nowhere. A pay phone hung on the wall to his left and halfway down the hall, on the right, a stairway led to the second floor. The building smelled of disinfectant and bug spray. Johnny could hear the crackle of the police radios from outside, but inside the Royal was still. There were no people, no sounds.

Johnny moved on and saw an open room on his right. He stepped in and did a slow turn. The walls were a uniform gray, the door frame a powder blue. They looked freshly painted, the latest layer of paint laid neatly atop a few dozen others. The room's linoleum floor was worn, faded, and bumpy but clean. A single bed, little more than a wooden platform, was built into the wall on his right. A new mattress, still wrapped in plastic, rested on the wood. A bare light-bulb dangled by a cord from the ceiling. The only plumbing in the room was a round sink, pitted and stained, wedged into the corner to his left. A wooden, triangular-shaped medicine cabinet with a cracked mirror was fixed to the wall above the sink. Next to the sink was an old white refrigerator.

There was one window, which looked onto the parking lot next to the hotel. Bars covered the window and just below the sill a metal lever protruded from the wall. Johnny looked at the lever for almost a minute before he understood. It was a fire release. He crossed the small room and stepped on the lever and was surprised when the bars popped free from the bottom of the window. He bent down and shoved the window up enough to reach through and push the bars. They swung easily on their hinges. Odd. In an old building where everything was layered with paint or rusted shut, the fire escape was greased and in perfect order. Maybe the new owner really cared about the people or, more likely, the fire marshal was hassling him.

Johnny stood, crossed the room and stepped back into the corridor. He looked down the hall at the line of doors ahead, left and right. For a moment he wondered if Hightower had lied to him, spun a tale about a mysterious Asian warlord and then fed him the hotel just to get rid of him. What could possibly be so important about a skid row hotel?

He moved to the first door on his left, but it was secured with a hasp and a heavy padlock. So too was the one across the hall. He moved to the next one and looked at the lock. It was new. He glanced back toward the front door, but as he turned back he heard a muffled noise from a room farther down the hallway. He moved quickly to the door and pressed his ear to the wood. He could hear a voice, an odd, almost bored monotone. He closed his eyes to concentrate. It sounded like a television, maybe a documentary.

Johnny tapped lightly on the door.

The noise stopped. Johnny listened to the silence and tapped again. Then a quiet voice asked, "Yes? Who is it?"

"My name's Rose. I need to talk to you."

But Johnny didn't get to talk to the man behind the door. At that moment, an iron grip closed on his arm. He was spun around and slammed against the wall. The drunk from the steps stood facing him, his hand digging into Johnny's bicep. He was stone-cold sober and his breath smelled of tobacco, not alcohol.

"What do you want?" His teeth were clenched and his voice was barely above a whisper. "What are you doing in here?"

The windbreaker pulled up slightly and Johnny could see the grip of a handgun in the man's waistband.

"I'm looking for a room."

"How'd you get in here?"

"The door was open. I walked in. I'm just looking for a room to rent, man. Jesus, chill out."

The man released Johnny's arm, stepped back and jerked the windbreaker down, covering the gun. "We don't have any rooms, we're full."

"But I saw an empty one down the hall."

"We're full. Now get out."

Johnny shoved himself away from the wall and as he did, the door to the room opened slightly and a short, thin man with a wrinkled, callow face and a bald head looked out. "What's going on out here?"

"Nothing, Major. This man was just leaving," the man in the windbreaker said. He stepped past Johnny and pulled the door shut again. "Get out. Now," he said.

Johnny walked down the hall and out into the sunshine. The man with the windbreaker was two steps behind. As Johnny went down the steps he saw the tall neck of a brown whiskey bottle sticking up from the brown paper bag. He caught only a glimpse, but it was enough to see that the seal had never been broken.

The cruisers were gone and the people had gathered again on the curb. There was no evidence of the police struggle or that a crowd had circled to jeer just a few minutes before.

Johnny walked on past the parking lot and turned into the bar he'd seen earlier. He waited a moment while his eyes adjusted to the dim light. The details emerged slowly from the darkness. The bar ended near the door and stretched straight back almost to the rear wall, to Johnny's left. Tables were pushed against the right wall. Posters for Budweiser, Michelob and Corona were tacked above the tables. Two men sat at the bar, the only customers.

The man nearest Johnny wore a soiled baseball cap, filthy jeans and a coat, despite the summer heat. He hung his head and stared at the bar, a beer bottle at his elbow. The second man wore neat khaki trousers and a white T-shirt that looked freshly bleached. It fit him snugly around his soft arms and stomach. Johnny chose a stool between the two and ordered a Corona. The bartender set the bottle down and walked away without asking if Johnny wanted a glass.

"Let me ask you a question, okay?" Johnny said to the bartender. "I wanted to get some information on the hotel on the other side of the parking lot. The Royal. You know anything about it?"

The man in the white T-shirt spoke even before the bartender. "Maybe I can help you. I used to live there. I was there for ten years."

Johnny turned and looked at the man three stools away. Johnny guessed he was in his early forties. His blond hair, fading to gray, was combed back in a duck-tail and his soft, pudgy fingers testified to a lack of manual labor. A tall glass, half-full with a dark liquid, sat on the bar in front of him.

"So, you used to live there?"

"Yes. I was there with Manuel, my lover. We were there for five years. At another place for three before that. But after they sold it, they threw us out. Gave everybody one week's notice. End of the month come and that was it—so long, it's been good to know you."

"So, where are you living now?"

"At another place around the corner here. But the rent is tough, it's five hundred a month. Manuel works days in the toy warehouses, when he can get it. I'm on disability. We get by."

"Yeah, I know what you mean. Things are hard. You say they gave you thirty days' notice? When was that?"

"Oh, let me think. We had to be out of there about two, no, three months ago. Just wham, got to get out. Didn't matter how long you'd lived there. Everyone was tossed out. One guy'd been there twenty years. Nobody cared."

"What happened after that?"

"What do you mean, what happened? Everyone left."

"I mean with the Royal. I was just there and the guy out front told me they were full."

"Yeah, funny, you know. They told us they were going to tear the place down. But nothing happened. Not yet, at least."

"But there are people living there, right? I mean, the guy told me they were full."

"I'll bet I know the guy you talked to. Long hair,

baseball cap. Blue windbreaker. He sits out on that step all day. Never goes anywhere."

"That's the guy. But are there people there?"

"Who knows? I never see anyone going in or out. Just see the guy with the windbreaker on the steps. That's all. I figure someone's got to be there cause I've seen a couple of guys on the balcony a time or two. But that's all. Never seen nobody else."

"You have any idea who bought it?"

"No, none. Say, why all the questions?"

"Just curious. Here, let me buy you another drink for helping me out. What are you drinking?"

The man smiled, picked up the glass and tilted it toward Johnny. "Thanks," he said, "I'm having a Tab."

Back at the Z Johnny dug through the box he'd loaded at the *Chronicle* and found his Rolodex. He flipped through it, pulled a card out and walked to the nearest pay phone a block away.

"Ted Inskeep, how can I help you?"

"Hey, Theo, it's Johnny Rose. How's it going?"

Johnny and Theo had become friends more than fifteen years before. Johnny had been researching a story and spent three frustrating days digging through old property records with little to show for his efforts until Inskeep, then a young clerk, offered to help. With Theo's assistance, Johnny had the information a few hours later.

"I'm fine. You still with the *Chronicle*?"

Johnny paused a moment. No point in lying. Not to an old friend. "No. I quit a little bit ago. I'm working on something now, though. It's kind of a freelance thing."

"Really? Anything I can do to help?"

"Well, how much trouble is it to find out who owns a piece of property?"

"Trouble? It's no trouble at all. What's the address?" Johnny told him the number on San Julian and heard the clicks of a keyboard. "Here it is. Looks like a new owner. Bought it about five months ago."

"Great, who is it?"

"It's a company called E&M Enterprises. They've got a mailing address up in Lancaster. You want it?"

"E&M Enterprises, are you sure?"

"Yeah, why? You know 'em?"

"Sort of. What's the address?" Johnny copied it, then asked, "Can you check and see if they own anything else in the city?"

Again Johnny heard the clicks as Inskeep worked the keyboard. "Nope. The place on San Julian is the only thing."

Johnny thanked him, set the phone back in its cradle and stood, his gaze fixed on the phone. He could feel the heat of the morning on his back and smell the diesel fuel as a bus accelerated on the street behind him. He looked at the notes he'd made and felt his pulse race again. E&M. It was the name on the credit card receipt he'd copied at Ben Ng's restaurant. He was starting to put things together. Maybe Hightower had come through after all.

Johnny read the address again. Lancaster, on the northern border of Los Angeles County on the edge of the Mojave Desert. He closed his eyes and tried to visualize a map of California. It was, he guessed, forty or maybe fifty miles on a straight line from Lancaster to Arvin, from E&M Enterprises to where Sandra Ruiz had drowned. And somewhere along that straight line a man with only dog tags to identify him had died of exposure.

Back at his car, Johnny again dug through the box

he'd carted out of the *Chronicle*. It took less than a minute to find the printout and a moment longer to find the stories about E&M and the overturned tanker car. He read the first few lines of each piece, then tossed the printout back in the box and stood with his hand, almost shoulder high, on the edge of the open trunk lid. His head was bowed slightly as he stared at the asphalt beneath his feet and tried to figure the connection between E&M Enterprises, a maker of agricultural fertilizer and a skid row hotel. He stood for another minute, then two, then three. Finally he raised his head and turned to stare back toward San Julian as if the answer were there, right in the middle of the city's dirty and neglected streets. But he found no answers and finally got back in his car and headed for the desert.

20

The northern edge of Los Angeles County caught the spillover from the city during late 1980s when real estate prices jumped a rocket ship and headed straight for the moon. Suddenly an hour and a half on the freeway to work every day didn't look so bad if it meant you could buy a house. The whole area boomed with new suburbs and new businesses. Land was cheap, houses were big and cheap; white stucco walls, red Spanish-style tile roofs. People anxious to escape the city flocked to the area. Later, when the recession settled onto California like an early killer frost, housing prices fell and unemployment rose, the dream tattered and the thinness of the promise became apparent. The new communities that had offered escape in the desert saw a jump in domestic violence as out-of-work husbands and wives fought. Desperate families couldn't sell their homes and walked away from their dreams or were evicted. Squatters and welfare recipients moved in, straining the fragile community. Gangs sprang up in the desert like so many weeds after a rain.

But a few years earlier, it was all still new and everything seemed possible. The newness of it all helped explain why a chemical fertilizer factory could be close to the homes. It was still miles away, but close enough for an evacuation when the rail car jumped the tracks. The plant had been there first, back when nothing but sand, scrub, rocks, lizards and coyotes were nearby. Even today the plant was remote by L.A. standards, where people drive a half-block to the 7-Eleven for a pack of cigarettes.

Nearly five miles of empty desert separated the plant from the nearest building, a big empty grocery store stuck in the middle of a stretch of undeveloped land like a cavalry fort in Indian country, blazing a trail for the settlers and tract homes that never showed up.

Johnny checked the address and followed the map east out of Lancaster. He drove along a two-lane road toward the plant, rushing toward but never approaching the shimmering heat waves that rose off the blacktop in the distance. The first sign of E&M was a smokestack, a brick silo that rose off the desert floor and seemed to stretch to the sky from beyond the horizon. Then came the fence, with rolled razor wire at the top. It ran for more than two miles and Johnny slowed and looked at the desert behind it. The fence appeared to hold back little beyond sand, rocks, cactuses and a few jackrabbits. Finally he came to a narrow road that ran from the highway to the plant's main gate. Just outside the gate stood a brown aluminum-sided portable building on the edge of a small parking lot. Johnny parked in the lot, the only car there, and walked toward the building. A large, tall woman, wide in the hips and shoulders, stepped out. She wore a brown shirt, brown slacks, boots and a baseball cap that said E&M Enterprises on it. A walkie-talkie rode on her left hip, a nightstick dangled from her right. Her face and hands were red and rough, her fingernails unpolished and broken. She pulled sunglasses from her breast pocket and slipped them on before speaking.

"What can I do for you?" she asked.

"Oh, hi, this is E&M?"

"Yup."

"Well, I'm a writer and I was hoping to talk to someone, maybe get a tour of the place. It would fit in with a story I'm working on."

"We don't give tours."

"Well, I drove all the way out here from L.A. It would sure help if you could just check. Maybe call the PR guy or something."

"We don't have a PR department and like I said, we *don't* give tours. *To anybody.*"

"You know, it's a long way back to L.A. I hate to go all the way back there empty-handed."

She said nothing. Johnny looked at her eyes, and failed to see through the dark shades. The walkie-talkie crackled on her hip and she looked down, pulled it from its holster and twisted a knob. A moment later it came to life. "You got a problem there, Sally?"

"No. It's some writer wanting to look around the place. I told him we don't give tours."

"Good. You need any help, just holler."

"No, I don't think I'll be needing anything." She returned the walkie-talkie to its holster and rested her hands on her hips, facing Johnny.

"What kind of fertilizer do you guys make here, anyway?" he finally asked. "Seems kind of funny to have all this security just for something that makes your grass grow better."

She stood silently staring at him, without answering, speaking or moving. The silence stretched, then a sudden gust of wind filled the air with dust and sand. Johnny turned his back, his eyes shut. A moment later it was gone and he turned back to look at the woman, who seemed unfazed by the dirt. He could feel the grit on his teeth and wanted to spit.

"It's a long way back to L.A.," he said again.

"Look, mister, like I said, we don't give tours to anybody." She moved her hands from her hips and dug her thumbs into her belt, her palms resting on the walkie-talkie and the handle of the nightstick.

"Yeah, okay," he said. He walked back to his car and drove back down the long driveway to the highway.

For the next hour Johnny drove through the desert, following dirt roads that were little more than ruts and rumors of past vehicles. The Z spewed a cloud of dust in its wake and constantly scraped bottom as it crawled from one pathway to another. He kept the windows up but the dust still invaded, filtering through the smog-eaten rubber sealer. The air conditioner was set on High, but it still labored against the heat and Johnny's face and arms glistened with sweat.

He had to guess at the distance and use the sun to figure his direction. Finally, though, he stopped the car and climbed to the top of a small hill. The wind had stirred sand and dirt into the air, reducing the visibility like some desert fog. But in the distance, Johnny could see the entire E&M Enterprises compound. It was a huge, sprawling complex, bigger than he'd guessed while driving next to it. It had to be dozens of acres, all of it surrounded by a chain-link fence topped with razor wire.

A swath of about one hundred yards of open desert separated the fence from the nearest building, a one-story rectangular cement-block structure that looked to be more than a hundred yards long. Another cement-block building, this one tall and built in the shape of a grain elevator, sat just a little way into the complex. In the middle of the fenced area was another tall building, perhaps five stories. Not far beyond that was the brick chimney that could be seen for miles. Farther beyond still was a water tower painted in red and white checks and beyond that a huge aluminum building that glistened in the sun and looked like an airport hangar.

The wind whipped Johnny's pant legs, and he had to shade his eyes against the sun. Still he stood and looked at the complex, taking the time to study each building in turn. He could see the rail spur that led from the complex into the desert. The fertilizer plant seemed abandoned, lifeless. He saw no movement, no people. E&M Enterprises, it seemed, was empty. He could make out two cars and one pickup parked near the long low cement building, but no one came or left the vehicles. After watching for almost half an hour, Johnny turned and walked back down the small hill, the sand crunching under his feet. He'd learned nothing that would explain E&M's connection to the Royal Hotel or help him understand why an empty fertilizer factory in the desert needed a high fence topped with razor wire and a full-time security force to keep people out.

He got in the Z and began the slow, jarring drive back to the main road. By the time he hit the blacktop,

Johnny had decided where he'd look for the answers.

It was midafternoon when he pulled into the parking lot of the *High Desert Report*. The paper was housed in a new one-story brick-facade building. A tall flagpole stood at the end of the short walkway from the building's main door to the parking lot. The American and California flags snapped frantically in the wind.

Johnny guessed it was ninety-five degrees outside, give or take a few degrees. But as he passed through the darkened glass door into the paper's lobby, the air conditioning engulfed him like an invisible arctic fog. He stood in the lobby, a narrow room stretching left to right, for a moment, feeling his damp shirt turn cool against his skin. He stood enjoying the stillness, the lack of wind. At both ends of the lobby, doors led to the offices beyond.

He saw the receptionist, a young woman with bleached blonde hair piled high on her head, sitting behind a waist-high counter watching him, and he finally approached. He told her he'd like to speak to the reporter who covered E&M Enterprises and wrote about the chemical spill.

"Just a moment," she said, punched the keys on the telephone bank and spoke into her headset. She looked at Johnny. "Someone will be out in a minute," she said. While he waited, Johnny studied the oversized photos on the wall: local accidents, sports highlights and visiting dignitaries. All taken by the *Report*'s photographers. About ten minutes later, a young man in a short-sleeved shirt with a loose tie walked into the lobby and introduced himself.

"Hi, I'm Gill Dexter. How can I help you?" He looked about twenty. Fresh out of school, with thin, disheveled blond hair.

"Hi, nice to meet you. My name's Johnny Rose. I'm a freelance writer. You cover E&M Enterprises?"

"Yeah, along with a few dozen other things. You know how it is on a small paper. Cop shop, city hall, school boards. You name it."

"Yeah, I know there's so much to keep track of. Still, I'm kind of hoping you can give me a little something on that fertilizer plant."

"Like what?" He seemed surprised that anyone would care.

"Well, for starters, why all the security around that place?"

"Beats me. Look, to tell you the truth, I just started here about two months ago. All I've done about that place is a couple of zoning stories. I mean, I read about the tanker car going off the rails, but that's about it. I wasn't here when it happened. I really don't know much about the place. I asked for a tour once and they turned me down flat."

Johnny was quiet for a moment, remembering the guard. He looked back at the reporter. "Any chance I could see your files on the place?"

"Why not? Nothing but a bunch of clips anyway."

He disappeared through the door and came back minutes later carrying a thin manila folder.

"Look, I've got to go out on a story and this is my personal file. You can just leave it with the receptionist when you're done, okay?"

"Sure."

Almost all the stories had been written the day the tanker overturned. About half were from the *Report* itself. The others were from the *L.A. Times*, the Bakersfield paper and several filed by the Associated Press. The AP had moved an aerial shot showing the tanker car on its side just beyond the fence of the E&M plant. The *Report* had run it big on the front page.

An E&M spokesman named Hernandez was quoted in every story saying there was absolutely no danger to the public's health. Nothing had spilled from the tanker. The houses were being evacuated as a precaution. One AP story pointed out that the nearest house was more than six miles away and reported that Hernandez refused to identify which chemicals had been inside the overturned tanker. It was a trade secret, he said. They were part of a new chemical lawn fertilizer the company was developing. In the days after the spill only the *Report* and the AP filed followup stories. The AP noted that it was the railroad, not E&M, that had reported the spill. It also reported that the EPA and officers from a special U.S. Army chemical unit, on loan to the EPA, had given the area a clean bill of health. The story quoted a Colonel Gaddy saying, "There was absolutely no spill and no danger whatsoever."

Everyone was back in their houses twenty-four hours after the whole thing started.

Johnny left the file with the receptionist and began the long drive across the desert, through the San Fernando Valley and into L.A. As he drove he thought about the clippings he'd read. It all seemed so routine. A tanker car flips, houses are evacuated. Everything is declared safe and everyone goes home. Routine. Except for two sentences in one AP story. Army officers, on loan to the EPA, had declared the area safe. And a quote from a full bird colonel.

Why the hell were Army officers helping out the EPA, and why such a high-ranking officer?

Johnny stopped at a gas station just off the freeway

near the bottom of the Sepulveda Pass. He called the Associated Press and asked for Steve Hounds.

"He's out on assignment." The voice was male, middle-aged and bored.

"I'm a friend of his. You have any idea when he'll be back?"

"Who knows? He's been assigned to the governor's race. He's up near Santa Barbara covering a speech by Gordon Geld."

"Well, he has my sympathies."

"Yeah, politics. It's always the same old thing. Different names, different people, but the same old shit."

"Well, tell him Johnny Rose called, will you?"

"Sure, he have your number?"

"Oh yeah. He's got it. Hey, listen, before you go, let me ask you one thing."

"Sure."

"You have any idea who covered a chemical spill at a fertilizer plant out near Lancaster a couple of years ago? A place called E&M Enterprises?"

"That was Hounds."

"You're sure?"

"Oh yeah, I'm sure. I took his dictation."

"Hey, that's great. Make sure he calls me, okay?"

"It'll probably be tomorrow. Like I said, he's up in Santa Barbara. Probably won't be back until late."

"No problem," Johnny said. "I've got lots of time."

21

Johnny stopped at the veterans' hospital but did not stay long. Jimmy was sedated and sleeping. The nurse said he was unlikely to wake before morning. Still, Johnny sat by the bed for a few minutes watching the blinking machines, the peaks and baselines on the monitors telling him Jimmy was alive. Finally he reached over, patted Jimmy's hand and left.

At home, he circled the block twice looking for unfamiliar cars, a delivery man who seemed to dawdle, an unmarked van parked nearby, anything that seemed out of place. Finally, believing it was safe, he parked in the carport and went in.

He ate a microwave dinner at the table and turned on the television. But the first thing on the screen was a commercial for Gordon Geld. It was the same one he'd seen dozens of times before. Footage of Geld working with the inner-city kids to clean up the beach, Geld in his office. Then a close-up of Geld looking straight into the camera and promising a new type of government, a new type of leadership. It ended with a announcer's standard line. "Gordon Geld. He gets things done."

Johnny turned the television off, looked at the dark living room and tried to think of things other than skid row hotels, fertilizer plants and death threats. He knew that sometimes the answers, the key puzzle pieces, were timid and shy and couldn't be forced or even coaxed from the darkness. They had to come when you weren't trying, weren't straining to make sense of it all. If he could just let them come, let it all find its own order, maybe then he'd know why Pham was dead and why Jimmy had tried to kill himself.

He tried to distract himself. He slipped an Asleep at the Wheel CD into the stereo, but the music made him think of Jimmy. The television didn't interest him and the book he tried seemed dull and stupid. His thoughts kept wandering back into the territory he was fighting so hard to ignore. In desperation he gave up and went upstairs. He showered away the dust and grime from the desert and then went to bed. But he lay awake, staring into the darkness and counting backward from 100, trying to remember the Dodgers' starting lineup the last time they won the Series. He rolled and turned for more than two hours until finally he slipped into a fitful sleep and dreamed.

In his dream Pham was walking across the park toward him. Johnny waited in the warm summer darkness watching his friend approach, knowing that Pham was going to tell him all about Kyle Loveless. All about everything. But as the man came closer it wasn't Pham anymore. It was Jimmy, and when he got very close he laughed and said, "How come you can't figure this out?

I already told you it was the captain, what more do you want?" Then he laughed and blood leaked from his mouth.

The dream was still with him the next morning, dancing in his head, refusing to fade away. He could see Jimmy and hear his words and laughter. He showered again and made coffee and toast. He had just finished a cup of coffee when the phone rang. He looked at it and listened to it ring again and again. The answering machine clicked on and Johnny heard a familiar voice.

"Johnny, it's Sheridan from the *Chronicle*. I just called—"

Johnny picked up the phone. "Hey, Sheridan, I was eating my breakfast."

"No problem. Listen, I only got a minute, so I thought I'd better tell you. Detective Earl was just here looking for you. He didn't know you'd quit. He seemed a little pissed. Thought you'd want to know."

"Thanks. I owe you one."

"No problem."

Was Earl on his way to the apartment? Was the detective planning on arresting him? Johnny knew he did not want to be there when Earl arrived. He left his coffee cup half-full and grabbed his keys from the counter. He hurried to the door.

Outside, he stuck his key in the lock and jerked hard on the doorknob, ready to turn the key. As he pulled back a bullet hit the wall with a thud, sending stucco flying. Johnny whirled and another bullet whizzed past him, smashing into the front window. He half-fell and half-dove forward, the unlocked door swinging wide. Scanning the street, he saw only the glare of the sun off the windshield of a Blazer parked at the curb. The shooter's face was dark and indistinguishable. Johnny didn't wait for a better look. He crawled the rest of the way into the apartment and kicked the door closed.

Johnny scrambled to his feet, locked the door and sprinted across the living room to the kitchen. He grabbed the phone and tried to jab 911, but his movements were rushed, jerky and uncontrolled. He gripped the phone harder and dialed again. He heard the shooter's shoulder against the front door. He was almost through. The door wasn't that strong. In a second he'd be in the apartment. Johnny dropped the phone and threw the sliding glass door open, took a step and leaped for the top of the wooden fence bordering the small patio.

The front door gave way and the shooter stumbled into the apartment. He dropped to a knee and sighted on the fleeing man. He shot just as Johnny leaped. The bullet missed by inches.

Adrenaline powered Johnny's legs, but it wasn't enough. He landed on his stomach, the top of the fence boards scraping his skin away. He kicked his legs violently and slithered over the top.

In the living room, the shooter shot again. Johnny's legs flew up as the bullet tore off a chunk of the fence top. Johnny landed in a head-first pile in the narrow cement pathway between his building and the next apartment complex.

The shooter ran easily across the living room, vaulted the fence and landed lightly on his feet. He looked both ways down the cement path. He took three quick steps toward the street, then heard a bang, the sound of a garbage bin lid closing, from the carport.

From his hiding place, Johnny could see the shooter only from the waist to the shoulders as he rounded the corner of the apartment building and came into the carport, gun hand raised and steady.

The man disappeared, heading for the alley. Was he gone? Johnny considered running, tumbling from his cover and sprinting away. But then he heard a scrape, leather on cement, and saw the gun swing past. The man with the gun was back, searching the carport. He turned in a slow circle, then moved to the Z and bent to look in. Johnny could see the back of his head as the shooter bent over. But he could tell nothing from the view.

"Shit," the man mumbled.

Johnny heard the Z's door slam shut and saw the gun suddenly hanging by the shooter's side. Then the hand swept up and the gun was out of sight. The man was moving again, approaching the Dumpster, and Johnny prayed his ploy with the Dumpster lid would work. He closed his eyes, held his breath and silently begged. The man with the gun gripped the lid with his left hand and flipped it open. A stench blossomed from the full garbage bin and Johnny could hear the shooter grunt. He walked to the other side, casual now, as though he had not a care in the world. He flipped the other half-lid open and looked.

Johnny saw the skinny old woman in the faded yellow muumuu and slippers shuffle slowly around the corner. He started to yell, but was too late. The shooter was already spinning around, bringing the gun up. Ethel was struggling, her thin arms barely able to carry the two plastic bags full of newspapers. She saw the man and the gun. She dropped the newspapers, screamed and fled. The shooter watched her go, elbows and knees pumping furiously but making little progress, but he did nothing.

He turned back to the Dumpster then and slowly, methodically emptied the gun into the garbage, spacing the shots evenly across it. He tucked the pistol in his waistband and headed toward the street.

Johnny pushed aside the black garbage bags full of crushed aluminum cans and brushed back the newspapers, then struggled from the rear of Ethel's Kingswood wagon into the front seat. He sat on the passenger side sucking in deep breaths. His hands still shook, and he clamped them on his knees, slowly lowered his head and thought of the man with the gun who wanted to kill him and the police who wanted to arrest him and try him for murder.

He exhaled deeply, shoved the door open and stepped into the carport. He moved to the edge of the building, hesitated and peeked around the corner. The path was empty and Johnny felt his whole body relax, almost collapse. He turned and leaned back against the side of the building. Finally, he started up the path toward his apartment but stopped. The man with the gun could be sitting inside, just waiting for Johnny to walk in. Johnny turned and walked back toward his car. He should call the police, he knew that. But he was already a prime suspect in a murder investigation and the shooting would just deepen their suspicion of him. He knew then that he wouldn't be home again until it was over.

22

Johnny got into his car but didn't start it. For a fleeting moment he considered taking a chance and making a quick visit to the hospital, but he knew he couldn't. He dared not visit again until it was safe; until he had the answers and used them to unlock the secret and stop the killer.

He waited a moment longer, looking past the steering wheel through the windshield at the Dumpster. The lids were still open, propped against the side of the building, just as the man with the gun had left them when he guessed wrong about where Johnny was hiding. His glance fell on the small cardboard box by the Dumpster that held Weird Harold's body.

Johnny turned the ignition. He had only one option left, one place left to look, one person who might have the answers. He had to find the woman who had impersonated Susan Loveless. He thought about it for a moment, seeing her get into the Jetta and drive away, and knew exactly where to start.

The full-service island was empty, but two cars were at the self-service lane at S&J Shell. Johnny drove past the pumps and parked at the far edge of the lot.

He hesitated a moment, unsure of whether to head for the office or the repair bays. Big letters painted in white and red on the office window touted a sale on radials. Johnny had to bend slightly to see past the letters. He could make out a young black woman running the cash register. She looked about sixteen. He decided to try the bays.

Entering the repair area, he walked carefully, skirting a small oil slick on the polished cement floor, and stopped by the rear door of a Taurus. A mechanic was bent over the engine. Johnny could hear him humming along to the radio playing on the workbench. It was a country song, but not one Johnny recognized. The mechanic's blue cotton pants, white socks and black shoes were all Johnny could see.

"Pardon me," Johnny said. "I'm hoping you can help me."

"Ah, shit," the guy said. He stood up and turned to look at Johnny. He looked about thirty and kept his dark curly hair tied back in a ponytail. He smiled, surprising Johnny with braces on all teeth. "Sorry, I wasn't swearing at you. Just that that thing won't budge."

"No problem," Johnny said.

"Anyway, I didn't catch what you said. What was it again?"

"I'm hoping you can help me. I'm looking for a woman."

"Aren't we all?" The guy smiled as he reached

back, pulled a maroon rag off the car's fender and began wiping his hands slowly.

Johnny smiled and nodded. "I guess we are. But I mean a specific woman. I'm hoping you know her."

"Yeah? What's her name?"

"Well, that's just it, I don't know. I just met her the other night and I didn't get a chance to ask her. You know how it is. Anyway, I know she gets her car fixed here."

"How do you know that?" He stuck the rag in his hip pocket.

"Well, I saw her car keys. They had one of those happy face discs with your address on it."

"Oh, yeah, those things." He shook his head slowly side to side. "We stopped giving them out about a year ago. Over the years we probably gave out a thousand of 'em, maybe two."

Johnny exhaled and felt an edge of desperation gaining a foothold. He held it in check and went on, speaking casually. "Well, she's a really pretty lady. Early forties, blonde hair, shoulder length. Wears a lot of makeup. I'm guessing five foot seven. Conservative dresser."

The mechanic shook his head again. "Sorry, man, doesn't ring any bells."

"She drives a black VW Jetta," Johnny added.

"You have any idea what kind of work we did for her?"

"No. None."

The two men stood facing each other, and then the country song ended and another started. Johnny tried to think of something else to say, anything to jar the man's memory. But there was nothing. No other clue he could conjure up.

Finally the man shrugged again, pulled the rag from his pocket and wiped his hands once more. "Sorry, man, that could be just about anybody. We get a lot of people through here." He waited a moment, but when Johnny said nothing the mechanic glanced over his shoulder at the Taurus. "Well, I got to get back to this. Guy's coming to pick it up soon."

"Okay, thanks anyway," Johnny said, and the mechanic turned back to the car, bent over the fender and started humming again.

Johnny stood by the car, unwilling to leave, unsure where he'd go if he did. He looked at the hoses and belts hanging from the ceiling. His eyes wandered to the stack of new radials against the wall and the air compressor near them. He looked at the boxes of parts on the workbench against the back wall. He looked at the motorcycle calendar pinned on a bulletin board that was full of black-and-white photos.

Each one was a publicity shot of an actor or actress. There were nearly two dozen in all. Stores and shops all over L.A. have them. Ask a celebrity who's eaten at your restaurant, had their clothes dry-cleaned at your place or car repaired at your gas station and they'll sign a photo for your wall.

Johnny walked to the workbench and studied the photos, most of them dust-covered and curling at the edges. His eyes slipped right over her the first time. Then he looked again. She was smiling brightly at him, her eyes sparkling, her coal-black hair short and spiked.

An actress. He should have known.

She looked about thirty. No wonder she'd worn so much makeup at his place. She had to look at least ten years older for him. Must have worn a wig, too.

Johnny glanced over his shoulder. The mechanic was still deep in the engine. Johnny leaned forward and read the scrawled inscription. "Thanks to the guys at S&J Shell. You do great work." It was dated more than a year earlier and signed "Nikki Masterson." He jotted down the name, then pulled the push pins out of the board and with another quick glance back at the mechanic, stuck the photo inside his shirt and headed for the phone booth at the edge of the S&J lot.

It took less than three minutes for Johnny to learn that Nikki Masterson wasn't listed with the Screen Actors Guild and to start flipping through the phone book a second time. He stopped at the American Federation of Television and Radio Artists. And again he came up empty.

"Sorry, we just don't have anything on a Nikki Masterson, have you tried SAG?" the young man at the federation asked.

Johnny exhaled deeply and clenched his teeth in frustration "Yeah, I already tried. Look, I'm in a real bind here. I know this woman's an actress and I've got to get in touch with her. You have any idea how I can find her?"

"You could try the Players Directory."

"What's that?"

"The Academy Players Directory. It comes out every three months. It has pictures of all the actors and actresses and lists their agents and phone numbers. At least all the ones that want to be listed. Most libraries around town have it."

The man at AFTRA was right. The Brentwood branch of the L.A. Public Library had all three volumes of the directory. Johnny grabbed the one labeled "Leading Ladies/Ingenues," took it to a reference table and flipped it open. Each page held two columns of five photos. Next to each was a listing of the actress's professional affiliations, agents and personal managers. He moved quickly to the Ms and found her. It was the same photo he'd seen in the garage. The space next to her photo was empty except for a single phone number and the word *messages*. It wasn't much, but it was enough. Using the reverse directory, Johnny had an address to go with the phone number within minutes. It was a Brentwood apartment not three miles away. He smiled. Finally he was getting the breaks.

But ten minutes later, standing in front of the manager of Nikki Masterson's apartment, Johnny wondered if he'd ever catch a break.

"Nikki Masterson moved out a couple of months ago," the apartment manager said. "You know, a place like this, people pretty much come and go."

Johnny looked at the man slouching in the doorway, one arm raised against the jamb. Bald and barefoot, he wore nothing but a bikini-brief bathing suit that disappeared under cascades of well-tanned fat. Johnny turned from the man and looked back across the courtyard, past the pool and Jacuzzi to the door of the empty studio apartment that matched the address in the directory.

Johnny guessed the apartment complex had a hundred units, maybe a few more. A place for college students and young professionals. Reasonable rents and weekends full of random movement. Not many people stayed long. A year, maybe two at the most. He hadn't really been surprised when he found the apartment empty.

He shifted his gaze again to the manager. Johnny guessed he was at least sixty, maybe sixty-five. Inside, a young man in tight black bicycle shorts and a T-shirt cut off just below the pecs crossed the living room and sprawled on a black leather couch. Above the couch a large painting of an Indian chief hung in a heavy frame. The younger man picked up the TV remote and flicked on the set, and instantly the noise of a game show filled the room. The manager glanced over his shoulder at the young man, smiled and turned back to Johnny.

Johnny held up the photo he'd taken from the Shell station and asked the manager, "This is her, right?"

"Sure is. So, why you looking for her? You a cop or a bill collector?"

"No, neither one. I'm a writer, freelance. I'm hoping she can help me with a story. Did she leave a forwarding address? A phone number, anything like that?"

"We're not supposed to give that stuff out."

"Yeah, I know. But like I said, I really need to talk to her. Usually young actors and actresses want to talk to writers, so I don't know that you'd be doing her any harm."

"Yeah, maybe you're right. Hold on a minute." He turned and walked back into the apartment, leaving the door open. When he came back he handed Johnny a slip of paper.

"Now don't tell anyone where you got this. It's strictly against regulations. But I know how tough it is to get publicity. Maybe you can help her out, you know?"

"Yeah, thanks," Johnny said and looked at the address. "You have any idea where Ravenswood Drive is?"

"Out in the Valley someplace. Said she was going to

be house-sitting for a friend of a friend for a couple of months. Some big director off in Italy shooting a movie or something. Wanted to save on the rent. Who can blame her?"

Inside the apartment, the young man moved off the couch and wandered to the door. He draped his right arm around the manager's shoulders, cocked a hip and smiled at Johnny.

"So, you really a writer?" he asked.

Johnny nodded. "Yup."

"Who you looking for?"

"Nikki Masterson." Johnny held up the photo. "You know her?"

"Oh, Nicole. Yes, I know her, the bitch."

"Oh?"

"Promised to get me a tryout, then cleared out of here without a word. Never did get it."

"Tryout for what?"

"I'm an actor."

"She in a movie?"

"A movie? Oh, please. No, she's in a play at the Odyssey. It's an Equity waiver theater."

"What's an Equity waiver theater?"

"A small theater where they don't pay you shit but you get to strut your stuff and hope someone notices."

"She still there?"

"I guess. It's supposed to run through the end of September."

"If you don't catch her at home," the manager said, "why not try the theater?"

"Yeah," Johnny said. "I'll do that. I'll definitely do that."

23

Nikki Masterson was house-sitting a single-story home on the north side of the Santa Monica Mountains with a view of the sprawling San Fernando Valley. It was the third house on a steep driveway running off a winding road that hugged the side of the mountains.

Even with a map, finding the house had not been easy. Johnny had missed the driveway, little more than a break in a high oleander hedge, three times before he finally found it.

He shifted the Z into first, worked his way up the strip of blacktop and made a sharp right turn into a small carport. Standing at the trunk of the Z, he waited and examined the house.

It wasn't ostentatious or even glamorous. Just a simple white stucco ranch with a wide used-brick patio that separated it from the edge of the mountain. The house's large windows offered a view of the Valley that had to be worth a few hundred thousand even today. The earthquake had been tough as hell on hillside real estate, but in L.A., if you wanted a view, you still had to pay.

He crossed the patio to the front door and pushed the bell. He heard a faint chime from inside, but no one responded. He waited a moment, then pounded on the door. When no one came, he went to the window, shaded his eyes and peered in. He could see a couch, glass-topped coffee table and a telescope, but no people. He stepped back and walked to the edge of the brick patio and looked at the Valley, shrouded in haze; the tall buildings below were mere outlines, almost illusions. He tried the door again, then walked across the patio to a chair and sat down to wait. The hours stretched slowly and he wished he had brought a book or magazine, anything to read. He paced across the patio and stood at the edge of the hill, looking at the Valley. He found a garden hose at the side of the house and drank from it when he was thirsty. By midafternoon he was hungry and bored, but he couldn't leave and take a chance he'd miss her. By seven, though, it was obvious Nikki Masterson wasn't coming. Johnny got back in the Z and headed for the Odyssey Theater.

He walked into the lobby just before the doors opened. He bought a ticket and when the door to the small theater opened, he was one of the first inside. He chose a seat in the last row and sat in the darkness, wondering why he'd bothered. He could wait outside. He didn't need to do this, to see the play. But it wasn't a matter of need. He wanted to. He wanted to sit in the dark and watch her, judge this woman who might be the best clue he had to finding a killer and saving his own life. He wanted to see just how good she really was.

And she was good. She delivered her lines with great timing and conviction, getting the audience to laugh. Of the six on stage, she was the best. She was in total control, just as she had been at his house. But as the audience chuckled and laughed, Johnny stared at the young woman and saw Jimmy lying in his hospital bed and the decaying body in the desert and Pham's head falling to one side, almost coming off in Johnny's hands.

By intermission he'd had enough and pushed through the people milling in the lobby to the outside. He found her black Jetta in the narrow parking lot on the theater's south side, moved to the back corner of the building and stood in the shadows, watching it, waiting.

The parking lot emptied quickly after the play ended, but Nikki Masterson didn't leave the theater for nearly an hour. Johnny stayed, waiting, leaning against the building below the spotlight that lit the parking lot. He stood in the darkness, knowing she'd appear, certain he was close to the answers. Finally, he heard the click of a woman's heels on pavement and looked up to see her crossing the lot from the front of the theater to the Jetta.

"Oh, Miss Masterson," he called from the darkness.

She turned, a smile on her face. Then he stepped from the shadow into the light, and she saw him. She stood frozen, as though caught by a strobe, her hand clutching the small purse dangling at her side. For a moment Johnny thought he saw fear in her face. But at that distance, with only the parking lot lights, it was hard to tell.

As he walked slowly toward her, she stood perfectly still, watching him come. Then suddenly she bolted for the Jetta. Johnny sprinted after her, catching her as she pulled the keys from her purse. He grabbed her arm and swung her around.

"Hold it. I want to talk to you," he said.

"Get away. Get away. I don't have to talk to you."

"Yes, you do, you don't have a choice." He shook her arm violently.

"Let go of me. You're hurting me. Let go or I'll scream. The cops will be here in a heartbeat."

"That's a great idea. Let's call the cops. You can tell 'em who murdered Pham and Sandra Ruiz and who tried to kill me."

"I don't know what you're talking about." She jerked her arm free suddenly and Johnny made no attempt to grab her. She stumbled slightly as she pulled away, then got her balance and looked at Johnny. "I just did a little acting job, that's all. It was just a job. Had you fooled, didn't I?" She smiled triumphantly at him as she rubbed her arm.

Johnny wanted to hit her. He squeezed his hand into a fist, his fingernails digging into his palms, then slowly let it go. "Oh, yeah, you were real good. But I've met the real Susan Loveless."

"Oh, well."

"Oh, well? That's it? That's all? People are being murdered and all you can say is 'Oh, well'?" He realized suddenly that he was screaming, close to losing control, feeling the adrenaline.

She turned, leaned back against the Jetta, folded her arms across her chest and looked at him, her face was suddenly full of boredom. In the half-light of the parking lot, her hair looked brittle and her skin almost pasty. Johnny wondered if she was only beautiful when she was in control.

"Look, I don't know what you're talking about. Okay? All I know is that you're bothering me and it's late and I'm tired and I want to go home. So, do you mind?" She jerked forward, and started to turn and unlock her door.

Johnny stepped in her way. He was inches from her and she moved back suddenly, stumbling and falling hard against the car.

"They've killed at least two people and they tried to kill me and you're an accessory. You're in this."

"What the hell are you talking about? I don't know anything about that shit. I was doing a job. That's all."

"You're helping them kill people and I want to know why."

"I don't know what you're talking about."

"Listen very carefully. They're trying to kill me, but that's not going to happen. You got that?" He stepped closer and leaned in, his face inches from hers. "I'm not going down on this. Now, tell me who hired you or I swear to God I'll drag you back in there and call the cops myself."

Johnny raised his hand, ready to grab her arm.

"Hey, wait a minute, I don't know anything. I really don't."

"Who hired you?"

"I don't know. I swear to God, I don't know."

Johnny grabbed her arm and turned as though planning to drag her to the theater. Suddenly her shoulders, which she'd held squared back and rigid, drooped. Her whole body seemed to fold slightly upon itself. She slumped back against the Jetta and he let go.

"Look, I swear I don't know anything about this

shit. I don't know anything about POWs and those people getting killed. Nothing. That's the truth. My agent called me and said he had a one-time gig. He sent me a little background on this pilot named Loveless and told me to show up at your place and convince you I was his widow and that the guy was long dead. That's all it was. A one-time thing. He said it was perfectly legal. Said it was some kind of practical joke. Told me to think of it as an improv job. They paid me five hundred bucks. And believe me, I need the money. Ask my agent, he'll tell you. Hey, he took his share, fifty bucks. What a tightwad."

"Who's your agent?"

"Mike Erskin."

"How do you spell it?"

"E-R-S-K-I-N, just like it sounds."

"Where can I find him?"

"The Madison and Morris Agency in Beverly Hills. You want his direct number?"

"Yeah." She told him the number and Johnny copied it in his notebook. "I hope to God you're telling me the truth," he said.

"I am," she said. She looked at him for a moment, holding his eyes, then quietly said, "I am."

Johnny looked at her for a moment, turned without another word and walked away, wondering if she were acting once again.

24

At the edge of the parking lot Johnny hesitated, turned south on Sepulveda Boulevard and drove toward Culver City, looking for a place to spend the night.

He passed a Best Western, a TraveLodge and a couple of independents that looked a little too nice. Johnny wanted a high-turnover place with little curiosity and no questions. It was unlikely the man with the gun would search every motel in L.A. looking for him. With any luck, the shooter would even think he was dead. But he could take no chances.

Just before the city limits he pulled into a Burger King and went inside. He ordered a hamburger, fries and a soft drink. He sat alone at a table near the window and watched the traffic on Sepulveda Boulevard while he ate.

Fifteen minutes after he walked into the restaurant,

he drove out of the parking lot and turned south once again. He found a small, old motel that seemed to squat lifelessly in the night, as though resigned to its fate and simply waiting for a developer to rip it out and put in a highrise. A red neon arrow in the shape of a spear blinked rhythmically and pointed toward the motel's entrance. The M in MOTEL was burned out, leaving only OTEL and VACANCY visible in the dark sky. The driveway led under an archway to where two long, low buildings faced each other over a strip of crumbling asphalt. Johnny stopped in front of the office and scanned the parking strip. He saw only six cars and a van. It was not a high-turnover place.

As he entered the small office, a bell on the door jingled. Behind the counter a tattered curtain hung across a doorway. He could hear a television from the room within.

"Hello," Johnny called, and a moment later a young man with long, disheveled brown hair pushed the curtain aside and stepped to the counter.

"Hi," he said and looked away from Johnny to the Z in the driveway. "Just you tonight?"

"Yes. What'll it run?"

"Sixty a night. Checkout by ten in the morning."

"Okay," Johnny said. He handed the boy his Visa card. He swiped it through the machine and a moment later gave it back along with the receipt. Johnny signed, and as he filled out the registration card, the clerk reached under the counter and pulled a key out.

"Number six. Third one down, across the courtyard."

The room was little more than shelter from the elements, a hard-used space that offered a double bed with no headboard and a thin, faded spread the color of kidney beans. A chest of drawers, its edge scarred with cigarette burns, and one nightstand and a lamp were the only other pieces of furniture.

Johnny walked to the bathroom and looked in. The tub-shower and the sink were gray and old. In both, rust stains ran from the faucets down the pitted enamel like two-lane brown highways through a desert. He stepped back into the bedroom, moved to the small closet and pushed aside the curtain hanging in its door. It was empty except for three wire hangers.

He crossed to the bed, sat on the edge and fell backward. The mattress sank in the middle. Johnny lay staring at the ceiling, its pale yellow paint chipped, peeling and water-stained. He thought of Jimmy and wondered who the captain was. Who was the man who had loosened Jimmy's fingernail grip on sanity and driven him to the rooftop?

Suddenly, without knowing why, he thought of Nikki Masterson and in an instant knew she had lied to him. He grunted, understanding it and cursing himself for not seeing the lie the instant she uttered it. She'd said her agent got her the job. But Johnny knew Nikki Masterson didn't have an agent. In the Players Directory, Nikki Masterson listed only a phone number and the simple word: *messages*. If she had an agent, she'd have listed him.

Johnny sat up and looked at the brown curtains pulled tight across the window. Even in the night he could tell they were worn and thin. He looked at his watch. It was almost eleven. He reached over, picked up the phone and dialed.

"Associated Press, Rickert."

"Hi, I'm trying to reach Steve Hounds. He around?"

"No, I think he's already gone. No, wait a minute, he's still here. Hold on a minute, okay?"

Johnny could hear the intermittent noise of an office in the background; then the line was dead. Then he heard a click, and Hounds was there.

"Yeah, this is Steve Hounds."

"Hey, man, it's Johnny Rose."

"Oh, hi. I got the message you'd called. I'd have called earlier, but I've been out of town. The guy who's been covering Geld got kidney stones, so suddenly I'm the political reporter. Anyway, sorry I didn't get back to you."

"No problem."

"Hey, I just thought of something. Now that you're not with the *Chronicle* anymore, maybe you can help me out, tell me a little something about Geld I don't already know."

"You heard already?"

"What? About you being fired? Yeah, but listen, don't let it get you down. Everyone in this business gets fired at least once. It's no big deal."

"Fired? I didn't get fired. I quit. Where'd you hear I got fired?"

"That's the word they put out. I got it from that asshole Barsh. He's Geld's new press secretary."

"Listen, Steve, I wasn't fired, I quit."

"Whatever."

Johnny started to say something more, to protest again, but stopped. There was no point in debating it now. He simply went on. "I need a favor."

"Oh? What?"

"You covered a chemical spill a while back out in the desert. It was at E&M Enterprises. You remember it?"

"Of course. It was all very strange. I mean, they called in the Army. Shit, you and I both know the military doesn't give a rat's ass about some fertilizer spill. Especially one way out in the desert."

"So why were they there?"

"I wish I knew. I worked on it for months afterwards, nights and weekends, just trying to figure it out. Tried every source I had but I never got anywhere. The lid was clamped tight."

"You have any idea what was in that tanker car?"

"No, none. But if you believe it was fertilizer, then I've got some land in Florida I'd like to sell you." Johnny sighed deeply and then Hounds shocked him. "Why are you asking me all this? You should be asking your former boss."

"What? Who, Barsh?"

"No, not Barsh, Geld."

"Geld? Why the hell would I ask him?"

"He owns it."

"He does?" Johnny was stunned.

"Of course. You mean you didn't know? I figured that's what you were getting at."

"Know? Hell, I didn't have any idea."

"Well, tell you the truth, I'm not all that surprised. That was about the only piece of the whole thing I could ever track down, and it took months. Not something that shows up a lot of places. You have to trace it back through a bunch of corporations and stuff, but yeah, Geld owns the whole damned thing. Just another link in the statewide chain of Geld Enterprises."

Johnny sat perfectly still for a moment, then slowly ran his fingers back through his hair. The silence stretched and finally he simply said, "I don't think I understand this."

"Understand what? What the hell's going on here, Rose?"

"I don't know. I really don't. Listen, I gotta go."

"Go? Wait a minute. You're not leaving without telling me what this is all about. Why all the questions about E&M? You got something on it?"

"No, but if I find something, you'll be the first to know."

Three minutes later Johnny was back in the Z heading for the one place he'd never have thought to look.

The *Chronicle*'s parking lot was locked at night, secure behind a tall chain-link fence. A guard patrolled the lot at regular intervals. All the paper's doors required a security card, which he no longer had, and just inside the employee entrance another security guard was posted twenty-four hours a day. All the security, they'd been told soon after Raby arrived, was necessary to keep the employees' cars and the *Chronicle*'s computers safe. But they couldn't really keep anyone out of the building. Not if that person knew the way in, and Johnny did.

He parked a block away and went in through the loading dock. He ducked between two trucks, climbed to the dock, went past the chute that soon would be spitting out bundled papers, skirted the pressroom, crossed a hall and slipped through the door into the pressmen's empty lunchroom.

The room was big enough for about a dozen tables. Vending machines lined the far wall. Sections of tomorrow's paper were scattered across the ink-smudged tables and the floor. Johnny chose a table in the far corner, and sat facing the door. He picked a newspaper off the floor and pretended to read it while he waited for the guard to come.

He arrived fifteen minutes later. He wore the uniform of the security force: dark blue slacks, a white, short-sleeved shirt with an insignia over the left pocket, a wide black leather belt cinched tight against his thin waist. A walkie-talkie and flashlight hung from the belt. He took two steps into the room, glanced around and turned to leave. He stopped and turned back. Johnny lowered the paper and the guard looked at him for a moment, then nodded and smiled.

"Hey, Johnny, I heard you were gone, man. In fact, I'm supposed to call Duckworth if I see you."

"You gonna call 'im, TJ?"

"Fuck no, not if you don't want me to."

"Good."

TJ was one of four roving night security guards at the *Chronicle*, the only one who still had a job a month after Raby's security team came to the paper. They'd kept him, Johnny figured, because he was smart and he was willing to put up with the schedule: working nights and weekends, split days off. TJ hated it. But he needed it. He was a student at Santa Monica City College and the gig at the *Chronicle* allowed him to study at night while getting paid. He dreamed of becoming a writer, and Johnny had read a few of his creative writing assignments and offered a few tips.

"So, why you here? I heard they fired you."

"That what they told you?"

"Yeah, told all the guards. Said to not let you in and if we saw you, we're supposed to call Duckworth himself first thing."

"Well, not that it makes any difference, but I quit, they didn't fire me. But right now I need a favor."

"What is it?"

"I need to get into Geld's office."

Johnny watched as TJ slowly smiled. "Hey, no problem. I got a master key. In case there's a fire or something, you know."

The hallways on the *Chronicle*'s lower floors were tunnels of gray linoleum and stark white walls. The red fire extinguishers offered the only dash of color. On the top floor, though, the elevator opened onto a lushly carpeted hallway imbued with perpetual twilight by the soft lights recessed into the ceiling. TJ stepped out of the elevator first, looked both ways, then waved Johnny out. A potted palm stood next to the elevator directly under a spotlight.

TJ pushed open the heavy wooden door. "They never lock this one. It's Geld's office that's locked up tight as Fort Fucking Knox."

They walked into the darkened office. Even in the darkness, Johnny could make out the secretary's desk just outside the door to Geld's inner office and the door to another office farther back on the left. The upper half of the far wall was windows, and Johnny could see the city's lights.

"Whose office is that?" Johnny motioned to the one farther back.

"That's Raby's, this is Geld's," TJ said as he turned and unlocked a door to his right. He pushed it open and stepped back.

"Look, I gotta get back on my rounds. If I'm gone too long Duckworth might go looking for me."

"Duckworth?"

"Yeah, he's been working nights lately. I don't think the guy has a life outside of this place."

"Yeah, I know. Look, thanks for your help. I'll just have a look around and find my own way out."

"Okay. I'm going to keep an eye out for Duckworth. He always comes up here at least once, just to check. I'll call on line 9565 if he's coming. It lights up in every office."

"How about if I just lock the door after you go?"

TJ shook his head. "No, he'll unlock it. Inspects Geld's and Raby's offices personally every night. Checks everything. He's very thorough. A fucking brown-noser, if you ask me. Wants to be able to tell 'em every day that he checked personally. But look, if he's coming I'll call and you'll have to split. Take the stairs out."

"Okay. Thanks, TJ."

"And no lights."

"What?"

"If they see lights on up here from the street, they'll come check. You gotta be real careful."

"Okay, I'll work it out."

"Hey, man, good luck."

"Thanks," Johnny said and moved past the guard into the office.

He heard the outside door close and turned to look around. Light from the streetlights filtered through the venetian blinds that covered the windows to his left. Even in the soft half-light, Johnny could see it was a large room. Geld's desk, a huge slab of wood, sat in front of the window, the light glinting off its polished surface. To his right the room was darker, and he waited a moment until his eyes adjusted. He saw a couch, an armchair and a coffee table that formed a small seating area near the far wall. He stepped toward the couch and realized that the wall behind it was covered with framed pictures, including one poster-size photo that held center stage.

He crossed the room to the couch, his feet moving

silently across the rug, then slapping lightly on the hardwood floor where the rug ended just in front of the coffee table. Standing next to the couch, he leaned forward and looked at the poster. It was the same *Forbes* cover he'd seen in the private office at Geld's house, only this copy was even larger. Next to it were framed commendations, and declarations honoring Gordon Geld as citizen of the year, chairman of this charity or that society function.

Johnny left the accolades to Geld's greatness and crossed the room to the desk. He stood for a moment at its edge and slowly wiped his fingertips along its smooth surface. He looked back at the rest of the office, then turned and sat in Geld's high-backed chair. He switched on Geld's computer and waited. A moment later it demanded a password.

He sucked in a deep breath and held it, then exhaled. He typed in "Geld." It was rejected. He tried "Gordon" and was rejected again. He tried *Chronicle,* then the initials GG. But every password he tried was denied, and Johnny felt the fine edge of suppressed panic. After a preset number of attempts, the computer would lock up. And Johnny knew he was quickly running out of tries. He figured he had two, maybe three left. Hit the bull's-eye blindfolded or go home. He sat staring at the screen, then pushed the chair back from the desk and stretched his legs out straight. He couldn't guess blindly. He had to think, be logical. What would Geld use as a password? Most people use their own or their spouse's name or initials or birthdates. It's always something simple so they won't forget. But Geld wasn't just anyone. Geld was a rich industrialist who planned to be governor. Who knew, maybe he really wanted to be president.

Johnny closed his eyes and saw Geld walking through the newsroom stopping to chat with the reporters, the squire discussing the weather with the peasants. And Johnny could see him on the dais, making a speech. Over the years, Johnny had discovered that you can learn a lot about people without ever asking any questions. People will tell you who they are, if you'll just listen and watch. So who was Gordon Geld? What would he use as his password? Johnny looked around the room, peering into the shadows, searching for an answer. His glance stopped on the enlarged *Forbes* cover and suddenly he knew with absolute certainty. The *Forbes* cover. The article was about his genius, his special touch, his ability to turn anything into gold. The headline was catchy: MIDAS MAN.

Johnny's fingers flew across the keyboard as he typed the *Forbes* headline. Instantly, he was into the computer.

His elation was short-lived. He found nothing to help him. He found copies of letters Geld had sent to political leaders and donors, thanking them for their help and asking for more. He scanned a long report on California's precincts detailing where Geld could count on support and where he was weak. There was a memo to the paper's personnel department ordering it to make sure everyone working there, especially recent immigrants, had proper work permits. There were even three recent invoices e-mailed to him for his review and approval.

But he found nothing on Vietnam or POWs, the Royal Hotel or even a fertilizer plant in California's high desert.

"Shit," he swore. Maybe there was no connection. Or maybe he just couldn't see it. He looked for almost an hour and, in the end, almost missed it. He clicked open a file that held a list of the companies in Geld Enterprises. Each company name was followed by a series of random letters and numbers. The *Chronicle* was near the top, and about halfway down the list was E&M Enterprises.

Johnny felt his pulse erupt. He leaned close to the screen, his nose inches away. There was no pattern to the numbers and letters that followed each company name, nothing in common from one line to the next.

He leaned back in his chair and heard a faint rumbling in the distance. He stood and moved to the window and looked out at the street below. The first delivery trucks loaded with the early editions were rolling, leaving the loading docks, heading for the circulation zones farthest from the presses, making the windows quiver slightly against their old putty. Soon the final sports and front page deadlines would be gone and the presses temporarily halted for the last replate. Then the trucks would hit the closest circulation zones, where the papers would be transferred to pickup trucks and car trunks to hit the vending boxes and newsstands.

Johnny started to turn from the window but stopped and looked again. Half a block away he saw the billboard he'd first noticed from the parking lot. Geld's picture seemed to be smiling directly at him. It was as though the publisher were watching his every move. Johnny looked at the billboard a moment longer, shook his head slightly and sat at the publisher's desk again. He searched the desk, found a disk in a drawer and copied the file that was still open on the screen. He took the disk, switched off the computer, pushed the chair back and left.

In the outer office he stopped and looked at Raby's

office door. He hadn't thought of searching there until that moment, but knew instantly that he would.

The door to Raby's office was unlocked and Johnny pushed it open. It was small, just big enough for a desk, shelves against one wall and a credenza with eight drawers, four top and bottom, behind the desk. The desktop held only a pen and pencil set, a lamp and a phone. Johnny stepped in and examined the room, trying to get a sense of the man. But unlike Geld's office there was nothing of Raby in the small space, no footprints of the man. No paintings on the walls, no plaques, no books on the credenza. One shelf held a few books, a small stack of magazines. The others were bare. Johnny ran his fingers along the books' spines and tried to read the titles in the half-dark. Politics and business. He glanced at the magazines: *Business Week*, *Forbes*, *Fortune*.

On the last shelf, set back from the edge, he saw a framed photo. He leaned toward it, snatched the picture off the shelf and held it close. Whoever had taken it knew his stuff. It was sharp and crisp, and the detail stood out even in the darkness. Johnny could see it had been taken years ago, when Raby was a young man. He stood in jungle fatigues in front of a row of helicopters with the heavily forested hills of Vietnam in the background. He was looking directly at the camera but was not smiling. Johnny moved to the window, held the photo up to the glass and looked at Raby closely, already knowing what he would see: two small black parallel lines on each shoulder, captain's bars. He moved back to the shelves and returned the photo.

He had just sat down at Raby's desk when he heard a muffled ring in the distance. He listened and heard it again. He looked at the desk. The red line on Raby's phone, 9565, was blinking. Johnny picked it up but said nothing, then heard the familiar voice.

"Hey, man, it's TJ."

"Yeah."

"Duckworth's working his way around to the upper floors, you got maybe five minutes."

"Thanks." Johnny hung up and turned to the credenza. He jerked open the first drawer and flipped quickly through a dozen hanging files: political strategy papers written for Geld, guard schedules for his security detail, a list of donors and their spouses. He pulled open the second drawer and pawed through the files and moved on to the third. At the back of the fourth he found a file with a two-word label: BLUE RAIN. The label, so out of place from the others, caught his eye.

He pulled it out and laid it open on the desk. A small pile of thin papers nestled inside. Johnny held the papers up to read them in the dim window light. One word jumped out: *Vietnam.* He blinked and leaned closer to the window. He could make out dates and the name Ho Chi Minh City. The other lettering was faint and hard to read, but Johnny could see enough to know the papers were copies of shipping invoices. He stood and leaned closer to the window, his shoulder almost touching the glass. He read the invoices carefully and in the back of the file he found a slip of paper with a series of numbers printed neatly by hand. The numbers looked like map coordinates and were followed by two names: Khun Sa, Doi Sanh.

Again he heard the phone. He reached across and grabbed it.

"Duckworth's on his way. I just saw him heading to the elevator. You gotta get out of there." TJ's voice was hurried, excited.

"I'll just be a minute, I gotta look at something I found."

"No! You don't have a minute. He'll be there any second. Go now, Johnny! Now!"

Johnny hung up, put the papers back in the folder and dropped the folder into the drawer, shoved it closed and ran from Raby's office. He hurried to the outer door and eased it open and peeked out. He could see the elevator call button lit. Duckworth was coming up. Johnny closed the door gently, quietly, then turned and sprinted down the hall. He heard the chime of the arriving elevator as he reached the stairs. He could hear the elevator doors slide back as he pulled open the heavy door to the stairs. He stepped through, then held the knob tightly as he eased the door closed. Duckworth's walkie-talkie squawked and Johnny's pulse pushed into overdrive.

Slowly and carefully, he slipped the door into the frame. The lock slid home with a click just as TJ's voice came over the walkie-talkie, asking Duckworth a question. Johnny took the stairs two at a time but stopped and caught his breath at the bottom. He walked slowly, casually, out of the building and strolled the city block to the Z. Five minutes after he left the *Chronicle*, he was heading to the motel, the disk snug in his pocket over his rapidly beating heart.

25

Johnny awakened just before six the next morning and lay staring at the pocked and water-marked ceiling. His muscles and joints ached from the thin mattress and worn springs, and he sat up slowly.

He sat on the edge of the bed in his underwear, his pants and shirt draped across the dresser. He thought again of the picture he'd seen in Raby's office. There was nothing to directly tie Charles Raby to Jimmy. A lot of people had been in Vietnam. A lot of men had pictures of themselves on their office shelves. But somehow, Johnny knew without need of an explanation that Jimmy was connected to Raby and that Raby led directly to the ghosts of POWs who seemed to walk the earth again. Johnny needed to understand more, to understand the connection.

He pulled the phone from the nightstand and set it on his lap. He got the area code for North Dakota,

called directory assistance and asked for Harold Kraznycka's phone number.

Jimmy and Kraznycka had served their first tour in
Nam together, flown on the same chopper. Kraznycka
had even written Jimmy a couple of letters after he got
home. Johnny could see the name printed in a sloppy
hand in the upper left-hand corner of the envelopes as
clearly as if he were looking at them today. Jimmy had
natural talent in music, but Johnny could spell. If he
saw a word or a name once, twice at the most, he could
close his eyes and see it right there in front of him
again anytime. Instant recall. He could spell words
backward if he wanted.

Harold Kraznycka of Minot, North Dakota. The
name was right there. Johnny had thought of Kraznycka
many times. Once he'd even picked up the phone,
ready to call. But he'd always hesitated, unsure if he
really wanted to know the answers to the questions he'd
have to ask. Instead he'd trusted the doctors and psychiatrists and simply hoped for the best. Now, though,
hope wasn't enough.

Directory assistance asked if Johnny wanted the
home or the business. He wrote down both numbers,
and when he got an answering machine at Kraznycka's
home, he dialed the business.

"Bait and Tackle." The voice was male, middle-
aged and white.

"I'm trying to reach Harold Kraznycka."

"This is Harry. What can I do for you?"

"Hi, ah, my name's Johnny Rose. I think you knew
my brother Jimmy, Jimmy Rose, in Vietnam."

"Oh, sure, hi. Hey, how is Jimmy? I wrote to him a
few times after we got back, but I never heard back
from him. How's he doing, anyway?"

"Hmm, well, he's not doing so well. He's in the hospital. The VA out here in L.A."

"Oh, sorry to hear that. Nothing too serious, I hope."

"Well, to tell you the truth, he's in the long-term psychiatric care facility. He's having some real problems."

"Wow, that's rough."

"I keep hoping things will get better, but you know how it is."

"I guess."

"Listen, I didn't call to burden you with Jimmy's problems. I'm calling in the hopes you might be able to help me help him."

"Me? I don't know what I can do. I mean, I'll try, but I knew Jimmy a long time ago. I haven't seen him in more than, what, twenty-five years?"

"I know, but the thing is, I think his problems go back to Vietnam. He was never the same after he came home and now things have gotten really bad."

Kraznycka mumbled something Johnny couldn't make out and then the line was empty for a few moments, so Johnny went on. "Lately Jimmy's been talking about a captain from Nam. I think it's someone he served with over there. He seems to be fixated on it. Maybe it's nothing, I don't know. I mean, I just don't know what to do. I finally remembered your letters and I knew you were over there with him and I was thinking you might know what he's talking about."

The phone was silent for a long time, and Johnny waited for Kraznycka to say something. He sat looking at the old brown curtains less than three feet in front of him, seeing the dust that clung to them and the light that poured through the gap where the sagging cur-

tains no longer met in the middle. And finally Kraznycka spoke.

"Look, Mr. Rose, like I said, that was all a long time
ago."

"Not to Jimmy it wasn't. He just tried to kill himself. He's tried before, but not in a long time. We all
kind of figured he'd stabilized, but when I saw him in
the hospital he was in bad shape. He kept talking about
this captain again. I think this guy came to visit him
and brought back all the bad memories."

"Wow, I'm really sorry to hear that."

"Mr. Kraznycka, if you know something, you gotta
help me out if you can. You gotta tell me what happened over there."

"I don't really know for sure. I just heard a bunch
of talk is all. Besides, I don't see how any of this will
help now."

"I don't know either, but I have to know what happened to him. It may be the only way I'll ever be able
to help him."

"I don't know, it was a long time ago, man."

"Please. I really need your help."

Again the silence, then Johnny heard Kraznycka
exhale deeply. "Yeah, okay. Like I said, I don't know
that much about it, really. Jimmy and me met during
his first hitch. We spent a lot of months in the bush
together. I was on the same chopper crew with him.
You know how it is, couple of young bucks. I tell you
what, when we pulled him out of the jungle, no one
was happier to see him than I was, believe me. I don't
know, it was like it was me out there. When I saw him
come walking out of that grass I wanted to run over
there and hug him. Well, anyway, we both re-upped
over there.

"I took some R and R, but I don't think Jimmy even left Saigon. Then he went into this special unit that went hunting for downed pilots and POWs and I didn't see too much of him after that. We'd bump into each other now and then and he'd tell me what he was up to. You know, this unit of his, they did some crazy shit. They'd fly choppers over an area where a plane had gone down and where they heard a beeper. Then they'd drop a big cable to the ground and drag it through the jungle. If the pilot was down there, he was supposed to grab this cable and they'd haul him aboard. Jimmy was a door gunner on the chopper. He said sometimes they'd be flying slow, dragging that cable, taking all kinds of ground fire.

"Funny thing is, I think he liked it. I remember this one time he told me about, they picked up a guy and they were hauling him up but the guy was VC. He'd dressed in fatigues and was planning on throwing a grenade in the chopper. Suicide mission. Jimmy saw it coming and blew his shit away while the guy was dangling on the cable."

Johnny closed his eyes and remembered Jimmy's story of the chopper flying low over the grass, rocking back and forth, and him firing away at anything that moved.

"Well, anyway, I guess a couple of times they got wind of VC camps where they were holding American POWs. His outfit went in to rescue them. Flew in the Rangers or whoever it was. But they missed each time." Kraznycka stopped talking, but Johnny knew he hadn't heard it all and prompted him.

"Yes?"

"Well, after the second raid, I ran into Jimmy in a bar. He was already drunk when I got there. I started drinking with him and after a while he starts telling me about the guy in charge of the raids, this gung-ho captain. The guy was absolutely fixated on getting our boys back. I mean, from what I heard this guy was off the scale. I heard it from a couple of other people, too. It was like this was his own private war.

"Those POW camps, he was the one that found out about 'em in the fist place. I guess he had a special way of getting people to talk."

Kraznycka paused for a second, then asked, "You sure you want to hear this?"

"No, I don't want to, but it may be the only way I can help my brother."

"Okay. Well, what this captain would do is he'd take three or four VC up in a chopper. You know, he'd load 'em up and have 'em just sitting there, hands tied behind their backs. Then when they got up high enough he'd throw them out the door one at a time. Just drag 'em to the door kicking and screaming and throw 'em out. All but one, that is. He always saved one. The last one would tell this captain whatever he wanted to know. Couldn't shut him up."

"So? How does Jimmy fit into this?"

Kraznycka sighed deeply again, and when he spoke he sounded tired, old. "Jimmy helped throw them out."

Johnny sat silent, holding the phone, hearing Kraznycka breathing on the other end, but his mind was numb and he could think of nothing to say.

"I always figured it was because of when he was left out there for those days alone, you know? It just did something to him. Those days out there alone with the VC all around. It just did something to him."

"Yeah," Johnny said.

"Look, I'm sorry I had to be the one to tell you this."

"I had to know. Listen, do you know the name of this captain?" Johnny asked, although he was sure he already knew.

"I can't remember exactly. Sounded like one of those Jewish ministers, I think."

"You mean a rabbi?"

"Yeah, something like that."

"Raby, Charles Raby?"

"Right, that's it." Johnny said nothing and Kraznycka, hearing the silence, went on quickly. "It was a war. We all did things we're not proud of. And you gotta remember, that was a long time ago."

But for Jimmy it wasn't a long time ago. It was as real as yesterday. Raby had made sure of that.

Johnny thanked Kraznycka, hung up and sat on the edge of the bed thinking of his brother, seeing him drag the short men in black pajamas to the door of a helicopter to force them out. Throwing them to their death.

Johnny didn't know how long he sat, waiting for the outrage at Jimmy's actions to creep in, the revulsion to well up inside him. But it never came, and after a while he realized the man he saw in the helicopter wasn't the brother he'd grown up with. It wasn't Jimmy the shy musician. The man in the helicopter was the man he saw lying in a hospital bed tormented by nightmares he'd woven more than two decades earlier. Whatever sins Jimmy had committed, Johnny had no doubt he'd paid for them in full measure. It wasn't Johnny's place to cast stones.

Finally he got up and walked into the bathroom. He unwrapped one of the small bars of soap and showered in a weak stream of tepid water, then dried off with the one thin towel the motel furnished and dressed again in the clothes he'd worn the day before.

Johnny left the motel at a little before nine, his hair still wet and his face unshaven. He drove straight to Nikki Masterson's house on the hillside. To avoid the tight cornering on the driveway, he left the Z on the road below and walked up.

He paused to catch his breath at the edge of the driveway. The Jetta was in the carport and Johnny went across the brick patio and pounded on the door. There was no answer, and he pounded again and pushed the bell. Finally he turned, walked to the edge of the patio and looked at the Valley.

"You got my money?" Nikki Masterson's voice came from behind him, on the left near the far end of the house. He turned and saw her. She'd stepped onto the patio, coming through two open French doors. Johnny guessed they led to a bedroom.

"Ah, shit, it's you." She seemed more angry than surprised. Johnny walked slowly toward her but she didn't move. She just stared at him, her jaw set.

"I want to know who's behind this. Is it Geld? Is it Raby? Who is it? I want to know. I want to know why you're doing it," he said.

She stood next to a glass-topped patio table and metal chairs watching him approach. She was in jeans, running shoes and a white T-shirt. Her hair was uncombed and she wore no makeup. Her right arm dangled at her side, a cigarette between her fingers, her left hand on her hip.

"I already told you. I don't know anything about it. I was just doing a job." She brought the cigarette to her mouth and inhaled deeply.

"That's bullshit. You don't even have a goddamned agent."

"Oh, brilliant, Sherlock, you figure that out all on your own, did you? Now, would you mind? I'm expecting someone."

Maybe it was her flip tone, maybe the contempt in her eyes or the way she exhaled, blowing the smoke directly at him. Johnny stepped forward quickly, almost running. He banged into a patio chair, knocking it aside. He grabbed Nikki Masterson's right arm and dug his fingers in deeply.

"Listen here, you bitch. Someone tried to kill me yesterday. Now you're going to tell me what this is all about."

"Let go of me." She jerked her arm free and Johnny made no attempt to grab her again. She wasn't going anyplace.

"Who hired you? Was it Geld? Raby? Who?" His voice was an insistent whisper.

"Fuck you."

"Who is it?" He glared and moved next to her. He was close enough to feel her breath and smell her hair.

She stepped backward quickly, lost her balance and fell into a chair. Johnny stepped to the chair instantly and grabbed her right shoulder with his left hand. She hit his arm, a weak, glancing blow.

"You think this is some kind of joke? People are getting killed. Someone's trying to murder me. I'm not going to let them. You get the point?" He raised his fist.

She pushed against the back of the seat and raised her arms to protect her head. "Wait, please. Not in the face. Please."

He saw it then. This time the fear in her eyes was

genuine. This time, he knew, she wasn't acting. He stopped.

"Who sent you?"

"It was just a guy. I'd never seen him before."

"Was it Geld?"

"I don't who you're talking about. I don't know anyone named Geld."

"He's running for governor, for Christ's sake."

"I don't pay any attention to politics."

"Don't lie to me. I'm sick of it."

"I swear. I don't know the guy. I never saw him before. He came to the theater, just like you did. He gave me the money there and told me what to say. He said it was a joke on a friend. I didn't know anything was wrong until you showed up. You've got to believe me."

"Name, he give you a name?"

"No, never. He never said his name."

"What did he look like?"

"Tall and thin. Dark hair. Maybe mid-fifties."

It had to be Raby. Johnny released his grip and straightened up, looking down at Nikki Masterson in the chair.

"Why? Why's he doing it?"

"I swear to God I don't know anything about it. The guy came to the Odyssey and hired me, just like I told you. That's all I know. I never saw him before that night. You gotta believe me."

Nikki Masterson pushed herself up out of the chair warily and edged away from Johnny, moving toward the door, watching him as she went, almost pleading. "Look, I told you everything I know. Believe me. That's it. I don't know anything about any shooting or murders or anything like that. Just some guy showed up and hired me. I'm an actress. I don't know anything about politics or anything." She rubbed her arm. "Shit, that hurts."

Johnny stepped back from the chair and let his eyes wander to the bedroom door. He saw two suitcases sitting inside the double doors to the bedroom and remembered her first words before she realized it was he. "You got my money?"

He looked at her again. Her eyes had followed his glance. "They're sending you money. To get you out of town."

"Yeah, so? I don't want any part of this anymore. None." The defiance was gone. She seemed tired, ready to quit.

"You told them I was at the theater, didn't you?" He took a step toward her.

"Yes."

"How did you contact them? What did you do?"

"A phone number. The guy gave me a number and said to call if there was an emergency. Said it was a pay phone downtown, so just leave a message."

"What's the number?"

"I don't know. It's in my purse. In the bedroom."

"Get it."

Nikki Masterson walked through the doors into the bedroom and returned a moment later with a large, black, soft-sided purse. She dropped it on the patio table and opened it. Johnny's eyes were riveted on the black bag while she dug, shoving things back and forth, searching for the paper like a raccoon in a garbage can. He was concentrating totally on the purse and Nikki Masterson's hands.

Neither one heard the Blazer coast to a stop at the end of the driveway.

"Here it is," Nikki Masterson said. She pulled her hand from the purse, the relief obvious in her voice. Johnny took the paper. They both heard the Blazer's door open. Duckworth stood next to the Blazer steadying a gun on the edge of the door, pointing it directly at them.

Nikki Masterson looked at him and froze, unable to comprehend the scene.

"Get down," Johnny screamed just as he heard the first shot and Nikki Masterson's face exploded, splattering him with blood and tissue and tiny bone fragments. Johnny dove for the bushes on the edge of the patio. The next bullet shattered the glass top of the patio table. He gained his footing and tried to run down the side of the mountain, but tumbled and fell headfirst and rolled out of control. He heard the gun again and the dirt next to him kicked up. He struggled to tuck his legs and gain his footing. But his momentum sent him sprawling again, face first, down into the dirt and dried weeds. Two more cracks came quickly and bullets whizzed past him, striking the soft dirt. Johnny kicked with his feet and flailed with his arms, fighting for more speed, more momentum. Anything to get away.

The slope ended abruptly at a cliff. Johnny rolled over as a bullet hit near him. He fell the five feet to the street below and landed sprawled on the asphalt. He lay for a second, dazed, then struggled to his feet and limped toward the Z, only yards away.

A mailman, leaning from his truck to reach a nearby mailbox saw Johnny, bloody and dirty, plunge off the hill, struggle to his feet and stagger toward the car. For a second their eyes met but Johnny didn't stop, didn't seek help. He grabbed the car door and swung it wide. He fired the engine without closing the door and popped the clutch. The Z leaped forward and the door banged shut as the car sped up the street toward Mulholland Drive.

He could hear the mailman shouting, "Call the police, call the police."

Johnny glanced in his mirror and caught sight of the Blazer as it hit the street from the driveway. It careened toward the edge of the road and the dropoff to the canyon below. A moment later, though, it was under control and speeding to catch him.

Johnny had the pedal almost to the floor. As the road met Beverly Glen Boulevard, he let up, downshifted and jammed the accelerator hard again. The car shot out of the side street across the oncoming traffic and turned up the hill. A moment later he was at Mulholland. He could see the red light ahead at the intersection but he didn't hesitate. He sped into it, crossing in front of a Chrysler LeBaron. The young blonde behind the wheel didn't slow, just flipped him the finger and screamed, "Prick."

A moment later Johnny was rushing down the side of the Santa Monica Mountains toward Beverly Hills.

26

Beverly Glen Boulevard descends the south side of the Santa Monica Mountains and jogs slightly west at the northern tip of a small wedge-shaped city park. As Johnny approached the park, he slowed and turned east off of Beverly Glen. He stopped on the far side of the park and pulled the Z to the curb between a new Lexus and a delivery van. He had a clear view of Beverly Glen and watched the traffic closely. After almost fifteen minutes he knew Duckworth wasn't coming. He'd eluded him.

For the moment.

Johnny could feel his shoulders and neck muscles go slack as the adrenaline seeped away and exhaustion crept in. He leaned his head back and closed his eyes. His thoughts drifted. Then suddenly the image of Nikki Masterson filled his mind. He could see her clearly again, her body knocked backward by the bullet even as he screamed to get down. He jerked forward and opened his eyes. His heart was racing and he blinked his eyes against the bright sun.

He twisted the mirror to look at himself. Jesus, it was bad. His face was flecked with blood and streaked with dirt and dried sweat. His hair was dirty and wild. He looked down at his clothes. His shirt was splattered with blood and tissue. A weed was stuck just above the pocket. His pants were ripped at the knee. He pulled the computer disk from his pocket, blew the dirt off it and put it back.

He got out of the car and followed the sidewalk to a small Spanish-style building with a red, rounded tile roof, the park office. Two Latino men dressed in the green of the city's parks department stood outside the building, leaning against their rakes and laughing. They fell silent and looked away as Johnny approached. He moved past them to the restroom. But the sink's faucet was broken and there was no water. He leaned on the porcelain for a moment and stared at the vague image reflected in the sheet of polished metal that served as a mirror.

"You've really screwed the pooch this time," he said to the image. He turned, shuffled out of the bathroom and fell on the grass. He lay staring at the sky straight above him, a donut hole of blue bordered by brown haze. He let the sun bake him and a moment later, with no thought of how tired he was, fell asleep.

He dreamed of a jungle. He was hiding at its edge. He glanced over his shoulder into the impenetrable darkness of the thick vegetation. Something evil was in the jungle searching for him, waiting for him to move and show himself. He crouched and waited for a helicopter to come and rescue him. Then it was there, flying low, coming in to pluck him to safety. But it seemed to veer away and Johnny could feel the panic. He wanted to stand and shout, but he couldn't reveal himself. Then it circled and flew toward him again. He awoke suddenly and sat up. Immediately he felt the soreness throughout his body. In the distance he saw a gardener riding a lawn mower in big lazy circles, coming closer, then turning away again. Johnny watched the man maneuver the mower for a few minutes, then struggled to his feet and moved back to the Z.

He sat in the car, leaning forward, his hands resting lightly on the steering wheel, staring straight ahead. He felt terribly alone, isolated and vulnerable. He knew he needed something, an edge, an angle, something that would give him an advantage that Raby and Geld didn't expect. But most of all, he needed help.

He found a pay phone in Westwood Village and dialed the AP. The assignment editor told him Hounds was out. Down near San Diego working the election. He'd be back late. Did Johnny want to leave a message? Johnny didn't bother answering. He hung up and paused for a moment, leaning against the molded plastic housing that gave the phone minimal protection from the sun and rain. God, he was tired.

He walked back to his car and sat for almost half an hour thinking of Nikki Masterson and Sandra Ruiz and Pham and wondering what was so important, so vital, that they had to die to keep it quiet. POWs? If so, why were they killing people to keep it quiet? But if there were no POWs, then what the hell was going on? And in the end he thought of himself and the attempt to kill him at his apartment. He'd escaped that time and avoided Duckworth at Nikki Masterson's by pure luck, but he couldn't run on luck forever.

Finally, he started the car and drove south on Westwood Boulevard. There was only one place left to go. One person who might believe him. One person who might help.

Susan opened her door moments after Johnny rang the bell.

"Oh my God," she said. "What happened?"

"I need help."

He was almost afraid to watch her, afraid of what her reaction would be. But Susan didn't hesitate. No debate filled her eyes, no question crossed her face. She responded instantly, pushing the screen door open.

Johnny walked stiffly past her into the living room and sank onto the first chair he saw; the rocker, the same one he'd occupied only days earlier when he'd first come to talk to Susan and asked her if her husband might still be alive.

Susan wore baggy white shorts that hung almost to her knees and a blue tank top. Her hair was pulled back, except for a loose strand that fell down the side of her head. Johnny looked up at her, standing next to the rocker.

"I don't know what—" he started to say, but she stopped him.

"Wait, don't say anything. I'll be right back." She turned and disappeared down a hall into the back of the house. Johnny leaned forward and rested his arms on his legs, his head down. He raised his head and looked around the living room, seeing the dust in the corner of the hardwood floor and the *L.A. Times*, unopened, on the coffee table.

What had he done? Had he brought danger into Susan's house? Was he risking her life by coming here?

How long until Raby or Duckworth or someone else on his security force found him here? He knew he should leave, just get up and walk out before Susan returned. But a moment later Susan was back. She carried sweatpants and a T-shirt draped over her arm.

"These belong to Will. You're about as tall as he is but probably don't weigh quite as much, so they may be a little big, but they're all I could find. You can wear them until I get your stuff washed." She held out the pants and shirt. When Johnny didn't rise to take them, she put them on the chair's arm.

"There's a shower in the bathroom off the hall. Clean up and then you can tell me everything."

"I shouldn't be here," he managed.

"Yes, you should. This is exactly where you should be."

Johnny smiled through the pain and exhaustion. Her strength and determination delighted him, filling him with an almost adolescent joy. He almost laughed.

"I put some stuff in the bathroom. It's down the hall to the right. Hope you don't mind using a woman's deodorant."

Johnny shook his head no. The exhaustion almost overwhelmed him as he stood, and he had to push on the arms of the rocker to gain his feet. They stood awkwardly, only a few feet apart, their eyes locked, neither one moving, each understanding what hadn't been said. Finally Johnny shuffled past her and moved slowly down the hall without saying a word.

He turned the shower to hot and let the bathroom fill with steam as he peeled off his filthy clothes. He glanced at the mirror and was glad to see it was already steamed over. He didn't really want to know how bad he looked.

In the shower Johnny leaned against the tiles and let the hot water beat on his back, then he turned and lowered his head under the hard stream. He turned slowly, letting the water pelt every side of his body for several minutes before reaching for the soap. By then his skin was stinging red, his muscles weak and rubbery. He moved slowly, washing himself carefully, deliberately. Susan had left a pink plastic razor and he lathered with soap and shaved with exaggerated caution.

After the shower, he dried off with a thick terrycloth towel and pulled on the sweatpants and then opened the medicine cabinet. He found a bottle of Advil, shook four into his palm and ate them. He didn't know how much good they'd do, but they sure as hell couldn't hurt.

The pants were just slightly too long and a little too big in the waist, but Johnny hiked up the ends and cinched up the drawstring. At least they were clean. He pulled on the T-shirt and some thick socks Susan had left. He pulled his wallet, the computer disk and the phone number Nikki Masterson had given him from his pockets and walked out of the bathroom, not bothering to look toward the mirror again. Some questions are best left unanswered.

In the kitchen, Susan was at the counter, pouring iced tea into a glass. She turned and smiled when he came in.

"You look a lot better," she said.

"Thanks."

"Good. You hungry?" she asked.

Johnny felt his stomach tighten. "Not right now, but I could use something to drink."

"Tea okay?"

"Yeah, that'd be fine."

She handed him the glass. "How are you feeling?"

"Better. Much better." He swallowed and when he spoke again his voice was soft. "Hey, thanks for letting me come in."

She smiled, almost shyly, and nodded just once. "I'm glad you came," she said.

He leaned back against the counter. "You're probably wondering what you've gotten yourself into."

"Well, yes, I am. But . . . well, why don't you tell me?"

The shyness, the hint of softness he'd seen a moment ago was gone. The independent, self-reliant woman was back. "Let's sit at the table and you can give me all the details."

27

Susan's head was bowed, her eyes focused on the table, and Johnny studied her openly. Even in the unforgiving brightness of the late afternoon sunlight flooding through the window, she was pretty.

Johnny sipped his tea and waited for her to look at him. How do you start a story like this? Where do you begin? Twice he started, then stopped, stumbling over the words, trying to decide. Do you start with Nikki Masterson's murder, his quitting the paper, his own narrow escape from Duckworth, or maybe it was just easiest to start at the beginning? He started with the last time he'd seen her.

"After we had breakfast, I drove out to Arvin to talk with Sandra Ruiz. But like I said on the phone, she's dead. She drove her car into an irrigation canal and drowned. Or someone drove it in for her."

Susan nodded. "I still can't believe it."

Johnny looked out the window past Susan's shoulder, thinking of Sandra's car heading nose first into the canal less than two miles from her home.

Johnny took another sip of tea and began again. "The thing is, it would be easy to do. The canal is right there, it would be easy for someone to fall asleep and the tire goes off into the gravel and the car spins out and then you're upside down in the ditch, trapped. No one would suspect a murder. I talked to her cousin and, well . . ." He was warming to the story now, telling it just as it happened, from Sandra Ruiz on to the *Chronicle* and Jimmy, the files in Raby's office and then Nikki Masterson, and finally to right there in her kitchen.

He looked at her from time to time and realized she was concentrating totally, and her quiet eyes told him she believed what he said. Suddenly he knew how important that was to him. Not just that anyone believed him. Important that *she* understand him, that *she* believe him.

"I guess I'd suspected for a while. But the moment Kraznycka said it was Raby, it was all clear. It's how they knew I was at the park the night Pham was murdered. It's why they offered me the job, to get me away from it. They knew everything I was doing because I told them. They knew everything about Jimmy because it's right there in the paper's records. They had a map of my life.

"You know, I couldn't figure out why the guy that Jimmy called captain asked if I had a girlfriend. But now I get it. He wanted to know where to find me if I wasn't home." Johnny realized suddenly what he'd just said and quickly added, "Don't worry, I never mentioned you to Jimmy. In fact, I never mentioned you to anyone."

"I wasn't worried," she said and Johnny believed her. "But," she continued, "why are they doing this? Why kill so many people? What are they trying to protect?"

As he thought about her question, Johnny's gaze drifted to the glass inches from his fingers. The ice had melted and water had puddled around its base, forming a small rim of moisture on the tabletop. He looked up at her again. The late afternoon sun had shifted, slanting through the window, lighting half of Susan's face, leaving the other side in darkness.

"I don't know. When I was in Raby's office I found invoices for shipments to Vietnam, but I didn't have a chance to read them, so I don't have any idea what they're shipping.

"You know, I keep coming back to what I said before. If there were POWs, Americans who survived, that Raby and Geld brought home, why keep it a secret?"

"I know what you mean. You can bet if Geld had anything to do with bringing them home, he'd be on the six o'clock news shouting about it. Think what that would do to his ratings. He could walk into the governor's mansion. He could probably skate into the White House, which may be his ultimate goal anyway."

"You think Raby could do something like this on his own, without Geld knowing?"

"No. No way." Johnny shook his head. "Whatever it is, I gotta believe Geld is involved."

"And if they're not really POWs, then whose body was in the desert and who did your friend Pham see?"

"I don't know. I have absolutely no idea. My head hurts just trying to think about it."

They were quiet, and Johnny took a long drink of

tea. The cubes had melted and the drink was weak. He set the empty glass back on the table, carefully replacing it on the circle of water it had left behind.

Susan spoke first. "Okay, where do we start? What can I do to help?"

Johnny thought for a moment. "Well, I've got the phone number Raby gave Nikki Masterson. I'm betting it's the pay phone I saw in the Royal. Can you trace it?"

"Oh, that's easy. That shouldn't take more than a couple of minutes online."

"Good. Maybe you can also find out something about E&M Enterprises."

"Okay. First let's have a look at that disk you got at the *Chronicle*. I wouldn't be surprised if all the answers are already on it."

"Maybe, but I sure couldn't figure it out."

"Well, we'll take another look. But before we start, you feel like eating something now? I'll make us something quick and easy. We'll start right after that."

"Great," Johnny said. He'd noticed she said *we* when talking about the search and wondered how much good he'd be. Computer jockey was definitely a solo gig, and not one he was much good at.

"How about an omelet?"

"Great."

"I usually chop a few onions and mushrooms, throw in some cheese. It's kind of a single person's meal, basic and easy. Actually, the only hard part is turning it."

"What can I do?"

"Start chopping and slicing."

She put the ingredients on the chopping board for Johnny, moved to the front of the stove and sliced two garlic cloves into oil in a skillet over a low flame. Johnny pulled a small bowl from the cupboard and filled it with sliced mushrooms and green onions.

She dumped the eggs into the skillet and slowly turned the pan, raising each side in a rotating motion until the eggs covered the bottom evenly. She turned down the flame and looked at Johnny. "Tell me something. Why'd you become a reporter in the first place?"

"Oh, I don't know. It sounded like a good idea at the time. You know, indoor work, no heavy lifting. Besides, I already knew how to type."

"And I thought it was maybe to fight for truth, justice and the American way," she said stepping to the counter.

"Yeah, that too. But only before happy hour."

She reached past Johnny, picked up the bowl of onions and mushrooms and moved back to the stove. She poured the mixture onto the eggs.

"You're a lot more complicated than you let on, aren't you, Johnny Rose."

"Complicated? Me? I wouldn't say complicated as much as thick-headed."

"Okay. Listen, this is almost done. Why don't you get the plates out, they're in that cupboard." She nodded at a door just above the kitchen counter.

Johnny put the plates on the table, then searched the drawers for silverware and set it out. Susan scooped up the cheese, dropping a few strands on the floor as she moved, and threw it on the eggs. He moved close to the stove and watched over her shoulder as she deftly flipped the omelet closed.

She looked up and smiled, and Johnny realized he was only inches from her. She stood her ground looking at him, a smile he couldn't read on her lips. He could hear the butter sizzling and smell the cooked eggs. He realized he was holding his breath and exhaled and stepped back, not quite ready. Not sure how she would react if he tried to kiss her.

She brushed past then, walked to the table and slid half the omelet onto each plate. Johnny ate fast, taking huge bites and chewing rapidly. Then he caught himself and slowed down. He stopped, only a small part of the omelet still on the plate in front of him, and looked up sheepishly at Susan and grinned.

"Hey, this is great. I'm more into microwave cooking myself. It's sort of a rule around my place. Nothing gets eaten unless it's been frozen for at least two months. I had some lasagna the other day; it still had some taste to it. I threw it away immediately."

Susan chuckled and Johnny realized it was the first time he'd felt relaxed, happy, in days. He smiled back at her.

"So what got you into research?" he asked.

"It was sort of an accident, really. After Kyle's plane went down I started looking for a job, just something to keep me occupied. I saw an ad in the paper for a proofreader. I was an English major in college and, well, I didn't want to teach, so I applied. I've been there ever since."

Their conversation drifted, a little personal history woven in among talk of movies, books and the beach. But, as if by silent, mutual consent, they didn't speak of her husband or Geld or Raby.

"Oh, I love going to the beach, I just don't like to go in the water," Susan said at one point.

"That's crazy, how can you go to the beach and not go in the water?"

"I just do, that's all."

Finally they cleared the table and did the dishes—
she washed, he dried—and put them in the cupboard.
As he put the silverware into the drawer, Johnny knew
he didn't want this interlude to end. He didn't want to
think about what was ahead of them. He just wanted to
be with Susan and let the rest of the world go to hell.

He dropped the last knife into the drawer and
looked at Susan. "Hey, you have any pictures?"

"Pictures? What kind of pictures?"

"You know, old family stuff. I feel like looking at
pictures."

She hesitated, then smiled and said, "I'll be right
back. I'll bring them to the living room. There's a bottle of wine in the refrigerator. Why don't you grab it
and bring it."

A few minutes later she shuffled into the living
room carrying a cardboard box, its top bulging, and set
it on the coffee table.

"A lot of these are slides, but there are a lot of
snapshots, too." She pulled the masking tape off the
dusty top and turned back the cardboard flap.

She giggled at the first picture she saw. "Oh my
God, look how young I was."

She handed him a photo of a young woman in an
ankle-length dress wearing a wide-brimmed straw hat
that cast a shadow across most of her face. But even in
the shaded area he could see her granny glasses and
her smile. Johnny stared at the picture and felt as if
he'd known her forever.

"God, you were beautiful," he said in a low voice.

"Thank you, I think," she said.

"Oh no," Johnny added. "I think you're still beautiful."

She looked at him for a moment, then dug back

into the box of photos and started showing and explaining them as she went.

The color had faded on many, the bright reds turning slightly rusty and the blues a little white. But Johnny didn't care. He loved them. There were a few of Susan with long-haired young men in tie-dyed shirts wearing headbands.

The mound of photos was already spilling off the coffee table and the wine was almost gone when Johnny found a picture of Susan leaning against a young man in a butch cut, jeans, a T-shirt and aviator glasses.

"That's Kyle. I'd known him about a week then," she said and sighed. "You know, I never did see him with long hair."

In the photo, Kyle stared at Susan with an intensity Johnny had seldom seen. He handed Susan the photo. "He was really in love with you, wasn't he?"

"Yes, we were very much in love," she said. Her tone was matter-of-fact but tinged with sadness.

Finally, after more pictures of Kyle and Susan, the love in their eyes growing with each photo, she leaned forward and pulled out a white envelope, folded and ragged along the edges, from near the bottom of the box. She handed the envelope to Johnny.

"Here, these are the last ones I have. He sent them from Vietnam. I got them about a week before learning his plane was down."

Johnny studied the photo of the man looking at the camera, holding his aviator sunglasses at his side. Johnny looked at her and said, "Susan, what if, ah, I don't even know how to ask this. What if . . ."

"What if your friend was right? What if Kyle is alive?"

"Yeah."

She leaned back against the couch and hugged her knees. She looked across the room and sat silently for a few moments. When she spoke, her voice was soft.

"Kyle's dead."

"But Pham sounded—"

Susan held up her hand and motioned to him. "Wait, Johnny." He stopped speaking and nodded toward her. "A few years after Kyle's plane went down I used to find myself wondering if I really wanted Kyle to come home. I told myself that it was stupid, that of course I wanted him to come home. After the war ended, it all became kind of hazy and I didn't know what I thought anymore. I knew I was supposed to be the faithful wife, always hoping. And I felt guilty because I wasn't. And I felt like I was somehow letting Kyle down because I liked being independent. I liked making my own decisions. I'd made a life for myself and for Will. I got a job, I bought a house. I even caught myself hoping he wouldn't come back. I didn't want him to be dead, I just didn't want to try to make everything the way it was before he left. I mean, it would have been very hard to change, to suddenly be with someone I hadn't seen in years. But I'll tell you this. If Kyle did come home, if he just walked up and rang my doorbell, I'd say, 'Welcome home, sweetheart,' and I'd try to pick up where we left off. I would do everything in my power to make it work. I owe him that and I owe it to Will. But I'm not kidding myself, I'm not carrying a torch for a dead man."

"I didn't mean to pry."

"No." She shook her head. "You didn't. You remember in the restaurant, when you told me about your brother? I wanted to tell you then, but I didn't. So no, you didn't pry. I guess we all carry some baggage with us."

Johnny stood. "Let's go find out what the hell they're up to and stop them," he said. He held his hand out to her.

Susan gripped his hand, rose and said, "Yeah, let's."

28

Susan used Will's bedroom as her office. A desk was built into the corner farthest from the door. It shared the room with a single pine bed and a dresser near the closet. She pulled the chair back, turned on the computer in the middle of the desk and sat down. A printer, a stack of CDs and books covered half of the desk.

"First let's try the phone number," she said. She looked at the paper and began typing.

As she typed, Johnny looked around the room. The walls were an off white and he imagined them covered with pictures of the fighter planes and Little League teams or Dodgers and Lakers pennants, and he thought how hard it must have been to raise a boy alone.

"Well, I've got one bit of good news," she said. She swiveled in her chair and looked at Johnny. "The phone number you got from Nikki Masterson is a pay phone in the Royal Hotel, property of E&M Enterprises."

"Good. But I'm not sure what it means. Just one more piece of the puzzle, I guess."

"Well, let's try the disk." She picked it up and blew on it. "What'd you do, take this to the beach?"

"It was in my pocket when I went down the hill getting away from Duckworth."

She nodded and blew again on the black plastic square. She reached over and moved a stack of CDs and picked up a small canister of compressed air. She blew air from the canister onto the disk.

"Let's take this for a test drive," she said and inserted the disk in the computer's drive. She leaned forward and began typing. "Yeah, we're in luck. I think it's okay," she said. "Come here." She waved him near and pointed to the screen. "Is this it?"

Johnny leaned over her shoulder and looked at the monitor. He saw the same rows of letters and numbers he'd seen in Geld's office. "Right. That's what I copied from Geld's office."

"Okay, let's take a closer look," Susan said. She leaned forward in the chair and a moment later was in another world, as though she'd passed through some electronic voodoo looking glass.

Standing behind her, Johnny watched the screen for a few moments, then paced to the other end of the room and stood by Will's dresser. Atop it was a small framed picture of Kyle Loveless. Johnny picked it up. It was a formal shot of Loveless in his uniform, smiling directly at the camera. He looked like a man Johnny would like, someone he would have enjoyed meeting. As he looked at the photo, Johnny wondered. Had Kyle Loveless really survived more than two decades in the jungle? Was he walking the streets of Los Angeles today? If so, why wasn't he here, in this house, sharing his life with his wife, seeing his only son?

Johnny set the picture down and half-turned to look at Susan again. She was still intent on the computer, leaning toward it, her shoulders hunched forward.

He crossed the room and stood behind her. Without thinking, he raised his hand and slowly rubbed her back, a gentle touch, an act of intimacy shared by people of long acquaintance.

Susan moved slightly, pressing into his touch. But she didn't take her eyes off the screen, and Johnny left his hand resting on her shoulder for a few moments.

"Let's try this," Susan said. She moved the mouse, clicked and quickly tapped the keys. A moment later she exhaled deeply in frustration and started again.

"What?" Johnny asked.

"Nothing. This will just take a few minutes, that's all," Susan said.

Johnny sat on the bed and leaned back against the wall, and watched Susan as she typed. He realized suddenly that she squinted as she stared at the screen and he wondered if she needed glasses. There was, he knew, still so much to learn about her.

"Hey, here we go," she said suddenly. "I'm in E&M's main computer."

"How the hell?" Johnny said as he scrambled off the bed and stood by her side.

"You've got to have the right password to get in, that's all. It's just like any system. That list of company names you got from Geld's computer?" she looked up at Johnny who simply nodded. "Those are Geld's personal passwords. It's like having the master key. Look at this. Personnel records, accounts receivable, every-

thing you don't want any outsiders to be able to get to."
Her fingers danced on the keyboard. "You name it, it's
here. Hey, you want to take a trip to the Bahamas or
maybe get a cash advance delivered to your bank?
With this access, I can do anything I want." She giggled. "All-expenses-paid trip to Hawaii for two? Coming right up, sir."

"What else is there?"

"Wow, check this out," she said. Her voice had lost
its playful tone.

"What is it?"

"I don't know. Looks like a bunch of chemicals to
me." She tapped the screen. "I mean, I can't even pronounce half of these things. And this." She typed again
and suddenly a picture appeared on the screen.

"I think it's some kind of a molecule," she said.

"Yeah, looks like the model of DNA we had to
study in high school."

"Right, but what are these chemicals?"

Johnny stared at the screen and slowly read, moving his
lips as he tried to pronounce the words: Phosphorus
trichloride, methanol, dimethylhydrogen phosphite,
methyl hydrogen methylphosphonate, bishydroxymethyl-
phosphonyl oxide and on and on.

Johnny slowly shook his head. "What the hell are
they doing out there in the desert?"

"I don't know, but I'm going to find out," Susan
said. "If there's an explanation for this stuff out there
anywhere, I'll find it."

But three hours later, Susan had found nothing.
"Damn," she swore lightly under her breath. "It's got to
be there someplace."

Johnny rose from the bed and moved to her side,
draping his arm across the back of the chair, bending

low, his cheek close to hers, and looked at the screen.

"Let's give it a rest," he said. "You've done enough for tonight."

"There are still a few places I haven't checked. A couple more hours and I'll find it. I know I will."

"No. Stop now. It's time to take a break."

She nodded, turned back to the computer, closed the files and switched off the machine. She stood and stretched, arms above her head, then looked at him standing only a few feet from her.

"I'm sorry," she said. "I'll try again. I'll figure it out."

Johnny said nothing. Instead, he held his hand out to her. She stepped toward him, her eyes locked on his, and took it. He pulled and she moved slowly to him and into his arms. He kissed her deeply, passionately, his arms holding her tightly to him.

She'd come to his arms willingly and kissed him with equal fervor, her hand reaching to the back of his head, pulling his head to her. She was, Johnny realized, tall enough that he didn't have to bend and she didn't have to stand on her toes.

Slowly he reached his hand to her breast, but she broke his embrace and took his hand in hers. She held it tightly for a moment, smiling at him, then turned and led him down the hall to her bedroom. She turned to him again as they stepped into the room, and wrapped her arms around his neck. This time she didn't resist as Johnny slipped his hand under her shirt and fumbled for a moment unfastening her bra.

Their breathing came quickly and heavily. Their mouths stuck together as they moved across the room and fell onto the bed. It bounced and groaned under their weight. Johnny fumbled with the top button of her jeans and suddenly stood. He pulled his T-shirt off over his head and hastily loosened his pants and jerked them from his legs. Susan slipped off her shirt and shed her jeans, and a moment later they were locked in each other's arms, their tongues exploring and their hands caressing unknown flesh.

Johnny rolled on top of her and Susan embraced him, wrapping her legs around his, holding him tight and pulling him with each thrust.

He came with a gasp and lay between her legs for a moment, then rolled onto his back next to her.

"If they find me tomorrow, I'll die a happy man," he joked.

"You men are all alike. Get a little and you think you're masters of the universe." She laughed, rolled onto her side and cuddled next to him, her head on his chest.

Later they made love again, more slowly and gently, then lay facing each other and slowly drifted off to sleep.

The sun was slipping past the edge of the blinds, filling the bedroom with a diffused light, when Johnny opened his eyes and looked at the empty bed next to him. He sat up and turned toward the nightstand to see the clock radio. It was already past ten. He swung his legs to the floor, feeling the stiffness from the day before. He sat for a moment, then bent and picked the pants off the floor and slipped them on.

Susan was at the computer and turned to smile at him when he walked in.

"How's it going?" he asked.

"Not bad. I didn't find anything, but I think I know where to go for help."

"Really? Where?"

"There's a chemist at the institute. He worked for the Department of Defense for a long time. If anyone knows exotic chemicals, he does. I'm going to call him."

"Are you sure you can trust him?" he asked.

"I think so. I'm not one hundred percent certain, but I don't know where else to look. I'm not getting anywhere on my own."

Johnny hesitated a moment, looking at Susan dressed in jeans and sweatshirt, her hair pulled into a ponytail held with a rubber band. He smiled and nodded. "Do it."

She grabbed a cordless phone from its base near the computer. A moment later she was talking.

"Hey, Mike, it's Susan. Oh I'm fine, thanks. How are you? How are Jamie and the boys? Really? That's great. Listen, Mike, I've got a favor to ask of you. I need you to look at something. It's a chemical formula. I want to know what it is. Can you try to identify it for me?" She paused for a moment. "No, I'm in a big hurry on this. I need it as soon as possible. Ah, it's something I'm working on. I guess you could say it's an outside project. You will? Great. Look, I'll put it in the master file. Go in there and find my personal file. My password is 'Boy Howdy.'" She winked at Johnny, then turned back to the phone. "No, he was a character in a book I read." She stopped talking for a moment and typed. "All right, it should be there. Now you got it open? It's labeled 'Chemicals.' Got it? Great, I'm working at home today, so get back to me as soon as you get something, okay?"

She hung up. "He should have something by noon. Maybe sooner. He's really good."

Johnny and Susan made a late breakfast and drank

coffee and read the paper, each trying to hide their anticipation, their anxiety. Noon slipped past and in the early afternoon, Johnny walked to the front window, pulled back the curtains and looked out.

"Expecting visitors?" Susan asked.

"No."

"I said I think we can trust him. It's probably just taking longer than we thought."

Johnny nodded. "Yeah, I know. I'm just nervous, that's all. I guess I'm pacing, aren't I?"

"Try to relax, Johnny. He'll call."

Mike called at four-thirty. Susan grabbed the phone from its stand and nodded yes to Johnny. She walked into Will's room and Johnny followed.

"Hi, Mike, what did you find?"

"Where the hell'd you find this?" he asked.

"I ran across it in a report. Why? What is it?"

"Man, this is some really nasty stuff. My guess is this stuff is highly classified. You better be careful who knows you have it."

"I will, Mike, but tell me what it is."

"Well, I can't say for sure, but it looks a lot like something I saw when I was working for Defense. If you process this stuff right, you'll have . . . Jesus, I hate to even think about it."

"Mike, wait a minute, I'm going to put you on the speaker so I can take some notes while we talk, okay?"

"You alone?"

"Yes."

"Okay, let me ask you this first. You ever hear of sarin gas?"

"You mean the stuff that crazy guy dumped in the subways of Tokyo?"

"That's the stuff. Well, this looks like someone was

planning on making a juiced-up version of sarin, next-generation kind of thing."

"You mean chemical weapons?"

"Sure looks like it. We used to make some of that stuff ourselves, but we destroyed all our stockpiles years ago. It was part of something called Operation Mist. This particular stuff got the name Blue Rain."

"Blue Rain?"

"Yeah. I never knew all the details, but from what I heard, the Pentagon got some chemist, a guy around here someplace, to develop some defoliants for them. One was particularly devastating. We called it Blue Rain. It was like Agent Orange, only it worked much faster. It pretty much dissolved plants on contact. There was some talk about using it against the coca fields down in Colombia and Peru, but nothing ever came of it. Anyway, the chemist took the Blue Rain work a step further. He discovered that with the addition of the right mix of chemicals, the Blue Rain worked even better on people. He also figured out a way to make it in different parts. You make it separately, then mix it just before you use it. The last part was like a trigger. Once you added them all together, you had a chemical weapon that was like nothing ever seen on this earth. Really powerful stuff. It could make even a tiny country into a world power if they ever got hold of it. It was a hundred times stronger than sarin."

"Whatever happened to it? To the stuff he developed?"

"Nothing," Mike grunted. "That's what's so interesting. It turns out the stuff has a half-life of about ten days after it's mixed. It deteriorates so fast it was almost useless. After about forty-five days, all you have left is some bad-smelling water. But the funny part is, word leaked out about this powerful chemical weapon we'd designed. I always figured the CIA leaked it just to scare the hell out of the Russians. Some people even say that's why the Russians were willing to sign the chemical weapons treaties. Of course, if they'd known how fast it deteriorates, who knows if they'd have signed."

"So it's possible some people still know about it, but don't know it's useless after a few days."

"It's possible. My guess is, if they've heard of it at all, they only got part of the story, the deadly part."

Johnny grabbed a piece of paper and quickly wrote a note and slipped it in front of Susan. She nodded.

"Hey, one last question. You have any idea where they were making this stuff?"

"No, not really, but it must have been someplace pretty hot. One chemist I know who worked on it, every time he came back, he was sunburned, even in the winter. So I figure it wasn't Michigan." Mike laughed. "Anyway, does that answer your question?"

"Well, yes, I think it does. That was wonderful, thank you, Mike."

"Listen, Susan, I wasn't kidding earlier when I told you to be careful. This is still highly classified. I don't know what you're doing, but this isn't something to mess around with."

"Thanks, Mike." Susan hung up and looked at Johnny. "Well, what do you think?"

"I think I know who developed Blue Rain in the first place and where they were making it."

"But what are they doing with it?"

Johnny shook his head slowly. "I wish I knew."

"Maybe I should search E&M's files again. Who knows, maybe I'll get lucky."

"No, maybe there's another way."

"What?"

"When I was in Raby's office. I found a note in that file labeled Blue Rain. It was just a couple of words and a few numbers. I think the numbers were map coordinates. I don't know what the words mean, but let's try 'em." He grabbed a pen from the desk and wrote the numbers and added the words "Khun Sa, Doi Sanh" on the paper. "See what you can find on these."

Susan read the paper and began typing. Johnny sat on the edge of the bed. It didn't take long. Less than five minutes later, Susan turned to him.

"You'd better look at this." Johnny stepped to the computer and looked over her shoulder. On the screen was a map of Southeast Asia from the northern tip of Australia to the southern edge of China. Susan maneuvered the arrow on the screen and clicked, and a moment later the juncture of Thailand, Laos and Burma filled the screen. She clicked again, paused a moment and clicked again.

"That's a hell of a map," Johnny said.

"It was developed after the Gulf War for the Department of Defense and then expanded for the DEA to use. The Center got a copy when we were hired to do a study on global oil routes. Something about finding alternate supply routes. I never did understand it."

She clicked again, stopped and tapped her finger against the screen. "Here. This is the exact spot Raby had written down. Looks like it's a small town or a village. It's called Doi Sanh."

"What the hell?"

"Wait, there's something more. There's a related file." Susan clicked on a small icon in the corner of the screen and the map disappeared, replaced by a page of type. She read it quickly.

"Looks like Doi Sanh is the headquarters of a warlord named Khun Sa who controls the opium trade in the Golden Triangle." She scrolled farther down the screen. "Looks like he's locked in a pretty fierce fight with some of the others. So far he hasn't been able to push 'em completely out of the area." She stopped and turned to look at Johnny.

"I'm beginning to get an idea about this," he said. "It's a very nasty idea, but it's the only thing that makes any sense. And I think I know how to prove it."

"How?"

"I've got to go back to the *Chronicle*. That's where the evidence is."

29

The press had started and the first delivery trucks were idling at the loading dock as the last of the papers were piled in the back. Johnny stood for a moment at the edge of the bay, his left shoulder rubbing the old red bricks of the building. He was close enough to reach out and touch the fender of the delivery truck and could smell the diesel fumes. He waited, and a moment later the truck's engine growled deeply and the truck glided slowly past him to the street. It stopped at the driveway's edge, and Johnny slipped behind it and into the loading dock and walked into the building.

He took the back stairway to the top floor, pushed the door open a crack and peered into the muted light of the deserted hallway. Johnny waited a second longer, studying the corridor's shadows, reassuring himself that he was alone. He crossed the thick carpet to the office door, pushed it open and moved quickly to Raby's office.

He found the file immediately and pulled it from the drawer. He opened it and moved to the window, holding the papers up to the weak light that came from the city through the window. He moved it closer to his face and leaned toward the glass. Still the light was too weak and he could not read it. He remembered TJ's warning. But he had no choice. He sat in Raby's seat, flipped the file open on the desk and turned on the lamp. Johnny began to read, forcing himself to go slowly and read thoroughly. He read everything, every scrap of paper, then started again and finally began to understand, to see the pattern.

It was the same pattern they'd seen in E&M's books. E&M was producing chemicals in bulk quantities and sending them to a firm called Cardinal Freight Forwarders. Cardinal got the shipments, logging them in the day they left E&M, and exported them a few days later. According to the customs documents, Cardinal was immediately exporting all the liquid fertilizer it bought from E&M. And it was all bound for Hanoi.

At some point, Johnny knew, the destination changed and the chemicals were rerouted to a village called Doi Sanh near the border of Burma and Laos. Johnny sorted the export documents into a separate pile, folded them and stuffed them into his hip pocket. He put the file back in the drawer, then stood and turned off the light. He walked slowly through the darkness to the edge of Raby's office. There he hesitated a moment, waiting for his eyes to adjust to the darkness in the outer office. As he moved toward the door, he sensed something, someone standing near. Before he could move, he felt the barrel of a gun jam against his left ear.

"Stop right there. You get cute and I'll kill you." Johnny recognized Duckworth's voice instantly.

The left side of his face was lit by a flashlight and Johnny turned away from it. Duckworth jabbed the gun barrel behind Johnny's ear.

"I said don't move." Duckworth's voice was calm, in control. "You know, Raby told me to watch for you, Rose. Said you might just try sneaking back in here. But I didn't believe it. Didn't think you'd be that stupid. Not after yesterday. I figured you'd be out of the country by now. In Mexico, or Canada, maybe. I guess the joke's on me." The edge of the gun barrel dug into his flesh. "Okay, now let's move back into the office. Slow. Move real slow."

Johnny turned in the darkness and moved back through the doorway into Raby's small office.

"Go sit down facing the window," Duckworth said.

Johnny sat in the chair and looked at the round tunnel of light from the flashlight for a moment. He knew Duckworth would shoot him without compunction. Claim he caught him burglarizing the offices. It would be justifiable homicide. Johnny slowly turned in the chair and faced out the window. Duckworth flipped on the lights and Johnny blinked for a few moments, then saw Duckworth's reflection in the glass. Johnny leaned back, put his feet on the edge of the credenza and watched in the window as Duckworth pulled a cellular phone from his hip pocket, flipped it open and dialed.

"It's me. Guess who I just caught coming out of your office." He paused for a moment. "Yeah, Johnny Rose. The man himself. Okay, fine, I'll hold him here," Duckworth said and flipped the phone closed.

"Look, you don't have to do this," Johnny said. "Don't let Raby do this to you. Don't let him make you into a mass murderer."

"You know, Rose, for such a smart guy, you don't know shit. I'd walk through hell without a canteen if that's what the colonel wanted. He's the best damned soldier I ever saw. He understands that you never abandon your men, never give up trying. So why don't you just shut the fuck up?"

"Tell me something, what exactly is worth all the killing?"

"I said shut up." Duckworth took a half-step toward him. Johnny started to speak but stopped, exhaled slowly and said nothing more.

Raby arrived less than thirty minutes later. He was dressed casually in khaki pants, a yellow polo shirt and loafers, but his bearing was still ramrod straight, military. Johnny watched his reflection in the window as he walked into the room. Raby stood looking at Johnny, ignoring Duckworth.

"Where was he?"

"Just came out of your office. Kelly said he saw a light on and I came up to check it out. I came in the outer office just as he switched the light off. I just waited for him to come to me."

"Okay." Raby looked at Duckworth for the first time then. "The Blazer's in the parking lot. Let's get him down there." He looked at Johnny, then motioned with his hand. "Come on, Rose, let's go."

Johnny dropped his feet from the credenza, stood and turned to look at Raby, who was watching him with a detached disinterest.

"Cuff him," Raby said. Duckworth spun Johnny around, pulled his arms behind his back and slipped handcuffs on. The metal was tight and the edge of the handcuffs dug into Johnny's flesh.

In the parking lot, they stopped about ten feet

from the Blazer. Duckworth stood just beyond reach, his gun dangling at his side.

"I'm going to get in the Blazer now, and then you," Raby said. "You can try running for it, but you won't get five feet." Johnny said nothing.

Raby got into the Blazer first but left his door open. He motioned to Johnny, who didn't move. "Get in," Duckworth said. Johnny looked over his shoulder at him. Duckworth had raised the gun and was pointing at him. Johnny moved to the vehicle and climbed backward into it. He started to topple toward Raby in the driver's seat but caught his balance and swung his legs in. As he twisted he glanced in the backseat and saw Raby's briefcase.

Raby pulled his door closed, but Johnny noticed he didn't strap himself in. Duckworth shoved the passenger door closed and stared at Johnny through the side window, still waiting, almost anxious for him to make a move.

Raby spoke then. "You're sitting there thinking about running, wondering where to make your break or thinking about all the ways you can take me out. Well, forget it." He reached across his body and pushed the central lock with his right hand. Johnny heard the *ching* as the car's front and rear doors locked simultaneously. Raby grinned at him. "Makes getting out just a little tougher, doesn't it?"

Johnny said nothing. Raby reached below the front seat of the Blazer with his left hand and pulled out a gun. He laid it in his lap so the handle rested against his left leg. He smiled and said there was something else Johnny should know. "I'm strong and fast. Make a move, any move at all, and I'll kill you where you sit."

In a swift motion, he swept the gun up and stuck

the barrel in Johnny's face. The move was practiced,
sure and so fast that the barrel was pressing against his
cheek before Johnny even realized that Raby had
moved.

"See my point?" he asked. Johnny just looked back
at him. Raby smiled, then put the gun back against his
leg.

Duckworth rolled the gate back and Raby started
the engine and drove out of the parking lot. He moved
the Blazer through traffic easily, his right hand on the
wheel, his left resting on his leg, his thumb inches from
the gun butt.

30

The city flowed past outside; the side streets and intersections, the gas stations and the oncoming traffic.
Johnny saw it all, his eyes picking up details that at
any other time would have slipped away unnoticed. He
saw a young Hispanic man in the harsh fluorescent
lights of a Chevron station. His jeans were patched at
the knees and his soiled baseball cap was pulled down
on his forehead. He was putting gas into an old, rusted
green Ford pickup, its bed piled high with flattened
cardboard. The man was staring into the night, and
fatigue filled his face. He saw the man, and in that
instant Johnny knew he was going to die within minutes.
Panic filled him, then disappeared as he denied the
reality of it.

Raby seemed to see none of the world outside the
Blazer. He drove casually but not recklessly. He maneuvered the Blazer through the streets and traffic with

ease, his right hand on the wheel, his left always resting on the butt of the gun.

They rolled to a stop behind a long white limousine, its windows tinted black. They were so common on L.A.'s streets that you could pick out the tourists by who turned to look when they rolled by. As he looked at the limo, Johnny felt the tension ease and slip away. The fear was replaced by a brittle calm, as though none of it were real, none of it were happening.

His hands were going numb and his shoulders had begun to ache. Still he managed to turn and look at Raby. "How many men did you rescue? How many did you bring home?"

Raby's eyes flicked from the road ahead to Johnny and then back again. Was he debating, wondering how much to say? If he were, he decided quickly.

"Eight."

"How'd you find them?"

"I never stopped looking. If you look long enough and hard enough and are willing to pay a high enough price, you'll find what you want. You can buy anything if the price is right."

"The right price," Johnny said and nodded his head slowly. "That's the Blue Rain, isn't it? You're trading Blue Rain for POWs. That's it, isn't it?"

Johnny saw Raby's left hand slip onto the gun butt, then release it again. The light changed and the limo pulled forward. Raby kept his foot on the brake and the Blazer sat idling. Raby turned to look at Johnny fully, but he said nothing.

"But why Blue Rain? Why not just guns or money?"

"Money? They've already got more money than God and they can get all the guns they want. I had to offer them something they didn't have and couldn't get anywhere else."

They rode in silence for a moment and Raby, his eyes still on the road, asked a simple question. "How?"

"It wasn't hard. After I got the phone number from Nikki Masterson, I traced it to the hotel. Found out who owned it. Called some people who knew E&M. People who knew what they really did. I put two and two together. It was simple, really. I already knew about the POWs. Pham Lich told me."

Raby smiled, a tight grin that showed no mirth. "You should have taken the job with Geld. He could use someone like you." The voice was even but hinted at disgust. But disgust with whom? Him? Geld?

Johnny twisted uncomfortably on the seat, trying to ease the pain in his shoulders and hands. He sat straight but turned his head to look at Raby.

"No. I'm not like you, Raby. I could never work for Geld. I could never let him use me, not like you did."

Then Raby did something that surprised Johnny. He laughed. It was genuine laughter and Johnny looked at him, suddenly unsure, off-balance.

"Is that what you think?" Raby turned back to the road and the Blazer rolled forward.

"Yeah, that's what I think. I think you're going to make Geld a hero. Shit, he could ride this all the way to the White House. What do you get out of it? Money, power? An ambassadorship? Maybe some place nice like Switzerland?"

"I don't give a shit about Geld and his goddamned election."

"Bullshit. Why else would you do all this?"

"Because I'm a soldier."

"What kind of a soldier murders innocent people?"

"Everyone who died died for a reason. To protect the mission."

"Mission! What mission? The men are already here. The mission's over Raby."

"No, no, it's not." His voice was suddenly tight, intense. "There may be more."

"More what?" Raby was silent, his eyes on the road, and Johnny looked at his face reflected in the windshield and suddenly he understood it all. "More POWs?"

Raby said nothing and Johnny whispered under his breath, "Jesus."

Raby looked at him and Johnny saw a flash of hate. "If the word gets out, they'll never get home. They'll die over there. It's as good as signing their death warrant."

"Bullshit," Johnny said. "We can rescue them. We can put pressure on the governments in Hanoi or Burma to release 'em."

"Jesus, you really are ignorant, aren't you? I'm not dealing with governments. I'm dealing with Khun Sa, the man who controls the area. He's the only one who knows where the men are. Once the word gets out, he'll move 'em, hide 'em back in the jungle, and no one will ever find 'em. He'll keep 'em until he gets what he wants for them. But no government will give him chemical weapons. They'd never do that, so the men will just die over there. Most have a year, maybe two, at the most. Old age isn't much of a problem in the jungle. Strong men die young."

He paused for a second, then spoke again. "Governments?" He snorted. "The governments can't even stop the fucking opium trade, how the hell they going to find a few men in that jungle? No. Blue Rain is the only chance any of them ever getting out, of ever coming home."

"My God, that's why you killed everybody? That's why you murdered Pham and Sandy Ruiz? Just so no one will know the POWs are home?"

Raby looked at him, holding his gaze for a moment, and in his eyes Johnny could see the truth of what he'd just said.

"You can't keep a lid on something like this. Geld won't keep it quiet. Hell, he'll tell the world himself. He'll sell you and everyone else out if it'll help him win the election. You turn your back for a moment, and he'll tell the world what a big hero he is. He lives for the big moment. He 'gets things done,' remember? You don't really think he gives a shit about the men still over there, do you? Not if it means getting elected, he doesn't."

For the second time within minutes, Raby's laugh caught Johnny by surprise. He shook his head from side to side and said, "God, you're pitiful. This had nothing to do with trust. I don't have to trust Geld. I have the documents. I've got copies and backups he'll never find. I have him by the balls. He's scared shitless that someone will find out he traded Blue Rain to the world's opium king. The word gets out that he's trading chemical weapons to a warlord for human lives and his career is finished. He might even go to prison, who knows?"

"Then why'd he do it?"

"Oh, he planned to use 'em to win the election all right. That's why he ran, because I told him I could bring the POWs home. We figured we could lie about how we paid for 'em and who we paid. But then I found out there might be others. He wanted to announce it anyway, but

I'm forcing him to keep it quiet. He brags about it, I expose him. You see, you got it all backwards, Rose. I have the power. Not him."

Raby said nothing more, and a few moments later turned onto Lincoln Boulevard and headed north. A mile beyond the Santa Monica Pier Raby pulled a U-turn and parked the Blazer at the west curb. "We're here."

Johnny looked out the window at the narrow span of grass leading to the cliffs above the Pacific Coast Highway and the Santa Monica beach: Palisades Park.

Raby grabbed the gun with his right hand and pushed open the door with his left. He started to slip out but stopped and turned to look back at Johnny.

"You know, I'm sorry they all had to die. I really am, but there was no choice. I'm going to bring the men home. All of them. No one's going to stop me."

"What about my brother?"

"I'm sorry he tried to kill himself. I didn't want that to happen. But I guess my visit pushed him over the edge and sometimes you have to sacrifice the few—"

"You're sick, Raby."

"No. I'm just a soldier with a mission."

Johnny watched Raby silently as he stepped out of the Blazer and stood on the asphalt looking back through the open door at him.

"I'm going to cross in front of the Blazer. When I'm on the other side, I'll signal you to get out. If you think you can get the door open and make a run for it while I'm moving, go ahead and try. But don't think for a moment that I won't kill you right here."

He watched Johnny for a moment and finally nodded slowly, then shoved the door closed. A second later he was at the hood, the gun in his hand dangling at his side, staring through the windshield at Johnny. "Okay," he yelled.

Johnny exhaled deeply, feeling the panic grow, the desperation crowd in. There was no denying it now. In a few minutes Raby would kill him. He sat unmoving and stared out the window, his mind blank, a desperate form of denial gripping him.

"Let's go," Raby shouted. The voice seemed to startle him awake. Johnny turned his back to the door and fumbled for the handle. He found it and pulled. The door opened and he swung back around and kicked it. He slipped out of the car, scraping his arms along the seat's edge, and stood on the grass next to the Blazer.

"Turn around," Raby said. A moment later Johnny felt the gun barrel at the base of his skull as Raby unlocked the handcuffs. They fell to the grass without a sound. Johnny rubbed his wrists and flexed his fingers, trying to restore feeling. He hugged his arms across his chest, easing the pain in his shoulders.

"Go on, walk over toward the railing," Raby said. He motioned to the cement railing that separated the long narrow park from the unstable bluffs and Pacific Coast Highway below. Every year the winds and rain eroded more of the cliffs. At some point, the park itself would disappear.

Johnny looked at him for a moment. He held the gun in front of his leg. Johnny figured it would take a second, maybe less, for Raby to raise the gun and fire. A second. A lifetime, and not close to long enough.

Johnny turned and moved toward the railing. He scanned the park as he walked, searching for help, praying for a miracle. But he saw no one, nothing that could help. He glanced over his shoulder at Ocean

Avenue, hoping for a patrol car, but the street was empty.

He turned and walked on toward the railing above the cliffs. His feet moved off the grass and across the dirt, each step bringing him closer to the bullet that would end his life. He thought of Susan for a moment and wanted to ask Raby if Kyle Loveless was one of those he'd brought home. But the question would just tell Raby about Susan and endanger her life. Raby would kill anyone he considered a threat. Johnny forced himself to concentrate on the moment, to find something, some edge he might use to save himself. He crossed the jogging trail worn through the grass and stepped onto the stretch of grass separating him from the railing and cliffs.

"Stop right there."

Johnny was inches from the cement railing. In the distance he could see the ocean, inky black in the night. He could feel the breeze and thought of how much cooler it was here than downtown or in the Valley. In the far distance he could see the pier, the colored lights of the Ferris wheel twinkling like a far-off promise of Christmas. His eyes went to the highway below. Traffic was light and the cars were moving, flying past. Headlights sparkling for a second, then gone.

Johnny guessed what Raby was going to do. They'd find the steps farther south and descend, cross the pedestrian bridge and walk to the middle of the beach. That's where he'd kill him. Probably a single shot in the back of the head. It would be hours before the body was discovered.

Johnny already could feel the sand pulling at his feet as they crossed the beach, could feel it under his knees as he knelt and Raby held the gun inches from his skull.

"Now step over the fence and move to the edge of the bluff," Raby said.

"What?" Johnny whirled and looked back at him. He had the gun up now, leveled at Johnny's chest. Johnny glanced over his shoulder past the railing. The cliff jutted out to a point, forming a triangle perhaps ten feet beyond the railing. A tree, its roots and low branches exposed, clung to the cliffs on the base of the triangle.

"Do it," Raby barked. And Johnny understood. He wasn't going to be shot, murdered. He was going to fall just as all the Viet Cong had fallen from the helicopter. Only this time, it was in L.A. and this time it would be ruled an accident. And there was no question that the plunge to the highway would kill him. The cliffs were too high.

"I said climb over the railing." The words were barely above a whisper.

Johnny stepped over the cement railing. He moved slowly, shuffling his feet, his back to the killer, his eyes fixed on the ocean, the waves curling and smacking into the beach, the foam gleaming white in the darkness. He smelled the salt air, and goose bumps rose on his arms.

Raby climbed over the rail.

"Move forward," he said, louder now.

Johnny turned, his back to the ocean, and looked at Raby. He looked relaxed, casual. Just another job almost done.

"I said back up."

Johnny inched backward. His heel hit a tree root and he froze. He could hear the cars on the highway below, the noise of their tires rising through the night.

The sides of the cliffs fell away almost straight down to his right and left. He was standing near the pinnacle of the triangle. The only solid ground was straight ahead where Raby stood with a gun.

"If I go over, it's all going to come out. Cardinal Freight Forwarders becomes public knowledge. Probably raise a lot of questions."

"Cut the shit and back up."

"I got the invoices out of your office," Johnny insisted.

"What invoices?"

"From E&M to Cardinal. It ties it all back to you and Geld. The cops are going to want to talk to you."

"You're lying."

"No. It's true. All those tanker cars full of chemicals going to Hanoi. Someone's gonna start asking a lot of questions. Could blow the whole operation. Think about it, Raby. Word might even leak out about Blue Rain, how it's only good for thirty days. What's that warlord going to say when he finds out he's bought damaged goods? You'll never get the rest of the men out then."

Raby nodded slightly, then raised the gun again. "Okay, where are the invoices?"

"I tell you what. You let me go, I'll let you have 'em."

"No deal."

"Okay, but I go over the cliff, you won't find 'em in time. The shit will hit the fan. Now's the time to deal, Raby."

"Right. And I'll tell you what the deal is. You tell me where the invoices are and I let you die fast. You don't and I'll hurt you. You're dead either way. One way you'll give 'em up after a lot of pain. The other way is fast and quick. Now tell me where they are," Raby said.

Johnny waited, letting the silence between them stretch. "In my back pocket," he said and slowly reached into his jeans and withdrew the papers. He held the packet of folded paper in his fingertips, his arm dangling at his side.

Raby inched forward, his arm outstretched. He snapped his fingers. "Give 'em to me."

Johnny stepped back. His heels were on the edge of the bluff now. He could retreat no farther. He stared at Raby, afraid to look down. He heard the skittering sound of small stones bouncing off the cliff below his feet. The dirt under his heels felt soft and unsteady. It wouldn't hold his weight for long.

Raby's eyes were fixed on Johnny's hand. "Give them to me now." He leaned forward, stretching his left hand out, motioning with his fingers for Johnny to hand the packet over.

"Here!" Johnny flicked the papers in the air. The breeze caught them and they scattered like huge snowflakes, fluttering in different directions.

Raby's eyes were on the thin sheets of paper, which seemed suspended in the air. He leaned and grabbed for them. His weight shifted toward Johnny and his foot hit the root. He stumbled.

Johnny ducked and moved forward, slipping under Raby's outstretched arm. Suddenly Raby's momentum was against him and he spun. Johnny stood up and looked back at Raby, who teetered on the edge of the cliff. Raby's gun hand and free arm were flailing as he fought for balance.

"Help," he barked. Raby's left hand grasped air. He balanced for a moment on the cliff's edge, his arms pinwheeling backward as he fought desperately for control. Johnny stepped forward and grabbed a fistful of Raby's shirt, and for an moment their eyes locked and Johnny saw the total panic in Raby's eyes. He reached for Raby's outstretched, pinwheeling hand and bumped it as the edge of the cliff gave way. An instant later Raby tumbled over the side, jerking free of Johnny's grasp. Johnny made a desperate lunge for his hand but missed. He caught himself on the edge and watched as Raby hit the side of the bluff once and fell straight to the roadway below.

Instantly a big Mercedes was on him. Johnny heard it all as one noise; the *thud* as Raby hit the road, the rapid *thump, thump* as the front and rear tires smashed the body. Then came the squeal of brakes as the driver tried to stop. Johnny stood on the bluff for a second longer, staring at the red brake lights below, feeling Raby's shirt jerk loose from his grip. He turned and walked back across the narrow park to Ocean Avenue.

31

Johnny climbed back over the concrete railing and walked across the grass, the jogging trail and the sidewalk to the street. He moved slowly, numbly, unaware of time or place. He stepped onto the blacktop and looked south along Ocean Avenue. In the distance a car cruised silently away from him, its taillights barely visible red dots, then turned east, moving like a shadow, and was gone, leaving the street empty again. He turned and looked north at the narrow park, the palm trees tall, half-ghosts in the light that spilled into the park from the streetlights. The air was cool, but he felt flushed, clammy from the moments before on the cliffs. He exhaled deeply, lowered himself to the curb and, head down, stared between his knees at the gutter seeing nothing in the gray concrete, but Raby's expression the moment before the cliff gave way and he fell backward from the bluffs, his arms pinwheeling in the night.

Johnny felt an odd mix of emotion. He was elated, almost giddy, because he was alive, but the excitement felt distant, like faraway thunder, tempered by the knowledge that he'd been unable to save Raby. He heard sirens then, their sounds carrying far in the still night, and he lifted his head. There were two. An ambulance and a police car, Johnny guessed. He sat listening as the insistent wail grew louder and louder. The noise seemed to last forever, then stopped abruptly, and Johnny knew they were on Pacific Coast Highway just behind where he sat. The cops were probably standing on the shoulder looking at the bluffs, shining their flashlights up to the edge, figuring Raby was some tourist who got too close and slipped. How much time until they ID'd Raby and knew he wasn't just an out-of-towner trying for a better view or some poor drunk slob who felt like dancing along the cliffs' edge?

Johnny inhaled deeply again, sucking the cool night air deep into his lungs. He held his breath for a moment, then exhaled and stood up. His pulse was steadier now, his hands not so moist. It wouldn't be long before the uniforms came and started looking through the park for reasons why Raby had climbed over the concrete railing and approached the edge. Johnny turned and looked toward the cliffs. He thought of the papers he'd thrown in the air, saw them again as they scattered in the ocean breeze. The cops might find one or two of the papers, but would they connect them to Raby? Probably, and if they did, so what?

But Johnny was still a suspect in Pham's death. He couldn't wait for the police. He had no evidence, nothing to back up his story. He moved to the Blazer and picked the handcuffs off the grass, where they had landed when Raby uncuffed him. He got in the vehicle and looked around. He saw Raby's briefcase on the backseat. He reached into the rear and pulled it between the seats to his lap and opened it: a batch of papers held together with a paper clip, a small daily planner, two pens, Raby's passport, a thin cellular phone, a book of stamps, a yellow legal pad, a check-book and a small address book. Johnny flipped through the papers but found only references to the Geld cam-paign, nothing about E&M or Cardinal Freight For-warders or the Royal Hotel.

He started to close the briefcase but stopped, remembering Raby's words. Remembering how he'd described his hold on Geld. He alone knew about the chemical weapons sales to Vietnam, and it gave him the power to bury the rich and powerful Mr. Gordon Geld if he needed to. Johnny set the briefcase back in his lap. An idea played at the edges of his mind, form-ing and mutating and finally taking shape. He looked through the windshield at a traffic light down Ocean Avenue. He watched it turn green, amber, red and green again. He drummed his fingers on the steering wheel as the color cycle ran again. Johnny's mind played with the idea; a way to cry checkmate at Geld and save his own life. His fingers were still for a moment as he decided.

He found Geld's number in Raby's address book and took the phone from the briefcase. Johnny looked at the Blazer's clock. It was after three in the morning. He dialed and Geld answered himself, his words thick with sleep. "This is Gordon Geld."

"Raby's dead, Geld."

"What? What did you say?"

"You heard me, Geld's dead. Splattered all over Pacific Coast Highway."

"Who is this?"

"It's Johnny Rose."

"Rose, if this is your idea of a joke—"

"This is no joke. Raby just fell off the cliffs at Palisades Park. He hit PCH on one bounce."

Johnny waited and smiled, feeling the power his own words gave him and seeing Geld in his mind's eye. He was awake now. Probably sitting on the edge of his bed trying to figure what it all meant. Wondering if Johnny was lying and deciding instantly he wasn't and just as quickly wondering how dangerous Johnny Rose had become.

"I'm sorry to hear that. He was a good friend and a loyal employee."

"Good friend? Loyal employee? Save that bullshit for the news conference, Geld. I've got some real news for you. I know all about E&M and the Blue Rain you're sending to that Khun Sa."

"I don't know what you're talking about."

"Let's cut the crap, okay? I saw the shipping documents in Raby's files. I've already seen the records at E&M. I've got it all now. Every bit of it, and I've got you by the fucking balls. So listen up. Your secret just became my life insurance policy. Anything happens to me, the information gets made public in a hurry. You got that? So you better hope I stay real healthy. Because if I don't, you end up in jail, and it's going to be tough to run your campaign from behind bars."

Geld said nothing for a moment. Johnny could hear him breathing, a shallow steady inhale and exhale. *Yeah, take all the time you want,* Johnny thought. *All the time you need.*

"You call me up in the middle of the night and threaten me with this? I feel sorry for you, Rose. Maybe you should see a doctor."

"I got the documents. Check Raby's files."

"I never denied that I sold fertilizer to Vietnam. So what? I had the export licenses to do it. It was all legal. I never tried to hide anything. If something happened to it after it arrived over there, I don't know anything about it."

"Bullshit. It was Blue Rain and I can prove it."

Geld laughed dryly. "Rose, I don't know what you think you saw, but anyone who wants to can check E&M's records. There are absolutely no records of our making anything like this stuff you call Blue Rain, whatever that is. And anyone who wants can check Mr. Raby's office. Bring in a team of accountants and go through his files. I have nothing to hide.

"But then, who's going to listen to you anyway? Who's going to put any merit in the words of a disgruntled employee who was fired for insubordination? Who's going to believe you, Johnny?"

Johnny's gaze shifted toward the cliffs and the ocean that stretched like a black slate to the horizon, where it melted into the dark sky. Far out he saw a light blink, probably a freighter on its way to the far side of the world. He looked at the bushes along the cliffs and thought of Raby's papers scattering in the breeze.

"I've got all the evidence I need," Johnny tried again.

"You don't have anything." Geld's tone was suddenly fierce, determined. "Now you listen to me. As soon as I hang up, I'm calling the police and reporting this threatening phone call. I'm sure they'll find this very interesting."

"The cops don't scare me," Johnny said. "But you should be scared shitless, Geld. You're the one whose hired hand was a killer."

"You know, Rose, you sound desperate. You need

help. Like I said, I think you should see a doctor." And the line was dead.

Johnny held the phone to his ear for a moment longer, not sure at first that Geld had hung up. He closed the phone and dropped it into the briefcase.

He called a taxi from a pay phone a few blocks away and gave the driver directions to his own car a block from the *Chronicle*. As the cab snaked through the city toward the newspaper, Johnny thought about Geld. He'd probably already ordered Raby's office sanitized and the records at E&M altered. Duckworth would have it clean enough for a general's inspection within hours. By the next morning there would be no records of anything except fertilizer shipments to Vietnam. No records of Blue Rain or chemical warfare agents or warlords named Khun Sa. Johnny knew there would be nothing and he knew that in his eagerness he'd played his hand too quickly and it had turned against him. Geld would call the cops and they'd want to know how Johnny knew so quickly about Raby's death.

He paid the cabbie and got in the Z, but hesitated before starting it. He wanted to go to Susan's. Drive directly there, make love to her, sleep with his arms around her and forget Raby's fall from the cliffs. Forget Raby and Geld. Just forget all of it. But he couldn't forget any of it. He couldn't forget the police, who would want to haul him in for questioning. And he couldn't forget Geld. Would he turn Raby's men loose to find him? There might be even more people looking for him now. He couldn't track that kind of mud into Susan's house. She'd already risked too much for too little return. As Johnny started the car he knew that from then on, whatever he did, he'd do it alone.

32

Johnny could think of nowhere to go and so, tired and alone, he returned to the motel in Culver City. He left the car idling in the driveway in front of the office when he went in. The same young man was working the counter. He stood as Johnny entered. If he was surprised to see him again or taken aback that Johnny was seeking a room at an hour so close to dawn, he gave no sign of it.

He waited until Johnny was next to the counter, then said, "Just for tonight?" Johnny nodded. "Would you like the same room?"

"Sure, that'd be fine."

Three minutes later Johnny walked into the room and fell onto the bed. He lay looking at the ceiling and thought of Susan and knew he should call her and tell her he was okay. He rolled to his side and reached for the phone.

But as his fingers touched the receiver, he waited. He wouldn't hesitate to tell her what he had found in Raby's office or about the struggle on the cliff. He'd tell her everything. Or would he? Would he really tell her that he knew positively that the men in the Royal Hotel were POWs? What would she say? Would she want to rush there and search for Kyle? Johnny exhaled deeply and rolled onto his back. He lay still, trying to understand the woman he was in love with and understanding only that he didn't really know her at all. Was her husband even alive? Was he one of the men in the Royal, or had Pham been mistaken? He squeezed his eyes shut, trying to see Susan, to hear her voice and listen to the words she would say.

He awoke almost six hours later to a roar as a car with a worn muffler and tailpipe started in the parking lot near his window. Johnny sat up in terror, the sound of the engine loud in his ears. For a moment he didn't know where he was or what had happened to deliver him to his strange surroundings. Light flooded through the frayed curtains and Johnny squinted against the brightness, his eyes sore. It came to him quickly then, Raby's flailing arms, the ambulance's siren and Geld's cold self-assurance. He rolled to the side of the bed and waited as a moment of nausea passed and then grabbed the phone and called Susan.

"Oh, Johnny, thank God. I've been really worried. Raby's death is all over the news. Johnny, what happened?"

"He tried to force me off the cliffs, but he fell. I tried to grab him, but I couldn't hold him."

"Are you all right?"

"I'm okay." But even he could hear the confusion in his voice.

"Johnny?"

"Really, I'm all right. Look, I want to see you."

"Of course, I want to see you, too. But, Johnny, what happened?"

"I'll explain it all when we're together."

"Where are you? Can you come to the house?"

"No. It might be too dangerous. I don't want to get you any more involved in this."

"Johnny, I'm already involved."

"But Geld doesn't know that. They don't even know you exist. I want to keep it that way, okay?"

"Don't play hero with me." Her voice rose in anger. "I knew what I was doing when I first helped you and I know now. So don't tell me not to worry my pretty little head about this, Johnny."

"Look, maybe I didn't say exactly what I meant. But you're the only friend I've got. The only one I can turn to for help. I can't take the chance of leading them to you. I just can't."

She was silent for a moment, then said, "All right, just tell me where to come."

Where? He hadn't thought of that. Where? Johnny rubbed his face and raised his eyes to the curtain only inches away. He blinked at the brightness and lowered his gaze to the floor. He thought of several places. The Westside Pavilion shopping center. It was nearby and always crowded, but it was inside. They could go to Westwood Village or the Santa Monica Pier. Both would be full of people today. But Johnny hesitated. He didn't want a crowd. This might be his last afternoon with Susan. He couldn't waste those hours with her wandering in a shopping mall or bumping into kids carrying cotton candy on the pier. He wanted them to be alone.

"Do you know the Malibu Lagoon?"

"Of course. It's out on PCH."

"How about noon? I'll meet you in the parking lot."

"Okay."

Johnny showered and dressed again in his dirty clothes. Just before he left the bathroom he looked at himself in the mirror. His eyes were swollen, the skin under them dark. His unshaven face looked thin and worn. He looked old and tired. Johnny stood looking for a moment and understood, without knowing why or how he knew, that the end, whatever it was, was fast approaching.

Johnny walked from the small parking lot across the well-kept lawn to the large signboards covered with drawings and short descriptions of the birds you could see in the marsh. He was early and read the words idly, not concentrating and not remembering one sentence as he read the next.

At noon the sun overhead was hot on his arms and neck. Three women relaxed on blankets on the low grassy knolls separating the parking lot from the edge of the lagoon as their small children chased each other, giggling, up and down the slopes. Johnny sat on a concrete bench and waited, glancing at the parking lot every few seconds.

Susan arrived a few minutes later. He watched her car turn into the lot and felt his heart accelerate and his stomach muscles tighten. He stood and waited, pretending a casualness he didn't feel as she got out of the car. She wore baggy white shorts, sandals and a yellow blouse and her hair was loose on her shoulders, and he thought she was the most beautiful woman he had ever seen. She saw him, smiled and waved. As she came close, Johnny walked to her, put his arms around her and pulled her tight against his body.

He felt the warmth of the sun on her and smelled fresh perfume and a hint of soap and wanted to stand holding her forever. Finally he pulled back just far enough to kiss her.

"God, it's good to see you," he said.

"I was afraid I'd never see you again."

"Oh, you don't get off that easy," Johnny joked, but the humor felt strained.

"Come on, let's walk," he said. "I want to tell you about what happened."

They followed a raised dirt path through the lagoon and stopped on a wooden bridge. In the distance Johnny could see the seagulls and pelicans, brown and white against the bright blue sky, soaring and drifting on the sea breeze, then landing on the sand to stand statue-still, as though nothing had changed in the neighborhood for the last thousand years. He bent at the waist and leaned forward, resting his forearms on the railing of the bridge. He looked down into the clear water and saw a Dr Pepper can half-buried in the black silt of the lagoon. The Chumash Indians had lived in the area for hundreds, maybe thousands of years before the first white men arrived in the 1500s. But the Chumash were extinct now, pushed into oblivion by Manifest Destiny, progress and Dr Pepper. He grunted, thinking that the aluminum can probably would be buried by the mud and outlast them all.

Susan leaned back, her shoulder near Johnny's face, and waited for him to begin. Finally Johnny shifted his eyes from the aluminum can to the marsh and said, "Raby was pointing a gun at me. He wanted to force me off the cliffs. But as he moved toward me, he tripped and lost his balance. The cliff gave way and he went off."

"Jesus."

"Yeah."

Susan was silent for a moment and Johnny turned and leaned back against the railing.

"Why'd he want to kill you? I don't understand that."

"Because of what I found in his office. I saw some invoices that proved he was selling Blue Rain to that Khun Sa. It was all there. It was the final link from E&M Enterprises."

"You mean they were peddling chemical weapons to the opium dealers?"

"Yeah," Johnny said. He pushed away from the rail, looked at Susan for a moment and felt a sudden jolt of desire and dread. "There's more to it than that, though. Come on, let's walk and I'll tell you the whole story."

They followed the path to the sand and Johnny pulled off his shoes, rolled his pants to his knees, tied his shoes together and hung them over his shoulder. Susan pulled off her sandals and carried them in her right hand as they worked their way through the thick, hot sand to the ocean's edge. They walked slowly along the surf, pausing occasionally to watch the surfers ride the slow easy rollers to shore, and Johnny told Susan about searching Raby's office and finding the documents and his phone call to Geld. But he still didn't tell her about the men. Not at first. Not until she knew everything else. Then, when there was no longer a way to avoid it, Johnny stopped and looked out into the ocean, keeping his eyes away from Susan, not able to look at her.

"It's not just the Blue Rain that Raby was protecting. I don't think he really cared if someone eventually found out. It's what he was doing with it." He was quiet then and could sense Susan looking at him, waiting for him to go on.

"Yes?" she finally said.

"He was using it as ransom. For POWs. Americans left behind over there."

The time seemed to stretch into infinity as Susan stood quietly at his side, matching his gaze on the horizon, saying nothing. Then she hooked her arm through his and leaned against him.

"Kyle's dead, Johnny. I know he is."

"But Pham—"

"Pham was mistaken. That's all there is to it. Look, if Kyle were here, he wouldn't stay in a dump downtown. He'd contact me."

"Oh God, I hope . . ." But he didn't finish. He turned to Susan. How do you tell a woman you hope her husband's dead? He started to speak again, but she held her finger against his lips and smiled.

"Don't say anything," she said. She slipped her arm around his waist and turned back toward the lagoon. They walked in silence across the sand for nearly a hundred yards. Then, without breaking stride, Susan asked, "What are you going to do?"

"I don't know."

She stopped and watched him for a moment, her eyes a clear window into a heart brimming with passion and love.

Johnny avoided her eyes, letting his gaze fall to the sand, focusing on his rolled-up trouser legs, seeing the ring of wetness where a wave had rushed ashore and caught him off-guard. He saw the blonde, almost white hair on her golden red arm and listened to the gulls calling and a radio on a nearby beach blanket. She pulled him close then and they clung to each other until Johnny bent and kissed her. Finally, he broke their embrace and smiled.

"Come on, let's go," he said.

"Where?"

"There's a nice hotel in Santa Monica. I think we should go have some fun and let the world go to hell."

Susan smiled. "Your car or mine?"

"Mine. It's faster."

The shrieks of children playing in the courtyard pool drifted behind them as they walked down the hall to their room. Johnny had seen the kids with their water wings, flippers and inflatable toys splashing and running while their parents sat on deck loungers. The noise ended abruptly as the door closed and thoughts of the world beyond the room disappeared.

Susan was one step ahead of him, and she turned at the sound of the door closing and moved into his arms. She put her hand on the back of his head as he pulled her close to him. She smelled of sunshine and salt air and Johnny felt himself tumbling, falling away from the world, disappearing into Susan's arms as they kissed. Suddenly there was no other world beyond the hotel room and Susan's embrace.

They shuffled across the floor and down the short hall into the room, their mouths together. Then Susan broke away, looked at Johnny, laughed and jumped onto the king-size bed. Johnny stood at the end of the bed and pulled off his shoes, not bothering to untie them, hopping first on one foot, then the other as he ripped them from his feet. As the second shoe came off he lost his balance and fell onto the bed next to Susan, making it shiver with his weight.

"Well, that was graceful," she teased.

"I was hoping you would be so caught up in the passion that you wouldn't notice."

"I am passionate, but I'm not blind."

Johnny smiled. "No? Well, close your eyes and pretend," he said and rolled on his side to face her.

She was quiet and Johnny touched her cheek and stared into her eyes, saying everything he wanted to tell her about his love for her without uttering a word. He leaned forward very slowly and kissed her. They made love slowly, longingly, as if they were lovers of generations reunited after a long separation. Afterward they lay snuggled together, the curves of their bodies melding, their fingers interlaced. Susan leaned into him and kissed him on his temple.

"What will you do now?" she asked.

He had tried not to think of it. Indeed, he had avoided any thought of anything beyond the moment until then. He looked over her shoulder, seeing the thick curtains, pulled tightly across the window, and the cabinet against the wall at the end of the bed, its dark wooden doors covering the television.

"I don't know." His voice was soft, tired. He stroked the side of her head gently with his fingertips. "I suppose my fingerprints are all over the inside of Raby's Blazer. I could explain that away if I had to, but the cops probably won't run prints on it anyway. Still, there's always, well . . ." His words faded into silence.

"What?"

"There's a chance that Geld still thinks I'm a threat. I doubt it. I mean, like he said on the phone, I've got nothing. There's no way I can hurt him. Not now. Not with Raby dead. He was the only one who could really hurt him."

"And so?"

"I'm thinking of leaving L.A. for a while. Maybe a few months. Maybe a little longer. Just until this whole thing blows over. After the election, Geld isn't going to give a rat's ass about me."

"Johnny, I don't see you as someone who runs."

"No, I don't like to think of myself like that, either. But I'm pretty much fresh out of options. I tried to bluff Geld last night, but he wouldn't move. So if I stay in L.A., I might be asking to get myself killed."

"Where will you go?"

"I don't know, but I'll let you know when I get there."

She laid her head on his chest and Johnny draped his arm across her shoulders. They snuggled together and held each other, and Johnny drifted off to sleep. He awoke more than an hour later and was alone in the bed. He sat up and looked quickly from side to side, suddenly seized by a fear that Susan had abandoned him. Then he heard the shower running and fell back to the bed. A few moments later the water stopped and Susan came out of the bath in a white terrycloth robe, her wet hair falling limp down her back.

"Ah, look who's awake."

"I guess you exhausted me," Johnny said.

"Yeah, right."

"I think I'll take a shower, too." Johnny rolled from the bed and walked into the bathroom. The mirrors were steamed and the floor damp. But the water was already hot and he stuck his head under the strong, pulsating stream and stood for a moment, then stepped back, fully awake. He'd just reached for the soap when he heard Susan.

"Johnny, Johnny, come here. Come here and see this."

He hurried into the room and stood, his hair dripping down his chest and back, a towel around his waist, looking at the television. Susan sat on the edge of the bed, staring at it. A middle-aged man with hair neatly swept back over the tops of his ears smiled at the camera and talked about a major announcement expected from the Geld campaign tomorrow.

"Candidate Geld, whose top campaign aide fell to his death from Palisades Park onto the Pacific Coast Highway last night, is promising a major announcement at a nine o'clock press conference tomorrow morning. Our political reporter, Letty Donohue, is at Geld headquarters now. Letty, what can you tell us about this surprise major announcement?"

The camera switched to a young blonde woman standing on a sidewalk in front of a store, the huge windows covered with Geld posters. In the background, through the glass, Johnny could see people hustling about the busywork of electing a governor.

"Well, Bill," the blonde said. "No one here is saying much, except we should expect some exciting news. At first the thought was that Geld's announcement would be connected with the death of his top campaign aide, Charles Raby, but apparently that's not the case. One campaign staffer told me that Geld held a meeting by phone with the entire election staff today. He said he was saddened by Raby's death, but promised a major announcement tomorrow. He wouldn't say what it concerns, but did say it will prove his campaign slogan isn't just empty rhetoric."

"Yes," chimed in the anchorman, "I think by now we all know what that slogan is, don't we, Letty?"

"Yes, the staffer I spoke with promised Geld's announcement would prove he's a man who"—she paused for a split second—"'gets things done.' And that may be very important." She paused for dramatic effect. "Sources close to Mr. Geld tell me that in the last two weeks Geld's campaign has been losing ground. His internal polling shows his campaign slipping slightly. One political analyst who does consulting for the campaign said he now believes Geld's campaign may have reached its peak with Mayor Apodaca's endorsement. That's why there's so much speculation surrounding this announcement. It appears this may be Geld's last chance to regain some of the momentum he's apparently lost. It could be the decisive moment of the campaign for Gordon Geld."

Johnny reached over and turned the volume low. He turned to Susan. "The son of a bitch is going to tell the world about the men he's brought home. "

"He wouldn't. Raby said there were others. He said they'd die over there."

"They probably will. But Geld doesn't care. And I made it all possible."

"No, you didn't. You didn't have anything to do with all this."

"If I'd been able to save Raby, none of this would be happening. He was the only thing keeping Geld in check. Now he's dead, and Geld can do whatever he wants."

Johnny slowly lowered himself onto the end of the bed next to Susan but kept his eyes on the television. She reached across and put her hand on his knee.

"Johnny, you can't blame yourself. He was going to kill you."

"If there are any men left over there, they'll never

get home. They're going to die and it's my fault. I've got to do something."

"But the press conference is tomorrow morning."

He looked at her and smiled. "You know, there just might be a way."

33

Johnny drove past the Royal Hotel about three the
next morning. He slowed the car and looked closely
at a man in ragged clothes standing in front of the
hotel. A small open fire burned on the sidewalk at the
man's feet. He held his hands toward the flame, palms
down. Johnny could see little in the half-light that
spread from the fire across the man's front and flickered
on his dark face. His jeans were fastened with a thick
metal buckle and he wore a heavy coat, too heavy for
the warm weather. The flames glinted off something
shiny at the man's waist. But Johnny didn't slow for a
closer look and a moment later the hotel was fading in
the mirror, nothing more than an innocuous black
square building.

   He rounded the corner, pulled to the curb and
stopped, the motor idling. There was little question the
man in rags was a guard. Geld would not leave the hotel

unprotected. Johnny inhaled deeply, held his breath for a moment, then exhaled. The street was empty, the bars were closed and the street people had crawled into their cardboard boxes or sought shelter beneath the city's bridges and overpasses. Minutes before, as he'd turned off the freeway, he'd seen the lights that checkered the windows of the skyscrapers as the cleaning crews worked toward the dawn.

He turned the corner past the bar and a moment later turned into the alley heading toward the back of the Royal. He turned off his headlights and drove cautiously past the back of the bar and the building next to it. He could hear the tires crunching as they rolled over the crumbling asphalt and even in the darkness he could see the sides of the alley, a dumping ground for the discards of a neighborhood soaked in welfare, crime and poverty. He saw an old lamp, its base broken, a grocery cart on its side, a discarded carpet, a pile of magazines and a jumble of clothes that looked old, dirty and torn.

He stopped the Z just short of the parking lot next to the Royal Hotel. Easing the door open, he stepped into the alley, which smelled of urine, stale beer and vomit. He left the door open to avoid any unnecessary noise and moved to the edge of the building. He edged past the nose of the car to the building's corner, where the fenced parking lot began. From the darkness of the alley, Johnny could see the hotel across the empty lot. No light leaked from the interior, no television glow lit the inside of a window, no cracks of light slipped past a poorly hung curtain. The Royal looked old and abandoned. Leaning around the corner, he glanced toward the front but saw no sign of the sidewalk fire or the rag man.

He moved on quickly then, running past the chain-link fence topped with razor wire to the back of the hotel. He skirted a large Dumpster at the edge of the hotel and was behind the Royal. At one time the hotel had had a rear door opening onto the alley, but it had been bricked up. Johnny stepped back into the center of the alley and looked up at the rear of the building. He saw a solid brick surface, no windows, no doors, no balconies.

"Shit," he swore softly under his breath. He stepped farther back into the alley, almost bumping the wooden fence on the other side. He looked at the building again. There was nothing, no toehold, no opening he could slip through. His gaze swept up the alley and back and stopped on the Dumpster. He looked to the chain-link fence, then through the fence to the sidewalk at the front of the building. He ran back down the alley past the Z to where he'd seen the abandoned carpet.

The carpet was old, worn and thin. Carrying it to the Dumpster was easy. He laid it atop the garbage bin and climbed up himself. Hoisting the rug to his shoulder, he threw it on top of the razor wire and jumped the fence. He stumbled and fell as he hit the pavement. He lay still, watching the front of the building, waiting for the rag man. But there was no sign of him.

Johnny hurried to the side of the building and moved cautiously to the window closest to the front. No one had reattached the bars after he'd been in the room days before. They swung away from the wall silently and with ease. Johnny hoisted the window just enough to get through and slithered inside. He sat on the floor, remembering the place as the outline of the refrigerator, bed and sink slowly emerged from the shadows.

He cracked the door and looked into the empty corridor. The bare bulbs dangling from the ceiling filled the hallway with a harsh light. He paused at the first door and leaned close to listen. There was no sound from within. The second was equally quiet, as were the third and fourth. But at the fifth door he heard a man's voice. Or were there two? He couldn't tell. The words were soft and indistinguishable. Johnny rapped lightly, but there was no response. He knocked again and realized that he was holding his breath. He leaned back and consciously exhaled as he waited, and then there was a voice.

"Who is it?"

"My name's Rose. I have to talk to you. It's very important. I was here the other day. I think I stopped here. I told the guard I wanted to rent a room. Remember?"

"What do you want?"

"I need to talk to you."

"Go away. No one is allowed in here but residents."

"Listen, I know who you are. It's very important that we talk."

The unseen man inches away behind the door was quiet. No sound came from the room. Johnny waited but heard nothing. A minute, then two, passed in silence, as if the man's earlier words were but a dream. Johnny stepped back and looked at the door, his gaze running along the frame. He stepped close, his mouth next to the jamb, and spoke.

"You have to listen to me. Geld's going to tell the world that he brought you home. He's going betray the others, the men still over there. You have to know what's going to happen."

Suddenly the door opened a crack and the man,

short and thin, his face and scalp white and puffy, looked out. He wore an athletic shirt and boxer shorts.

"Who are you?"

"My name's Johnny Rose."

"What's this about?"

"I know who you are. Raby told me. But I also know that Geld is going to announce that he brought POWs home. Today. In just a few hours."

"How did you get in here?" The man leaned forward and looked past Johnny into the empty corridor.

Johnny ignored the question. "I have to talk to you. If we don't do something, Geld will use you. He's planning a press conference—"

"Wait," the man said and closed the door gently. Johnny heard feet shuffling. Then a moment later the door opened again, and the man turned away and moved slowly across the small room to sit on the edge of the bed. He looked old and tired, almost withered. From the doorway Johnny could see that the room was sparsely furnished. The single bed was on the right-hand wall; a small armoire, its dark brown paint chipped, was on the left wall; and straight ahead a small television sat on a wheeled stand. A stack of paperbacks balanced on the TV's top. A bare lightbulb floated above the room, tethered to the ceiling by thick white wires.

Johnny stepped into the room and a fist caught him hard behind the right ear. His head jerked forward and seemed to explode with white pain. The world went black and he fell to the floor, sprawling on his stomach. A second later he was conscious again and he felt a strong forearm wrap around his throat and jerk him backward, then shove him hard onto the floor again.

He lay there for a moment, his cheek against the dirty linoleum, saliva dripping from the corner of his mouth. He blinked, fighting the brightness that seemed to penetrate his eyes like a Hollywood searchlight. He closed his eyes and a wave of nausea swept over him. He opened his eyes again and could sense the man behind him but not see him. Johnny raised his head slightly and looked at the thin man sitting on the edge of the bed, not three feet away. Johnny lay for another two minutes, then struggled to his hands and knees.

The man who had stood behind him moved, walking past Johnny to stand next to the bed. He was tall, thin and black; his hair was short and streaked with gray. He wore baggy sweatpants and a loose fitting gray T-shirt with the emblem of the L.A. Kings hockey team. The clothes looked new.

"What do we do now, Major?" the man asked.

"Who are you?" the major asked.

"I told you, my name's Rose."

The major sat as still as a meditating monk, his eyes anchored on Johnny. Then he looked up at the man and said, "Get the guard." The man stepped past Johnny and disappeared out the door.

Johnny tried to stand, but the room seemed to spin and he slipped back to his knees. He looked at the major, trying to understand what was happening, searching for a way to convince the man that Geld was about to betray the Americans still over there.

"Look, you've got to believe me."

"Why should I?"

"Because Raby told me . . . Geld's press confer-ence . . . the others . . . Geld didn't want . . . the Blue Rain but now." Johnny knew he was rambling, not making sense. He could hear his own words as if he were an observer floating above. But his head throbbed and the man on the bed seemed to slip in and out of focus. Gently he reached up and felt the swelling at the base of his skull. A baseball bat probably wouldn't have caused more damage.

Still on his knees, Johnny turned, moved a few inches and grabbed the edge of the open door. He braced himself and stood up slowly, clinging to the door's edge.

"Look, I'm here to help, you gotta believe me. I may be your only chance."

Before the major could speak, a man in his early thirties with pale skin, red hair cut toothbrush short and green eyes pushed past Johnny into the room. He was stocky with powerful shoulders. A gun dangled in his hand at his side. He turned and looked at Johnny still hanging onto the door and grunted.

"What the fuck is this?" the redhead demanded.

"Said his name is Johnny Rose," the major said.

The redhead swung the gun up, stopping with the barrel millimeters from Johnny's face. "Oh yeah, I know him. Geld warned us he might show up. He's the one that killed Raby." Johnny's eyes shifted from the gun barrel to the major, searching his face for a clue that would help, but there was nothing.

"I didn't kill Raby," Johnny managed.

"Shut up!" the redhead snapped. He looked at the major. "How'd he get in?" The major shrugged. "Doesn't matter. I'll find out," the guard said. He looked at Johnny. "Let's go," he said.

"You'll never get the others out. They'll all die over there. Khun Sa will never let them out, not after today," Johnny said, his eyes almost pleading with the thin man on the bed.

For the first time, the major looked at Johnny seriously. "What do you mean?"

"It's Geld. I've been trying to tell you. He's going to announce it. Today. This morning. In a few hours. At a press conference." Johnny squeezed his eyes shut for a moment and forced his mind to focus. "At his house. You can call the AP. Ask them."

"Shut up," the guard said again and jammed the barrel against Johnny's forehead. "I'm taking you out of here. You've already caused enough trouble."

"Wait," the major said. He looked at the guard. "Is Geld having a press conference?" Johnny looked at the man, too. He looked unfazed, confident.

"How the hell should I know?"

The major's eyes shifted to Johnny. "What do you know about the others?"

"Raby told me. Said there were others. That if word of the Blue Rain gets out, no one will ever find them. They'll die if that happens. You know that. You know they can't live much longer over there. Raby told me that's why everything was being held under wraps. He didn't know about the others when he brought you out. But Raby's dead and Geld's going to tell the world he brought you home. He's going to brag about it at the press conference."

"Why?"

"He wants to be governor."

"Oh, this is just a bunch of shit. I'm getting him out of here," the guard said.

"I said WAIT." The major's voice was sharp and direct. "You have any proof?"

But what proof did he have? What could he say to the thin, shrunken man sitting a few feet in front of him who held his life in his hands?

"No. But Raby told me he was the only one keeping Geld quiet."

"I told you he was full of shit," the guard said.

"If he takes me out of here, he'll kill me and you'll never stop Geld," Johnny said.

"Yeah, right. This guy's crazy," the guard said.

"Was Roberto Ruiz crazy?" Johnny stared at the major. "He tried to walk home, didn't he? He was trying to get back to his wife, back to Arvin."

"What do you know about Ruiz?" He had the major's attention now.

"He died in the desert. Exposure. He was still wearing his dog tags."

"This is bullshit," the guard insisted. "He probably got this from Raby before he killed him."

"No. I saw the body. He was wearing new Nike sneakers and a polo shirt and pants. Been dead about three or four weeks."

"So Ruiz is dead?"

"Yes. So's his wife, Sandra. They killed her to keep it all quiet."

Johnny was watching the major's face and saw the recognition leap into his eyes and the suspicion fade.

"What do you know about Ruiz?"

"He's making this up," the guard said.

"I can prove it. In my wallet there's a newspaper story about Sandra Ruiz. It says she drove her car into an irrigation canal. Check the date. It's just about the time Roberto disappeared. Someone drove her into that ditch."

"Show me."

Johnny reached behind him and slowly pulled his wallet from his hip pocket. He opened it and took the clipping out. He held it out between his finger and thumb. The major leaned forward and took it. He scanned it and looked at the redhead, the question obvious on his face.

"It's a bullshit coincidence," the guard said, but the edge of confidence was wearing thin.

"Sergeant, get the others. I think this is something we need to talk about."

"Wait a minute, you can't do this," the guard said. He stepped back toward the door. "I'm going to call Geld right now. We'll get this straightened out."

"Sergeant," the major called.

The tall black man blocked the doorway. The guard turned slightly and raised his gun, pointing it directly at the major, still seated on the bed. Johnny looked at the major, but the man showed no fear, no concern.

"Put it down," the major said.

"No. I'm not going to do that. Now you listen to me. I've got my orders. I'm supposed to call Geld if this guy shows up. I'm supposed to take care of it. You're not stopping me. You got it?"

Johnny didn't wait for an answer. Holding the edge of the door for balance and support, he spun, pivoting on his left foot, driving his right knee into the guard's scrotum and knocking the pistol skyward with his right hand as he moved. The sergeant grabbed the gun from behind and jerked it from the guard's hand. The guard doubled over in pain, unable to speak beyond a low-voltage moan.

"Lock him in one of the rooms, get the guard from the front and lock him up, too, then wake the others," the major said. The sergeant grabbed the guard under the armpits and pulled him to his feet. A moment later they were gone and the major looked at Johnny and said, "I'm Major William Langdon."

"Johnny Rose."

"So you said." He paused for a moment, studying Johnny as though he were seeing him for the first time. Then, his hands folded neatly in his lap, he began speaking.

"Raby told me the same thing, that there might be others. He said it was important that no one know we were here. In the beginning they took us to a place in the desert. It was a huge, sprawling place with a barbed-wire fence. That's when Ruiz left. He said he knew where he was and could walk home from there. He took off in the middle of the night. We never saw him again."

"He got lost or maybe he just didn't remember how far it was," Johnny said.

"It was right after that that they moved us here. Told us it would only be for a few days. But it's been more than three weeks. The whole time, Raby was telling us it would be just a few more days until he could get the others."

"Did you believe him?"

The major was quiet for a moment, then pursed his lips. "I think he really was trying. Besides, if getting the others out meant we had to be quiet, that's what we were going to do." He turned suddenly, as though startled awake, and looked at Johnny. "Did you really kill Raby?"

"No. He fell off a cliff. I tried to save him, but couldn't."

"I think you'd better tell me what's happened."

Johnny spoke slowly at first, but as the words began to come he spoke more rapidly. He told the major about the Blue Rain ransom and Geld's overriding ambition and Raby's blackmail. Three times he caught himself speaking too quickly, rushing the story, and forced himself to go slow, not hurry on just to get to his own most important question. When he'd finished, he took a deep breath and exhaled slowly. He glanced at the empty doorway and into the hall, then looked back to the major.

"There's one thing I've got to know. The men you brought back, is one of—"

"Major." The voice came from the doorway and Johnny's eyes followed the major's gaze. The sergeant stood in the doorway blocking the view.

"Okay," the major said. "We need to tell them now. We have to decide what to do." He stood and walked through the door. Johnny followed.

Six men, including Langdon and the sergeant, stood in the hallway. They had gathered in front of the stairway leading to the second floor. All were thin, their eyes dull, their skin devoid of color or tone, as though they had spent years inside. They were clean-shaven. Their hair was cut close and their sideburns ended bluntly just below the tops of their ears, as though they were raw recruits in their first day of basic training. But they dressed casually, their clothes new. Two wore fresh T-shirts and jeans that looked stiff and uncomfortable and white Nike running shoes. Another wore only boxers and an athletic shirt, as did the major, and one had a robe tied in front, his bare ankles and feet sticking from beneath the robe. They looked at Johnny, their faces blank, as though expecting nothing.

Johnny stood in the doorway and watched as the major talked. Johnny's eyes drifted from one man to the next as he searched each face, trying to match it with the twenty-five-year-old photo on the dresser in Susan Loveless's bedroom. The major told them of

Roberto Ruiz's death and of Raby's fall from the cliff. Then he hesitated, looked back at Johnny for a moment and moved on, telling the men of Geld's plans.

"Mr. Rose, let me introduce the men. You already know Sergeant Washington, Army. This is Lieutenant Clever, Air Force," he said, nodding to the man in the robe. "PFC Edwards, Army." He gestured to the man wearing his boxer shorts. "Sergeant Muller's the man in the jeans, he's Marines, and the one next to him is Major Kingman. He's Army, too."

As Langdon recited the names, Johnny felt a joy grow within him and he smiled as though he were seeing the sun after a long, gray winter. None of the men was Air Force Captain Kyle Loveless. Susan's husband wasn't here. Johnny wanted to cry out and laugh, but instead he retreated into his own thoughts. He saw Susan's face and thought of holding her, of being with her every day. Of giving her his love and receiving it in kind.

"What are we going to do?" asked the man named Clever.

"I don't know," the major said. He looked at Johnny. "Any ideas, Mr. Rose?"

Johnny looked up, back in the present. He nodded slightly. "Yeah, I think I know something we can do. But first tell me, do all of you know where you'd go, what you'd do if you left tomorrow?"

"We all know," Langdon said. "We haven't talked about much else for the last few months."

"Good, I'm going to make—" Johnny stopped. A man was slowly descending the stairs from the second floor. The man paused at each step, as if each movement required a reprieve. At first Johnny could see only his feet and ankles, then his legs and knees. They were heavily scarred and Johnny guessed it was from leeches. The man moved slowly into full view. The men silently watched him descend the stairs. Like the others, he was thin and appeared malnourished. He stopped on the bottom step and looked over the heads of the others at Johnny. He had once been tall but was now bent at the shoulders, a frail old man with an ashen complexion who could have been seventy, perhaps older. But Johnny knew the man standing on the stairs was his own age.

"This is Captain Kyle Loveless," Langdon said. "Air Force."

"I know," Johnny said in words so soft he barely heard them himself. Johnny turned his head away and looked down the narrow empty corridor. He saw the worn red carpet that led to the door and the night beyond. His eyes lingered on the black pay phone hanging on the wall just inside the door and he felt himself collapse inside. The joy that had filled him moments before was gone, vaporized in an instant, replaced by a vast, dark, empty space that seemed to expand throughout his body and crush his spirit.

"So what do you want to do?" Langdon asked.

Johnny squeezed his eyes shut for a second longer, then turned back to face the men. He cleared his throat and tried not to look at Kyle Loveless, focusing his eyes instead on Langdon.

"I'm going to make a phone call and then I'm going to put each of you on the line. I want you to tell the woman your name and where you want to go. She'll make all the arrangements."

"Who's paying for this?" Langdon asked.

"Gordon Geld."

Johnny walked down the hall and called from the pay phone. Susan answered almost instantly.

"Johnny?"

"Yes."

"Oh, thank God. What happened?"

"Look, Susan, do you remember when we were going through E&M's computer files you said you could get us a free trip to Hawaii?"

"Johnny, what's wrong? What happened?"

"Nothing."

"I can hear it in your voice. Something's the matter. What happened?"

"Look, I'll explain in a minute. Just tell me. Do you remember E&M's files?" He stared at the carpet as he talked, fighting for control, struggling to hold the blackness at bay.

"Yes, of course, but what does that—"

"Wait, just listen to me, would you, please?" He was speaking too sharply. He heard it himself and paused.

"Johnny, you're scaring me."

He ignored her and pressed ahead. "I'm going to put some men on the phone. One at a time. They'll give you their names and where they want to go. Can you book airline flights for them out of LAX? First available. This morning if possible. Put it all on E&M's books."

"Johnny, are these—?" She didn't finish and Johnny ignored her again.

"Here's the first man." He handed the phone to Lieutenant Clever and walked slowly up the hall past the men who had formed a motley line, to the stairs and Kyle Loveless. Deep lines creased Kyle's brow, and the skin of his neck was as rough and scaly as an old gobbler's.

"I'm a friend of your wife's. She helped me find you," he said.

"You know Susan?"

"Yes."

"How is she?"

"She's well. She's on the phone now."

Loveless looked at Johnny for a long moment, holding his stare, seeming to ask and answer all the questions he had. In the end he just nodded and moved off the step and down the hall, where he took the phone and said, "Susan?"

Johnny turned his back to give Kyle Loveless and his wife privacy and walked into Major Langdon's room to explain what they would do in a few hours.

34

The press conference wasn't scheduled to start for another forty-five minutes, but already broadcasting trucks and TV vans lined the street in front of Geld's house. This time there was no valet parking and Johnny had to drive almost two blocks before finding an empty stretch of curb. He backed the Z into a tight space between an Infiniti and a Buick station wagon. As he stepped out of the car, he looked toward the San Gabriel Mountains. The morning was bright and the sky unusually clear. The smog veil that so effortlessly hid the mountains all summer had been blown away by early morning winds.

He stood on the blacktop for a moment, the car door still open, and looked up at the mountains. He'd heard about people who moved to Los Angeles in the summer when the smog was so thick and heavy you could smell it and taste it and then woke up one morning in the fall and were stunned to see huge high mountains looming above the city as if some special effects technician had conjured them up overnight. Sometimes, Johnny knew, things are too preposterous to be anything but the truth. He shoved the door closed and walked down the street toward Geld's home.

Near the house, black cables began to spread across the sidewalk like a multitude of orderly pythons snaking up the cement and across the driveway and over the front porch. Johnny pulled open the screen door and held it for Langdon, who walked in and stopped a few steps into the room. Johnny paused next to him, remembering the last time he'd been there. Just like that night, it was empty, little more than a funnel for people, moving them to the back door and into the yard. But that night he'd been thinking of joining Geld and Raby. He'd been playing with the idea of a fat paycheck.

Johnny crossed the dark hardwood floor to the windows and looked down onto the terraced backyard. A crowd had already gathered on the lowest level and others were working their way down the steps like pilgrims to a shrine. The television cameras were in place across the lawn from an empty podium that bristled with microphones. Three people passed him as he stood by the window. They walked out the back door and began descending the steps into the arroyo. Johnny watched them go for a moment, then scanned the crowd for Geld. He spotted Barsh a moment later, but Geld was not outside.

Johnny turned back and saw Langdon still standing in the middle of the room, looking up at the dark wood-beamed ceiling.

"Come on, I know the way to the study. He'll be

there," Johnny said and started across the room toward the stairs. But Langdon didn't move.

"You know, I spent the first year or so in a cage," he said to the ceiling. "Then later they moved me to a prison camp. In the beginning I used to dream about coming home and getting rich and building a big house like this. I worked out every corner of the house in my mind. I could tell you about every single room, every piece of furniture. Everything. But later, after I knew the war was over and I wasn't coming home, it all sort of just drifted away. Now I can't remember any of it, except one thing."

"What's that?"

"Beamed ceilings. I remember the place had beamed ceilings." Langdon smiled. "You know, they don't look as good as I thought they would."

"You feel up to this?"

Langdon nodded and said, "Yeah, let's go do it."

They climbed the steps to the second floor and walked down the empty corridor to the end. The door was closed.

"How do you know he'll be here?" Langdon asked.

"I don't, really. It's just a hunch." Johnny said. He grabbed the knob and pushed through the door.

Geld was standing at the windows on the far side of the small study, watching the crowd below, a voyeur at his own coronation. He turned at the sound of the door opening. He was smiling, peaceful, triumphant. He saw Johnny and his face clouded, but he recovered quickly and even smiled.

"You are persistent," he said. "Raby warned me about that. Said you were too stubborn for your own good." He stared at Langdon for a moment, wondering who he was, the question visible in his face. Then he looked at Johnny again.

"But now that you're here, you'd better leave. I'm calling the police." He moved to his desk.

"You should hear me out. I'm here to trade," Johnny said and Geld stopped and looked up. "I know all about the Blue Rain you traded for the POWs. I've got everything I need to bring you down."

Geld laughed a soft, low chuckle, then turned away from his desk and moved back to the window again. He pulled the curtain a few inches to the side and peered out. When he spoke his voice had a high, clear quality, a saturation of hubris that Johnny had seen only a few times when people like Geld pushed their arrogance way past the red line.

"Look down there. There are more than a hundred people, maybe two hundred, waiting for me. Most of them are reporters, television people. Your buddies. You probably know some of them. But do you know why they're here? They're all waiting to hear me." He glanced over his shoulder at Johnny. "And you know what I'm going to tell them?"

"I have a pretty good idea."

"Yeah, I'll bet you do." He was speaking to the window again, looking out. "I'm going tell them that I brought American POWs back when everyone else failed. I'm going to tell them about the secret negotiations that Raby conducted and about the millions of dollars of my personal money I spent to bring them home."

He stopped, turned around and moved to the edge of his desk again. His eyes were as black and shiny as obsidian and he seemed to be staring a thousand yards away. Then his gaze shifted and filled with malice and for an instant gave Johnny a glimpse into the soul of the obsessed and twisted man who lay just beneath the finely attired surface. He leaned forward, his thighs touching the desk, and looked from Johnny to Langdon, then back to Johnny. When he spoke his voice was a hoarse whisper.

"You think you can tar me with some bullshit story about chemical weapons? Jesus, you're dumb. I told you last night, you're nothing. You're a nobody. You're a reporter who was fired and is now trying to smear me. Worse than that, you're a murder suspect. No one will listen to you. Not even your friends down there. You can't touch me, Rose. Now get out and take your friend with you because this time I *am* calling the police."

He grabbed the phone from his desk and began dialing.

"Mr. Geld, I'd like you to meet Major William Langdon, U.S. Army. He's one of the men you brought home. One of the POWs." Johnny said and nodded toward the major.

Geld stopped, his finger just over the phone buttons. He stood still, only his black eyes moving as he looked from Langdon to Rose.

"We just came from the Royal Hotel," Johnny said. Geld set the phone down.

Langdon stepped forward. "Mr. Geld, I want to thank you personally for what you've done for us. For me, Sergeant Washington, Captain Loveless and the others. We'd all given up any hope of ever coming home. You saved us. You really did."

Geld hadn't moved. He stood, frozen, sensing a trap but unable to see it. Finally he said, "I did what I could." His voice was low, barely above a whisper.

His eyes shifted back to Johnny, who smiled.

"He's my proof."

"What?"

"You said I had no proof. But he's my proof. Captain Langdon and the rest. They'll back everything I say. Khun Sa's guards told them before they left about the Blue Rain. Raby confirmed it for them. Even showed some of them the documents."

"That's bullshit." Geld's voice was a controlled tremble. "Raby didn't tell anyone. I was the only one who knew. He sure as hell didn't tell these men. And the guards wouldn't know. That's preposterous." He turned to Langdon. "You're lying."

Langdon nodded slightly. "Yes, Mr. Geld, I am lying. But I'll lie and so will every man who came back with me. If you tell anyone that we're here, the Americans still over there will never get home. You know it, too. If you tell, we'll destroy you."

"But you have no proof."

Johnny smiled and said, "They won't need proof. Who's going to doubt their word? It will certainly be enough to launch a congressional investigation. You think Watergate was bad, or Iran-Contra? At least Nixon and Reagan had some congressmen and senators on their side. But just imagine what all those politicians you've been tearing apart for so long will do when they get a chance to take you down a peg or two. I can see congressional hearings now. Subpoenas. You'll have a tough time explaining it all."

"This is bullshit, no one will believe you, Rose. I make one phone call and you'll be in jail."

"This isn't about me anymore. I'm not the one going to the press. He is," Johnny nodded at Langdon. "It doesn't matter what happens to me. If you talk, you're going down. But I'll tell you this. I'm staying in close touch with Major Langdon. Anything happens to me, anything at all, and the story comes out."

"That's right, Mr. Geld. We feel a great debt of gratitude to Johnny. We know you saved us, but Johnny's trying to save the men still there."

There was a light knock at the door and a low voice. "Mr. Geld, the press conference is scheduled to start in two minutes. Is everything all right?" Johnny recognized Barsh's voice.

"Yeah, fine. I'll be there in a minute." Geld's voice was harsh but low.

"What?"

"Yes. I said yes, goddammit. I'll be there in a minute." This time he screamed.

"So what'll it be?" Johnny asked. "What about it? Do I call my own press conference? The major and I can catch those reporters as they leave. Like you said, I know a lot of them already. Some of them are pretty good friends. I could arrange exclusive interviews for the AP and maybe a television network or two."

Geld pulled the chair from the desk and sat down. He folded his hands on the desktop and stared at his fingers, which curled so tightly on each other that his knuckles turned white.

"I won't say anything." His voice was low, barely above a whisper.

"And me?" Johnny said.

"No one will touch you."

Barsh's voice again drifted through the door. "Mr. Geld, it's time."

Geld stood and walked past Johnny and the major, his eyes straight ahead, as though neither man were in the room. He opened the door, paused, straightened his shoulders and walked past Barsh without acknowledging him. Barsh looked through the open door into the study and saw Johnny.

"Rose!" He stepped toward the door but stopped and looked at Geld walking down the hall to the steps. He leaned toward the study, then pivoted and hurried after Geld, who had already begun to walk down the steps.

Johnny stopped in front of the terminal at Burbank Airport but didn't turn off the engine. "They'll have the ticket at the counter. You're sure you're going to be okay?"

"Yeah. My family's going to meet me. I talked to them. They understand."

"Good luck." Johnny held out his hand and Langdon took it.

"You think Geld will, ah . . ."

"No. I think it's all over. I don't think he'll come after me. Besides, I have your address and phone number. I'll be checking in."

"Good." Langdon pushed through the door, then bent low to look in the window. "Thanks again."

Johnny nodded. "You're welcome," he said.

Langdon stood, turned and walked through the small crowd and disappeared into the terminal. Johnny eased the clutch out and the Z pulled away from the curb. With any luck he could be over the pass and in West L.A. within twenty minutes.

As he was coming down the south side of the Santa Monica Mountains, Johnny turned on the radio and dialed an all-news station. He didn't have to wait long. Geld's announcement was one of the top stories. The announcer's voice seemed to swoop and dip as he spoke.

"Gordon Geld stunned his supporters this morning by announcing he was withdrawing from the race for governor. He made the announcement at a news conference at his home in Pasadena. Our Patty Ramirez was there."

A heartbeat later, Geld's voice was on. "Thank you all for coming. I'll make this brief. After a long and heart-wrenching assessment of my campaign, the impact of the loss of my closest aide, Charles Raby, one of the finest men I've ever known, it has become apparent that I do not have a realistic chance of being elected governor. This campaign has been hard on my family and has distracted me from my business. I have spent much of my own money. Now, though, I think it would be best for me to withdraw and let the voters of California choose between the other two candidates. I want to thank all my supporters and those who have worked so hard to help elect me. Believe me, we will continue to fight for what we believe in, but this is not the proper time or place to do it." The recording faded with shouted questions and the announcer was back.

Then a young female voice was there. "Geld's announcement stunned his supporters and staff alike. They've been talking since yesterday about the announcement today, hinting that what he had to say might be enough to push him over the top. His campaign has faded in recent weeks, but Geld was still considered a major threat to both parties. California political analysts say they—"

Johnny ran the dial to a rock 'n' roll station, caught the last of "Lying Eyes" and turned off the radio and drove in silence.

The temperature dropped and the gray leaked out of the air, replaced by light blue as he neared the ocean. He parked next to Ethel's Kingswood wagon, taking care to leave enough room for her doors to swing wide and still not dent the Z. He looked at the Dumpster and saw that Animal Control had picked up the box with Weird Harold's body.

He sat for a minute in the car, the window down, his arm resting on the frame, listening to the sounds of his neighborhood. From the apartment building across the alley he could hear a dryer turning, a metal buckle banging against the drum with each rotation. He could hear the muted roar as someone fired up a leaf blower perhaps half a block away. A young boy, wearing blue jeans, no shirt and a bandanna tied over his head, rode his skateboard down the alley past the back of the car. Johnny caught only a glimpse of him in the mirror as he went by, but the sound of the skateboard's wheels faded slowly.

It was, Johnny knew, just another afternoon. He turned and looked at bulging plastic bags and piles of newspaper in the back of Ethel's car and remembered slithering under them, praying for his life as he watched Raby shoot into the Dumpster. All of it seemed so far away now, in another dimension, another world. A time far away.

And then he thought of Susan. He could see her, hear her voice and smell the fresh soap and hint of perfume from her neck. He closed his eyes, leaned his head back against the seat and thought of Kyle Loveless. He envisioned Kyle walking slowly up the sidewalk to Susan's house and through the door and back into Susan's life. He opened his eyes. It was over. He loved Susan deeply and she loved him. But, Johnny knew, that was totally irrelevant.

He shoved the door open and got out of the car. He had one thing left to do. The red light on the answering machine was blinking when he walked into the apartment, and he crossed to the kitchen and punched the button.

"Hey, Johnny, it's Sheridan. Thought you'd like to know. I just heard from a source that Earl's eyewitness turned out to be a wino who couldn't remember much of anything. More importantly, that dead guy's boss, some Vietnamese named Ben something or other, told the cops about Mr. Lich thinking he saw a POW and calling you. Said the guy was really scared. So I guess you're no longer a suspect." The tape continued for a moment, then the voice began again. "A POW, can you believe it? Isn't that a hoot?"

Johnny hit the Stop button and crossed the living room to the stairs. In his bedroom, he slid the closet door back and reached up to the shelf. He moved a stack of paperback books aside and stretched his hand to the back. He pulled a shoe box out and held it gently. The cardboard had faded and dust covered the lid. A once-white piece of string was wound around the box, end to end and side to side, and ended with a knot in the middle. Johnny plucked at the string and the knot gave way with a puff of dust.

He sat on the edge of the bed and lifted the lid. He looked at the black-and-white photos with crinkle-cut edges; he and Jimmy, side by side, standing next to their ten-speeds. They were about ten and eleven. He found a sixth grade report card and a valentine he'd made for his mother. He set the pictures aside and then reached back into the box to get the last item. He dropped it into his shirt pocket and, leaving the photos lying on the unmade bed, walked back down the stairs and went outside.

Jimmy was watching television. His face looked thin and pale. His hair was oily and he needed to shave. Thin wires attached to his chest disappeared under the sheet, and the jagged lines on the monitor next to his bed maintained a steady march across the green screen.

His eyes shifted from the television to Johnny, then back to the screen, but showed no recognition or curiosity. Johnny took the chair from near the window, moved it next to the bed and sat down. He watched the television for a moment, an afternoon talk show, then looked at his brother.

"How you feeling, Jimmy?"

"Yeah. I'm okay," Jimmy said without taking his eyes from the set.

"Good. The doctor tells me you're going to be all right. Soon as the legs and hips heal."

"Yeah. I'm okay."

The silence fell on them again and Jimmy said nothing, his empty eyes on the television. Johnny studied his brother openly for several minutes, seeing the lines near his eyes, the white in his hair and the stubble on his cheeks. He saw a small scar faded almost to oblivion on his chin and wondered what story it held.

"Turn it off for a second, okay?" Johnny finally said.

Jimmy clicked the remote and the television went blank. He shifted slightly to look at Johnny.

"Captain Raby's dead, Jimmy."

"Yeah?"

"Yes." Johnny nodded. He looked into his brother's empty eyes and wondered if anything he said could reach through the mists of time and despair to that faraway place where Jimmy lived.

"We brought 'em home. Seven POWs. They're all going to be home today. You and me, Jimmy. We finally brought 'em home."

"Yeah?"

"It's the truth. Seven of 'em. It's what Raby was doing. I'll tell you all about it later. We'll have plenty of time."

"Yeah, okay."

"Look, I brought you something."

"What?"

Johnny pulled his father's harmonica from his pocket and laid it on the bed next to Jimmy's hand. Jimmy picked it up and brought it close to his face, and then looked at Johnny. His fingers seemed too big, the knuckles swollen, the fingers awkward as he held the instrument.

"It was Dad's," Johnny said.

"I know. Why?"

"I don't even know how to start. I guess it's . . . I don't know, Jimmy. I just thought you ought to have it."

Jimmy's eyes shifted from the harmonica to Johnny's face for a moment and in that instant the haze was gone and Johnny saw his brother again, like an old friend in the distance. Then Jimmy's gaze moved back to the instrument in his hand and the look was gone. But it didn't matter. It was a beginning and that was all Johnny wanted, a chance to begin again.

He stood up and moved the chair back to its place by the window. He looked at his brother.

"Jimmy, I'm going now. I'll be back soon."

"Okay."

Johnny moved to the door but stopped and turned back. He looked at the man in the hospital bed, his feet in casts sticking out from under the sheets.

"You know, Jimmy, there's something I don't think I ever said when you got back from Nam."

"What's that?"

"Welcome home, Jimmy. Welcome home."